A MISTAKEN HOSTAGE

J.F. FORAN

Rebecca –
In appreciation,

Jeff

A MISTAKEN HOSTAGE

J.F. FORAN

Cover design by Paul Palmer-Edwards

Printed in the United States of America
The Troy Book Makers • Troy, New York
thetroybookmakers.com

To order additional copies of this title,
contact your favorite local bookstore
or visit www.shoptbmbooks.com

ISBN: 978-1-61468-650-7

For Karen

CHAPTER 1

A Chance Encounter

San Francisco, California

Brooks Davidson strode down the marble foyer of the San Francisco Opera House, past the ornate fluted columns that lined the corridor. His long body moved with speed through a dense, meandering crowd. The evening lecture over, he darted around couples and focused exclusively on reaching the bar. He spotted his friend Fergy, seated on a leather-backed stool, and muscled his way beside him.

"Jesus, Fergy! You had me delay my flight to Cairo to hear this?"

Fergy blushed. He was a head shorter than Brooks, and his stocky body filled the seat. His hip and thigh pressed against Brooks' long legs as they squeezed into the tight space.

"Easy man. There's much to learn from his philosophy. I felt it would tickle your curiosity."

"The Dalai Lama?" Brooks clapped Fergy on the back. "Well, his soft, gentle approach to life and political problems don't fit today's realities. Never mind. Let's have a drink. Then I need to get to the airport."

Fergy pointed to his drink.

"Join me; it's good. It's our first drink together in 2001.

Brooks nodded and waved to the bartender as Fergy spoke.

"You think the rough philosophies of your Middle East friends are superior to the Dalai's preachings?"

Brooks turned to the barman.

"Grey Goose, straight up, with a twist."

A smile broke across Brooks' face. A few seconds later, he nodded a thank you to the barman, then shifted in his seat to face Fergy.

"No. I think my friends, as you call them, are having the fight of their lives trying to settle on the best way to govern their countries. They don't have the luxury to be passive or patient."

Fergy sighed.

"I guess we can get into this when you return, but the whole world," he said and waved his arms, nearly upsetting his drink, "could benefit from the Dalai Lama's peaceful approach to political problems."

Brooks regarded his friend, his lips curled in a smirk, and lifted his glass.

"Salud! And thanks for inviting me."

"Always, old man. I'll get you to a more idealistic frame of mind yet."

Brooks laughed.

"Don't hold your breath."

The bar had become crowded with people gathered behind them seeking the bartender's attention. Amid the noise of many voices, Fergy turned as he heard his name called.

"Oh my!" he exclaimed as he turned in his seat to face three fast-approaching people: a man and two women. They were clearly about his age, in their early sixties. He put a hand on Brooks' shoulder as he spoke.

"Please meet my friend, Brooks Davidson. He goes way back to my college days and is with me in the Bullion Club."

Brooks turned to meet them and exchanged greetings with Doug and Judy Jameson and Sarah Pierce.

"A pleasure," he said as he shook hands with each of them.

Then his eyes lingered on Sarah. She was taller than her friends—even taller than Fergy. Yet it was her eyes that caught his attention. They were round, not oval, and they bored right through him. Her posture was erect, yet relaxed, which emphasized her height. She moved gracefully when she extended her hand to him. Her blue pin-striped suit fit her slender body beautifully, and its color accentuated the blond waves of her hair.

"What brings you to the lecture?" Brooks asked her.

"They invited me," said Sarah, nodding in the direction of Doug and Judy. "My late husband climbed with them in Tibet. That's the link to the Dalai Lama."

She pointed to Brooks' drink.

"That looks refreshing. What is it?"

"Would you like one? It's a Grey Goose—vodka."

"Oh, no; too strong for me. I'll have a glass of wine."

"A chardonnay?" he asked, catching her nod. He signaled the barman, placed the order, then turned to her.

"I'm sorry to hear about your husband. You're too young to be a widow."

She sighed, and her face lost some of the sparkle and vitality he noticed moments earlier.

"That's what everyone tells me, but death comes when it will come, doesn't it?"

Her comment surprised him, and while he thought of a response, the wine arrived. Sarah reached for her purse. Brooks held up his hand with a credit card extended.

"Please allow me."

Sarah thanked the barman, then turned to Brooks.

"Most kind. Thank you."

She lifted her glass to him and clinked his.

"Cheers," she offered.

Brooks smiled. She held her glass at eye level and gazed at him. She hadn't paid attention to men since her husband had died and, to her surprise, let her eyes linger on his face. She knew he was around Fergy's age because they were at college together, although he looked younger. Unlike Fergy, he had a full head of wavy brown hair turning gray at the temples. His face, with its faint tan, had no lines or wrinkles. The skin was smooth across his cheekbones and down to his angular jaw. His dark green eyes exuded confidence; they seemed calm and friendly, yet expressed vitality and curiosity. She brought the wine to her lips and took a sip.

"To your health," he responded. "I'm intrigued by your comment of death being the necessary end. Are you philosophically aligned with the Dalai Lama's Buddhism, or do you follow some other philosophy?"

"Oh, I guess I'm somewhat a Buddhist and somewhat a mix of other spiritual ideas. I'm not really into Buddhism like Doug or Judy. How about you? What did you think of the lecture?"

Brooks moved his feet to face her directly and slumped his six-foot-three frame to reduce the height difference between them.

"I found his view noble and admirable but perhaps in the realm of wishful thinking when it came to political thought."

"What do you mean by political?"

"When he said the Chinese will eventually give up Tibet through persuasion, I thought that was quite naïve."

4

Sarah seemed to stiffen. Her lips compressed. She spoke carefully, measuring her words.

"His philosophy is centuries old. It's deeper than you heard tonight. There's much more there. Are you familiar with Buddhism?"

"No—you have me. My spiritual foundation is Christianity, and I've spent a lot of time in the Middle East, so I'm more acquainted with the spiritual/philosophical thinking there."

"Really! What have you done in that part of the world?"

"For about thirty years, I was a diplomat in that region. Now, I teach and still do some work in the region. How about you?"

He knew the reference to a diplomatic career was misleading, but it avoided the usual endless questions that arose when he'd mention to newcomers that he was in the CIA.

"I'm a psychologist. I focus on executives who've been the casualty of a merger or acquisition and are out of a job."

She paused for a second and seemed to blush slightly.

"I apologize," she sputtered. "I'm always a bundle of questions. I guess that comes from being a psychologist, but..."

She tossed her head back and smiled.

"What do you teach? And how do you find time to work thousands of miles away?"

He watched her, thinking he'd never seen a smile more vibrant or dazzling.

"I'm an economist; I teach at Stanford. It's only one course a term, so I have ample time for my projects in the Middle East. In fact, I'm headed there tonight, so I'd better get going."

"Where?"

"I'm off to Cairo. I won't bore you with the details."

"Oh, please. What are you up to?"

He stepped back from her, amused.

"You are indeed a ton of questions; that's refreshing," he said. "I'm working on a project to bring a large manufacturing operation to Egypt."

"That's like an investment banker, isn't it?"

"Similar. I tend to work alone or with a small group of partners. I'm not with one of the big firms."

"I see."

She seemed to ponder his response. She placed a long finger on her cheekbone, then rubbed it with delicate strokes.

"When do you leave?"

He turned toward Fergy and addressed the group.

"Sarah and I have been talking about my schedule. Regrets. I must get moving. I have a flight tonight."

Fergy nodded.

"Ah, yes. It's Cairo isn't it? When will I see you next?"

"I'll be back in a week. I'll call."

He stepped back from the group and extended his hand to Sarah. "A pleasure."

He repeated the exchange with Doug and Judy and walked briskly to the doors of the Opera House and down the steps. He headed up Van Ness toward the Opera Plaza Garage. At the light on McAlister, he had to stop for passing traffic, relieved to halt his rapid pace. His mind drifted to the meeting at the bar and Sarah. Rarely, if ever, had his initial meeting with a woman secured his total attention. Her beauty was eye-catching, yet it was her serenity over her husband's death that lingered in his mind. He had struggled for years after his wife, Clary, died and had never become comfortable with a new female companion. His thoughts turned back to Sarah.

Damn! he thought. *Just a few more minutes. I didn't get a business card or her phone number. Well, she came with his friends. Fergy will have her number.*

The light changed, and he marched on toward the garage. He knew one thing for certain: He'd telephone Sarah when he returned from Cairo. He wanted their conversation to continue.

CHAPTER 2

Omar Sayed

Cairo, Egypt

Idris el Buradi, Egypt's minister of agriculture, was alone in his office. It was a spacious, square room furnished with his desk, a couch for his daytime naps, and two chairs facing the couch. The plain white walls were covered with photos of el Buradi with former President Anwar Sadat, President Hosni Mubarak, and an array of cabinet ministers. There were also shots of him shaking hands with Saudi Arabian sheiks and Ethiopian, Niger, and British senior officials. The floor was covered with a worn beige carpet left over from leaner times in the Egyptian government. The one touch of individualism evident was his wide, glass-topped desk. He was bent forward with his forearms and elbows resting next to a thick legal document on his desktop. His eyes, aided by Coke-bottle glasses, focused on an agreement transferring ownership of a cotton field in the Nile Delta to one to of President Mubarak's colleagues. The flashing light on his telephone console interrupted his concentration. He sighed as he recognized his secretary's button. He pushed the button and picked up the phone.

"Yes, Masika?"

In her clear, efficient tone, she announced, "It's Minister Sayed of Trade and Industry. He mentioned it's urgent. Are you available?"

El Buradi looked at the document on his desk and marked the paragraph with a red pen to hold his place. He removed his reading glasses and placed them on the document.

"Thank you. Put the call through."

When he heard the familiar click, he spoke quickly.

"Hello, Minister Sayed. To what do I owe this pleasure?"

The voice on the other end sounded surprised.

"'*Minister* Sayed?' Must we be so formal? We are family—distant, but still family."

El Buradi clenched his jaw.

"It's best to be formal at work," he said. "You never know who's listening."

He shifted in his chair and looked longingly at the legal document.

"What can I do for you?"

El Buradi listened as Sayed talked. At first, he sat in his chair without moving much, but as the monologue dragged on, he lifted the telephone off the console, cradled the black phone on his shoulder, and walked around his office. For several minutes, he listened to Sayed with interest, offering no comment.

Sensing repetition in Sayed's arguments, el Buradi asked, "Omar, what is it you need from me?"

"My projects," Sayed began, "specifically designed to work with your ministry, are being delayed. I don't understand the president's thinking on the best projects to create employment. You've met with him. I'd like your help to understand what's going on."

"Your information is correct," El Buradi said. "I have met with President Mubarak. In fact, I saw him today. The purpose of our meeting was to discuss my project of revitalizing cotton production. That discussion went well. Also, our joint project on investing in more textile plants is still being considered. But you must remember that the president has many programs to consider. He has a very full plate at the moment."

On the other end of the phone, Sayed bristled with impatience, shifting his compact weight back and forth in his chair. His suit jacket was off, and now he loosened his blue tie. His phone was jammed into his jaw and ear.

"Sons of dogs!" Sayed shouted. "Why not push him on that project? It's my top priority. It's not moving. What can I do?"

"These ideas take time, my friend," el Buradi said. "You must be patient. The president has much on his mind. We must work him skillfully. We can act only when the time is right."

Sayed cursed.

"Did the president mention my name or the list of my other projects that tie into your ministry?"

El Buradi grimaced as he listened to Sayed. He was pleased to be on the phone and not face to face with Sayed. He knew his facial expression would have revealed the president's lackluster attitude on the young minister's proposals.

"Well, Omar, as I said before, he has a lot on his mind. It's not the right time."

Sayed spewed a volley of curses.

"I'm the minister of Trade and Industry, and I'm being ignored! You're more experienced than I. I need your backing to get closer to the president."

"As you said, we're distant cousins, Omar. So believe me, I have your interest at heart.

You must be patient. The president is working hard on a project with the Americans, and you know he wants to keep American money flowing. "

Sayed erupted.

"The Americans! He talked about the Americans? Is it military? Or is it infrastructure, like ports or roads?"

"From what the president said to me, I couldn't tell and didn't press. It's not my business."

"You know that the president asked me to manage the access of the European and American banks to our country," Sayed said. "I'm supposed to keep unpromising business ideas from the likes of Lazard, the Rothschilds, and Goldman Sachs away from the president. So why is he talking to the Americans and not with me? Are you certain he was talking about the Americans?"

"Absolutely! He was quite enthusiastic about meeting with them. He apologized to me for rushing our meeting. He made it clear he did not want to delay his session with them."

"They were there?"

"Yes," el Buradi affirmed. "As I left his office, there was a group of them in the anteroom. I don't remember how many."

"Did you recognize any of them?"

"Only one: Dr. Davidson. I knew him when he was stationed in Cairo years ago."

"Davidson? *The dealer?*"

"What do you mean 'dealer'? I know he's retired from government, but I've not heard he deals anything."

"Davidson? You're sure it was Brooks Davidson?"

"Absolutely. We spoke for a few minutes before his group was called into the president's office."

Sayed uttered another string of curses, thanked el Buradi for the information, and hung up his phone. He frowned and shook his head from side to side. His hand lingered on the phone for a moment, then he rose and began pacing. His short, stocky body, never graceful, plodded toward the window. He saw his reflection in the glass. His round face was wet, and sweat from his brow trickled into his dark brown eyes. He pulled a handkerchief from his jacket pocket, dabbed the moisture off his eyes, and wiped the dampness off the fine skin of his olive-colored brow. Still feeling the heat, he ran the cloth over the short bristles of his thinning black hair. He stretched his arms for relaxation and felt his jacket strain across his thick chest and shoulders.

I've got to lose some weight, he thought.

He stood staring out the window, gazing down at the Nile. Often, the view of the wide river and its constant flow of traffic soothed him. But not today. The conversation with el Buradi worried him. The textile project had been put off, and—worse—he wasn't involved. The president told el Buradi the timing was wrong. Why? El Buradi—that coward—wasn't sufficiently confident to push for answers or to ask what could be done to accelerate the project. In the forefront of Sayed's mind was the distinct worry that Mubarak was ignoring him. Or was it just his imagination? He took a few deep breaths to calm his nerves.

Sayed turned his thoughts to Dr. Davidson. At President Mubarak's request the previous year, in late 2000, Sayed had hosted Davidson in his office for over an hour while the American talked about a project to build sport utility vehicles in Egypt. Sayed had dismissed the idea of SUVs as too much capital to generate too few jobs. Davidson, so perfectly mannered, was polite and thanked him for his time. In the intervening weeks, had Davidson gone around him, gone directly to Mubarak, to push the SUV project? Or had Mubarak, back in December, sent Davidson to him to assess how he might respond to a business idea from a foreigner? Was the president using Davidson to test the skills of his department and especially Sayed's strategy for economic growth in the country?

Too many possibilities, he thought.

Academic life was so much simpler.

Why did I agree to leave the London School of Economics and come back to Egypt? he wondered.

Though he asked himself that question often these days, he already knew the answer. He had come by invitation from the president himself, who claimed Sayed's academic ideas could be turned into projects to stimulate Egypt's economic growth. At the time, he was seduced by the idea that he could help his country. Fame and major financial rewards beckoned. And he knew his family and members of the Muslim Brotherhood would agree with his economic ideas because they focused entirely on Egyptian capital, skills, and resources. There would be no outside capitalists involved, an idea perfectly aligned with the principles of the Brotherhood. While he pushed his Egypt-only projects to Mubarak alone or in concert with other ministers such as el Buradi, he kept his ties with the Muslim Brotherhood quiet. He remembered his final interview with President Mubarak.

Mubarak had said, "Your articles against Sadat years ago gave me the impression that you were with the Muslim Brotherhood. Were you in that organization, and are you aligned with their politics?"

"Mr. President," Sayed had replied, "that was over twenty years ago," he lied, "and I was not a member then, and I'm not one now."

"What about your family, especially that uncle—I can't remember his name—was it Khalid?"

"No, Mr. President, his name was Gehad. And yes, he was active and a belligerent. During President Sadat's regime, he spent many years in prison. I observed his actions and saw the consequences. I learned from that experience and stayed away from him. I turned to an academic life, where I felt my ideas would be viewed as politically neutral. This will be my first foray into the political arena if you appoint me."

Mubarak had seemed to accept the answer, then added, "While the Muslim Brotherhood has successfully elected several members to our parliament, I agree with their initiatives in one area only— that is, improving employment in rural areas."

He paused and stared hard at Sayed.

"But I do not agree with many of their radical ideas for health care and education, and their resistance to commercial projects initiated by Western capitalists."

At the conclusion of the meeting, Sayed was certain he could balance his ideas for economic development between government-supported projects and those advanced by Egyptian investors. Now, four years later, he worried about the president's opinion of him. Did the president think some of his economic ideas were Brotherhood-sponsored or derived? Had the president concluded that he was against the use of foreign capital?

As Sayed thought about his years in the government, he learned that Mubarak tolerated the Brotherhood as long as they did not openly oppose him or expose his corruption. If the actions of their leaders became too aggressive in opposition to Mubarak, jail time or worse was the consequence. In the forefront of his consciousness, Omar knew the president would dismiss him, even jail him, if he knew Omar had maintained his ties with the Brotherhood.

In Mubarak's Cabinet, he knew he was the only member with Muslim Brotherhood affiliation. During his interview process, Sayed had questioned other cabinet members carefully to discover their position on the programs of the Brotherhood and found hostility, even fear. From the day of his appointment, he kept his association with the group quiet. He planned to keep it that way. He would advance the Brotherhood's goals of economic fairness subtly from his post in the Ministry of Trade and Industry. There were others in the lower ranks of the bureaucracy aligned with the Brotherhood. They kept their association well-hidden also.

Today, and increasingly over the past several months, he felt disjointed, a little out of sorts, and isolated from the president's inner circle. His mind jumped in and out of topics too frequently. He recognized the behavior and knew this was not like him. He went back to his disappointment with his cousin. El Buradi was not helpful in persuading Mubarak to approve their joint projects, nor was he useful in determining what Davidson and the Americans were doing with the president. He wanted to know what they were proposing and wondered if they were a threat to his work.

Who can I trust to ferret out the truth? he wondered.

His mind drifted back to Davidson as he returned to his desk and sat back in his chair. He placed his hands behind his head and stared at the ceiling fan slowly circulating above him. His staff had defined the American as a dealer because of his success in securing two major projects in Egypt: the rail extension down the Nile, and the Alexandria oil refineries. Sayed didn't worry about those projects; they were beyond the scope of his ministry. But they were close to his responsibilities—too close.

What was Davidson's next move? he wondered. *Was he becoming a risk to my position in the government, to my relationship with the president?*

He didn't like that Davidson, and the American companies associated with his projects, took major amounts of capital from

Egypt through the profits produced by their firms. And David-son's investment fees for organizing the projects were more than five million for each project. This had to stop. He needed more information. He wanted to know what Davidson and the other Americans were doing in Egypt. He went to his notepad and jotted down the name "Fathi Ashur." His first cousin was deputy director of the Mukhabarat, Egypt's Intelligence Ministry. Within that organization, Fathi was responsible for what happened in Egypt, the feared Internal Operations unit. Sayed picked up his phone and called his assistant.

"Telephone Minister Ashur for me. If he can't pick up, schedule a time for us to talk."

Sayed placed the phone down and began to think of his request to Fathi. He knew his cousin was a quick and impatient man. He'd known that from childhood. This request must be precise. His phone rang; he jumped in surprise.

"Amir?" he said.

"Yes, Minister. I have Minister Ashur on line two."

He quickly pressed that button.

"Fathi, what's it been? Too long. Since the feast of Eid al-Fitr?"

"Yes, cousin. That was a joyous gathering. Omar, I regret that my time is short. How can I help you?"

"I appreciate your time. My request is twofold. I want to know what Brooks Davidson and a group of Americans are doing in Egypt. And secondly, I want to know how I can track—maybe the best word is 'spy' on—this Davidson. He's bringing capitalism into the country, and it's against my values, your values. I believe I need to stop him."

Ashur was quiet. Sayed spoke.

"Fathi? Still there?"

"Yes, thinking. I'm pulling up the file on Davidson. It's old data, but the basics are that he is married to a journalist and living in Washington. This American, Davidson, is considered a friend of Egypt. He's revered in high places, which you well know. What's bothering you?"

"As I said, he's a Westerner bringing capitalist projects into the country and maybe planning more," Omar said. "It's the opposite of what I want my ministry to do, and it's not what the Brotherhood wants. I need to get him out of Egypt."

"Careful with the word 'Brotherhood' on the phone, Omar."

"OK, yes, of course."

He clenched his teeth over the mistake.

"But, cousin, I could use information on the man to demonstrate to the president and cabinet members that this man is not acting in the best interests of the country."

"As I said, I do have a file on Davidson, although it's not current. He lived here for three years, and we know he's been in and out of Cairo recently. I repeat: This is old data, and I'm not certain of his marital status. He's older now, so his wife could be dead, or they could be divorced.

You can view the file if you wish. You'll need to come to my office. I don't need to tell you this, but keep it confidential."

"That's helpful; I'll look at my schedule and propose a time."

"Now, Omar, the file covers the past. Considering his new projects in Egypt, that's much more complex."

"How so?"

"You'll need active surveillance on him."

Fathi paused, then said slowly, "That, I cannot do."

"No?"

"No; the reasons are many. Perhaps a topic for another time."

"I'm interested to discover if he's whoring, doing drugs, alcohol?" Omar said. "Activities the pious Mubarak, especially, despises. Information like that will turn the current reverence against him."

"Again, I will not authorize surveillance by my staff," Fathi insisted. "Still, if you want more information on him, I can suggest a name in the United States. This man—for some money, of course—will track him and possibly get the information you want."

"Davidson lives in California," Omar interjected. "His phony job is that he teaches at a university."

"I must go now, but one name comes to mind. In fact, he may be perfect. He was a good agent who had to flee the country because he notified some people we know that they were about to be wiretapped."

"Ah, yes, I remember the scandal."

"His name is Jabari Radwan, and I believe he lives in San Francisco, in California," Fathi said. "He's trained in electronic surveillance. He's clever, but be careful with him. He's too willing to take risks. Remember—I had nothing to do with this. Understood?"

"Of course. But, cousin, you understand the need to get Davidson out of Egypt? I've been able to control the access of other capitalists to the president. This Davidson is different. His capitalist projects seem to appeal to the president, and they are against our values."

There was no response. Fathi Ashur had hung up.

CHAPTER 3

Connection

Sunset Cove

The bike path in Sausalito was bordered on one side by the western edge of San Francisco Bay and on the other by the constant hum of traffic on Highway 101. Sarah and Judy, cycling side by side, passed hundreds of floating homes attached to piers and connected by a network of walkways. Sarah, ever fascinated by the vibrant water-based community, pointed to one of her favorite houses.

"Don't you just love that design? I always wonder what it's like inside."

"Yeah, yeah, they're cool, but let's pick up the pace," said Judy, head down and eyes fixed on the mileage indicator on her handlebars. "I've got an eleven o'clock."

Sarah rose from her saddle and accelerated the pace as she shot ahead of Judy.

"You want some speed? Well, let's go."

"I should have never mentioned changing the pace," said Judy, legs pumping furiously as she fought to catch up. "You'll bury me."

Seconds later, the two were side by side, and Judy thought it was time to broach the question she had been dying to ask.

"By the way, Fergy tells me Brooks Davidson is back in the U.S. Have you heard from him?"

"What?" Sarah asked. "Why would I hear from him? No, of course not."

"I want to tell you what I learned about him, but I'm getting too winded to do that."

Judy pushed hard on her pedals trying to keep up with Sarah, who seemed to propel the bike effortlessly. Sarah eased off the pace while keeping her eyes on the path ahead, avoiding potholes and rips in the concrete.

"Perhaps at another time," she said.

"You don't seem interested."

"We met for what—fifteen minutes? He was very interesting, but I haven't heard from him, so I assume there's no interest on his part. And, trust me, Judy, it's not a big deal to me."

Even with the slower pace, Judy was breathing hard.

"Gosh! I'll make this quick before I pass out. After the opera house lecture, Fergy said he's never seen Brooks more engaged with a woman like he was with you. That's why Doug and I thought the two of you might connect. I thought you'd be interested in hearing more about him?"

"Still trying to get me to date. You don't give up, do you?"

Between breaths, Judy elaborated.

"You need to hear this: According to Fergy, Brooks is much more than an academic. He was a top diplomat and is currently a very successful investor in the Middle East. Fergy said Brooks is unique—one of a kind. He said he's very aggressive in where he goes and what he does. He'll go anywhere in the Middle East. He has no fear of the radicals in the region. Apparently, he knows some of them."

"Are you trying to impress me?"

Sarah's face was full of amusement.

"Where are you going with this, Judy?"

"He's intriguing, maybe mysterious, but I think he's a real catch. It would be fun to have him around. He'd bring some life to the old crowd, don't you think? You should invite him for a bike ride."

"Not my style," Sarah said. "I don't chase men."

"Would you like to talk to Fergy about Brooks?"

"No thanks; I have the picture."

"Fergy gave me his phone number for you. Would you like it?"

Sarah cut her speed, sat up in the saddle, and turned her head to Judy.

"That's nice of him, but no."

She shook her head.

"That's not me, Judy. Let's get back for your eleven o'clock."

She rose from the saddle and picked up the pace again. She'd heard enough of Brooks Davidson.

★ ★ ★

Later that day, Sarah watched the sun set over the Golden Gate Bridge from her kitchen window. As the bridge turned gold from the descending sun, she prepared her dinner of salad greens, French bread, and tea. Weekdays, she preferred simple meals. Tonight, like most nights, she ate at a coffee table in her family room and watched the evening news. Frustrated by the mess, as she called it, in Washington, she finished her meal, turned off the set, and went to the sink to wash the dishes. With the plates put back in the cabinet and the dish towel stored beneath the sink, she returned to the family room for her books. She preferred this room for reading and catching the news because it was smaller and cozier than her living room. Her flat-screen TV was fastened to a wall that faced the coffee table and the comfortable, roomy suede couch. A few feet away, tucked into a corner of the room was a stone fireplace. In the winter months, she'd ignite the gas logs while she read by the fire. She preferred to read three books at a time, enjoying different topics and genres. This week, it was a mystery by Tom Clancy, a Lincoln biography, and James Baldwin's *The Fire Next Time*. She'd read a chapter or two from one book, then switch.

She nestled on the couch, pulled a cashmere shawl over her legs, and had opened the Clancy book when the phone rang. Calls at this hour usually came from robocallers selling something, and she normally ignored them. But this night, a slight curiosity stirred her. She picked up the phone with a curt "Hello," ready to replace the receiver if it were a sales call.

"Sarah, this is Brooks Davidson."

There was no immediate response. Sensing that she didn't remember him, Brooks continued.

"We met at the bar of the Opera House at the Dalai Lama lecture a few weeks ago. I was talking to our mutual friend, Fergy. Do you remember?"

Sarah hesitated.

"I'm sorry. I didn't get all that. Who is this?"

"I'm a friend of Fergy's. I'm Brooks Davidson. We met at the Dalai Lama lecture."

"Of course. Sorry. It took a moment. You've been traveling. Where was that?"

"My work took me to Cairo. It's good to be back."

"Where are you now? You're from Palo Alto—is that correct?"

"Yes, indeed. I'm sitting at my desk looking at piles of bills and thought, 'I have a better way to use my time: I'll call Sarah.'"

"But Cairo? What did you do there?"

"It was a good trip. A group of us concluded a project with the Egyptian government. Great to have it approved. I won't bore you with the details. I promise."

He laughed.

"A few details won't hurt."

"I have an idea: How about joining me for dinner and an opera? There's one coming up on February fifteenth."

He glanced at the calendar on his desk and grasped a pen to underscore the date.

"We can cover my trip, if you'd like, and I can hear more about what you do. Are you interested?"

"Can you hold for a second?"

Phone in hand, Sarah hustled over to her control tower to examine her schedule. Her calendar covered the desktop with a square for each day in the month. Appointments with clients, doctors and dentists, and meetings with friends filled nearly every square in the register. She selected a pencil from her circular penholder and poked at the dates in February.

"Oh gosh," she said as she saw her brother's name scribbled on the fifteenth. "Can I call you back on that?"

"Sure. Here's my number. The answering device works well if I'm not here."

She placed the phone back on the receiver, surprised at herself. She was pleased that he called. She went to her black book of phone numbers, recorded Brooks', then thumbed through it to get to her brother's number. She called and left him a message: *"Charlie, can we meet for lunch on the fifteenth instead of dinner?"*

The next day, Sarah called Brooks and left a message—she could make the opera. When she placed the phone down, she stared at her calendar and realized the opera was three weeks away. Judy's discussion about his background gnawed at her. It raised a lot of questions about his life. He lived abroad for so many years, worked in government, and now taught at a university. It was a life quite different from hers. Was the difference in career and, perhaps, lifestyle important to her? Would an evening with him be interesting? She had a rising curiosity to get answers to her questions and thought three weeks was a long time to wait. She remained seated at the control tower staring at the calendar. The tingle of curiosity about Brooks was a new and pleasant emotion. She knew she wanted to get a better understanding of him, but how to do it?

That evening, he called.

"Sarah, so good to catch you. I'm delighted you can make the opera. You'll love it; it's *La Traviata*."

"I don't know opera well. You'll have to give me some background on the work, but—"

"I can do that. Luckily, the real pleasure is in the listening. Verdi is a dream to the ears." He rushed on.

"But it's three weeks away. I'd love to connect before then if your schedule allows."

She relaxed back in her chair, her free fingers twirling a long shank of hair that had drifted across her forehead.

"My schedule is a little unusual this time of year as I have guests coming with some frequency. I guess they want to get away from East Coast winters."

"I can understand that," Brooks said. "I've lived there."

"You have? I have too. More on that later, but here's an idea: This Saturday, my biking group is doing the Marin Headlands. Fergy told me you like to bike. Are you interested? There'll be seven riders. You know Fergy, Doug, and Judy. Then there's you and me, so there will be two strangers. That's one possibility for us to connect."

"Give me a sec."

He was standing when he made the call. Now he slid into his desk chair and placed his arms on the desk. He opened his calendar and thumbed through the dates. He was scheduled to ski with colleagues who were to meet at his condo Saturday afternoon.

"Shit!" he murmured to himself.

To Sarah, he said, "It's a great offer. I can make it, but I'll have to leave by noon. Does that complicate your plans too much?"

"What's the complication?"

"I'm committed to meet some folks at Squaw Valley later that day. Do you think I could do the ride, or part of it?"

She laughed.

"That can work."

A second later, she had misgivings.

Oh, dear, she thought. *I'd better let him know what he's getting into.*

"We start riding at seven-thirty, which means you'll have to get here by seven to seven fifteen. You'll have to hit the road at some ungodly hour. That's asking a lot. I hadn't thought of that."

"Yeah, you're right, that's an early start, but I'm used to early mornings. So, you think we'll finish the ride by noon?"

"Oh, definitely. So you can make it?"

"Yeah, I think so."

"You sound hesitant."

"Oh, I'm probably a little uneasy about climbing the Headlands. I'm likely to be a bit slower than you and your crew."

"Not from what Fergy says."

"Well, I'm delighted he's tooting my horn, but we'll see on Saturday."

"Please give me your email address. I'll give you directions to my home. As you'll discover, it's not easy to find."

"Here you go," he said as he supplied the codes. "OK. I'll see you Saturday."

He hung up and immediately put his hand on his forehead. He could feel the furrows on his brow.

What had Fergy said about his biking? he wondered.

He biked casually and had done a few recreational bike trips in Europe, one to Tuscany. He remembered the Italian hills demanded hard work. He considered himself to be quite fit, yet he became breathless on some of the climbs in the Chianti region. The Headlands were much more difficult. He'd driven to the top many times with guests to show the remarkable views of the Golden Gate Bridge, the city of San Francisco, and the vista to the vast Pacific Ocean as it opened away from the bridge. He leaned back in his chair.

Well, he thought, *at least I'll get to know her a little better.*

The Marin Headlands, six hundred feet above sea level, rise sharply from the city of Sausalito. Once a fishing village and now an upscale residential community with a population of around seven thousand, Sausalito sits facing San Francisco. Sausalito's hills, with its vertical, winding streets, look down at the entrance to San Francisco Bay. The 1.7-mile Golden Gate Bridge covers the narrow strait and connects the two communities. The road to the Headlands twists and turns as it rises to the peak, with some inclines requiring even strong riders to get out of their saddles and pump hard to maintain a steady pace. At other sections of the road, the degree of incline reduces and riders can drop back to their seats and pedal more comfortably. Regardless of age or conditioning, most riders would agree that the Headlands are a tough climb.

★ ★ ★

On Saturday, Sarah and Brooks joined the group at a parking lot in Sunset Cove. In the early morning, their breath was visible as they exchanged greetings. Everyone was bundled in warm cycling jackets and tights to stay comfortable in the cool fifty-degree weather. Sarah waved her hand toward the group and called out.

"Let's go. We have fifteen miles of warmup before we get to Sausalito."

She looked over at Brooks with an expression that hinted at amusement as well as concern.

"That's where the climbing begins," she said.

For Brooks, the first steep incline left him wondering if he could make it without getting off the bike and walking. As the first sharp rise flattened out, he felt confident and tried to catch up to the group. Just as he came close to Sarah, she and her friends were out of their saddles accelerating into the next pitch. This happened again and again as he climbed to the top. His only solace was that Fergy was behind him. Now he knew why Fergy had extolled his prowess as a cyclist. He was faster than Fergy, which, with Sarah's crew, wasn't saying much.

Sarah greeted Brooks at the top, her arms above her head, exultant.

"You made it! An unfair introduction to Marin cycling."

She moved closer to him, studying his face.

"That was tough, wasn't it? You OK?"

He was panting.

"Yeah, I don't quite know how I made it, but I'm here."

He moved over to the guardrail to get a better look at the Golden Gate Bridge and the city beyond, both hundreds of feet below.

"I've been here many times, yet my appreciation for the view has just soared."

"Does that mean you'll come back for more?" Sarah teased.

"I think I need to improve my conditioning."

"You did marvelously."

She glanced around the group, seeking affirmation. Seeing heads nod, she turned back to him.

"Now, Brooks, on the descent, don't hit your brakes too hard. It's a very fast downhill."

Back on the road, Brooks realized quickly that he'd never experienced a descent so steep and so fast. This time, he decided not to keep up with the group. As he watched them disappear around the first bend, he thought Sarah and her friends were certifiable. They flew down the road without a care in the world, oblivious to the risks.

Sarah waited for Brooks in Sausalito, and they cycled side by side on the bike path back to Sunset Cove. She pointed to the houseboats along the shoreline.

"Have we frightened you away from riding here again?" she asked. "I think I gave you a rough introduction."

Her face was quiet as she watched for a reaction. Brooks reached a gloved hand to his chin and wiped away some sweat.

"I was surprised at the difficulty today, and I welcome that. It may seem like I'm avoiding another ride when I mention I'm heading back to Cairo."

"Cairo? Again?"

She watched him as he pedaled.

"You must tell me more about what goes on there. You're Mister Mystery."

"Oh, it's quite straightforward, Sarah. The deal I've been working on will be announced to the country. The project champions want me there for the celebration."

"You do hide your accomplishments, Mister Mystery, and I'd love more detail. But back to cycling—did you enjoy today's ride? Are you game for more?"

"I thought I was in good shape with all my skiing, but I have a ways to go before I can keep up with your crew. To answer your question: Yes, I enjoyed it. I like a challenge, and this was a great challenge."

Uncertain over his responses, Sarah realized she wanted to leave him with a good experience.

"When we get back to my house, let me take you to lunch. We have several good restaurants in town."

Brooks sat back in his saddle, looked over at her, and smiled, pleased with the invitation. He pedaled effortlessly now that he was off the mountain.

"Sounds good, though I need to get off to Tahoe. Can it be a quick lunch?"

It wasn't a quick lunch. After grilled salmon at a seaside cafe, the two talked for four hours in Sarah's living room. In late afternoon, he called his friends in Tahoe to say he'd meet them that evening.

CHAPTER 4

The Boiling Point

Cairo, Egypt

The gaggle of reporters—with their notepads, television cameras, and cloth-covered microphones—jammed the front steps of the Heliopolis Palace. The mass of them looked like birds pecking corn in a park—dozens of them, packed together, squawking questions. With the doors held open for him, Omar Sayed strode into the crowd and waved an arm. He clenched his jaw, and he pushed the members of the press aside.

"Give me room!" he growled. "Give me space!"

Someone thrust a microphone into his face.

"Minister Sayed...Minister Sayed! A few words, please."

Sayed couldn't tell who asked the question, and he offered no response. The journalists and hangers-on were blocking the path. He moved through the horde and down the steps as fast as his short legs would carry him. He raised a hand to block the flashing cameras as he plowed ahead.

"Allah, help me," he intoned. "Drive these maggots away."

He could hear the rumble of the engine. His driver had started the car and was standing by its side. He would be away from the throng in a few moments. He moved quickly toward the curbside and the black sedan. His driver opened the rear door, and Sayed stepped in. Disgusted and embarrassed by President Mubarak's speech, he settled into the limousine's soft leather seats. He leaned back, and the vision of the president in front of TV cameras with his advisor Brooks Davidson and a Ford Motor Company executive brought bile to his mouth. He was ready to vomit.

Idris el Buradi, the minister of Agriculture, had followed Sayed from the building. He accelerated his pace to reach the limo and rapped on the passenger door. With his hand, he motioned for Sayed to roll down the window. As it slowly descended, el Buradi rushed his question.

"Omar, why were you not on stage with the president and the others? That project with the Ford Company is yours, right?"

Sayed told his driver, "Hold the car for a moment."

Looking out at el Buradi, he said, "The president, in his wisdom, along with the capitalist viper Davidson, bypassed me and my department again. Enough is enough."

El Buradi wiped a fleck of perspiration from his brow, then placed a hand on the window frame, arresting Sayed's opportunity to close the window and speed away.

"Omar, what will you do? Nothing rash, I hope. It's just the way Mubarak does things. It's not personal."

For a moment, Sayed faced el Buradi. He then dropped his head and stared at his knees.

"I must get back to my office and think," he said, his head still pointed toward the floor of the car. "These economic projects are mine."

His jaw was set as he spit out the next sentence.

"This is the last time the president and Mr. Davidson will go around me and ignore me and my department."

"Meditation and prayer, my friend," said el Buradi as he gently touched Sayed's shoulder, inadvertently splashing a dash of moisture on the latter's blue silk jacket. "Meditation and prayer."

Sayed shook his head.

"I must brief my staff before they see this on television."

He waved off el Buradi, pushed the button to elevate the window, and gave instructions to his driver.

"To the Ministry."

He pulled a cell phone from his jacket pocket and called his office. When his assistant answered, he ordered him to convene a meeting of his top officers immediately. Midday traffic was heavy. The limo moved slowly through the crowded streets. Sayed's right leg twitched nervously.

"Be more aggressive," he implored his driver. "Go faster."

When he arrived at the garage, he called his assistant again and asked, "Did you get everyone?"

Amir replied, "Yes, and they're all in your main conference room, waiting."

Sayed stepped from the car, straightened his jacket, and smoothed the creases on his trousers. Comfortable with his appearance, he walked to the private elevator and inserted the key to the eleventh floor. Arriving, he went straight to the conference room. When he opened the door, his eyes shifted left, then right, canvassing the room, confirming who was there. Satisfied that his full staff was present, he took his normal seat at the head of the long, polished table. For a moment, he relaxed in his wood-backed chair, then rubbed the dark, puffy circles beneath his eyes. His cheeks were red. Sweat glistened on his forehead. He removed an immaculate white handkerchief from an inside pocket and mopped his brow.

"Thank you for responding on short notice," he said. "Give me a moment."

Amid the clutter of papers, ashtrays, cups, and half-filled water glasses on the table, his staff faced him. Twelve of them were gathered around the table. They ranged in age from their early forties to the bald, caustic Ahmed, who was sixty-five. Their bodies were still, their faces passive, as they awaited his news. Sayed's eyes swept the table, connecting with each member. Then he began.

"Gentlemen, I rush this announcement before it goes on national television. An hour ago, the president announced that the Ford Motor Company will build a sport utility vehicle plant in Minya. It will employ thousands."

Stunned, his ministers were silent. Then a hand rose.

"Tell us more."

Sayed waved his arm, circulating it to include everyone.

"Let's follow our normal procedure. We'll go around the table."

One at a time, they spoke freely. Some were disappointed, others angry. His deputy, Hadn, summarized the sense of the group when he said, "Omar, we were not involved. Why?"

"It's true," Sayed stopped to find the right words. "The president, advised by the American Davidson, has gone on his own again."

With a sharp thrust of his right hand, he said, "Remember, that's his prerogative."

As the talk babbled around him, Sayed thought about Davidson. In the Middle East, people who did not like the American said he was a dealer, implying that he provided services in which he was the main beneficiary. Mubarak called him an investment advisor, but others in the government preferred the less-flattering term "dealer." When someone at the table used that term, Sayed's ears perked up. He glanced down the table. Ahmed stood up.

"Gentlemen, Minister," he began, "the dealer is embarrassing us. He has ideas we don't have. Maybe we should approach him to work with us. Put him on a retainer."

Heads nodded in agreement, but Ahmed's comments bothered Sayed. He was concerned that his staff seemed interested in working with the man. As he thought about his position in the Egyptian government, he knew Davidson was a threat.

When the tense meeting was over, Sayed hurried down the long corridor to his office, his short, pudgy body moving at surprising speed. Puffing from his walk, he loosened his tie, removed his jacket, and paced around the edges of his spacious office. Alone and standing by a tall window, he felt his pulse, shook his head in dismay, then faced the difficult fact that the president had bypassed him again. He hadn't acknowledged Mubarak's insult with his subordinates but silently agreed with the tenor of his staff's comments. The Ford deal had diminished his ministry and his stature in government. To calm down, he placed a hand on the window and stared down at the wooden feluccas, some with passengers, others carrying commercial freight. Their white sails and bulky hulls moved lazily beside the modern tourist vessels, each plying its way down the Nile. The sluggish flow of traffic normally had a soothing effect on him. Today, the river was busy, as always, but he hardly saw the activity; his mind reeled from Mubarak's meeting.

"Yes, I am the minister of Trade and Industry," he said aloud to the window, asserting what the president and crafty American had ignored.

He wagged his finger at the glass and promised that the American had pushed too far into his sphere of operation. He berated the window.

"I've isolated and pushed aside other bankers, other advisors. Now, this man must go. Davidson will never push me aside again."

He let that vow roll around his mind as he walked to the plush leather chair at his desk.

He sat with his hands linked behind his head. He knew he had to act, do something to disarm Davidson's influence and undo the damage to his department. He'd been aware of Davidson for some time and knew of his high-level connections in the Arab world. What surprised him was that Davidson kept his activities legal, aboveboard. He did not get involved, as so many foreigners did, in bribes, drugs, arms, or laundered money. The man was too astute to get involved in that world. How to get rid of a man with such powerful connections? Sayed rose from his chair and decided that was his challenge.

To his chagrin, he acknowledged that Davidson had spent more time in the Middle East than he had. While the American was working with governments in the region, Sayed had been in London escaping political reprisal from Sadat's secret police. Unraveling Davidson's reputation and contacts required a strategy, a plan. As he paced around his office, an idea began to form. The phone buzzed, but he ignored it. As he thought about the American, he fumed. Not only had Davidson bested him, the Ford project ignored his principles of national economic growth and violated the tenets of Islam by allowing Western capital, influence, and profiteering into a Muslim country. He sat at his desk for a moment but was uncomfortable. He squirmed in the chair, then rose and began to pace again.

How much, he wondered, *did Mubarak pay the American to arrange the deal? And how much had he paid him for brokering the railway extension down the Nile or for the oil refineries outside of Alexandria? How much of Davidson's fee was kicked back to Mubarak?*

As he thought of specific actions, he was still bothered by larger questions. This project was another insult to the sovereignty of Egypt, another admission that a Muslim state needed Western technical innovation. While in London, he had constantly been reminded of British dominance in Egypt, a historical fact that he could not forget. Now the American was replicating the British role but in a more clever, devious manner, using capital investments rather than the British colonial system of overall government control. How could he remove the American's influence in Egypt? He left his desk and returned to the window. He stared at the busy street below for a moment, his mind bubbling with ideas. In his mind, a plan was forming. He picked up the phone and punched in a private number. He needed to talk with his cousin, Fathi Ashur.

CHAPTER 5

Off Together

Sunset Cove

Whenever Brooks entered Sarah's home, he would go straight to the glass wall that faced San Francisco Bay and drink in the view. Sarah's house sat on the side of a hill elevated well above the trees and other houses in the neighborhood, providing an expansive and uninterrupted vista.

On arrival, he would walk to the glass wall and check on the activity of sailboats, ferries, and freighters in the bay. Sarah had learned that Brooks had lived most of his career abroad in rented flats or houses packed together on busy streets. Sarah recognized that her home was a different and relaxing experience for him. Though he was careful with his comments about her place, she knew he welcomed her artistic taste. She'd been thoughtful in selecting chairs, couches, side tables, and she saw him often lingering by the objects of art that offered comfort yet enhanced the sense of open space in the main living room.

She had placed two dark-brown leather chairs near a sliding glass door that opened onto her deck. At first, she did this in jest to wean Brooks away from his incessant presence at the glass wall, eyes transfixed by the sea. At least, she thought, he should sit if he were so absorbed by the movement on the water. After she purchased the chairs, the cozy corner became a favorite place for them to relax at day's end and have a cocktail before dinner.

As she walked by the leather chairs, she paused and placed a hand on the back of one, deep in thought. She was excited and nervous about Brooks' impending visit today. She had a list of questions for him but wasn't ready to broach her queries. They'd known each other for more than three months, and it had become, for her, a fast romance. He was there nearly every weekend for their bike rides and dinners in San Francisco's best restaurants. Along with that, they often attended theater productions and symphony concerts.

In her mind, as the weeks accumulated, she had marked down the differences between them. She started to count the contrasts on her fingers and realized she didn't have enough fingers. The biggest one, for her, was his lifestyle of roaming the globe, first as a diplomat and now as an advisor and investor. She understood his academic responsibilities, but she knew, after three months together, that his work at the university was a small part of what drove and captivated him. His life, she reflected, was fast-paced, cross-cultural, full of governmental policy and intrigue. Hidden in his descriptions of life was a sense of danger in what he did. Yet, he neither spoke of risk in his work nor seemed worried about it, past or present.

She had asked why he did what he did, and his reply still bothered her because it prompted questions about her career and the careers of her friends.

He had said, "You've raised the two key existential questions about what we do with our lives. Has my work been worthwhile, not only for me, but for others in my community, my country? And have I done it well? Many have benefited from my work, so I believe it is worthwhile, and I've done it well. And I'm not yet done."

At first blush, she thought his response was arrogant, but it came out with such confidence and ease that it made her think. Was her career worthwhile? Did she do it well? She wasn't certain, but she liked her life. It was contained, bounded by activities and places that gave her meaning and comfort. She had her psychology practice. Her clients in San Francisco said they benefited from her advice. She had her home and friends in Marin and visits, occasionally, to her children in Dallas and Chicago. Her life was a comfortable, suburban existence where all neighbors and friends were similar in culture, language, values, and habits.

He had no children. She had two daughters. Lynne, the eldest by three years, was in Dallas with her husband and two children and had become protective of her mother once her husband, Peter, had died. When Sarah mentioned that she'd met someone, Lynne urged caution. They talked once a week at a minimum. Adrienne, the younger, lived in Chicago with her husband and three children. She was relaxed about her mother's life and delighted that she had begun to date.

After a few months with Brooks, she realized he did not live the conventional American life. His life was full of movement, adventure, and international associations, while hers was conventional, local, and quiet. With all these differences between them, she was finding it hard to believe that she was falling in love. They had not had sex or physical excitement to draw them together. Her love had grown from their biking, operas, dinners, and endless conversation. She marveled at the fact that Brooks had never pushed for lovemaking, and she wondered—at his age, her age—had the drive disappeared? She knew the frequent visits of her nephew, whose work had placed him in San Francisco for two months, precluded many opportunities for intimacy, but Brooks never seemed to mind. Yet even without sex, she felt closer and closer to him as the weeks, then the months, went by. Could her feelings be simply recognition of loneliness? As a widow and a widower, were they both starved for companionship? Why did she look forward to his excursion to Marin each weekend? This was unlike her. In the years since Peter's death, she rarely felt enthusiasm in meetings or visits from anyone. Since she met Brooks, she felt more connected to life again.

The knock on the door broke her reverie. Brooks' voice boomed in the entry hall.

"Sarah, where are you?"

She broke away from the leather chairs and rushed toward him in the entryway.

"You're early. Ooh, that's so grand. Did you skip a class?"

"No class today—just office hours with students."

His words tumbled out.

"I couldn't wait to get here. I received some news today that I'd like to go over with you."

"What's that?"

He gave her a hug, then a longer kiss, which she let linger. When she pulled away, she seemed slightly annoyed.

"Come on, Brooks. Don't hold me in suspense. What's this news?"

"OK. Is it time for a drink? We could sit in my favorite spot, sip a nice Manhattan or martini, and I'll reveal all."

She nodded and pointed him toward the cabinet, where they had begun to store the liquor he liked.

"I'll have what you're having for a change," she said.

He pulled the Ketel One from the cabinet and poured four

ounces of vodka into the metal shaker, followed by a dash of Lillet. She followed him into the kitchen, where he added ice from the fridge, shook it vigorously, and placed the mix on the kitchen counter to chill.

"Now, let me start with an unexpected phone call."

He looked at her on the off chance that she might want to start with a different topic. She smiled and placed an arm around his middle and hugged him.

"Go on."

"I got a call from an old friend and colleague at the UN. He wants me to speak at a conference they're having regarding Western investments in the Middle East. It's next week. Apparently, another speaker lined up had to cancel."

"So you're second choice. How's that feel?"

She laughed and poked him in the ribs.

"I'll ignore that."

He shared laughter with her.

"Actually, months ago, I turned the UN down because it conflicted with my talk at the annual bank conference on development economics in New York. Now the UN has changed their date, so I can do it."

"What about your short trip to the conference?"

"Here's the amazing news. Let's sit down."

He poured the martinis into long-stem glasses, and the two clinked them.

"To an interesting evening," he offered.

They crossed to the leather chairs. Brooks opened the shades to reveal the sea as Sarah placed her glass on the table and sat down, the leather creaking. He gazed at the sea for a second, let out a deep breath, then turned to the chairs.

41

"Every time I'm here, the view takes my breath away. I love the sun on the island at this time of day. The brown and green shadows are so calming."

He sat, and she lifted her glass toward him.

"I'm quite pleased. Now go on."

"The UN date is the same week as the other conference but later in the week. I can do both. I'm delighted about that."

"That sounds like a feather in your cap, but now you'll be gone a whole week or more.

That's not good. You'll miss the Largents' dinner and our bike rides."

He sipped his drink, stretched his long legs in front of him, then placed the glass on the round table between them. He leaned forward and reached out to take her hand.

"What I'd like most of all is for you to come with me. We'd have a little over a week in New York. In between my talks, we could do some plays, a concert—experience the city's great restaurants."

He paused.

"I know that's a lot and fast, but what do you think?"

She caressed the back of his hand with her thumb.

"That's so nice of you to think of me, but what about my patients, my volunteer responsibilities?"

"Oh, fantastic," he exclaimed, enclosing her hand with both of his, then pulling them away in a gesture of enthusiasm.

"You'll join me! That's grand! More than grand! We can figure out how to reschedule your appointments and cover you on those responsibilities. It will be no different than when you've taken vacations in the past."

A sparkle of amusement rose in her eyes as she absorbed his offer. If only he knew, she mused, how few vacations she had.

"Give me time to organize my thoughts. If I can, I'd like to do it."

She studied Brooks for a moment, thinking more about the implications of his offer.

"So with this offer and the fact that we've been seeing each other often over the past three months, I'd say we're getting pretty close."

He took a long sip of his martini, then placed the glass back on the table. He reached over and took her hand again.

"That's a very safe statement from my perspective."

★ ★ ★

During the days before the trip, Sarah packed and repacked her suitcase several times. She called Brooks frequently to check on the clothes he planned to wear and which dress would be appropriate at a UN reception or at the Lincoln Center concert on Friday evening. She stewed over her desire to bring running shoes, tops, and tights to run in Central Park. The shoes were a problem; they took up too much space.

Her planning and anticipation settled down only when the limousine picked her up. Sarah liked the luxury and feel of it and the relaxation of not having to drive to the airport. Having arrived from Palo Alto, Brooks was waiting at the curb when the limo pulled in. She jumped out and gave him a warm kiss. She pointed to the car.

"That was relaxing. Thank you for providing it. I'm so delighted to see you."

She had flown to Europe several times. Long flights were not novel to her. Yet Brooks had introduced her to a new form of travel with spacious seating in first class and a limo from the airport to the Four Seasons Hotel in midtown Manhattan. As they arrived at the entryway, the sense of adventure excited her and confirmed that Brooks had a travel style that was different from hers.

She watched him carefully as he approached the desk clerk. He had said in planning the trip that he would continue to recognize their privacy, indirectly stating the obvious—they had not slept together. In her home, with her nephew frequently in and out, privacy was not available to them. She knew that safety net of protection was good for her. Their deep kissing from time to time stirred her, but she would pull away, conveying that she was not ready to go further. She felt he was not ready either. How would he handle their preference for privacy in the confines of one room?

The clerk looked up from his computer and greeted Brooks.

"Evening, sir. Reservation name?"

"Good evening. It's Brooks Davidson, and I've requested a room with two queen beds. I've been assured that type of room is available."

Sarah's large green eyes danced at Brooks' request. She stared up at him with admiration and appreciation.

What a gentleman! she thought.

"Oh, yes, sir. A frequent guest, I see. Welcome back. The manager has a note for you and wants to say hello when he gets free. The room is ready. Would you like some help with your luggage?"

He glanced up from his computer, his eyes surveying the couple, then sliding his attention to a bellman standing nearby.

"George, please take Dr. Davidson to Room 1412."

Upon entering, Sarah wandered around the spacious suite and glanced out the window, viewing the bustle below on 57th Street. The honk of horns, and the clamor of people and traffic were barely audible fourteen floors above the street. Turning from the window, she walked toward Brooks and placed a hand on his shoulder.

"We're at an age, Brooks, when intimacy is still a part of it, I guess."
She paused, her eyes on him.

"And both of us are still getting over the loss of a loved one. I appreciate your sense of privacy."

"Sarah, it would be totally inappropriate for me to spring it on you; don't you agree? The double queens will work fine. When we're ready, we'll know."

She rose up on her toes and kissed his cheek.

"I like your phrase, *'We'll know.'*"

Brooks placed an arm across her shoulders, gave her a gentle hug, and held it for several seconds. Releasing her, he gestured to a couch next to the window.

"Let's take a moment. I'll go over my schedule for the next few days. Then we can decide when you want to join me at the conference and what adventures you'd like to have on your own."

They sat, and he opened a folder he had placed on the seat of the couch, then tapped her knee.

"And you don't have to go to any of the talks at the conference."

"Oh, good; I'm relieved. I hoped you'd say that. I do want to hear your speech, but, you know, the rest is not my field. I'd be lost and—hate to say it—probably bored."

"At least you're honest about it."

He laughed as he picked through the pages of his folder, showing her the itinerary for each day and the times when he was free for a lunch or coffee. They planned where to meet at the end of each day for dinner and a play or concert. He pointed to Thursday on the schedule.

"That's my day at the UN and the day of the reception. I think you'd enjoy that event. It's at four and in the grand hall, which is easy to find. OK. Here's the last surprise: When you're on your own and doing the shopping you enjoy, I have a small gift."

He pulled a credit card from his pocket and gave it to her. It had her name on it. She stared at the card, speechless. He registered her surprise.

"Here's the trick: I've put some money on the card, and the amount is a surprise. When you've expended it all, a clerk will tell you the amount's been exceeded, and you'll have to pay the rest with your own card. Sound like a fun challenge?"

"You can't do this."

"Of course I can. The fun is what you'll buy and how close you'll come to exhausting the card? Will it take one day or all week?"

"This is a dangerous game. I could go broke when I fly by the limit."

"To be seen. Let's have some dinner."

He rose, beckoning Sarah, and walked toward the door. She stood up, following him a step behind.

"I think this is the oddest game I've ever heard. I know you're a numbers guy. What's the scheme?"

She stopped as they came close to the door. He halted and faced her. She reached up and, with her forefinger and thumb, tugged on the lapel of his suit jacket, pulling him closer. She lifted her lips to his and kissed him deeply.

"I'm going to surprise you."

"You've been doing that since I met you. This time, it's my turn."

CHAPTER 6

Sarah and Brooks

New York

The week went by quickly for both of them. When not admiring the early April blossoms of tulips and hyacinths in the nearby parks, Sarah shopped, trying to determine the limits of the card and, by Thursday, had not exhausted the funds. She had coffee with Brooks one day and on another heard him speak to hundreds of men and women at the conference. She didn't understand all the material he covered but felt confident that she had absorbed the talk fairly well and was pleased that it had been so enthusiastically received by the audience. That evening at dinner, he chided her.

"What did you purchase today, my dear, and have you found the card's limit yet?"

She pulled slips from her purse and examined them, running totals in her head.

"I purchased this dreamy sweater and replaced a worn-out pair of flats today. And still no summit's been reached."

He stopped eating and pointed his fork toward her.

"It would be a big mistake to leave money on the card."

"You're having too much fun with my conservative spending pattern and low-risk approach, aren't you?"

"I want to see what happens when you let go, if you ever do."

"Oh, mister, when I do, you'll be shocked!"

He put the fork down, then patted her arm.

"I'm waiting."

He kept his hand on her arm, his eyes playful, trying to read her mind.

"On to another topic. Remember, tomorrow is the UN at four. I'll meet you in the Delegates Dining Room, where the reception will be. Go to the front desk. They will give you your badge and guide you to the right room."

"Is that when I'll meet some of your clients from the Middle East?"

"Yes. You'll see some interesting and different kind of people."

"Are they your Saudi clients? I think that's what you call them."

"Yes, close enough. I've done several projects with the men you'll meet."

"Will I meet their wives?"

"No, not there."

He looked at her quizzically.

"You do know the male-female relationships in that culture?"

"I'm not sure—maybe, maybe not."

"Well, very quickly: It's a male society in most of the Muslim world. The men often have several wives. The women rarely work. Very few have any education to speak of, and very few have a career. The women stay at home, manage the home or homes, and take care of the children. That's why it's unlikely you'll see any of them at the reception. You'll receive a lot of attention from some of the men, not all."

★ ★ ★

By the middle of the next day—one decidedly warmer than most for April in New York City—Sarah found herself trolling the sidewalks and shops on Fifth Avenue, but her mind was not on shopping or attempting to max out Brooks' credit card. Unlike her normal shopping sprees, she had made no purchases.

She was worried about the UN reception, meeting and talking with global power brokers—all strangers. By the time her wristwatch buzzed three-thirty, she had worked herself into a state of high anxiety. At a swift pace, she headed from a shop on Madison Avenue to the Delegates Dining Room on East 44th Street across First Avenue from the UN headquarters. She felt warm from her six-block walk there. She stopped at the entryway to wipe her brow with a handkerchief before she joined a short line at the reception desk. The guards were pleasant as she secured her identification badge and received directions to the dining room.

As she entered it, her eyes were drawn to the tall windows that opened the room to the city. She stared out at the city for a moment, then turned her attention to the mass of delegates dressed in a wide array of stylish robes, leggings, turbans, Nehru jackets, and Western business suits. But she did not spot Brooks in the crowd. The buzz of hundreds of conversations caused her anxiety to flare up again. To reach a calmer state, she looked for the buffet tables. When she eyed them, laden with food, she headed to it; Brooks could wait.

Sarah moved down the buffet line, filling her cocktail plate with shrimp, pickled herring, smoked salmon—more than she could ever eat. Next to her, a middle-aged woman in a tailored pants suit tapped her arm.

"Isn't this buffet marvelous? Sure beats mixing with all those stiffs, doesn't it?"

"Oh," Sarah sighed in relief, "I just arrived and haven't talked to anyone yet. I'm not too excited to enter that fray."

She pointed outward to the crowd.

"These delegates," said the woman with a slight shake of her head. "They talk shop all day and do it again at these parties. I need a break."

Sarah placed her plate on the buffet table and pointed to the mass of bodies that filled the room.

"I'm a guest today. All this is new to me. Many of these faces are on the evening news—they're big deals."

"Trust me: I work with many of them. They like to think they're big deals, but they're just like you and me."

The woman faced the room with Sarah and pointed to a short, stocky man energetically talking to two other men.

"See him—the short, bald one? He's my boss at the UN, and, believe me, he's quite average."

She paused.

"Over there, I see a man waving to us. I think that's Brooks Davidson."

Sarah scanned the scene and saw Brooks, standing amid three men in long white robes, beckoning her to join him. She turned to face the woman.

"You know Brooks?"

"Not really. I'm told me he's active in the Middle East—lots going on. Are you with him?"

Seeing Sarah nod, she touched her hand.

"George—he's the short one over there—has had several meetings with him. I don't know much about those discussions, but he has a high regard for Dr. Davidson."

"Thank you; that's nice to hear."

She touched the woman's arm.

"Please excuse me. I'm being summoned."

She took her plate and walked toward Brooks. As she moved closer, Sarah could see the other men more clearly. Their robes were trimmed in brown and gold; double dark bands held their headscarves. All three stared intently in Sarah's direction. Brooks stepped forward, smiled, and extended his hand toward her plate.

"Let me take that while I make introductions."

He put the plate on a table and introduced her to Sheik Ahmed Zaki Suleiman. The long names of the others became a blur to Sarah as she bowed delicately. Her lips pressed tightly as she silently said the sheik's name over and over. The sheik's eyes danced. They never left Sarah's face.

"May I use informal English and call you Sarah?" he asked.

Brooks placed a hand gently on Sarah's shoulder.

"Permit me to finish my conversation with Hamid and Alim. Then I'll join you and Ahmed."

Sarah gently straightened her shoulders, which lifted her body to her full height. She was as tall as the sheik. Eye to eye, she spoke directly to him.

"It looks like I have you to myself, Sheik Ahmed. Is that the correct way to address you? And, yes, you may call me Sarah."

"Ahmed is fine with me. Please tell me: What brings you here? Are you with the UN or a financier with Brooks?"

Sarah scanned his face. His eyes were lively. She wondered what he thought of the dress codes and working habits of American women. She wanted to ask these questions but felt the inquiries might be inappropriate. She wanted to remember his name and repeated it silently again.

"I'm a psychologist from California and a friend of Brooks'.

This UN world is new to me."

Sheik Ahmed stepped closer to Sarah.

"How delightful—someone different! I want to hear more about your world, but my friends tell me I'm too inquisitive."

"What questions do you have?"

"Oh, how did you decide to have your own career? Do you work all the time? How did you meet the fast-moving Dr. Davidson? Questions like that and many more."

She stared into the man's copper-tinged face and noticed how his short beard accentuated the angularity of his jaw.

"Your questions would generate a long monologue," she said. "I'd be boring you in seconds."

He threw his head back and laughed.

"I doubt that, but here's Brooks."

He gestured toward Brooks, who was accompanied by Hamid and Alim.

"May I suggest we continue this at dinner tonight?" the sheik offered.

Brooks' eyes swept over the three Saudis.

"Most kind, Ahmed. As always, you are most generous in your invitations. However, Sarah and I have a prior engagement."

He extended his hand to Ahmed, then to the others.

"We'll all dine together soon."

The three Arabs bowed and slowly retreated toward other delegates. Brooks guided Sarah toward the doors of the hall. She took his arm, then tilted her head into his shoulder for a second as they walked.

"Brooks, that was so interesting. I loved it. But I'm delighted that you protected our dinner tonight."

"It's been a busy set of days," he said, exhaling a day's worth of conversations. "I'm very ready for some private, quiet time. How about you?"

"Absolutely."

She pulled her hand tight against his arm, pressing her body close to his, then looked up. "All I want is you tonight."

CHAPTER 7

Cousins Meet

Cairo, Egypt

Fathi Ashur saw the red light on the phone and waved his deputy out the door.

"Come back in five minutes."

He rose from his desk to stretch his bad leg before picking up the phone. From time to time, he regretted that he'd given his cousin access to his private line. But it was done at the request of his family to assist Omar in navigating the intricacies of the Egyptian bureaucracy.

He returned to the desk, crushed his Cleopatra cigarette in a metal ashtray, and punched the red button.

"Hello, Omar. You've been calling every week for the past month—or is it two? It's a bad time right now. Is this urgent?"

"Yes, since our buildings are close, can we meet at our usual spot at noon tomorrow?"

Omar grimaced at the curt response.

"Is it Davidson again? Does it require privacy?"

"Yes and yes." Fathi sighed.

"I'll be there at noon."

He remained seated at his desk, aware that he should call his deputy back to the meeting. He wanted a moment to think about Omar's request. It was likely that his cousin needed help.

What would it be this time? he wondered.

He wanted no trouble with the Americans. Too much money was coming from that source.

He thought about his twenty-six years in the Mukhabarat, and how Sadat and later Mubarak used his Special Ops group to hound their enemies inside and outside of government. He had information on thousands of individuals. He placed his hands on the keyboard of his computer and tapped the icon for the foreign personnel section. He spotted Davidson's file and opened it. He smiled at the photo. It must be ten years old, he realized. Then he scrolled through the pages. It was a thick file and all positive. He reflected on one entry in which Davidson, then in the CIA's Cairo station, alerted him that the Russians were launching a program to bribe and infiltrate Egyptian ministries. He used the intelligence to expose the Russians, and more than two dozen agents were expelled from the country. He winced every time he thought of their revenge. A midsized truck had broadsided his Mercedes at an intersection a few miles from his home on the outskirts of the city. The driver and the vehicle were never identified. The crash took a painful toll on his body: his left knee was shattered, resulting in a permanent limp; his left wrist was broken and now arthritic; and his left cheek bore a long, white scar from broken glass.

He was tall and angular for an Egyptian, and the scar on his thin face gave him the appearance of severity that added to his image as a distant, austere leader. He picked up his phone and called his deputy.

"I'm clear again."

The deputy opened the door and burst in with news.

"Did you see the president's press conference this morning? I just saw a replay."

Ashur shook his head, rose from his desk, and gestured for them to sit at the small conference table near the window.

"No, anything significant?"

"It was the groundbreaking for a commercial venture. The Americans are coming—this time with a manufacturing plant for motor vehicles."

"Anything else?"

"No, but the president seemed particularly pleased with this venture. He boasted that thousands of jobs will be created."

"Yes, I'm aware."

Ashur glanced at his watch.

"It's getting late. Let's get back to work on the budget. Before we leave tonight, I want to cover all the changes I'm considering. Let's move fast. I want to be out of here fairly soon."

★ ★ ★

A bright, yellow sun welcomed the next day. Haze rose from the river, bringing humidity with the May heat. Fathi had left his jacket at the office and opened his shirt collar to get some relief from the sodden air. As he walked the few short blocks to the Nile, beads of sweat formed on his forehead. He slowed down. When he saw Omar leaning against the iron railing with his back to the sluggish river, he waved to him, and a smile creased his face.

Omar had been lost in thought while waiting by the river. He knew his cousin respected precision in speech, and he was rehearsing his comments. This was a critical moment in his career. He needed his cousin's help. When he spotted Fathi's wave, his shoulders relaxed slightly. He moved from the railing and greeted his cousin with a handshake and a kiss on each cheek.

"Did you see the president on television yesterday?"

"Yes," Fathi said. "I knew that would be our topic."

"Were you surprised by Mubarak?"

Fathi took a step back. He was surprised at the apparent nervousness of his cousin. Omar could not stand still. He moved from foot to foot, unable to stay in one place. He decided to try to calm his cousin.

"I'm never surprised by the president, and I sense your dilemma," Fathi said. "You're still annoyed with the American's project."

"Annoyed?!"

Omar moved from the railing in rapid steps toward Fathi. His arms pushed forward as if preparing for a fight.

"That doesn't begin to describe my crisis. My blood pressure is sky high. I can feel the pounding in my ears. Annoyed? It's more like I'm boiling over, about to explode. The president brought me here from England for my knowledge of developmental economics. And what's happened? On important economic decisions, I'm ignored, and today's announcement enforces the humiliation."

Fathi placed a hand on Omar's shoulder and let it rest there. "Come, come. We've talked of this before. What's new?"

Omar, momentarily, seemed lost in thought. His eyes were dead, staring at nothing. He shook his head to regain focus.

"I'm agitated, as you see. I can't seem to get over what the president's done. It's wrecking me."

Fathi pointed to the dirt path along the river. Short trees and shrubs separated the walkway from the cars on the street. Fathi liked that the hum of the traffic provided a buffer to their conversation, muting any possibility of prying ears listening to their discussion. Side by side they walked, avoiding other strollers and seeking open spaces to talk. As they got into their stride, Fathi picked up the pace despite his noticeable limp.

"What do you want to do, Omar? I assume you don't want to surface and complain about this issue at a cabinet meeting?"

Fathi pursed his thin lips to hold back the laughter that was bubbling within.

"Pardon me, but we've all seen what happens to a minister who challenges the president. I can see you in those prison clothes now—not consistent with your Savile Row suits."

"Stop this, Fathi. It's not humorous."

Omar kept walking but turned his head, giving his cousin a severe look.

"This is my career we're discussing. I need your advice. I have an idea that I think is good."

Fathi stopped and faced his cousin. His lean face was dark as he raised an arm and pointed his finger.

"What? Are you going to resign in protest, then run back to London? Back to the London School and teach there again?"

Omar stepped back, avoiding the finger as if it were a punch in his face.

"No. Something to directly help Egypt. An action that is sinister and, I believe, very effective."

Omar waited for Fathi to comment and let the silence linger for a few seconds.

"OK, I'll continue. I want to use the Mukhabarat, the skills of your highly trained agents, to silence the man who made this deal and so many others like it. If I can get rid of him, I'll be back on top, and I'll regain control over the economy."

Fathi, still standing quietly beside Omar, lifted his eyes and hands to the sky.

"Allah! He wants to murder this man; forgive him."

"No, no, no—listen to me. I'm serious. This is an American. He's a danger to our country."

"It's one man, Omar. You're overreacting."

"Not at all, Fathi. There are what—twenty-two countries in the Middle East? About ten have substantial economies."

He held up both hands, extending his ten fingers. He started to count off the countries finger by finger.

"Egypt, Saudi Arabia, Iran, Iraq, Jordan—"

"Stop, Omar! Where are you going with this?"

"I'm pointing out that Davidson, all by himself—well, maybe with a couple of partners—has introduced a new form of colonialism to our country and to one-half of the larger countries in the Islamic world. He's having a huge impact on the way these economies work."

He paused, then pointed a finger toward Fathi again.

"He's brought Western companies into our lands. He's slowly pushing our economies from state-run enterprises to open-market capitalism."

"I'm no economist," Fathi said. "You know that. But if Davidson is bringing more jobs than other plans can, what's the problem?"

"He's destroying Islamic principles of economic life—principles that existed centuries before the rise of capitalism."

Fathi stood his ground, shaking his head slowly.

"Well, let's hear you out."

"One more fact for you: Davidson's reaped a fortune for initiating each deal, and the fees coming from our treasury alone amount to over six million U.S. dollars."

Fathi pointed to walkers approaching them and suggested they start walking again. With his hand, he motioned them forward.

"That's probably cheap compared to what the London and Paris bankers would charge."

Omar acknowledged the comment with a shake of his head. As they moved ahead, he spoke.

"It's time for us to decide what happens in our economy and stop the Westerners, like Davidson, from bringing ventures into Egypt and running off with all the profits."

Side by side, they continued down the path, each digesting the thoughts of the other. Fathi broke the silence.

"Let's get back to where you started. You want help from the Mukhabarat? I told you yesterday that's not possible nor desirable from my perspective."

"Can we come back to that? I'd like to explore my Davidson idea with you."

Fathi sighed and pointed to more couples nearby, and they walked on quietly. At an open railing overlooking the Nile, he stopped.

"If we keep our voices down, the rushing water will protect our conversation."

Fathi leaned against the railing and flexed his gimpy leg to relieve soreness.

"OK. Let's hear your plan."

Fathi watched his cousin begin to assemble his idea, and he was amused at how Omar's head went back and his lips pursed before he spoke. He'd always admired Omar; the family considered him the bright one, the one to reach the highest peaks in his career. And Omar had done it in academia and had reached the top level in the Egyptian bureaucracy. Yet, Fathi was aware of his cousin's impulsive tendencies. There was that strong streak of rebellion that pushed him to criticize Sadat's corruption in essays—essays that ultimately forced him to flee the country and take up an academic career in England. When Mubarak claimed that was water over the dam, Omar came back. But, as Fathi observed, Omar's contempt of Western influence in Egypt had not abated.

Omar tugged at the collar of his shirt, opening it to cool his neck and chest.

"Yes, I appreciate your interest. My idea," he said, spreading his arms wide, "is this big."

Fathi rubbed his hands together and let out a sharp breath of air.

"What do you want to do? I gather you want to silence him. How—kill him?"

"No killing."

Omar was calm, his voice steady, his eyes riveted on Fathi's face.

"You've done many clever operations in the past, cousin. Look at what you did to the Russians."

"Ah, yes," replied Fathi, pointing down to his leg then up to his cheek. "Facial scars, an arthritic wrist, and a bad leg. I was younger then. I'm wiser now."

"My idea has three parts," said Omar, holding up his hand to stop Fathi from interruption. "First, we kidnap Davidson's wife and set a ransom number. Second, we demand he resign from all work in the Middle East. Third, we threaten him with blackmail on the secret memo he gave Mubarak—the memo that covered U.S. agricultural trade with Egypt. When those conditions are met, we release the woman."

Fathi flexed his jaw to pop his ears, wanting to ensure he'd heard the plan correctly. He was speechless. Omar felt his own excitement building. He plowed on.

"Understand this, Fathi: It's original, bold. We don't go after the man; we go after his family."

He stood up straighter, feeling unburdened by the weight of the plan.

"For ransom, we require a payment, say two million dollars, then the signed agreement. Obviously, that's the most important piece."

He stepped back, a look of triumph on his face, as he summarized.

"That means no more work in Egypt for Davidson."

Fathi pulled away from the railing and began walking as Omar followed.

"I need a place to sit, to think. This is huge, Omar. We talked about Davidson before, remember? Are you sure he has a wife?"

Omar laughed.

"All rich Americans have a wife. It's what they do. And he was seen with a very attractive woman by one of my staff at a New York conference. Hadn said they were very devoted to each other."

Fathi's leg had stiffened while resting at the railing. They slowed their pace, quiet now, letting the plan sink in. Fathi scanned ahead for a place to sit. Seeing none, he picked up the pace.

"What is it you said about Davidson and some trade deal with President Mubarak?"

"Oh yes. A blessing from Allah. You showed me this last year. It was a memo in your file from one of your agents. It claimed that Davidson had notified Mubarak that a new U.S. trade policy on export quotas was about to be inflicted on Egypt's purchases of agricultural equipment. The information enabled Mubarak to negotiate better terms. Davidson got the Alexandria oil refinery deal in return."

"I don't remember this," said Fathi, eyes widening. "I agree—it's blackmail material."

Omar added to his argument.

"I'm no expert on the law, yet when an individual supplies confidential government information from one government to another, I believe that's treason."

Fathi snorted.

"Well, Omar, you've done some thinking and some homework, but let's get at some facts."

"This is why I'm here. Your experience and insights are invaluable."

Fathi stopped walking and turned to face Omar. He raised his right hand and began ticking off his points finger by finger.

"I'll start with the kidnapping. First, who's going to do the kidnapping? It won't be the Mukhabarat, so who? We'll come back to that. Next, this is a prominent American. I can see his former employer, the CIA, all over this in seconds. And Davidson is likely to have high-ranking friends in their FBI. They'll be on it too."

"I have responses to those…"

The pathway was empty of other walkers. They stood in the middle of the dirt path. Fathi kicked a few pebbles away from his feet. He lifted his head and spoke directly to Omar.

"Let me finish. Next, where's the two million dollars coming from? This is one man, a former government employee, not a capitalist millionaire. Also, there is a one-man issue. Let's say he signs the agreement, pays the ransom. What's to stop Lazard, the Rothschilds, Goldman Sachs from coming in and doing what he's doing?"

Omar paced in a tight circle. He turned to Fathi as he spoke.

"Let's talk about the kidnapping last. I'll start with Davidson.

We go after his family. We have damaging information on him that he doesn't want his government to know, so he'll act fast. I doubt he'll want our information publicized and have his FBI or CIA digging into his shady deals."

Fathi had an odd look on his face as if he didn't agree with the argument, but with the wave of his hand, he urged Omar to continue.

"Next, as I said earlier," Omar said, "I have information from our Treasury that he's been paid millions for the refinery and rail deals in Egypt. That's just his work in *our* country. He's done projects in Kuwait, Saudi Arabia, Jordan, and elsewhere. My Treasury friends tell me that the checks for his fees were sent to banks in Panama and the Isle of Man. He can pay the ransom with a quick telephone call to one of his banks. Plus, he's avoiding U.S. taxes. That's a problem for him too."

Fathi reached out to grasp Omar's arm.

"Omar, stop pacing—you're driving me crazy."

Omar stopped in front of Fathi. He lifted his hands in surrender.

"OK, I admit I'm overexcited about my plan. Let me continue."

He hesitated for several seconds, seemingly to get his thoughts in order.

"Don't you agree? He'll have to act fast and without his government's involvement. The abduction will be over in a few days. He'll step away from Egypt quickly to avoid our releasing damaging information."

Fathi motioned to Omar to resume walking and turned to head toward their offices.

"I need to get back, so let's summarize where you are."

"I want to comment on your 'one man' concern and then conclude on how to kidnap the woman."

Fathi quickened the pace, moving his gimpy leg with some alacrity. Omar started to sweat, and his breathing came in short, uncomfortable bursts. Between breaths, he spoke.

"Fathi, for a man with a bad leg, you certainly can move fast. Slow down so I can get my thoughts out."

Fathi looked over at him and eased up slightly.

"Sorry, but I do need to get to the office. Please finish."

"I agree Davidson is one man, but think of the message we're sending to capitalist bankers. They'll be thinking that Egypt is not friendly to their projects and ideas. I think this action will scare them away. And that's what I want."

"I hear your comment, but it's wishful thinking," Fathi said. "Nothing scares capitalists."

"Not true, cousin. We don't see too many foreign capitalists in China or Russia."

"OK, OK. That might be true. However, Mubarak may offer Western capitalists protection."

"I don't agree. Capitalists will fear abduction. No government in our part of the world can guarantee protection from the radicals and rogue groups. You've said that yourself. You said the radicals in the region are getting bolder, more aggressive, toward their own governments and toward the West."

Fathi didn't look at Omar. His attention seemed drawn to the traffic on the river. An eighty-foot-long cruise boat was motoring past them, midstream on the Nile. Passengers on the upper deck were laughing, drinking. Their conversations spilled across the water to the pathway.

"Look at that."

Fathi pointed toward the boat.

"Ninety percent of Egyptians couldn't afford one day on that boat, and there go a hundred drunken Europeans and Americans taking ten days to travel our river."

"We don't need them here," Omar said. "That's why Davidson and his ilk must go."

Fathi unleashed a rich set of Arabic expletives—a burst rarely heard by Omar or others.

"Listen, Omar, your idea may have some merits. We're not through discussing it, but be clear on one thing: You're going beyond our Muslim Brotherhood beliefs when you say we don't need outside ideas, money, and projects."

"I'm being very precise, cousin. I'm saying we don't need Western projects that remove solid economic projects designed by my organization. I want projects that will build Egyptian competence, capital reserves, and jobs. We don't need foreigners coming into our country and violating Islamic principles of alcohol and drug use like those parasites on that cruise boat."

Fathi clapped Omar on the shoulder.

"Let's keep moving. How do you plan to capture and hide this woman?"

Omar wiped his mouth with the back of his hand and walked in silence for several steps. When he looked up at Fathi, his eyes were pleading.

"Are you certain your highly skilled staff cannot arrange or complete this task? It will be over in two to three days."

"I've done many abductions. Some are quick, some drag on. It's never easy to predict where or when complications will arise. To answer your basic question, no. My staff is fully deployed now, and this is not the right work for us."

"Other than capacity, why not?"

"Do you have any idea what it's like to take on the Americans?

They don't like their people kidnapped. And you want to harm a man that was once CIA and very high in the CIA. Believe me, you don't want to cross the CIA."

"Are you saying my idea is wrong, bad?"

"Not necessarily. I'll come back to that, but first another question: Are you doing this for revenge on Davidson, to get even?"

"No, not at all. Though I despise the man, my action is for the good of Egypt."

"I understand."

Fathi faced Omar and looked him straight in the eye.

"I'll give it serious thought."

"Does that mean you'll have ideas on how to conduct the abduction?"

"If I think you have a chance of success, I'll have ideas on how to do it."

"That's all I ask."

CHAPTER 8

A Call to Action

Sunset Cove

Brooks entered Sarah's home and, predictably, went straight to the glass wall to absorb the view of the bay. Hearing a noise at the front door, Sarah dropped the dish towel onto the kitchen counter. Her long legs propelled her from the kitchen to the living room, where she placed her face in front of his and gave him a kiss.

"Am I the attraction, or is it the view?" she teased. "In June, the colors on the island are more vivid, aren't they?"

He didn't reply. He gazed down at her, tucked a hand behind her neck, and returned her kiss. She grasped his hand and led him to his corner of the living room, where the maroon leather chairs faced the sea.

"Let's sit here tonight."

She pointed to the chairs while she stood by his side.

"I've made a special appetizer, and I have your favorite drink chilled and ready."

"You have something on your mind," he tendered, settling himself comfortably in his chair. "What's up?"

"You just wait—I have gobs to discuss."

She tapped his shoulder.

"I'll be back in a minute," she said as she retrieved their drinks from the refrigerator.

Sarah used the word "gobs" frequently. Brooks had come to learn it had a fluid definition. It could mean she had many topics to address, or it could mean she had one large and worrisome item on her mind. She was like his late wife. Both were introverts, yet each dealt with information differently. Clary, as he called her, held her worries and activities inside until the issue at hand became a crisis. She was perpetually reluctant to reveal her inner thoughts even though, in a large social setting, she was a bright and lively conversationalist on the topics of the day. Sarah was her opposite. She tended to reveal all worries through immediate conversation on any matter, large or small. They all came out, yet, in a crowd, she tended to be a listener, an observer. She preferred to find a quiet inner place and stay there.

Sarah placed the drinks and a plate of sushi on the small table between the chairs, then reached for her Manhattan.

"Dig in."

"This looks grand."

Brooks lifted a salmon roll to his mouth and swallowed.

"Wow, one of the best—agree? Now back to your 'gobs to discuss.' Is it a long list or just a couple of big topics?"

She flashed her vibrant smile, her eyes opened wide, bristling with energy.

"You know a Claude Anderson fairly well, I take it."

"Claude? Good God! How did you come up with that name?"

"Oh, Brooksie, I'm—"

"Sarah," he interrupted. "We agreed; it's never 'Brooksie,' right?"

69

"Yes, OK. I did agree. Don't be so dogmatic."

She tossed her head back.

"It's cute though."

Then she smiled that wide smile that dazzled him. He'd never seen a smile like Sarah's—her lips open to reveal the rows of immaculate, white teeth, her face lit up, and her round eyes sparkling. He watched her face and let her warmth invade him.

"What's with Claude?"

"He called here, and I'm thrilled."

"Sarah, you have me on the edge of my seat. Say more."

"Don't be silly. I'm pleased because you've given one of your friends this number. I'm glad you're comfortable doing that."

"I am. I hope you know that."

He'd been sipping his martini, then placed it on the table and extended his hand gently to her knee.

"Claude's quite a talker, yet he can be all business too. Did you have a conversation?"

She glanced down at his hand and placed hers on top of it.

"Oh yes; he was quite chatty. He had many stories about you. They're on my list of gobs to discuss."

"I can't wait to go over those, but why did he call?"

"He got to that eventually. He said it was important. Actually, I think he said it was urgent for you to call as soon as I had a cocktail in your hand."

Brooks gave Sarah's knee a squeeze, then pulled his hand back. He shifted his body in the chair and reached for the long-stem martini glass.

"I have my cocktail, and it's still early in D.C., but I can call him after dinner."

"No. I promised him you'd call as soon as I had you settled

with your drink. I'll head to the kitchen and arrange some of my deli delights. While I'm doing that, give him a call and tell him I say 'hello.' I really liked the way he was on the phone."

"No surprise there. He's very charming, very good with people."

"He said you were in grad school together and in the same government agency for years. You've known each other for over three decades."

"Yeah, true. For most of our careers, we were in the same region: the Middle East. Did he tell you about our years there?"

"I remember something about your being there in the seventies and eighties, and both of you coming back to headquarters in the nineties. He said you were his boss for a while, and now he has your old job."

"The two of you had quite a chat."

"Well, I loved it. You're too quiet about that part of your life."

"The nineties were troublesome for me. I don't dwell on that time much or bother reliving it."

"That's the time he mentioned. That's what I want to talk about."

She held up her hand before he could speak.

"But later. Give Claude a call while I prepare."

Claude had five phone numbers, and Brooks had them all locked in memory. It was eight-fifteen in Washington. Brooks called the private home number. It rang three times before a growled voice answered, "Davidson, this better be you."

Brooks could picture the scene in Claude's home. He was in his study, a cramped ten-by-ten room jammed on three walls with bookshelves packed with books. Newspapers and periodicals were piled on wooden chairs monogrammed with Columbia University on the back. On his small wooden desk, he stacked reports that he pushed around in some form of organization only he could decipher. His phone was lost in this jumble. The one open space on the desk was reserved for his tumbler of scotch. It was at half-mast when Brooks called.

"Brooks! Goddamn—'bout time! I'm on my second scotch. One more, and I won't be taking calls."

"You got to slow that shit up, old man. We're too old for more than two a night."

"This aging shit is for the birds. OK. Glad I found you. Like your lady. Got to hear more about her. I called because something's going on out there. I've got some work I need done, and the folks on top have asked for you."

When Claude Anderson mentioned folks on top, Brooks knew there was trouble afoot. Anderson's job, as deputy director of Middle East operations, was one level below the top post in the Central Intelligence Agency. From the way Claude phrased the request, Brooks knew either the CIA director or someone in the White House had a problem they wanted addressed outside the realm of normal government operations.

"This doesn't sound good to me. What's up?"

Brooks heard a slurping noise on the other end of the line.

"Goddamnit, Claude! Are we going to talk or drink?"

"Sorry, old man. It's been a rough week. Here's the deal: Bush's people think the Saudis are planning another oil embargo. Obviously, the president doesn't want it and needs to know if the rumors have any basis."

"So?"

"The folks in the big house know you have solid contacts with all the princes who matter, plus you know lots of people at the well sites and refinery level. I'd like you to visit the kingdom next week. The Bush people want it even sooner."

"Jesus, Claude. Are these people tone deaf? They pass me over for agency head then want me to do work they can't get done with their appointees? Why the fuck should I help them?"

"Brooks, calm down. Take another sip of that martini that your delightful Sarah concocted. You can't still be pissed at Bill Clinton and Bush Junior because they picked other people for the top job."

"I hear you. Every time I think I'm over it, I find the resentment coming back. Sorry."

"Face it, Brooksie—you and I are bureaucrats. They normally pick an outsider to run the company at Langley. We went as high as we should. We're not made for the compromises and treachery that goes on at the top. We're not made for that world."

"Yeah, yeah—we could debate that forever. I'm quite comfortable where I am."

"Professor and investment banker. I don't know how you do it. I could never function in that investment banking world of yours."

"A topic for another conversation. Back to your request. I thought the Bush people were pissed over my SUV deal with the Egyptians. I'm surprised they want anything to do with me."

"The president's practical. It's the Commerce people that have their tits in a wringer. More important, like the president, I want to emphasize that I'm not only practical, I'm realistic. As you know, a lot of our best Middle East folks left when you left. We're weaker here than I'd like. I'm calling you back because the issue's important. We need your knowledge and skills."

"Flattery, flattery—it always works."

"You'll do it?"

"The schedule's a problem. Let me work on that. I can get

back to you in a day or two. Is there anything else before we talk about compensation?"

"There is something else, and this is my concern—mine only."

"Say more."

"As I scan and scrub the field reports coming in, I'm getting a strong sense that something big is about to happen. It's going to get done by one of the fucking rogue groups in the Middle East."

"What are you seeing or hearing—where, when?"

"That's it. Our people think an assault of some kind—rockets, bombs, a big artillery type of attack—will be launched against a U.S. site. It could be a military base in Europe or the Middle East, it could be an embassy, it could be a civilian target in the U.S. The information's fuzzy and hard to pin down, but our field people are picking up this type of rumor. The one idea I have is to use your very good contacts with the Saudi Mukhabarat. If you agree to visit the kingdom on the oil embargo, you could do a very quiet inquiry on what they know about the dissidents in their kingdom."

"The Saudis? Really?"

"Yeah, bin Laden's group. They're a worry."

"He's effectively been kicked out of the country."

"Right. We know they're tracking him as close as they can. Increasingly, they're worried he wants to bring down the regime. They may know something. If they'll share it with anyone, they'll share it with you."

"Interesting," Brooks mused. "First, let me look at my schedule to see if I can get free for a week in the near future. It won't be next week, but I can look ahead. Will that work for you?"

"I wish it was tomorrow. Tell me what's possible."

"OK. I want full fees, first-class travel. You know my requirements."

"I'd like to use the contract that we have on file. Is that good enough?"

"Is that what we used on the Jordan inquiry?"

"Yes, and I have one more request."

"OK. The contract's fine. Send it. I'll sign if I can get the dates to work. What's the one more request?"

"Jean has a friend who's marvelous and coming out of a difficult divorce. Jean thinks you should meet her since you put no pressure on women for permanent ties. This woman is in no mood for a long-term relationship."

"The lady you talked to today, this Sarah—she's quite special," Brooks said. "You'd like her. I think I need to play this one out. I'll pass on Jean's friend. Please thank her for thinking of me."

"Does this Sarah know you were CIA and you still do some work for us?"

"No, I'm old school on that. Until we're much closer, I'm still a retired diplomat."

"Good. Best to keep it that way."

CHAPTER 9

Gaining Traction

Cairo, Egypt

Ashur's office was a direct reflection of his personality. It was spare and clean. There were no awards, memorabilia, or photographs of notables on the walls. A single print, Picasso's *Dora Maar*, was mounted behind his desk. The other walls were bare. His desk was a contemporary Italian design: blond wood with a black stone top. It was empty except for his desktop computer and a black telephone. Two Biedermeier chairs faced his desk. The wood frames were the same color as the desk, and the black-fabric seats matched the color of the desktop. Two tall windows looked out to the Nile; their gray shutters could be raised or lowered by cord depending on the location of the sun. A small conference table sat near the windows. The four functional office chairs tucked into the table were rarely used.

Ashur stepped out from behind his desk and arranged the chairs so they faced each other. Today, his father, Gamal, was making a short visit from Kom Ombo, his home a few hours south along the Nile. He came north a couple of times a year to spend an hour or two and discuss politics with his son. He'd also meet with old friends and comrades from the Muslim Brotherhood.

Ashur looked at the chairs and was satisfied. It was how he liked it. He and his father would face each other. He would not greet him sitting behind his desk.

When his father arrived, Fathi welcomed him with a hug and a kiss on each cheek. He pointed to the chairs, and they sat comfortably extending their legs. His father was shorter and slightly heavier than Fathi. His gray suit was a snug fit on his body, a sign that he'd recently gained weight. As he settled in his seat, he rested his hands on the arms of the chair.

Fathi's eyes were always drawn to his father's hands. They were gnarled from torture in prison during the Nasser years. He had paid a price for his commitment to the Muslim Brotherhood. It was a lesson Fathi had absorbed and mastered. He learned to keep his interest in the Brotherhood's philosophy quiet and take steps to support a Brotherhood project only when the activity could not be traced to him. His father opened the conversation.

"Fathi, you look well—perhaps a little tired. Is General Murad working you too hard?"

Ashur's hard, cold eyes softened as he gazed at the man seated across from him. He was always pleased by his father's concern over his well-being.

"No, Father. The work is well balanced. My staff is excellent. My health is sound. But I do have one problem on my mind. We'll get to it later."

"Very well. Your mother sends her love. She's in excellent health as usual and is sorry to miss this trip. Too many obligations at home, she claims."

He smiled at the recollection of their conversation.

"Also, I have special greetings from Gehad and all your uncles."

"Gehad? Really? He's one of my topics today. Before we start, would you like some coffee or tea?"

He moved a hand toward his telephone. His father shook his head and spoke.

"Let's get right into the politics as our hours and days are precious. I'll start with Gehad's message."

He looked at his son and moved his body so he directly faced him.

"As you know, Gehad's moved to the top of the Brotherhood. He's heard rumors of great unrest in the ranks of Al-Qaeda."

Fathi's lips parted as he began to speak, but his father raised a hand to arrest his son's question.

"Let me finish. Gehad's also worried that there are new movements, fresh political pressure by the Russians, and the Americans in Egypt. He's curious—what do you know about these developments?"

He paused again, watching Fathi's face.

"If you have no information, he's requesting that you put an operation in place to track the key people," Gamal said.

"What's his real concern?"

"He thinks if Al-Qaeda starts more trouble, it will force Mubarak to shut down all opposition in the country, and our gains in the parliament will be erased. He thinks the Americans and Europeans are attempting to increase their influence on Mubarak to shut down terrorists in the country. That could lead to arrests of the Brotherhood activists."

Fathi tapped his father's knee.

"On Al-Qaeda and on any of the so-called radical operators in the country, my people are on top of this," Fathi said. "No worry there. We're watching the Americans and others as well. If Mubarak or his secret police want to target the Brotherhood,

I'll know about it and get the information to you. We'll use our normal channels."

His father sat back in his chair, extended his legs, and released a puff of air through his nose.

"Excellent. Gehad will be relieved to hear this. Our secret channel has worked well. Let's keep using it."

He pulled a Cleopatra from his pocket and lit it. He puffed twice, then let it rest in his fingers.

"You mentioned Gehad. Do you have something for him?"

Fathi hesitated a moment. He wiped his eyes with the back of his fingers.

"This is a longer story. It's about my cousin, your nephew, Omar Sayed."

His father sat upright in the chair. His eyes focused on Fathi.

"Allah be praised; what's the famous economist done this time?"

Fathi laughed.

"Dear Father, in the most efficient summary I can muster, my cousin has been ignored, actually insulted by the president. He blames the circumstance on an American and claims the American is undermining the country's economic opportunities. He wants to remove the man from Egypt."

"What...what do you mean 'remove'?"

His father leaned forward, started to rise from his chair, then settled back in the seat. "That's too brief for me, Fathi. Say more."

"Omar told me about the American's economic projects. There are three of them. The most recent venture involves a foreign automaker."

He took a few minutes to describe the Ford project. His father snorted.

"I get it. The Americans see a big market, and all the Egyptian cash will fly out of the country into those capitalist hands in Detroit or wherever."

Fathi paused, then continued.

"As I understand Omar, he believes the actions by the American promote capitalist values, and these projects are displacing Egyptian projects—projects that advance the economic ideals of the Brotherhood. He insists that the American has introduced a new form of colonialism."

His father remained relaxed in the chair, shaking his head.

"And Omar thinks he can get rid of the American? That his ideas for the economy will once again have Mubarak's attention and support? Do you believe that?"

"As you know, I'm not in the inner circle on economic policy. I don't know where Omar stands with the president."

His father raised a gnarled hand to his ear and tugged it.

"I imagine Omar's like a bull in a restaurant. I never thought he was a good choice to work with Mubarak."

He shook his head again.

"So the American is winning the battle for Mubarak's attention. Is there corruption involved?"

"I doubt it, but I don't know," Fathi said. "What's certain is that the American's projects will mostly benefit the educated."

"The economic ideas we value in the Brotherhood—job training for the unemployed, jobs for the poor, opportunities for the lesser educated, a broader-based economy—these ideas are ignored by the American, by all Americans?"

"I imagine that's true, but I don't think this American or any American has the entire Egyptian economy on their mind. They think of individual deals and opportunities."

His father stood up and stretched his arms over his head. He glanced over at Fathi.

"I need to move around every once in a while. I get stiff so easily. How's that leg of yours?"

"Like your back. It gets stiff more often each year."

Fathi remained seated in his chair.

"Back to Omar. He wants to kidnap the man's wife and, in addition, blackmail him. The purpose of all this is to force the man to sign an agreement that he will not work in the Middle East, meaning he can't work in Egypt."

"So that's the idea," Gamal said. "He came to you because he wants the Mukhabarat to do it?"

"Yes, and I gave him a firm no."

His father extended an arm toward Fathi, stopping him from further comment.

"Listen, blocking American consumer products from Egypt is a good idea. Scaring Americans with a kidnapping isn't totally crazy. This man, and others like him, will think twice before bringing their capitalist projects into Egypt."

"That what Omar thinks," Fathi said. "I think differently, but what I think doesn't matter. My agency will not mess with the Americans. General Murad and Mubarak will never act to embarrass or confront the Americans. I agree with them. We don't want to aggravate their CIA."

"Why worry about their CIA?"

"This American was the CIA chief in Egypt and later rose higher in the intelligence agency. I imagine he still has lots of friends there. And trust me, Father, you don't want to be a center of their attention if they believe you've hurt one of theirs."

His father reached to his head and scratched the thinning hair covering his scalp. He looked at Fathi thoughtfully.

"Is that why you wanted to talk to Gehad?"

Fathi stood up, walked over to the windows, and peered down at the river. He turned slowly back to face his father, still standing by his chair.

"Father, I want to know if the leadership of the Brotherhood wants to employ extreme methods, like taking a hostage, to get the capitalists, and their influence on Mubarak, out of Egypt."

"Well, as you realize, there are two problems here. If there is a foreigner kidnapped, Mubarak and the West will blame the Brotherhood. That's not good, but we can attempt to deflect the blame to the Al Hura or Al-Qaeda. Even then, Mubarak may use it as an excuse to round up some of our people anyway."

He paused, then lifted two fingers toward Fathi.

"Secondly—and this is equally important—how...," he snorted as he released a lengthy series of Arabic curses. "How is Omar going to do this without the skilled assistance of your people? Is he going to send a team of his fairy-assed economists to America to get the woman?"

With that, he doubled over in laughter. Fathi laughed with him. He walked over to his father and placed his arm around the older man's shoulders. He shook them affectionately.

"You always bring me wisdom, perspective, and humor. But let me try an idea on you. I'm not certain this is a good idea, but it's worth taking to Gehad if you agree."

"I agree that any action which reflects or could reflect on the Brotherhood needs leadership agreement," Gamal said. "You would be wise to advise Omar on that."

"I'm not certain that will stop him, but I will be forceful, insisting on Brotherhood approval."

"What's your idea to help him?"

"First, I will stay out of this, but I can suggest some people to Omar. We have several ex-Mukhabarat employees living in America. One of them is Jabari Radwan. Do you remember him? He was behind me in engineering at the university—very bright, a bit too aggressive. He's from Kom Ombo too."

"Yes, I knew the father. Died in prison—a victim of Sadat's reprisals."

"That's the one. He escaped to America after informing Gehad and others that they were the target of Mukhabarat wiretaps and bank examinations. Somebody in the Mukhabarat informed on him."

"He ran—got away. Good for him. Is he still a believer?"

"Yes, from time to time I'll hear from him, asking if it's safe to return," Fathi said.

"What would Omar do with Jabari?"

"I'd tell him to give Jabari the idea and for Jabari to give him a plan of how he would do the abduction. If it sounded feasible, and Omar could find the money to pay the team, it might be a way."

"You don't favor this action, do you?"

"No. I don't support bringing Western business practices into Egypt, but I acknowledge the Americans and this Davidson have some good ideas to improve our economy. You should see the file we have on him. It's extensive and mostly positive. If his wife is kidnapped, he'll bring all hell down on every contact he has in the Middle East. He'll have everyone looking for the woman."

"I hear you, my son, but what I like is that we're sending a message to the capitalists: Don't bring your new style of colonialism here. I'll bring that idea to Gehad and see what he thinks."

Fathi nodded and remained quiet, observing his father, his eyes resting on his face.

"You don't agree?" Gamal asked.

"I agree on one point: let's hear what Gehad thinks. But I warn you that Omar is a loose cannon. He might do this regardless of what you, I, or the Brotherhood thinks."

His father stepped closer to Fathi. There was barely a foot between them.

"Why do you say that?"

"Remember many years ago when Omar penned those critical essays on Sadat and had to run to England to escape prison? He was a hothead then and still is. Too much emotion, not enough thought. He doesn't see the risks."

"I understand, my son. You're careful. You're smart. Those qualities brought you to a high position in the Mukhabarat. I'll speak to Gehad. He or I will get back to you. You could then inform Omar of our thinking."

He paused. A smile creased his lined face.

"I like the idea. Any way we can stick it to the Americans, we should."

Fathi looked at his father and wondered if he was serious.

"I repeat: Tell Gehad my concerns. In the meantime, I'll let Omar know I passed his idea onto the Brotherhood."

CHAPTER 10

Omar Sayed

Cairo, Egypt

Omar Sayed placed the phone back on the cradle and gazed out at the declining light. It was nearly dusk on the first of June. The light filtered through the trees outside the tall windows of the three-bedroom apartment. The narrow rays of golden light dusted his shoes and spread onto the carpet. After twenty years in London, he chose the Zamalek neighborhood because it was modern, uncluttered, and unlike the densely packed streets and buildings in central Cairo. It was a favorite community with the expat crowd, and he could enjoy the company of Euro friends, international cuisine, and a secular lifestyle more similar to the way they lived in London. There was green in Zamalek—trees, grass, playing fields—and views of the Nile, unlike most of Cairo. His wife and two children adjusted well to the life in this international enclave. That he chose a location apart from many of his colleagues at the ministry didn't faze him.

The phone call delighted him. Actually, it caused him to bounce up from his chair. He pumped his hands toward the window, a bright smile on his face. He wanted to shout but didn't want to alarm his wife, son, and daughter, who were reading quietly in the living room. He wanted to celebrate, so he turned to the teak cabinet behind his desk and unlocked it. Inside, he kept a bottle of Sapphire gin, a bottle of Noilly Prat vermouth, four Baccarat crystal glasses, and a tall glass pitcher. The dry martini at twilight was another acquired habit from London that he loved. It had become a day's-end ritual. The phone call added another reason to enjoy the evening's beverage.

Occasionally, his secular Egyptian friends would join him for a drink, though his wife never did. Like him, she was not a pious Muslim, but alcohol did not please her. From time to time, she would urge him to stop this ritual. Politely, and consistently over the years, he ignored her request. Normally, he went to the refrigerator to collect ice for the pitcher but, at this hour, doing so might disturb his wife. He pulled the pitcher and bottles from the cabinet and began his diligent preparations to get the proportions right. Satisfied with the perfect mix, he swirled the ingredients twice, then poured the martini. He took the glass over to a chair near the windows and glanced down at the street. He sipped the drink and sighed.

"Done," he said aloud to the window.

A Brotherhood spokesman by the name of Begat Othman had called and said the group approved of his plot to abduct the American woman. He wanted to celebrate with someone, but this action would have to remain his secret.

"Your idea of kidnapping is bold, but it is dangerous and complex," Othman had said. "It has risk for you and the Brotherhood. While I and other Brothers approve of your action, it must be a total secret. You must tell no one. "

"That's why I chose Radwan," Omar had replied. "He's out of the country. There'll be no trace to me or to the Brotherhood.

The action is designed to scare away those in the West who seek to influence—even dominate—our country."

"That's what I like about your plot," Othman had replied. "No right-thinking banker is going to meddle in Egypt's economy without the fear of disappearing—either being held hostage or found dead."

Othman told him that although Jabari Radwan was a sound choice to lead the project, he was not to tell Fathi Ashur that his former agent was chosen. He was not to talk to Ashur again about the kidnapping.

He went over Othman's comments again and again. He wanted to write them down, but Othman was insistent: There was to be no record of this conversation or any notes taken on their future discussions. Othman was adamant. Any changes to the plan were to be made in person or with calls on throwaway cell phones. As Othman described the Brotherhood's reaction to it, Omar knew they were supportive but cautious about its complexity. If it went right, they did not want credit; if it went awry, they would claim no knowledge. When he coupled Othman's thoughts with those of Fathi, Omar knew he had the moral and philosophical support of key Brotherhood members. Yet he was concerned that no Brotherhood leader was willing to put his name and career on the line for the project. He was alone. Despite the lack of full backing, he was pleased that he had the self-confidence, imagination, and drive to do what he believed was right: He would get a prominent capitalist away from Mubarak and out of the country.

Othman, though, surprised him with his parting thought on the abduction. The Brotherhood leader concluded that the plan was appealing because Davidson's removal from Egypt would embarrass Mubarak. The implication to a majority of Egyptians,

Othman claimed, was that Mubarak and other Egyptian officials would be suspected of taking bribes from Americans to bring projects to Egypt. This could be a public relations disaster for the president. He was certain that most Egyptians would assume this form of corruption had been going on for some time. Omar realized the smell of graft at the top would benefit him as well.

He sipped his martini, thinking of next steps. Othman had given him the names and backgrounds of other exiled Mukhabarat agents and former Egyptian military personnel in California. Omar had written down a list of ten potential candidates. All were living in San Francisco or in the cities and towns not far from where Davidson lived. The pieces for the abduction were beginning to fall into place.

He glanced at his watch. It was five-thirty in Zamalek, eight-thirty in the morning in San Francisco. It was Sunday; Radwan should be home. Now all he had to do was convince this Radwan to lead the kidnapping. He took one last sip of the martini, thinking if the call went well, he'd have a second before dinner. He picked up the phone and tapped the numbers.

★ ★ ★

Jabari Radwan had found a small hub of Middle East ex-patriates in the Mission District of San Francisco. Friendships were established. Most were with fellow Egyptians, and he kept in close touch with several of them who had Mukhabarat or Egyptian military experience.

While he settled easily into the mixed cultural pot of the Mission District, he found the American economy a bit of a puzzle. His engineering background, considered a strong asset in the Mukhabarat, was not impressive to the firms in the city and in Silicon Valley. He made his living as a contract programmer with a small firm that provided "rent-a-tech" personnel to small companies that could not afford full-time computer staff. He supplemented this work as an evening instructor on Excel spreadsheet software at San Francisco State University. His two children attended the local public school, and his wife was seemingly satisfied with her friends and surroundings in America. But in quiet evening conversations with her, Jabari acknowledged that he missed the excitement and importance of his work with the Mukhabarat.

When the telephone rang, he was at the breakfast table with his family. The kitchen, with its comfortable table for four, was a center of activity in their two-bedroom apartment, a place for meals and discussions of the day's activities. At the second ring, his wife rose from her chair.

"I'll get it," she said. "It'll be for me."

As she listened, her eyes grew wide, and she turned to Jabari. "It's for you."

She extended the phone to him and whispered, "It's a minister from the government."

She shook her head in disbelief. Her quizzical look seemed to be asking Jabari: *Who is this?*

Jabari was suspicious at first, posing questions to prove the caller's identity. Sayed took several minutes to describe the work of his ministry and to reveal his friendship with several Brotherhood leaders. He spent more time testing Jabari's willingness to work again on behalf of the Brotherhood.

"For the right amount of money and the chance to return to Egypt, I'm listening," Jabari responded.

He leaned, elbows on the table, and relaxed. He concluded that the man on the phone could be trusted. With a quick sweep of his arm, he gestured to the children and his wife to leave the room.

"Give me a few minutes," he whispered to them.

In the quiet of the kitchen, Jabari talked to Sayed for more than an hour. At first, the idea of kidnapping an American woman seemed bizarre, but as the conversation proceeded, he could see the originality and the powerful impact of the plan. As his curiosity grew, the attraction of the plot expanded from satisfying Brotherhood goals to the personal rewards for himself. He swallowed hard and went quiet for a moment when Sayed mentioned the compensation for the kidnapping. Jabari repeated it.

"Minster Sayed, did I hear you correctly? My compensation will be $250,000 for leading the project? And I have the opportunity to return to Egypt and work in the Ministry of Trade and Industry?"

"We'll work out the payment details once you've assembled your team," Sayed said. "I will pay a modest amount of cash up front for preliminary work, then one-half the full amount once the woman is captured. The second half will be paid when the American, Davidson, pays the ransom."

"The financial offer is attractive, and I do want to return to Egypt," Jabari said. "But how can you ensure my safety in Egypt? I must avoid arrest by Mubarak's police."

Sayed sensed that he had agreement.

"As a cabinet minister, I have power over such things. I can get you reinstated."

He winced as he said this but felt it necessary to convince the man to accept the task.

"You asked about risk of failure," Sayed said. "It's low because Davidson will want his wife back, and the ransom demand is small for him. In addition, we have blackmail information on Davidson which he will not want revealed, so he'll act fast."

"I'll need a team of at least three others and money for them as well," Jabari said. "Plus, I'll have expenses for vehicles, food, and the location for storing the hostage. Do you have the money for this?"

Sayed stared at his martini glass, wishing there was more of the drink left.

"For your team, I have a list of people who are Brotherhood members or friendly to our cause. I will get you those names, their locations, and how to reach them. And yes, as minister in the government, I have access to any money I need."

Jabari had reached for notepaper next to the phone and was scribbling notes.

"I have good friends and contacts here with exiled Egyptians. I'd prefer to select my own team."

"That's fine, but send me their backgrounds. I want to discuss each candidate's skills with you before we reach agreement. I have one more important detail: I have contacts with Egyptians in America and Canada who do business with my ministry. They have perfect locations to hide the hostage for a few days. I'll supply that to you when I get your plan."

They agreed to talk again in three days.

Jabari had been involved in taking hostages in the past. The process of abduction and holding abductees was not new to him. Doing it in America, though, was quite different from his experience in Egypt. He returned to the living room to begin the day with his wife and children, but his mind remained fixed on Sayed's extraordinary proposal and the possible rewards. He gathered the children, clapped his hands, and announced a trip to the park for a biking excursion. He pulled the children's bikes from a closet and, in the excitement of getting them out of the house, forgot his own bike. His wife could see his mind was not on the task of organizing the children.

"Jabari, you're in another world! Was the phone conversation about what happened years ago? Are we still in trouble?"

He turned toward her and placed his hands on her shoulders.

"No, my dear. I'm sorry, but I'm likely to be distracted until I figure out what to do. The call was from the minister of Trade. He presented an idea that may get us back to Egypt. That's all I can tell you."

"Do you want to go back? Life is good here. I love it. The children love it."

"There is much to discuss," Jabari said. "I'm open to return if I can get a job that recognizes my skills. I don't feel valued in America."

Over the next two weeks, Jabari took time off from his programming work to track the daily movements of Sarah Pierce and Brooks Davidson. He secured the help of Mustafa, a good friend and fellow exiled Egyptian. Mustafa was a bachelor, short and overweight for his five-foot-ten body. He was a former soldier who had fled the country to avoid arrest for trading in stolen weapons on the black market. He drove a taxi in San Francisco, so his hours were flexible. With the GPS in Jabari's SUV, they found the home of Sarah Pierce. Using their available time carefully, they tracked her movements and those of Brooks Davidson for two weeks.

Jabari was annoyed with the requirement to purchase a new cell phone each day to communicate with his team and Sayed, but he maintained the security Sayed demanded. After two weeks, Jabari decided to contact Sayed and present his approach to the abduction and what it would cost. Sayed took the call at the study in his home and almost immediately bolted out of his chair.

"Are you crazy—four million dollars?"

Jabari was at the breakfast counter in his home, a new cell phone in his hand. His wife was off to her shopping. The children had left for school.

"I can email the details to you, unless you think emails are too risky."

He dropped the tone of his voice.

"It might be less; it might be more. I've done this many times—trust me."

They argued back and forth for several minutes. Finally, Sayed relented.

"OK. Send me the details."

He gave Jabari the email address of one of his children. Hours later, Sayed reviewed Jabari's costs and trimmed the budget by removing the cost of lodging the hostage and reducing the estimates for travel. He thought the kidnapping would be concluded in three to five days. Jabari had estimated a month. In final negotiations, Jabari insisted that Sayed keep the full estimate in reserve in case complications arose during the process of taking the hostage and securing the agreements for her release. Jabari had another point he wished to express.

"Minister Sayed, this American Davidson…he has odd habits for a married man. He comes to their house only on weekends. It's an odd arrangement for an American marriage."

Sayed was momentarily troubled by the comment.

"No, it's all right. My deputy, Hamid, saw Davidson with his wife at a conference in New York. We have other information too. They're a very close couple. It's one of those American arrangements. He teaches in Palo Alto, many miles away, I'm told.

It makes sense for him to work in one place and spend weekends in this Sunset Cove."

"I understand but wanted you to know."

Jabari stared at a calendar on the countertop.

"As soon as you say 'go,' Minister Sayed, my team is ready. We found the hiding place in Santa Rosa you recommended. We can get there quickly. There are four on my team. I've selected people who can free up the time. When you agree on the men for the team and wire the first payment, we'll get the woman."

"I accept your team. You've found the right kind of people. Expect the cash within two to three days. You'll pick it up at the Egyptian Consulate in San Francisco. It will be in a cardboard box addressed to your name. After that, you'll get additional cash, if needed, from our friends at the hostage location."

CHAPTER 11

The Hostage

Sunset Cove, California

Every Friday, Sarah left her San Francisco office in the early afternoon and drove across the Golden Gate Bridge to her hospice patient in Mill Valley. Her current patient was in the final stages of life—quiet, no conversation. All that was left was the labored breathing. Sarah was used to that.

On this day, she placed her hand on Marie's withered arm and whispered, "I'm here. I'm with you. You're not alone."

She sat on the chair next to the bed, looked at the pale, drawn face with purple splotches on her cheeks, then closed her eyes and meditated in cadence with the breaths of her patient. After fifteen minutes, she picked a book from her bag and read, waiting for her patient to stir, to talk. After two hours, she picked up her hospice bag and called the hospice center, informing the nurses' desk that the morphine drip was running low. A refill would be needed by evening. She touched the woman's arm once more.

"I'll see you next Friday," she whispered close to her ear, then left the room.

She thought Marie wouldn't make it through the weekend; she'd check with the nurses on Sunday. It was light traffic from Mill

Valley to Sunset Cove. Sarah, eager to get home, made a quick stop for groceries, then raced to Towle Lane. In the garage, she pushed the button to close the door and retrieved the groceries from the trunk of her car. With bags in hand, she entered the short set of steps that led to the kitchen. Her spirits, always on an even keel, rose as she thought about the surprise she had in store for Brooks. In her bag of groceries was a small, round chocolate cake from Whole Foods, one of his favorites. She placed it on the kitchen counter under a glass case, setting it precisely where he was sure to see it. She then stopped and listened. She heard footsteps on the entry deck, and then the doorbell rang.

Who could that be at this hour? she wondered. *Must be Zappos, though I don't remember any recent orders.*

She left the counter and crossed to the front door. On opening it, she saw two men. They were nicely dressed, of modest height, with black hair and sunglasses covering their eyes. Their skin was light brown. One of them lifted an arm toward her. That was the last thing she would remember on June ninth.

Jabari, who had doused a mask with desflurane, clamped it firmly over her mouth. Sarah was too surprised to react. One arm flailed ineffectively, then fell to her side. Mustafa grasped her arms as she began to sink and moved her slowly inside the front door. With Mustafa holding her upright, Jabari placed a large manila envelope with the ransom note on the floor of the entryway. He stepped back to the door and turned to the driveway, where Baligh and Hamid, the two other members of Jabari's team, waited in the front seat of the stolen van. Baligh scanned Towle Lane and saw no cars or people.

"All clear," he said quietly.

For Jabari, Towle Lane was a perfect street for taking a

hostage—a long and narrow private road. There were six houses tucked into a hillside overlooking the sea, each separated by stands of tall pines. After two weeks of watching Sarah come and go, Jabari knew there were no walkers or traffic on the street in the late afternoon. Her short, wide driveway had enough room for three cars side by side, and Baligh had pulled the van right up to the garage door. Now, Jabari and Mustafa placed their arms under Sarah's shoulders and sleepwalked her to the van, placing her on the rear bench seat. They wrapped her hands and then her feet with duct tape and secured her with canvas straps to the seat.

Jabari returned to the house, double-checked that the ransom package was in an obvious place for Davidson to see, then locked the door and returned to the van. Baligh put the van in gear and drove slowly out of Towle Lane through Sunset Cove and out to Highway 101. Jabari sat near Sarah and watched for her return to consciousness. He readied a needle containing propofol to plunge into her arm and ensure she would sleep for the drive to Santa Rosa.

★ ★ ★

Taha Jahin lived on a twenty-acre estate outside the city of Santa Rosa. He came from a family of rug merchants in Cairo, and he left Egypt in his twenties to expand the business into the United States. He settled in California because of its fabulous weather and to pursue another of his interests: the wine business. Sales of his Persian rugs flourished as the state's economy expanded. At the same time, his initial wine shop grew into a major retailer of California wines throughout the United States. On his home property, he built a substantial warehouse, where he stored the wines prior to shipment. The warehouse had a separate section where the rugs imported from the Middle East were stored. For all their business interests, the Jahin family maintained strong ties to Egypt's Ministry of Trade and Industry to ensure that all necessary import and export licenses were in order. Over the past five years, Taha Jahin had come to know Omar Sayed quite well.

Jahin greeted Jabari at the entrance to his property. He wore a blue pinstriped suit, white shirt, and red tie. To Jabari, he looked more like a San Francisco banker than a wine merchant.

Jabari extended his hand.

"It's most helpful for you to support Minister Sayed's plan," Jabari said. "We thank you. Where shall we park the van?"

Jahin took his hand and slowly studied Jabari's face.

"First, let me say that while I wish to support the goals of Minister Sayed, I must be careful in America. Understand?"

He watched Jabari for a reaction.

"Now, the van."

He pointed to a structure at the rear of his property.

"You'll be located in the large stucco building down there. Hide the vehicle behind the warehouse. Inside the building, there's a small apartment. Next to the apartment is a large washroom I use for my workers. They're away until my next shipment comes in. The building is yours for a week or so. Your men can stay in the apartment. Your hostage can be locked in the washroom. I've stocked the apartment with food and beverages. If you need more, call this number."

He handed Jabari a piece of paper. Jabari studied the paper and pointed to one of several numbers on the page.

"Do I call this number if we need transportation to get other supplies?"

"Yes. As I understand it, you'll drop the van in Santa Rosa. Is that correct?"

"Yes."

Jahin clapped his hands together as if to conclude the small talk.

"Let's get the van parked now. I'll show you around the warehouse."

Baligh drove down a pebbled drive to the massive building, while Jahin walked with Jabari. Jahin looked at the younger man.

"Jabari, I applaud what you're doing for our country, but I must warn you of two things. First, I've had great success in this country as well as Egypt that I don't want to jeopardize. You must use every care with your hostage. Sayed demanded that she be unharmed during captivity."

He paused for emphasis.

"And secondly, as I mentioned, my crew will return in seven days with a major wine shipment. You must be gone by then."

Jabari nodded.

"Minister Sayed thinks this will be concluded within that time. The timing should not be a problem."

Jahin clapped him on the back. Jabari acknowledged the approval with a wave of his hand as they walked in silence to the warehouse. The facade of the massive ochre building was dominated by two fifteen-foot-high sliding doors with a small, square window overhead. The doors sat on rails and were opened by a motor activated by a device in Jahin's hand. The warehouse sat at the end of a long, deep lawn. Looking across it, Jabari saw a swimming pool, its water sparkling in the afternoon sun. Adjacent to the pool was a low-slung hacienda-style home with many wings. The sprawling residence fit into the property as if it had been there forever. Jabiri could see that the man had done well in America.

As they entered the warehouse, Jabari eyed rack after rack of bottled wine, which gave off a noticeable scent of fermentation. It was a damp, cool fragrance, and it tickled Jabari's nose. They walked to the back of the building and came upon two doors. Jahin opened one with a key. Because there were no windows, it was totally dark inside. When Jahin switched on an overhead light, Jabari could see that it was a washroom for workers with a big metal sink. Mops and buckets were stashed against a wall. A stall enclosing a private toilet was tucked into a far corner. A small iron cot with a thin mattress was against the back wall.

"This is for your hostage," Jahin said with a sense of distaste. "You'll need to remove the mops, pails, and any implements the hostage can use. OK, let's walk over to the apartment."

The apartment had a small, fully equipped kitchen, a living room with a sofa, three chairs, and a dining table with chairs. A short hallway off the living room led to two full-sized bedrooms. Jabari studied the layout of the place, then thought about the washroom. He surveyed the room, not looking at Jahin.

"This can work. Thank you."

He and Jahin walked out of the building discussing the supply of food. Satisfied with the arrangements, Jahin walked back toward the hacienda, and Jabari went to the back of the building and the van. Mustafa, Baligh, and Hamid were outside the van, smoking. Sarah remained unconscious on the rear bench. They opened the van's sliding door and carried her to the washroom, where they lay her on the cot, her wrists and feet still bound. They turned off the light, leaving the room in total darkness, then went into the apartment. Baligh went straight to the refrigerator. He turned to the others, his eyes bright.

"Two six-packs here. Who's thirsty?"

Jabari glanced at his crew. He had a smile on his face.

"Well done. The first step is over. Jahin will give us the first payment. Let's have a beer."

"What about the hostage?" Hamid asked. "Feed her and...?"

He waved his hands nervously. Jabari stood up from his chair and walked around the room.

"Look, we're under strict orders not to harm her in any way. The minister wants no problems with the Americans except for this Davidson. Let's wait until she wakes up. Then we can give her some water and a little of the food in the fridge. No conversations. Let's wear masks until we get a blindfold on her."

He glanced at his watch.

"I'm to call Davidson on his cell around eight tonight. So we have a few hours before this gets real hot. We can drink that beer and wait for some noise from next door."

CHAPTER 12

A Mistake

Santa Rosa, California

When Sarah opened her eyes, she couldn't move her arms or legs, and her mouth was covered. Her tongue pressed against the material, and she felt air holes. It felt like duct tape with air holes punched in it. She could taste acidity. She realized that breathing was possible, yet she struggled for breath and began to panic. Her eyes darted around the room. It was pitch-dark; the only sliver of light seemed to come from the bottom of what might be a door. She kicked her legs and realized her ankles were bound. She tried to move her arms. She recognized they were tied fast at the wrist. She screamed into the tape. The sound was muffled, which magnified her sense of suffocating. She became dizzy. Her mind swirled between confusion and anxiety. She struggled for clarity of thought.

What's happened? she thought. *Where am I? Why am I bound and gagged?"*

She tried to slow her breathing to calm her mind.

What to do?

Her eyes drifted to the sliver of light across the room.

I must get to that light, she thought.

With immense concentration, she lifted her legs, bringing her knees to her chest, and rolled to her right. She crashed off the narrow cot onto the floor, landing on her knees and arms.

"No! Fuck! That hurt!" she cried into the tape, gasping for each breath.

Tears streamed down her cheeks. The pain in her elbows and knees began to subside. She resolved again: Get to the light. Adjusting her bound hands until they were beneath her, she lifted her torso and pulled her knees into a crawling position. She brought her knees toward her chest, then slid her hands forward. In this manner, she crawled toward the light but lost her balance and toppled over. She regained her position, repeating the hand and knee motion until she reached the sliver of light on the floor. Her fingers followed the crack of light around to one side, then the other, concluding it was a door. She shuffled her knees close to the door, about a foot away. She spread her knees as far apart as the tape binding her ankles permitted. She waited a second or two to secure her balance, then lifted her bound hands over her head and, like a hammer, hit the door again and again. After a few moments, she heard a man's voice from the other side, clear and loud.

"Stop banging," he instructed.

Stunned to hear a voice, she hammered on the door harder. Seconds later, she heard the doorknob being twisted.

"Stop!" the voice commanded. "I'll open the door."

Sarah tried to speak, but the tape over her mouth stifled her words. She banged the door again. The voice, rising in volume, shouted again.

"Stop the shit-assed pounding and move away from the door so I can open it."

Sarah felt the door pushing against her as a vertical shaft of light split the darkness.

"Move back more Goddammit, move back!"

Short brown fingers wrapped around the edge of the door, pushing it into her knees and thighs. She placed her hands on the floor and, with her hands, pushed her body a few feet from the door. Gradually, the door opened, and the voice became a compact man wearing a black ski mask. The wrists and hands that extended from his black shirt were light brown, thick and powerful. Sarah froze at the sight. Her heart pounded. The man entered the room, lifted Sarah from the floor as if she were light as a feather, and placed her standing in front of him. He studied her body from head to toe and, with one of his powerful hands, ripped the tape off her mouth.

"*Aaaaaagh!*" she screamed, stunned, as she brought her bound hands to her mouth.

"Who are you?" she choked out, breathing in deep gulps.

She took another deep breath, then wiped spittle from her mouth with the gray tape that covered her wrists.

"What's happening?" she wanted to know. "Why am I here, bound and gagged? What are you doing to me? What do you want from me?"

"Shut up," he said, "or I'll put the tape back on."

He pointed to her hands.

"Give them to me."

With his fierce grip, he ripped the tape from her wrists, then dragged her toward the bed.

"Lift your feet."

She sank onto the bed and lifted her ankles. He pulled a knife from his pants pocket and cut the tape.

"Stand up!" he commanded.

Unsteady, she stood, eyes wide with fright. Three other men entered the room. They also wore black ski masks. They spoke rapidly in a language Sarah didn't recognize. The man who entered the room first was Jabari. His compact, powerful body and hard eyes induced a strong sense of fear in Sarah. Her initial instinct was to avoid him. She looked away from Jabari to focus on another man, Mustafa, who was chubby and had soft brown eyes. Compared to Jabari, the skin on his hands and wrists was a lighter shade of brown. For reasons she could only link to her intuition, she concluded this man was not dangerous. The third man, Hamid, was eerie. Behind the ski mask, his dark, lifeless eyes were surrounded by skin that was unlike the others. It was bronze or a rust color. He was taller than the others and thinner. He held his hands by his side, and they twitched as if he wished to do something with them. The fourth man, Baligh, stood behind the others with his eyes fixed on the floor. Sarah assumed he didn't want to be seen. Quickly, she studied him and noted that he was of average height and medium weight. His brown eyes never looked up. Mustafa spoke to Jabari.

"Shall we give her some food?"

Jabari ignored him and turned from Mustafa to face Sarah.

"I have a cell phone here."

He took it from his shirt pocket and waved it in front of her.

"I will record a message to your husband on this phone. You will say that you are safe and well. You will tell him to pay the ransom and sign the agreement immediately. When he's paid the money and signed the form, you'll be released, and he'll be informed where to find you. Is that clear?"

Sarah flexed her fingers, still stiff from the tape, then rubbed her eyes. With her eyes wide open, she looked at him and concluded that he must be the leader.

"I'm lost, confused by what you said. Please repeat it."

Jabari repeated his instructions.

"Did you get it this time?"

Sarah eyes swept the room, taking in the men.

"Are you crazy? I don't have a husband. Holy shit!" she screamed. "He's been dead for five years. You've got the wrong person! Who are you people? You've made a mistake! Let me go right now."

Jabari moved so fast that Sarah never saw what was coming. The inside of his hand slammed into the side of her face. She fell back against the bed and slid to the floor. She stayed there, startled, looking up at him and touching the side of her face gingerly with her fingers. She began to cry.

"You'll get more of that and worse if you anger me. We know who you are. We know Brooks Davidson, and we don't make mistakes. If you make a mistake, you may never see him, your children, or anyone else in your life. Do you understand me?"

She looked up at him and said nothing. Jabari bent over and slapped the other side of her face, this time less brutally.

"Do you understand me?"

She nodded.

"All right then. That's better. Now, I want you to give me Davidson's phone number and we'll record a message. If you do that perfectly, then I can offer you some water and a little food. Would you like that?"

Tears wet her cheeks, and she sobbed.

"Water, please," she said.

Jabari reached into a rear pocket of his cargo pants and placed a small bottle of water in her hands. She drank greedily. Jabari watched her drink, then put his phone in front of her.

"Put the water down, stand up, and type this message on my phone."

Sarah placed the bottle on the floor and took the cell phone. She typed in Brooks' number and the message: *I am safe and well send the money and sign the agreement. Sarah.*

She handed back the phone.

"He won't believe it's me. It's not how we talk."

Jabari turned the phone toward her.

"Then put it in your own language."

She stepped away from him, fearing another slap in the face.

"You're making a mistake. He's not my husband. We're friends, and I doubt he'll do anything. Certainly, you won't get money from him. He's a professor, a former government employee, and, again, we're not married. We have no children."

Jabari moved his right hand. Sarah backed away from it. It was a feint. Jabari's left hand came from the other side and slammed into her face.

"I said, 'Don't piss me off.' We know who you are, and we know all about your Dr. Davidson."

She toppled to the floor and stayed there, sobbing. Hamid, his hands twitching, moved close to Jabari and Sarah.

"Let me have a few minutes with her. I'll get what we want."

Mustafa pulled Hamid away and, shifting the verbal exchange with Sarah from English to Arabic, he spoke to Jabari.

"Remember what the minister said: Leave her untouched. It will cause problems with the Americans."

Jabari, a look of disgust on his face, handed the cell phone to Mustafa and spoke in Arabic.

"We'll send the woman's message to Davidson after he's seen the ransom note. Later tonight. Right now, I want you to get Minister Sayed on his cell. He should be headed to work."

CHAPTER 13

Pills in a Pocket

Santa Rosa, California

Jabari stood above Sarah, then reached down and pulled her to her feet.

She's acting—or worse, he thought as he stared at her. *Much worse if she has no idea who Davidson really is.*

He grabbed her shoulders with both hands and shook her hard.

"Listen to me. Your man, this Professor Davidson, is much more than an academic, and you know it. Don't hide information. It will be harder on you."

With her hands now free, Sarah rubbed her cheek.

This man is on the edge of violence; be careful, she thought.

She tried to read his eyes, but his black mask unnerved her. Sarah's head had stopped buzzing. She felt a dash of confidence.

"Where are you from, and what do you want?" she asked. "Why me? Why am I here?"

Jabari resisted the temptation to slap her again.

"You're a fucking nuisance. I'll speak to you this one time. We're from a country that your man knows well. He has harmed our country. You're here because you know him. We're keeping you to get him to change his mind."

Sarah inhaled sharply.

I'm a hostage, she thought. *A pawn in their plan. Are they crazy?* Her mind raced.

I'm a psychologist with a small practice, a hospice volunteer, she thought. *I've only known Brooks for a few months.*

She tried to slow her thinking, but her thoughts swirled too fast. She felt her face get hot. She was certain this strange man could hear the beat of her heart. She clenched her hands, released them, then did it again. He was serious. She was the target. This was not a mistake. The fear returned. Her stomach began to rebel. She felt nauseous. She breathed deeply, trying to drive the nausea away.

"Let me understand," she started. "You're using me to get something from Brooks Davidson? You've made a mistake."

She stood tall, nearly equal to Jabari's height.

"I hardly know the man," she insisted. "Whatever game you're playing," she stammered as the words came out in a rush, "I'm not just a small fish, I'm the wrong fish."

Jabari's wide brown eyes moved up and down Sarah's body. He pushed her back down on the bed.

"You're lying."

Mustafa bellowed from the living room.

"Your call is here."

Jabari turned, crossed the room, locked the door, and went to the living room, grabbing the phone from Mustafa.

"Not good," he muttered to himself. "Not good at all."

He lifted the phone to his ear.

"Minister Sayed," he began. "Sorry to call you this early in your day. We have good news and a problem. As I said in my earlier voice message, we have the hostage safe, sound, and hidden perfectly. The problem is that she and Davidson are not married and hardly know each other. He may ignore our demands. Plus, she says he's an academic who can't and won't pay."

It was early in Cairo, not yet five in the morning. Omar Sayed was in his office because he could not sleep and didn't want his wife or children wondering about telephone calls at odd hours. He put the cell phone on his desk and set it on speaker because there was no one else in the building at this hour. He paced around the room as if he were preparing for a track meet, his eyes at all times on his phone. After listening to Jabari, he screamed a string of Arabic obscenities.

"You don't listen to her!" he shouted. You listen to me, you dumb fuck!"

Jabari winced.

"I wanted to warn you. Davidson may not worry about our hostage. That's all. I need guidance."

"You have your guidance," Sayed said. "Don't bother me with your worries. Wait another few hours, then call Davidson at the number I gave you. If he gives you trouble, call me. I want no more bullshit from the woman."

He walked back to his desk and slammed his finger on the phone, ending the call.

Back in California, Baligh had been on the couch and quiet for the past hour, sipping his beer. His short legs extended out in front of him. His hand had a firm grasp on a beer bottle. He glanced at Jabari. Baligh saw anger on his face and thought it wise to calm him down.

"Let me prepare our meal," he offered. "I saw cooked lamb in the refrigerator. I'll heat up some rice, and there's hummus. There's plenty for us and the woman. When the meal's done, we can have some of my magic pills. After all, we kidnapped the woman successfully. Let's relax a little. Tomorrow's another day."

He rose from the couch and moved slowly toward the kitchen.

In her room, Sarah sat up in the bed and twisted her body to get her feet on the floor. Her legs and arms were still stiff and sore. She moved slowly toward the bathroom stall. She needed to urinate. She opened the stall door and saw there was no toilet paper. She shuffled over to the main door to the room.

"Help!" she shouted.

There was no immediate answer, so she began banging on the door with her fists. In a matter of seconds, Hamid opened the door and leered at her through his black mask.

"I have a surprise for you."

He placed a blindfold over her eyes and stretched the elastic cord behind her head.

"If we peek into your room, and the blindfold is not on, we'll beat you to a pulp. If you make more noise, we'll put the gag back on and tie you to the bed."

He put his hands on her shoulders to push her back toward the bed, then changed his mind and slid them down to brush against her breasts. His eyes swept up and down her body.

"You're pretty cute for an old lady, aren't you? What do you want—me?"

He laughed as the narrow opening of the mask revealed a mouth full of stained teeth that reeked of tobacco breath.

"Sure—we'll have some fun later."

He poked her chest.

"Food is coming. I'll be back."

He left the room, pulling the door behind him and then locking it. Sarah walked back to the bed and sat, rubbing her wrists and rotating her ankles to restore circulation and feel the freedom of movement.

Oh my God, she thought. *I have no control. I'm a hostage. They'll rape me while I'm their captive. How do I protect myself?*

The loss of decision-making and the removal of any form of control bore into her mind. The fear she felt took on new dimensions. She started to shake as if a chill consumed her body. She walked around the room, trying to shift the terror she felt into the mechanics of counting steps. It didn't work, and her mind came back to Hamid's threat: *We'll have some fun later.* She was still shaking as she walked. As she paced, Sarah took inventory of what she had and what she knew. She had nothing in her hands when she had answered the door of her home.

My home! she thought, shuddering at the fact that she could lose it. *There is no one to pay my bills, particularly the mortgage. Could or would Brooks think of that—paying the property tax, the utility bills? Oh, God!*

She walked around and around the room. Nothing made sense. She couldn't act to solve her largest worries: getting free and managing her home. As she paced, she felt the pockets of her jeans—nothing there—and her hands went into the pockets of her outer jacket. In the left pocket, buried deeply in the crease at the bottom, were her pills. She had picked up her prescription for walking pneumonia at the pharmacy on the way home. She was fully recovered from the infection, and these penicillin pills were a final insurance that the disease was under control. Her mind slowed down as she thought about the pills. But no strategy emerged, and she returned to pacing and counting the steps around the room.

After a while, she heard a key in the lock. The door swung open, and chubby Mustafa entered with a plate of food and a cup of tea. He placed it on the bed. Sarah noted again that his eyes were soft. He appeared to be kind or have kindness in him.

She turned to the food, and the wave of nausea that plagued her earlier returned.

"I can't eat," she said. "Take it away. The smell makes me sick."

"Knock on the door when you're finished. I'll come back."

When Mustafa left, Sarah walked over to the bed and stared at the food. It appeared to be some kind of meat with rice, along with hummus on the side. She bent over and sniffed the meal. The meat looked like worms crawling and weaving through the kernels of rice. She gagged, then placed the dish on the floor and stepped away. The smell of the meat overpowered her. She gagged again, then vomited over the food until the heaves became dry and wracking.

Oh, damn, damn, damn! she told herself.

She moved away from the stench of her own vomit, then went to the door and banged on it.

Mustafa appeared.

"Finished?" he asked.

Stepping inside, he realized what had happened.

"Oh shit!" he exclaimed. "Lady—what a fucking mess! I'll get a towel. You'll clean this up."

He held his nose and muttered.

"Fuck! Use the toilet to remove the crap and wash the dish in the sink."

Continuing to hold his nose, Mustafa left to find a towel. When he returned, he tossed the towel in the room and quickly closed and relocked the door. Sarah scooped the vomit onto the plate and discharged it into the toilet. She wet the towel, mopped the floor, then rinsed the towel in the sink until the stench was gone. Satisfied that the fetid odor had disappeared, she sat on the bed and, feeling better, sipped the tea.

She knew, unlike any time in her life, that she was alone and without any information. She didn't know the duration of this captivity or the plan for release—if any. Death was a possibility. Rape now seemed like a certainty. These thoughts caused her body to again shake uncontrollably. She tried to meditate, but she couldn't focus on her mantra.

How can I regain some form of control? she wondered.

Her mind fought for insight on how to do so, but she couldn't focus on the challenge. The turmoil in her mind caused her to get up and pace again. She measured the steps going forward across the room. There were fifteen. Then she walked backward and counted eighteen. She was puzzled that going forward yielded a result different from that of going backward and knew that her mind wasn't working well.

She lifted her hands over her head, then stretched from side to side. She took off her Bogner jacket, and the pills rattled as the coat hit the bed. Her modest yoga exercises helped calm her. She repeated the exercises until she felt some heat in her body and the shaking had subsided. A thought occurred to her.

The pills in my jacket could be useful. No one would rape a diseased woman.

She toyed with the idea, then sat on the bed to think it through. The clarity of the idea brought a degree of excitement to her. She walked to the door and banged it vigorously.

Jabari opened it.

"What the fuck is it this time?"

Sarah reached her full height.

"You need to know this. I have TB and need medication or I'll die."

"There's an American expression I've grown to appreciate,"

Jabari said. "Bullshit!"

Undaunted, Sarah stood up to him.

"You appear to have some brains, so you'll understand this. You've heard my dry cough. You've seen or heard about my vomit. These are natural TB symptoms. I need my medicine to control the disease."

"Oh, you're good, tall lady, but full of shit. Nobody from your precious little rich town gets TB."

"Recently on a trip to Africa, I got exposed to the disease," Sarah said. "When I received medical attention, the doc said if I came in a day or two later, I would have died. The last of the pills are with me, but the rest are at home. I need to get them."

"I repeat: Bullshit."

"OK, but if any of your men touch me, they'll get it. My saliva is toxic. Better wash my dishes carefully. The disease is very contagious. I think you're smart enough to know that much."

"OK. When I talk to your Professor Davidson, I'll have him send your pills along with the ransom money."

Sarah coughed in his face. He recoiled, stepped away, then wiped his face.

"You fucking bitch!"

Stifling the urge to strike her, he decided that he'd better not touch her. He turned and raced to the bathroom.

CHAPTER 14

$2 Million or Else

Sunset Cove, California

On Friday afternoons, Brooks Davidson routinely left his campus office at two o'clock to avoid rush-hour traffic on I-280. On this day, he left later than usual and pushed his Lexus 450 to make up time. He was eager to see Sarah. As he drove, he listened to an EMI recording of opera highlights. Along with Placido Domingo, he belted out the lyrics of Handel's *Ombra mai fu*. Pulling into Sarah's driveway, he reached for the garage activator and pressed the button to open the door. As the door lifted, he saw her BMW parked in its normal space, and it gave him a rush of pleasure.

She's home, he thought.

He climbed the steps into the kitchen and saw the bag of groceries on the counter, then the chocolate cake in the glass case.

How grand, he thought.

"Sarah, where are you?"

Leaving an unopened grocery bag was unusual for her. She was methodical in her household work. Groceries were put away immediately. A premonition hit him.

Something's wrong! he thought.

The uneasiness he felt triggered a shiver down his spine. He walked to the entrance hall and shouted at the stairwell to the bedrooms below.

"Sarah—you hiding?"

As he listened for an answer, he spotted a manila envelope on the floor of the hall. When he advanced toward it, he was startled. His name was prominent in large, bold letters. He tore it open and read:

"To Davidson – June 9, 2001

We have your wife. She is safe and will stay safe as long as you comply with these directions.

First, for her release, you are to pay $2 million to a bank we designate in a forthcoming phone call. We will provide the codes at that time.

Second, you are to stop all investment and financial advisory work in the Middle East from this date forward.

Third, you will sign the agreement attached to this letter that confirms your removal from business activities in the Middle East. Directions to mail the agreement will come in the phone call.

Fourth, if you do not comply with these three demands within four days (by June 13) we will release documents revealing your corrupt and treasonous activities with several governments in the Middle East and kill your wife.

You will be reached on your cell phone later tonight. Keep it open.

Allahu Akbar"

Brooks' hands trembled as he read the ransom note.

"No, no, no!" he shouted into the empty house.

The sound echoed off the walls of the high-ceilinged hallway.

He threw the note on the floor and stormed off to the living room, out to the kitchen, then back to the living room again.

What have I done? he asked himself.

Though typically calm in crisis situations, now he was plagued with anxiety. He started to panic. He ran his hands through his hair.

How could—why —would anyone kidnap an innocent like Sarah? he wondered.

His mind was spinning. This was done to harm him? It made no sense. And they called her his wife? These people didn't know much about his life, did they? They obviously didn't know that his wife had been dead for years. He could feel the heat rising within him.

They just made a grave mistake! he thought.

He stormed around the rooms, subconsciously hoping that his movements might bring sense to this insane act. A short while later, he went to the kitchen sink and drew a glass of water. He willed his breathing to slow down as he sipped from the glass. The situation was not new to him. He'd had field operators taken hostage in the past. He thought those frightening days were over. At least he had experience with hostages, and the thought enabled him to breathe more slowly.

From his experience, he knew he had to be deliberate and thoughtful in dealing with hostage takers. He remembered that avoiding making threats usually achieved desired results. As he stared into the sink, he spoke to his mind as if it were another person. He emphasized that he must recall the skills that served him well in the past.

Be calm with the abductors, he reminded himself. *Talk, listen, and sort out what Sarah's hostage takers really want.*

That strategy had previously enabled his field personnel to come home safely. He needed a plan before Sarah's captors called.

He went to her "control tower" and sat in her chair. He selected a pen and placed a sheet of paper on the desk and smoothed it out; he was ready to work. Nothing came to mind. He shook his head in dismay. He was too agitated to work. He put the pen down, stood up, and walked to the kitchen. He wanted to think. He looked through the kitchen window above the sink. His eyes drifted out to the sea in the distance. Its constant movement was lost on him. His mind was riveted on Sarah—a poor, frightened innocent who had no idea what was happening and why. She will be frightened to the core; that was his only thought at the moment.

CIA agents knew the risk they took and what the United States would do to secure their release if captured. Sarah was totally unaware of the risks in international work. He had not shared that aspect of his life with her. He knew, at this moment, he had failed her. She didn't know that the people he commanded often worked in places of grave danger. She, unlike his colleagues, was totally unprepared to be held as a hostage. He pounded his hands together in frustration. He had done this to her. He returned to the desk.

"Calm down," he said out loud. "Get in control. Analyze the situation, develop a plan of action, and find the bastards."

He picked up the pen and began to write. He listed the countries where he, and his partners, had worked since he left the CIA: Israel, Jordan, Saudi Arabia, Kuwait, Egypt, and Qatar. He crossed out Israel. He noted the signature on the note: *Allahu Akbar.* This was an Arab action. That left five countries. He listed all the people he worked with there. The list was long, but the effort gave him a sense of progress. He worked each list to see where he might have created enemies. He circled the names of key people in each country and resolved to call them. He believed he could count on them to uncover information about the abduction. The first on his list to call was Claude Anderson.

He removed his cell phone from his jacket pocket and called his former CIA colleague's private line at home. The phone rang five times.

"Pick up! Pick up!" Brooks yelled.

The call went to voicemail.

"It's urgent, Claude. Call at any hour."

He placed the phone on the desk. The moment he removed his hand, it rang.

"Claude!" Brooks nearly shouted.

The voice on the other end was rough, crude.

"Don't speak, and listen carefully."

English was clearly not the caller's first language. Brooks tried to discern the accent but wasn't certain on the country of origin.

"I'm listening."

"We have your wife. She's safe. Have you read the ransom note?"

"I need proof of her safety."

"Shut up. I dictate the conditions."

Brooks interrupted the caller.

"You must know my country does not pay ransom for hostages. There have been many examples of that."

"I said 'shut up' and listen! If you want your wife back and don't want your treasonous actions made prominent in the American press, you'll do what the note demands."

Brooks let out a few breaths.

Be calm, he repeated to himself.

He released each phrase slowly.

"My wife is dead. She died years ago. Secondly, I cannot and will not pay a ransom. It's against my government's laws as I just told you, and third, I don't have that kind of money. Even if I did, it could not be raised in four days."

"Bullshit! We know of your accounts at Swissbanc, the money stashed on the Isle of Man, the accounts at Inter-Bank in Panama. Millions kept away from your taxman. You can write a check for two million in a day. Don't pull that shit on me! Do it, or the death of the woman will be on your hands, and your treason will be revealed!"

The caller let out a few short breaths and continued.

"Get a pen. Here is where the money is to be sent."

The caller cited the Ar-Eastern Bank in Tripoli and rattled off a series of digits. Brooks was surprised as he copied the information onto his paper.

How would they know about his foreign bank accounts? he wondered. *Where could they have found that kind of information?*

"It's not that simple," Brooks said. "The banks require my presence with papers to identify and validate that I authorize transactions of that amount. I need time if you really expect me to act on your demands."

"Do you think you're talking to amateurs? We know how international finance works. Just do what I said. Now I'll continue with the other demands. You are to send a cable to Egypt's President Mubarak, Jordan's King Hussein, Saudi's King Fahd, and the Emir Jaber al-Ahmad al-Sabah of Kuwait indicating that you now and forever are removing yourself from advisory services and commercial projects to concentrate on your academic work. Is that clear?"

There was no response. The caller repeated the question.

"Is that clear?"

"I'm writing your demands. You want a lot."

The caller ignored the comment.

"You will place a blind 'cc' on the message to the following cell phone number so I can ensure it was sent."

He gave the number to Brooks.

"Send the cable to those parties in the next four days. Just like the money. Got it?"

The caller didn't wait for an answer.

"If the cables are not sent, if the money is not in the Ar-Eastern Bank by next Tuesday, we'll release your treasonous acts to the press and your Justice Department. Then we will kill the woman whether she's your wife or not."

"Listen—I need proof that Sarah's alive."

"It will be on your cell phone in thirty minutes. And our last demand: Keep your police and FBI out of this. It's between us. You do what we want, and you get the woman back unharmed. If we sense your government's active, we kill the woman."

CHAPTER 15

Spreading the Net

Sunset Cove, California

The click on the other end of the phone ended the conversation. Brooks looked down at his notes. There was more information there than in any of his past hostage situations. He listed their two demands: money and stop work. Kill Sarah and expose his treason were the consequences if he failed to comply and involved the FBI.

Somebody's crazy and working with bad information, or both, he thought.

He circled "money and stop work."

Who would have those conditions and why? he wondered.

His work, his projects in the Middle East, were well received and were generating benefits to their economies. This was a riddle, and it was giving him a headache. He needed to concentrate. He pushed the notes aside and returned to his list of countries. He crossed off Qatar—the emir was not on their list for a cable.

And treason—what were they thinking? How could that be true or construed as true?

He needed to think about that.

What information had this group seen and used to arrive at the conclusion that he committed treason?

He wanted to pat himself on the back. He hadn't yelled and screamed at the caller. He didn't indicate that he was about to drop a shitstorm on their heads. He believed he communicated that he was thinking about their demands yet not necessarily agreeing to their terms. He felt he sounded negotiable and didn't provide a threat to Sarah. Yet, as he said her name, he felt the cold chill in his heart that he had put her in a horrible situation. He went to the liquor cabinet to find the vodka. He saw the Grey Goose bottle, tossed a splash into a glass, added several ice cubes from the freezer, and sat at the kitchen counter staring at his notes. He tried to trace the caller from his cell phone. It didn't register. It was a throwaway phone, as he expected.

He sat back to think. Claude came to mind. Had he gotten his message? He needed to talk with him. The vodka wasn't working. He wasn't calming down. He slammed the drink on the coffee table. Drops flew onto the table and onto his shirt. He brushed the vodka off his shirt.

"Shit! Shit! Shit! Fuck! Fuck!"

He knew his thinking was ragged as he pushed his mind toward the kidnappers' motive.

Why would anyone do this? he wondered. *Who would do it?*

He pushed himself to think and concluded that the kidnappers had to be from one of the four countries on his list. Although, he mused, it could be a pan-Arab group like Al-Qaeda. He didn't have enough information. There were too many possibilities. He listed them: Mubarak, Hussein, Fahd, and al-Sabah. They admired him, benefited from his work, and paid him handsomely. Not one of them would initiate this abduction.

So who? Why?

He speculated that a new group might be forming to try to

embarrass the monarchs and drive the capitalists out of the region. His mind shifted again.

What about a radical group within a country that was hostile to its leaders, such as the Muslim Brotherhood in Egypt? Was that worth exploring? But why Sarah? If this group didn't want his presence in their country, why not capture him?

His thoughts danced through the possibilities. He returned to personal motives.

Who benefits from removing me? he wondered. *Whom could I trust in the Middle East to unravel the mystery?*

He needed to determine who could help him and who his enemies were. He settled in the living-room chair that faced the sea, but he didn't see the waters beyond. His mind turned inward and drifted to the day when he was passed over to be the head of the CIA and decided to leave. He shook his head. That was when he decided to get into this work—work that now resulted in Sarah's abduction.

His mind wandered back to how the work got started. He knew the books he'd written and his government experience had paved the way for a secure academic track ahead of him. Adding to his options, when he left the government, he had been approached by several investment banks to do deals in the Middle East. He realized, after discussing their plans, that he didn't need them. He had better contacts and knowledge than they did. At first, he worked with partners from England and France, men he knew from his tours in Jordan and Israel. He'd teamed up with them often but not always. At times, he conducted business alone, as in Egypt, because it was faster and more efficient. His investment plans had succeeded far beyond his wildest dreams and resulted in several industrial projects that created local jobs and established new economic opportunities. Initially, he didn't imagine that his contacts in Egypt, Saudi Arabia, and other countries would be so lucrative, with each party willing to pay substantial fees to organize and complete these deals. He admitted that he preferred to sequester the funds offshore to keep the appearance of his advisory work low-key to university officials who sought to focus their faculties exclusively on academic matters. And he had many friends who parked funds offshore for tax reasons. He was only doing what thousands of others in business were doing. Deep in these thoughts, he was startled when the phone rang.

"Brooks! Glad to catch you," came Claude Anderson's booming voice. "I was planning to call you today about my Saudi request, but you rang first and sounded agitated. Did I get that right?"

"Claude, it's a serious mess. There's been a hostage taken. Sarah's been kidnapped."

There was momentary silence on the line.

"Holy Jesus H.! A kidnapping! Who? What do they want?"

"A group unknown to me seized her. I'll read you the ransom note and talk about the phone call that came later."

He summarized the essence of the ransom payment, the threat of personal blackmail, and the demand to avoid police notification. He mentioned his thinking about the countries where he'd worked, then stopped to listen for Claude's response. It was slow in coming. The tone and normal crispness of Claude's speech were missing. Davidson suspected that Claude's evening included some drinking. After what seemed liked minutes, Claude spoke.

"This is very serious," he said. "You're right to call me not only as a friend but also as a government official. This is an international incident, so I'll contact the normal people here. We know how to keep it quiet, as you are well aware."

After a short pause, he continued.

"I assume that's OK, regardless of their demand for no police."

"Of course," Brooks said.

"And I'd include State, my boys here at the CIA, and your friends in the FBI. Still OK?

"Yeah, but no media releases. No press from high-level officials."

"Yeah, I agree there," Claude said, "but I suggest we get the ambassadors in each of the countries to discuss with their counterparts what they know about radicals who would do this. We'll imply that a delay of the military goodies they've ordered could be affected if we don't get the woman back fast."

"That sounds right. Good God, it's helpful to know something can be done and someone with your skill is doing it."

"Flattery always works."

Brooks appreciated Claude's levity, the first break in tension since he'd read the ransom note.

"My thinking's a bit tangled, but I'd like to explore a few ideas with you," Brooks said. "I've just done a deal with Mubarak. I plan to go right to him. I'll do the same with Hussein, Fahd, and al-Sabah, or at least get to someone close to them. I'll claim that a rogue group in their country is embarrassing them with a kidnapping of an American and using that threat to remove options to improve their economies."

"That's good. Our ambassadors can put pressure on them too. What about the money?"

"I plan to ignore the demand, and I won't send the letter they want—the one removing my services from each country."

"Stonewall them?"

"Yeah. You agree?"

Claude hesitated for a moment.

"Brooks, what's this about the kidnappers having blackmail on you? Any credibility on that?"

"I've thought about the threat, and I can handle it."

"Before I act, old friend, I'd better know the details. I don't want my ass hung out to dry."

"OK. Fair enough. A couple of years back, I was trying to get a refinery deal done with Mubarak. At the time, his officials were having trouble with our import-export people on some agricultural equipment. I advised them on how best to present their case."

"Any of that in writing?" Claude asked.

"You know me better than that."

"So that bumped you over the top for the refinery project."

"It didn't hurt."

Brooks relaxed enough with the comment to release a chuckle.

"I may have skated close to the edge on that one, but I'll point out two things: There's no written proof of what was said. And secondly, I explained what was available in the public record. Egypt's Ministry of Trade and Industry bureaucrats were lazy or unable to master the details of our trade regs."

"Holy shit, Brooks. Do you know what you just said? You said one of the blackmail sources was from something you did in Egypt. Are there other juicy blackmail situations hiding in Saudi, Jordan, or Kuwait?"

"Jesus! I didn't think about the possible sources of blackmail. You're right, Claude. That's the only time I guided anyone in those countries through our trade regulations or helped them navigate our bureaucratic mazes. My God—the hostage takers could be Egyptian."

"Think hard on that, old boy. See if you have any other dirty little details that the hostage takers could use against you. That information might tell us about the group that took Sarah."

"You've got me thinking, but I'm pretty certain that was the one and only time I talked about U.S. policy and procedures. And it's not that damaging if it does surface."

He paused to recall his statement.

"Yeah, I'm one hundred percent certain I never talked about U.S. military or economic policy. In the instance we're discussing, I worked directly with Mubarak, and nothing was written down."

"This sounds good to me," Claude said. "I'd be very surprised if you'd done a dirty to make some money."

"Not my style or inclination."

"OK, back to my reason for the checking in with you: Can you get to Saudi Arabia in the next week or two on the oil embargo question?"

He laughed—a long growling noise.

"And now you have a second and more compelling reason: The Saudi Mukhabarat and your friends there may know something about the group that's involved in this abduction. In getting there real fast, you can kill two birds with one stone."

"OK, I hear you," Brooks said. "I'll get your job done, and I'll talk to friends at the Mukhabarat."

"Call on a secure line as soon as you get the oil production data. We'll stay in touch on the hostage situation."

He paused.

"One more thought: I know Bill Turner at the FBI. He's just taken over their San Francisco office. I'll tell him you'll be calling."

"Will do. I can't thank you enough for your support on Sarah."

Brooks placed the telephone down and let out a deep breath. A plan going forward was beginning to emerge. He knew that when Claude contacted his counterpart at the State Department, the ambassadors in the four countries would act. How fast and how aggressively would depend on what other crises or top-priority issues were on their desks. He could get what they called the State Department's slow waltz. He'd seen it happen before.

He wanted to stimulate action and worried if his sudden departure during the Clinton administration would affect efforts in the CIA. More of a worry was his criticism of the Bush administration's policies in an op-ed of his that ran in *The New York Times*. That could affect the speed and intensity of action he wanted from the FBI and State Department.

He sat at the dining-room table and opened his computer. He sent an email to Claude suggesting that suspected terrorists from the Middle East held at the Guantanamo Bay detention camp could be offered as trade for Sarah. He pondered over other messages but couldn't think of any and closed the computer.

He was still bothered by the why. He felt that if he could define why the kidnappers targeted Sarah and him, he could confirm who did this. It would speed up the search for her. He sat back in his chair, placed his hands behind his head, fingers interlocked, eyes soft. This was a pose he often took when meditating. His mind turned to a recent broadcast he heard on Al Jazeera in which the news anchor was decrying the avalanche of Western investment in the Middle East, calling it the new form of colonialism. He'd heard this comment before, but now it began to resonate with him.

What if he were the first investment advisor to be harassed and forced to quit the Middle East? he wondered. *Would others pull away in fear? Who would benefit from this scare tactic?*

The puzzle brought him straight up in his chair. There were many radical groups seeking to drive out Western influence. One of them, the Muslim Brotherhood, proclaimed its long-standing philosophy of Islamic economic independence. A sense of satisfaction flowed through him. That group, founded in Egypt way back in 1928, was now a major force in the politics of the country. It was another clue that pointed to the Egyptians. But Brooks leaned toward dismissing that idea. His relationship with Mubarak was solid, going back years, and the benefits flowing to Egypt from his projects were immense. Pondering possible enemies in Kuwait, Jordan, and Saudi Arabia, he went online to check out flights to Saudi Arabia. And he made a note to call Bill Turner at the FBI.

CHAPTER 16

Gunshots

Santa Rosa, California

The captors had taken her Cartier watch and, with no windows in the room, Sarah had no idea of day or night. Twice a day, they brought her olives, bread, and a new plastic glass for water from the sink. Occasionally, there was a dish of rice and vegetables. Each time they knocked on the door, they yelled at her to put on the blindfold and kneel facing a wall. She took their threat of a beating seriously and followed instructions. When the food was delivered, she asked the same question.

"When will you let me go?"

Beneath his black ski mask, the food carrier's mouth never moved. For Sarah, being isolated in a dark room with a sink, a toilet, and no windows was a nightmare. She was used to an active life with her clinical work, her hospice volunteering, her family and friends, and her cycling three or four times a week. The empty room was sucking energy from her inner being.

This is a form of psychological torture, she thought, *and it's working.*

She fought to retain a grip on reality and tried to converse with her captors, but her fear of them and their clear avoidance of her quashed her attempts. Her voice sounded hollow in the empty room. She sought to determine day from night by the noise level in the next room but lost track of her captors' movements—they were too erratic. Eventually, she concluded that the food was delivered at noon and again in the early evening.

After endless hours of being alone, she realized that nothing happened between meals. The tedium of sitting on the bed during this time was a welcome relief from constant dread, but she knew her inactivity was no help. She decided that she had to take control of something to maintain her sanity. She committed to keeping busy and was willing to try anything to help time pass. She walked around the room, counting the steps, as she'd done during the first hours of her confinement. On her first excursion, she did twenty laps, calculating her movement across the room and back as one lap.

During this regimen, she found it comforting to talk to someone and would select a person. It would be one of her kids, a friend, her sister, or Brooks—although that got her angry—and she'd say aloud whatever topics came to her mind. When she thought about Brooks, she was overwhelmed with confusion that often spilled into anger. How could this man not tell her of the enemies he'd acquired over the years or the danger in his current life? Her kids gave her a different feeling. They came to mind most often, and she told them about what had happened. She explored how they would feel and what would they do about her disappearance. She had rarely been out of touch with them for more than a day or two.

Had Brooks told them? she wondered. *Had they seen her kidnapping on the news? How were they handling the crisis?*

There were many topics to discuss in her mind, and her conversation list grew to dozens of people who helped her consume time. After the walking became boring, she switched to her yoga exercises until her muscles were exhausted. At first, she kept her clothes on, hoping that would be a deterrent to rape. When it was evident that they ignored her until a meal was delivered, she shed her shirt and pants, placing them on the bed. She walked and exercised in her underwear and bra. The room was cool, but it felt good on her body as she exercised. This enabled her to keep her clothes clean and without odor. She washed in the steel sink after each exercise, drying with the one coarse towel left on her bed. Staying clean helped her feel better.

After exercise, she rested on the bed and daydreamed. The bed had a thin but firm mattress protected with a heavy cloth cover and a thin sheet. A single wool blanket covered the sheet. She lay on the blanket and let her mind fantasize journeys into different careers.

What if she had studied more hard science and less psychology? What if she had met different men or been born in Germany, as her mother was?

She avoided thinking about her captivity; it was beyond her control, and dwelling on it, even for a few minutes, brought her anxiety to a high level. When that happened, her motivation to walk and exercise disappeared, and she had to fight the tendency to lie in bed and worry. She estimated time by figuring she could do three sets of yoga a day. When she'd completed eighteen sets, she wondered if that meant she'd been in captivity for six days. She had no idea if this was accurate, but after the eighteenth yoga set, the knock on her door startled her. Mustafa barged in as she raced to put on the blindfold and her pants and shirt.

"What the fuck you doing?"

He put his hand to his face to disguise his appearance.

"You came in too fast. I didn't see anything," she stammered as she sank to the floor, tied the blindfold across her eyes and faced the wall. "Please don't hit me."

It struck her that her captors spoke English quite well, although with a noticeable accent. Yet when talking with each other, they used the foreign language that she had now concluded was Arabic.

"Get up!" he ordered, then lifted her from the floor and pushed her toward the bed. "Sit and wait."

Changing languages, he called out.

"Jabari! She's ready."

Jabari walked into the room, pushed Mustafa aside, and stood next to the bed, hovering over Sarah. He carried a bag of clothes and gave them to her.

"It's been six days, and your clothes are beginning to stink. There's a fresh shirt, pants and underwear."

Sarah raised her head as if she could see him despite the blindfold. She could smell his tobacco breath.

"Thank you," she said. "I'll put them on later."

She dropped the bag to the floor. Jabari placed his hand under her chin and lifted her face so her blindfold was directly before his eyes.

"Lady, your man has not responded to phone calls. He has not done what we asked. Also, he has ignored what you told him to do in your text message."

"I can't explain what he does or doesn't do."

She lifted an arm in frustration, pointed at Jabari and muttered, "Fuck! Fuck!"

"What'd you just say?"

He clipped her hard under her chin.

"You don't talk until I tell you to. Now I want you to telephone him."

She started to cry. She rubbed her jaw, then moved her hand to point at the blindfold.

"I can't see. I have no phone."

"I have a cell phone. Tell me his number. I'll punch it in. You will repeat the message I give you. But first we'll take a long drive before we call so the call can't be traced to this location."

They drove in Jahin's 2000 S-Class Mercedes for about an hour. There was ample room in the sedan for all of them. Sarah sat in the back seat between Mustafa and Hamid. They had manacled her wrists and feet. She tried to listen to noises as the sedan sped to its destination but heard nothing except the hum of the tires on the road. When the car stopped and the doors opened, all she could conclude was that they were in farmland. She could smell the lush grass and cow manure. With the sedan pulled over to the side of the road, they unshackled Sarah's ankles and wrists. On Jabari's command, Sarah gave him Brooks' number. Jabari punched in the numbers.

"I will shoot this pistol in the air," he told Sarah.

He let her feel the barrel of the weapon.

"When your man answers, you will hear a shot. Then you'll say to Davidson. 'That's what they'll do to me if you don't deposit the money and send the cables. Your actions are overdue.'"

He paused.

"OK. Have you got it?"

Sarah nodded as he called. She could hear the ring tone clearly when Jabari put the phone on speaker mode and handed it to her.

Pick up, she pleaded silently.

Brooks answered. He was in his office at Stanford, having just gotten off the phone with Bill Turner of the San Francisco FBI office.

"Hello?"

She nearly collapsed at the sound of his voice. A split second later, the gunshot rang in the air.

"Brooks, they're not shooting at me," she said, then quickly added, "I have a message for you."

She then dutifully stated Jabari's message.

"Jesus, Sarah, is that really you? Are you OK? I know you can't talk, and I assume they're listening on a speaker phone. But how are you Sarah? What can I do?"

"Oh, Brooks—your voice."

Her own voice started to waver.

"Just do as they say and get me out of here. Please."

"Trust me, Sarah, everything that can be done is being done. Trust that. I've talked to your girls—they're brave. I'll take care of your bills. I love you."

He paused.

"Put one of them closer to the phone."

She handed it to Jabari.

"He wants to talk with you."

Jabari grabbed the phone.

"You heard the shot. I'll use it on her tomorrow if you don't pay and sign the agreement."

"Listen to me," Brooks began. "I've talked to my banks. Remember, they're in foreign countries. For funds of that magnitude, they want me present to sign in person for the transfer. It will take days before I can get there to conduct this business. You'll have to wait."

"You heard me," Jabari said. "Get it done now, or we release the evidence of your treason, and we shoot the woman."

"Pay attention to what I say," Brooks demanded in a voice steady but stern. "If you do that, I'll still be working in the four countries where you want me removed. You'll have the security services in all those places searching for you plus three U.S. agencies and the local police. Do you want that, or are you willing to wait?"

There was a moment of silence on the line. Then Brooks spoke again.

"Before I undertake any of the actions you want, I want a five-minute video of Sarah Pierce that clearly shows she's alive, healthy, and in good shape mentally. I need that proof before I do anything."

Jabari yelled into the phone.

"Do it now!"

CHAPTER 17

A Cock-Up

Cairo, Egypt

Fathi Ashur's red phone rang. It was tucked in a drawer beneath his desktop. This was his private line to General Galal Murad, the director of the Mukhabarat. It was unusual for it to ring; General Murad rarely called him directly. Ashur opened the drawer, placed the receiver to his ear, and, before he could offer a greeting, heard the general's voice.

"Come to my office immediately."

Ashur had taken the call standing up, as if called to attention by a superior officer. He remained fixed in that position for several moments, then stretched his jaw to release the tension forming behind his eyes. He let his breath out slowly, wondering if the general had heard about the kidnapping of the American woman. He assumed that was the purpose of the call. He glanced at his calendar. It was June 15, and the woman had not been released. He needed to call Omar. He put on his suit jacket, rubbed his sore leg, and began the trek to the general's office.

As Ashur proceeded slowly down the long halls, he was irritated at being summoned. He never felt welcomed in the general's office. To him, it looked more like a prison cell with its blank white walls, gunmetal desk, and a few steel-backed chairs set around it. The cold-gray carpet gave the room a dreary appearance. The only pleasant aspect of the place was the picture window that let in sunlight and provided a view of the city streets below. Yet the general avoided this aesthetic touch by covering the window, during most of the day, with black louvered shutters.

The room was dark when Ashur entered, the only light coming from a single desk lamp.

Murad waved him to one of the chairs. Galal Murad was a Cabinet member and a long-standing ally of President Mubarak. He was in his fifties, a veteran of the Six-Day War against the Israelis back in 1967. He had the battle scars to attest to his bravery and commitment to Egypt. Of medium height with close-cropped gray hair, he had an austere and commanding presence.

He leveled his hard, brown eyes at Ashur. He had an odd pattern of speech, sprinkling his vocabulary with English idioms he'd acquired in his early military training at Sandhurst.

"Ashur, we've had a cock-up with the Americans. Our president is on fire. He's worried that the bastards will withhold or stop aid for military equipment totaling billions of dollars."

"General, I don't understand. What's happened?"

"You didn't hear the news? Apparently, an American woman was kidnapped. She's the wife of a former top CIA official. His name is Davidson, a man I know well and respect."

"What's that got to do with Egypt?"

"The American ambassador—you know Francis Ticonne, don't you?"

Murad twisted the corner of his mouth, emphasizing the question.

"The ambassador read a ransom note over the phone to foreign minister Hamdi, then to Hagazi, one of the president's assistants.

The president was stunned and called Ambassador Ticonne. The note said that Dr. Davidson had to resign from all advisory services to Egypt in order to free the woman as well as pay an exorbitant ransom to the kidnappers. The president is enraged by the implicit accusation that someone in our government may be involved in this mess."

"Were other countries mentioned in the ransom note?"

"Yes. Saudi, Kuwait, and Jordan."

"Then it may have nothing to do with Egyptians," Ashur said. "It may be a group like Al- Qaeda trying to get Western investors and advisors out of the region. What did the president request you to do?"

"He wanted to make certain that this plot does not involve Egyptians."

"General, do you believe Egyptians are involved?"

"You know the president. He exploded with his paranoia about enemies in the country. He's worried, as always, about their willingness to use any means to expose and embarrass him. He brought up Al-Qaeda and the Muslim Brotherhood right away."

"General, this cock-up, as you call it, may have nothing to do with us."

"That's what I want you to find out," Murad said. "Put your best people on this and dig into every radical and opposition group in the country. I want you to determine if any of the actors responsible for this stupid deed are Egyptian."

Ashur stared at the general, attempting to maintain a calm, measured presence. Inside, he pushed his worries deep into the recesses of his mind.

"Of course, at this moment we have some of the bad actors in prison," he told the general. "I'll get the right people to squeeze them for what they know and may have heard."

"Check out Al Muharib as well as the two groups the president mentioned. Report to me as soon as you have anything. Let's talk every day."

He waved a scarred hand at Ashur, dismissing him. During the meeting, Ashur felt that he'd held his composure. Once out of the office, he asked the general's secretary for some water. He sipped it slowly, trying to cleanse the stomach acid rising to his mouth. His heart was pounding. He forced breaths in and out.

"Minister Ashur, are you all right?" the secretary asked. "Should I call someone?"

"No, Merit, it's a passing reaction, a slight dizziness. It happens every now and then—a holdover from my incident with the Russians."

He waved goodbye, certain that she would report his discomfort to her boss. He walked as fast as his gimpy leg would carry him back to his office and called Omar. There was no answer on the private line, so he left a message with Sayed's assistant: "Lunch tomorrow, same time, same place."

★ ★ ★

When Omar picked up the message later in the day, he knew Fathi's cryptic message meant their meeting was of top importance. This injected a dose of fear in him. He called Fathi for additional information. His assistant said he was not available, and Omar confirmed the next day's meeting. His cousin rarely called. Omar, his nervousness increasing, then crossed a forbidden line and called Fathi's home phone. The call went to voicemail.

That night, he tossed and turned in his sleep, uneasy over Fathi's terse message. At breakfast, he limited his conversation with his wife to yes and no responses and left the apartment after quickly consuming a slice of dry toast and a cup of dark coffee. The morning dragged by as he reviewed proposals for trade agreements with his deputy and the chief of his budget office. At the close of the meeting, his deputy had a question.

"Minister Sayed, is there more I can do? You seemed impatient with us."

"No, not at all," said Sayed, smiling. "My mind drifts to a forthcoming meeting with the president. You understand."

When the midday hour approached, he rushed from the building and walked hurriedly toward the Nile. The afternoon was hot and humid, much less pleasant than it had been for their meeting in May. He felt the sweat on his forehead and wondered if it was the heat or a premonition of messages to come. When he arrived at the river, he saw his cousin sitting on a bench, smoking a cigarette.

"Fathi!" he exclaimed. "Good to see you."

Fathi gazed through a veil of smoke at Omar. His face was drawn, his eyes cold. He gestured with his damaged hand to a seat beside him on the bench.

"Let's talk here. There's no one nearby, we're safe, and it's too hot to walk."

Omar sat, looking expectantly at his cousin.

"This must be important. You're so serious and, I might add, mysterious. What's this all about?"

Fathi inhaled and let a stream of smoke flow out his nostrils.

"An American woman has been kidnapped by an Arab group, and the Americans, through their ambassador, have complained directly to the president."

"So? Did you expect—"

Fathi put up his hand.

"I don't want to know anything. I simply want to warn you that the ransom note was read to the president. It demanded that a Dr. Davidson was not to work in Egypt. You can imagine how upset the president was to learn his country was named in a terrorist act."

"So what? Other countries were mentioned."

Fathi raised his hand again.

"Stop. No more talking. Listen."

He leveled his tired eyes at Omar.

"I've been given the task to discover if the kidnappers, one or all, are Egyptian. The president and General Murad were emphatic. They want to know if any of the terrorists were affiliated with radical groups in the country. He wants the answer now."

Omar brushed the top of his head with his right hand. He wiped the sweat in his palm on the thigh of his pants.

"Dog shit! Camel shit!"

He spewed a string of Arab curses at the river in front of him. He didn't look at Fathi. "What are you going to do?" he finally asked.

Fathi tossed his cigarette to the ground and erased it into the gravel path with the heel of his shoe. He let out a long sigh, then directed a crooked finger at Omar's chest.

"I will drag the investigation out for a few days. I can do that, but no longer than a week. Get the job done, get the woman released safely, unharmed. Or...I don't need to finish that sentence."

"You better finished that sentence, cousin. You're in this too."

Fathi rose from the bench and stood over Omar.

"This can be cast as an Al Hura or Al-Qaeda action as long as you close it fast. I can keep it away from you as long as you act fast. Do it!"

CHAPTER 18

Allies Step Up

Palo Alto, California

Brooks was in his book-filled study, organizing his papers, notebooks, and laptop for the trip to Saudi Arabia. It was eleven p.m. when the telephone rang. The blare of the ring tone rattled him.

Nobody calls me at this hour, he thought.

He braced for the worst.

"Turner here," announced an energetic voice that Brooks recognized as Special Agent William Turner. "Brooks, how are you doing?"

Brooks was not expecting such a late call from the FBI, nor was he prepared for Turner's upbeat voice. He struggled to find the right response.

"What are you doing, Bill? Working hard at this hour?"

"I've been thinking about the kidnapping. I'd like to discuss an idea with you. And I'm so energized by this idea, I want to act on it tomorrow morning. I want my staff on this as soon as I hit the office."

Turner had met with Brooks the day after Sarah's kidnapping at the bureau's office in San Francisco. Younger than Brooks, in his early forties, and bristling with energy, Turner had moved his six-foot frame in a steady pace around the room, occasionally approaching his desk to look at his notes, but he never sat down. Brooks remained standing by Turner's desk and watched his active movement of arms and hands as he described the FBI's strategy to find Sarah by tracking cell phone calls and working with informants in San Francisco.

In his study now, a faint smile crossed Brooks' lips.

"Bill, I like the initiatives. What's happened?"

"We got a break, but I must admit I'm stretching quite a bit to call this a break. That's what I want to discuss with you, hear your thoughts."

After six days with no progress and no obvious steps he could take other than pay the ransom and sign the agreement, Brooks felt powerless. But he knew U.S. policy—no payment of ransoms—and had even been one of its architects. After he informed Sarah's daughters of the abduction, they trusted his advice to let the FBI take the lead. He also told them about his contacts in the Middle East and how he planned to use his insider's access. That seemed a distant and unproductive avenue to them, and, with each ensuing call, they asked what more he could do. Their veiled request implied "pay the money," and he had begun to consider it. His emotions were pushing him to give in to protect Sarah's life. He was fighting the impulse with the logic that it was wrong way to deal with terrorists. At this late hour, on the edge of mental and physical exhaustion, Brooks was pleased to have his attention diverted to another's thoughts.

"Bill, you sound encouraged. I definitely want to hear this."

"Brooks, you've been down the hostage road many times, so tell me if my ideas make sense."

Before he could comment, Turner was already talking.

"We found an abandoned van in a Santa Rosa parking lot."

"Yeah. What's that—?"

"Let me finish. The owner of the van reported it stolen on June ninth from a residential street in the Mission District. The date works. Later that night, the manager of a Safeway in Santa Rosa noticed a van had not been moved by closing hours and called the police. The vehicle identification number matched the stolen vehicle number circulated by the city department."

"Again, so what?"

"Listen to this," Turner began. "Not only does the date work, the van was scrubbed clean. No fingerprints on it, inside or out. Now, that's very unusual. Somebody was being very careful. This was not your usual stolen vehicle profile."

"I'm listening."

"The van may well be the vehicle used by the hostage takers."

"That's a stretch."

"Think about it: A vehicle had to pick Sarah up. They can't fly her out of Sunset Cove or move her by train or bus. She must be driven somewhere. So where did they go? How could Arab speakers find a safe place to store her?"

He hesitated, wondering if he was pressing his case too fast.

"Are you with me?" Turner asked.

"Go on."

"Yeah, OK. I'm thinking if the van was the vehicle used, she might be at a safe haven in the Santa Rosa area. So, you ask, where's a safe haven in Santa Rosa? Here's my strategy: We, in coordination with the Santa Rosa police, interview every homeowner and building operator with a Middle Eastern background. Shouldn't be too many. I'll have my team on these names first thing in the morning. I'll talk to the chief in Santa Rosa as well."

"I like your aggressive position, Bill, but you may wind up talking to dozens of people. It seems like a long shot."

"Here's another piece of the puzzle. Get this: My wife works part time at a boutique on Folsom Street. Each month, they get a software firm to back up their data and store it. Their normal guy didn't show up. When Mary asked where he was, the manager said he's been out sick for a week. She told me his name was Jabari and that he looked Middle Eastern. We checked the name with his company. All they knew was that he was sick and wasn't available to come to the phone. According to his visa, his full name is Jabari Radwan. He's Egyptian. My top priority will be to talk to every citizen in Santa Rosa with an Egyptian background."

"Amazingly fast work, Bill, but there's a ton of Egyptians working in the city—maybe Santa Rosa too."

"My gut tells me this is good. The final reason I want to pursue this Jabari Radwan is his visa. It indicates he's former military in Egypt. He damn well might have the capability to pull off a caper like this."

"I like your thinking," Brooks said. "It's a lead. Other than the phone calls, it's the only lead. I say go for it. Is there anything I can do other than make contact with my friends in the Middle East?"

"You stay on that course. We'll take the U.S. side. If they try to move her via public transportation or across international boundaries, somebody's bound to see a woman surrounded by Middle Easterners."

Brooks shuddered at the thought of Sarah being taken out of the country but silently agreed with Turner. It would be difficult to move her without a passport and avoid detection by customs agents.

"Yeah, my big hope is that some of my contacts in the four countries will have heard of this abduction and have some leads for us."

★ ★ ★

The next morning, Brooks made his second call to Francis Ticonne. The American ambassador was an old acquaintance. They'd served in the Saudi embassy years ago and had gone in separate directions after that assignment. Brooks knew that he had rubbed Ticonne the wrong way a few times, so he worried the man might have little motivation to help him. In his first call to Ticonne, Brooks had been assured that the ambassador would make direct contact with President Mubarak. He had followed up the meeting with a brief message to Brooks indicating that Mubarak was genuinely surprised by the abduction and did not want Davidson's services removed from Egypt.

When Brooks got Ticonne on the phone, the ambassador was apologetic.

"Brooks, my schedule is an embarrassment. I've wanted to connect much earlier. How are you doing?"

"Thank you, Frank. I know your schedule. I don't envy it. I'm OK and feel better when I'm taking action. It's hard to be on the sidelines on this one."

"Let me bring you up to date on my conversations with Mubarak and some of his people. First, we've kept this quiet as you requested in your first call. However, it will come out eventually if the tops in Washington want to get into the act."

"I think pressure might work on this pack of terrorists because my responses to their conditions don't seem to scare them," Brooks said.

"Well, let me tell you more about my meetings with the Egyptians. As I said in my last message, Mubarak and Foreign Minister Hamdi were truly surprised by the action. In fact, Mubarak was outraged that Egypt was mentioned in the ransom conversations. They value your work. I gather you've heard the same from the Jordanians, Kuwaitis, and Saudis?"

"I have, and I plan to visit each in the next week or so."

"Good. And please come by here. President Mubarak wants to see you and, of course, it's always a delight to have you at the embassy. Back to my meetings—I'll keep pressure on the Egyptians and will work to identify any internal malcontents who might have been involved."

"Frank, thank you. You're going the extra mile. But I do have one more question for you. Are there dissidents within Mubarak's government who want to embarrass the president as well as harm me?"

"You're on to something, but I can't put my finger on it. There's rumbling here in Cairo and across the region that anti-Americanism is rising. In Egypt, it's the Muslim Brotherhood we have to watch. They have twenty percent of the seats in parliament and are more and more outspoken about corruption among Mubarak's top officials, implying the Americans are part of this problem. When the Sarah Pierce abduction is over, I wouldn't be surprised if we find that some Egyptian group was behind this to embarrass Mubarak."

"That's helpful insight, Frank. I had a conversation yesterday with Bill Turner of the FBI. He's pursuing a lead involving an Egyptian guy. Maybe our information is beginning to point toward Egyptian involvement of some kind."

"Really? Forward that name to me. I'll find out what I can about the man. Good luck on this, Brooks. Please give my personal assistant your travel schedule. I hope to see you in a few weeks. By then, my bet is that we'll have found Sarah."

Brooks placed the handset down and slumped onto a leather stool at the kitchen counter. He studied his notes from the conversation and thought of Frank's comments. In an attempt to placate him, Brooks recalled what Frank had said.

Hostage takers rarely kill. They want money for their cause.

Brooks didn't agree, and that worried him. Several names came to mind—journalists, NGO workers, and government officials who had been captured and beheaded. What stuck in his mind was that Sarah's future faced the same uncertainty that these other unfortunates experienced.

He knew he'd been incredibly lucky to find such a great woman at this stage in life. Yet, she had been snatched away because of his business interests. For now, she was gone. He would not see her face this weekend. He would miss the brilliant smile that kept sliding into his consciousness. This abduction, no matter how terrible, was bringing her closer to him. The uneasiness he felt, the gnawing dread, the bond of caring were not typical for him. He wanted Sarah safe, but he began to realize how much he wanted her back. Not just back safely, but back to him. Her presence in his life had crept up on him, and, without him fully realizing it, she'd become important.

Why did it take this dreadful experience to make me recognize that she was slowly moving into the center of my life? he wondered.

He'd had affairs after Clary's death, and a few of them had lasted a lot longer than his relationship with Sarah, but none had touched him as she had. He wanted to do more but did not want to interfere with Ticonne's dealings with the Egyptians or with the FBI tactics in Santa Rosa.

He followed the call to Ticonne with calls to the embassies in Riyadh, Kuwait City, and Amman. He wanted the same thoroughness in investigation from his contacts in those countries as he was getting from Francis Ticonne. He'd have to wait. In each call, the staff at the embassy said the ambassador would get back to him. Instead, Brooks checked his flight schedule and asked for appointments on the dates he would be in their country. The Saudi and Egyptian embassies were on the top of his list.

CHAPTER 19

Flight

Santa Rosa, California

Sarah tried to keep track of the days with her exercises and the delivery of food. After a week, or what she thought was a week, there was no indication from her captors that she'd be released. The thought gave her the shakes—that sense of terror that wouldn't go away. The gripping fear that characterized her first two days in captivity was changing—but not for the better. She knew that her current state of mind was not healthy. This morning, or what she thought was morning, she rose and did her workout. Afterward, she was sweaty and tired. She remained in her bra and panties, then lay on her bed and did not get up. The accumulated boredom and tedium in this barren room, she recognized, were getting to her. As a psychologist, she knew the signs of depression and recognized that she was headed in that direction.

Today, she rested, sometimes sleeping, but each drift into slumber was interrupted by a nightmare from which she woke up screaming. This had happened in the past few days, and now she found her bra, panties, and sheet soaked in sweat. She dried herself with the dirty towel at the stainless-steel sink and went back to bed. In the fog of somnolence, a misty point between sleep and wakefulness, the pattern was interrupted by a tumult of voices. Her door opened with a bang. She looked up, expecting food. Instead, she saw the black ski mask of the man she thought was the leader. Jabari's dark eyes glared out of the mask.

"Dress and put on the blindfold!" he barked. "Be fast! We're watching!"

When she was led out of her room, she peered through the bottom of her blindfold and saw that she was walking on a gravel path. She could see the feet of the men surrounding her as they guided her forward. They wore blue jeans or khakis that touched the top of their Adidas runners. One man had on soft, gray silk trousers that creased the top of a pair of polished leather loafers.

How odd! she thought. *One man has shoes that cost more than all the clothes on the other men. He must be the boss.*

That man seemed to be talking as his feet moved, while the other shoes stayed in place. His voice was loud; his speech, occasionally in English and Arabic, was fast and sounded frantic. He spoke now in English.

"I've just had a visit with government people, and they said they'd come back with a search warrant. The hostage must leave. Take my car to this address. The chopper will take you to the next place."

The men pushed Sarah forward, and she stumbled, her balance impaired by the blindfold. One of the men grasped her arm and led her up the path into sharp, dry heat. She heard the loud man speak.

"Every year, the immigration people come by to check the visas of my workers."

After a short silence, one of the kidnappers spoke.

"Are you certain they're coming back?"

"Yes."

Then the same voice spoke again.

"Hurry! Leave!"

The fast conversation and the command to leave confused and frightened her. The nagging despair that lingered in her mind gave way to a burst of fear. Before she could assemble her thoughts and ask a question, she was shoved into the back seat of a car, panic rising and causing her chest to tighten. Her feet and hands were manacled, and she was strapped in tight with a shoulder seat belt.

What next? she wondered.

It was roomy in the back. Two men sat on either side of her. The leather was soft and cool to touch. The air conditioning blasted cool air throughout the car as it roared away from the building. Sarah lost track of time. No one spoke, and she went into her head once again.

Why are we moving? she wondered. *Where are we going?*

A bump in the road and the creaking of a gate got her attention, and she listened intently. The car came to a stop. She could hear a whine of engines and the roar of what sounded like propellers.

They're running, she thought. *Someone's after us, them. Must be.*

Feeling a hint of confidence, she queried the men next to her, her voice barely above a whisper.

"Where are we? What's happening? Tell me something."

The one with the soft voice spoke to her.

"Things are happening. We're moving to a new place. We're getting on a plane."

She heard a slap, then another. She pulled back in her seat in terror. She figured that she'd be hit hard again, punished for talking. But the slap was not directed toward her. She heard the rough voice again.

"Shut up! Don't say another word! If you need to talk, do it in our language!"

She knew the rebuke was administered by the leader and directed at another member of the kidnappers.

Was there dissension in their ranks? she wondered. *Was the frantic conversation before they got in the car an indication that they were in trouble?*

Sarah realized that their change in plans was a good sign for her. They were running away. She felt a surprising jolt to her spirit. Something—she didn't know what—but something was happening. Deep inside her, she felt a slight stirring of hope. The depressed state of lying in bed, nibbling little bits of food, but mostly just drinking water, had induced lethargy. Now she felt a surge of energy, which prompted a request.

"Do you have any food?"

There was a bustle of talk in Arabic.

"We have an energy bar here."

She felt the bar placed in her hands. The wrapper felt familiar, and she eagerly stripped it away and dug her teeth into its soft chocolate. She sighed. The first taste was delicious. It was a PowerBar, one of her favorites when she cycled.

"Thank you."

She devoured it in seconds and followed that with gulps of water from a bottle offered by the man next to her. She could taste the salt from his lips as she placed the bottle to her mouth. It was repellant; it was his lips, his sweat she was inhaling, drinking. She tried hard not to gag because she wanted, *needed*, the water. She took the bottle from her mouth and, with her forefinger and thumb, wiped the top before she drank again.

With the infusion of food and the sip of water, she felt more than a spurt of energy. She was suddenly alert and began to focus on what was happening. They were leaving one place in an apparent rush, maybe even an emergency. It must mean the police were on their trail.

Were Brooks and the police looking for me rather than trying to come up with the ransom? she wondered.

This thought shifted into another worry. Would an aggressive search bring more danger to her? She welcomed the concern. It meant her mind was getting in gear.

What can I do to help myself? she thought. *Should I try to escape?*

Then came the realization that she was passing from a stage of psychological torture to a new one. It had been the isolation, zero conversation, and no sunlight or outside exercise that had pushed her into depression. She made a vow that no matter what happened next, she would challenge herself and them. She would continue her yoga and exercise routine. She would force the captors to talk with her. She would drive them crazy with conversation, whether they responded or not. She would find where they were weak and take advantage of it.

Stepping from the car, they led her toward a *thump-thump* sound. She felt the air whipping around her. She mounted a few short steps into what she knew to be a helicopter. A new voice asked a question, and she could not decipher the inquiry.

The man with the loud, aggressive voice spoke.

"Shut the fuck up! We'll talk to you! You don't talk to us!"

Sarah could feel the body of a man seated next to her as the helicopter took off.

"Where are we going?" she shouted.

The rude voice came at her like a blast from a bullhorn.

"Shut up!"

"What are you running from?" she persisted. "Are the Feds or police after you?"

She felt stronger, even confident, and was about to ask another question when a fist slammed into her ear, driving her head into the wall of the cabin. Both sides of her head screamed in agony. The blow stunned her. She felt a surge of nausea and fought to hold back the vomit. She held back tears, deciding that she would not be silenced. She was defiant.

"Not necessary, jerkwater."

She spat at him.

He slammed her head against the cabin wall again.

"Shut up unless you want more of this!"

Her head was screaming in pain, and she bit her lip to hold back the tears that began to surface in her eyes. Yet she felt her courage stirring inside her while the numbing reality remained: This nightmare was far from over.

CHAPTER 20

Search Warrant

San Francisco, California

Brooks Davidson had a lifelong interest in office décor. He knew that the furniture or photos and awards placed on walls were not complete insights into the nature and character of the occupant, but it was a useful starting place for him. What was this person all about? What was important to them?

Brooks knew Bill Turner had been promoted, and his new office was more spacious than the cramped cubicle he had previously visited. This time, the office was consistent with Brooks' impression of the FBI man—direct, no frills, all business. The wood-paneled walls had photographs of the president and the FBI director standing with Turner. He displayed no other notable items from his past or present to advertise his accomplishments. The wood desk was handsome, of simple construction. Only a telephone and a computer marked its top. A light gray carpet covered the floor. Brooks sat on the couch, upholstered in a slightly darker gray.

Turner had greeted Brooks, then faced him while leaning his powerful frame against the edge of his desk, his buttocks nearly resting on its top. Blue slacks and white shirt with a thin clip-on tie looked to Brooks like the standard FBI uniform. Yet, he dismissed these passing observations of institutional conformity. He appreciated Turner's skill and determination. And the man was obviously enthusiastic about his recently developed evidence.

"Brooks, I wish I'd been there. Yeah, when my agent pulled up to Jahin's grand hacienda, some weird shit happened."

Brooks sipped his coffee as he took in the room.

"I like your office, Bill—very cool."

Turner waved the comment away with a brief smile. Brooks spoke again.

"Before we get into Jahin, did your people get any useful information from other Middle Easterners? Was Jahin unusual?"

"He was."

Turner stopped to sip his coffee.

"There was virtually nothing from other interviews. Here's a quick summary: A records search indicated that twenty-three families with Middle East origins were currently living in Santa Rosa. Four or five of those families have been in the area for years. This Taha Jahin is one of the latter group. He's quite well known around the Bay Area—a successful wine importer/exporter. My guy figured, 'Why bother with Jahin? He's a good citizen.' Terrorists would be unlikely to get him involved with a kidnapping. But on second thought, Jim—that's my guy—decided to visit him in case he heard about the Pierce abduction and could offer us some names."

"And it got weird?"

"Now this info comes from Jim's report to me. At first, Jahin was gracious, polite. He had all the normal polish that prominent businessmen have. Then he got testy. He asked why they were questioning a good American like him. Jim didn't like the change in tone or attitude, so he said, 'May we look around?'"

"Smart move."

"Yeah, well, according to the report, Jahin got huffy. Said he'd been cleared by our immigration agents on the visa status of all his workers. He said, quite forcefully, 'I've complied. This is harassment.'"

"That's—," Brooks started.

Turner put up his hand.

"Let me finish. Jim must have gotten kind of tough, but when I questioned him, I could see that he persisted in a cool way. He said, and I'm quoting, 'Mr. Jahin, a woman's been kidnapped; other than murder, there's no crime more serious than kidnapping. We know from the ransom note the hostage crew is from a Middle Eastern country.' Here Jim maybe went beyond what the FBI knew. 'Our evidence indicates the team was from Egypt. Since you're from Egypt, we hope you might have heard something about this.'"

Brooks was relaxed and listening attentively.

"I get Jahin's position. I'd think that was intrusive if directed at me."

Turner again quoted from the report.

"At that moment, Jahin started to fidget. His eyes moved in that way the psychologists detect a person is lying or scared."

"My CIA experience tells me Jim's on to something," Brooks said.

Turner stared hard at Brooks.

"Agreed."

Turner looked at his notes.

"Here, Jim pushed harder and said, 'May I look around?' Apparently Jahin got real clear and said, 'Since you don't trust me, I don't trust you. If you want to look around, get a fucking search warrant.'"

Turner looked at Brooks with a big smile on his face.

"I can see Jim now, all five-ten of him, standing straight like the hard-core Marine vet he is. He looked at his watch and said, 'Judge Gerner will be in his office now. I'll be back in few minutes with a warrant.' He turned on his heel and left."

Brooks laughed.

"Turned on his heel, did he? I bet he saluted and marched off like an officer. I like his presence of mind. Good, fast thinking."

"Jim's real good on the right procedures, the right steps. However, if I'd been there, I would have parked outside Jahin's estate and watched for any cars or trucks making a fast exit. I'd have waited an hour or so. If a vehicle left the place, I'd have gotten the Santa Rosa police to chase them down."

"Your idea of surveillance is on the money," Brooks said. "Anyway, Jahin is hiding something."

Brooks was quiet for a moment. Then he rubbed his hands together as if ready to pounce on something.

"Are you going to bring Jahin in—squeeze him?"

"Yeah, we can, and I think we will. But don't get your hopes up. He'll get his lawyer and deny, deny, even if he knows something or is involved in some way."

"I've seen that happen too many times."

"But there's another freak occurrence."

Turner stood up, his face enthusiastic again.

"You remember my wife called her computer consultant, and he wasn't available—he was sick? We looked into his background. Jabari Radwan is on our list as a former Egyptian military officer, possibly in their intelligence service. I got his home phone number from the company and called him. His lady said he's not here—he's away seeing relatives, traveling. The stories don't match. First, he's not feeling well; now, he's out of town. I think we may have a lead on Ms. Pierce's location and a suspect."

"Sounds like sufficient grounds for you to act."

"Oh yeah! We got the search warrant for Jahin's estate, and I have a plan to smoke out Radwan."

"What did the search of the estate reveal?"

"Jim got the warrant that same morning and was back by afternoon. Unfortunately, that gave them time to move Sarah, if she was there. At any rate, the outbuildings where they might have held her were busy with workers. Their presence removed any chance of finding evidence of Sarah Pierce's possessions or fingerprints. I imagine Jahin, if he is in on this, moved his crew into the building to spoil our search and to obscure any clues. Jahin knows more than he's telling."

"Close, but no cigar. Shit! We both know he's not going to talk."

Turner stood up and moved away from his desk. He waved an arm across his chest as if to sweep away his frustration of the lack of hard evidence.

"I agree, but I'm personally going to pay him a visit. I want him to know he's being watched. Back to Radwan—I have a photo of him from his employee file. I'll post it with the police departments and all the transportation terminals in this region. If this Jabari Radwan finds out the police are looking for him, and he's innocent, he'll come in to clear his name, and we'll move on to other avenues of inquiry."

"No public announcements, right?"

"Yeah, we agreed to that. My hope is that they're traveling by car. They'll need gas, food, and a place to take a crap. If law enforcement gets the photo around, it might help."

"The question that bugs me, Bill, is why in hell did they kidnap Sarah?"

"They staked you out, Brooks. They really want you to do what the ransom note says. Sarah's the lever in this plot."

Brooks gritted his teeth.

"Since the group is Middle Eastern, there's a risk they'll move her there if we don't meet their terms real soon. We both know what happens to hostages in that part of the world."

Turner shook his head.

"Don't let the terms rush you, Brooks. You know the deal. If these jackasses want to move someone out of the country, we both know that takes a lot of money and organizational skill to cross borders. Just imagine the trouble they'll face trying to move an uncooperative hostage by the gate staffers and customs agents. I can't imagine these assholes are stupid enough to try that."

"I hear you. Let's get Radwan's and Sarah's pictures around, see what happens."

"That's my plan, along with talking to every Middle Easterner on our watch list."

Turner observed Brooks to judge if these steps seemed sufficient to him. Seeing no reaction, he spoke.

"When you get to Saudi Arabia, Brooks, let's stay in touch. Your contacts may have ideas on who is out to hurt you. That will help the search here."

As Brooks left Turner's office, a sinking feeling came over him. His gut feeling was that Sarah would be moved out of the country. He pushed the elevator button for the first floor. Just as the doors slid shut, he wondered if he should return to Turner's office and ask him to enlist assistance from Canadian and Mexican authorities. He decided to hold off on that request.

When the elevator reached the lobby, he walked outside to a cool breeze laced with fog. He shivered despite the June day.

The fresh air pushed a new thought to mind as he walked toward the parking garage. He wanted to think about the idea before he cleared it with Turner. He could initiate contact with the hostage crew by calling one of the cell phone numbers they had left him the prior evening. He'd say he was ready to negotiate the ransom payment on the condition that he could continue his work in the Middle East. He felt that if he could tie them up in a long a conversation over money or his work arrangements, the FBI's tracer on his cell phone might identify the location where Sarah was held. And he'd demand, again, to see an active video of her holding today's newspaper as proof of existence. He knew this went against U.S. policy and that he should clear it with the FBI but, for him, it was an idea worth pursuing.

CHAPTER 21

Deprivation

Seattle, Washington

T he helicopter dropped awkwardly to the ground, the wheels hitting unevenly and jostling Sarah in her seat. She thought they must be running from the police.

It's been at least a week, she thought. *What's taking Brooks, the police, so long?*

With a blindfold on, she had no idea where she was but sensed from the smell as the door opened that they had landed in a field. As soon as the chopper blades stopped whirring, she was guided down three steps to the ground. As her escorts, one on each arm, walked her across the field, she felt the squishy turf beneath her Nikes, the grass tickled her ankles, and she tried to count the seconds but lost track of time when the numbers reached the hundreds. She started counting again but gave up when she stumbled, whereupon the two men swore and yanked her upright. It seemed like several additional minutes until they entered a place that smelled like a horse barn. Her handlers left her inside a room that reeked of horseshit and hay. The door slammed shut with a clang and the telltale sound of a deadbolt.

"You can take off the blindfold now."

It was the chubby, soft-voiced man.

At least someone is offering a tiny amount of decency, Sarah thought.

She exhaled slowly and removed the scarf that covered her eyes. She pushed the breath out of her mouth to dampen the stench. She knew, as she glanced around the room, that she was inside a horse stall. It was a rectangular box for a big horse, or maybe two. The walls were tall and reached the ceiling. Although there were no windows, a wire mesh over the stall's wooden door let light in, which was at least an improvement from her first prison cell. She spotted a rolled-up sleeping bag in one corner but no bed. Bits of hay were scattered on the dusty floor. She saw a large, round metal pail and gagged when she realized that this was her toilet. There was no sink or hose for water, and no stool or chair to sit on, so she sank to the floor in a corner, placed her hands over her eyes and began to cry. The strength and emerging confidence that she had felt on the flight drained away.

As her first day gave way to darkness, a set of overhead lights snapped on and illuminated the barn. She got up and gazed out to the interior. A central corridor made of thick planking ran the length of the building to a vast set of doors at one end. She saw dozens of stalls, yet no horses. She shuddered at the thought that she was this big barn's only occupant. The chubby man brought her a meal of bread, olives, and water. He left a new pail for her toilet and removed, holding his nose, the existing and slightly used bucket of piss.

The evening wore on. When the massive array of overhead lights turned off, clearly on a timer, it was her first inkling that she could tell day from night in this location. She unrolled the sleeping bag and crawled into it for warmth. The bits of hay in the stall were insufficient for a mattress, and the floor was hard. It was difficult to find a comfortable position for sustained slumber.

In the late morning of the second day, her guards donned their ski masks and let her outside without her blindfold. Inwardly, she was pleased with this small degree of freedom. She walked toward a long, deep meadow. At the back end of it, a forest extended as far as her eyes could see. Beyond the woodlands, mountains rose to majestic peaks, crested with snow. The lanky man with the menacing voice leered and snarled at her.

"OK, lady, let's see you do your exercises. I want to see your boobs bounce up and down."

She again warned them she had TB and coughed to remind them the risk of contamination was still there. The tall one, his hands twitching at his sides, backed away as she began to stretch. Without her blindfold, she relished the sights, smells, and sounds around her. She smiled at the thought that her confinement was like that of a farm animal let out to pasture. In the distance, she surmised that the tallest peak must be Mount Rainier. She'd seen many photos of the Cascades and was certain that she was in the state of Washington. The primitive quarters and farmland puzzled her until she surmised that the location meant her captors were on the run and had little time to prepare more comfortable quarters. She began to think that their plan was not working. She worried that the change of scene boded ill. If the kidnappers panicked, they might kill her or dump her, miles from civilization. She picked up her pace, trying to dismiss her rising fear with physical exertion. She thought of escape, of sprinting to the trees in the distance.

Could I outrun them? she wondered. *Where would I go for help? But this was a wilderness area. No, I'm not ready, mentally, to attempt such a bold move.*

Mustafa and Hamid had anticipated her desire to escape. To block any attempt to flee, the beanpole with the dead eyes and twitchy hands walked five feet in front of her, and "Fatboy," as she now thought of him, guarded the rear. She turned her head and queried Fatboy, the only one of the men who'd shown any consideration for her well-being.

"Why have you captured me? I'm a nobody."

"Ma'am, I can't have this conversation. Don't try."

"What? Will you beat me like your leader does? He's an animal. You're not that kind of person. This I know."

"You don't know that, ma'am. How can you possibly know anything about us?"

"I'm trained to understand human drives and motivations. I can tell by the way you act and how you talk."

"That's pure bullshit."

"No, it's not. So why am I here?"

"Do you ever stop talking, asking questions?"

Sarah stifled a laugh. Brooks had made that same point again and again.

"No, I won't stop until I know why I'm here. If you tell me, I'll quit pestering you."

She halted and turned to look him in the eye.

"Tell me."

Mustafa felt the sweat gathering beneath the mask. He wanted to tear it off to cool down.

"Camel farts and dog shit! Lady, leave me alone, or I'll put you back in the stall and leave you there for days!"

"What harm is there in telling me? Maybe I could help you with Brooks Davidson if I knew why I'm here."

"Oh, fuck! All right! Will you please shut up if I tell you?"

"Yes."

"It's as our leader told you on the first day: You're important to this man who has harmed our country. We're using you to get him to change what he's doing to our land and to others' in the Middle East."

"I heard the man but thought it couldn't be true. It makes no sense. If you want Dr. Davidson to stop something, why didn't you just take *him*? He and I are just friends. It's no wonder he's not paying a ransom."

"It makes no sense for me to talk with you. You don't understand the Arab grievance nor the Arab mind."

"What I do know is that whoever designed this kidnapping and the reasons for it…," she began, pausing for effect and because she knew what she was about to say was insulting, but she was feeling bold, "…well, if brains were dynamite, that person doesn't have enough to blow his nose."

Fatboy called to the man in front of him. She thought his name sounded like Hamet or Hameed.

"Fuck it," Fatboy said. "Let's bring her back."

Sarah looked into the ski mask quizzically.

"What? We're stopping my exercise?"

"Yes, ma'am. Any more talking from you, and I'll call our leader. He likes to whack you around."

"Oh, yes, he's real brave. Bursting with courage, that man. He beats a woman who is bound and gagged. Like to see what he'd do around Dr. Davidson."

Mustafa grabbed Sarah by her shoulders, turned her body, and pushed her in the direction of the barn.

"Angry camels have better manners and act smarter than you. Back to your cage."

Sarah kicked at clumps of grass as they walked back to the barn. She knew she had made a mistake. She had talked too much and irritated the one kind man in the group. And she'd lost her opportunity to be outside. Her brief experience of walking in the pasture and seeing the trees and mountains gave her a sense of freedom and hope. With her head down, she marched quietly back to the barn and stood near the large wooden door as they shoved her through it and locked her in the stall.

"If you let me talk to your leader, I know I can help you," she called from inside the building. "I'm trained in dealing with conflict."

There was no response. She heard the muffled noise of their feet as they walked away. She turned toward the back of the stall, went over to far corner, stretched out her elbows, and pressed her body into the corner. She held this stretch position until her shoulders and upper back began to ache. She slid down against the wall.

How can I get them to talk with me? she wondered. *I could offer to ransom myself. I have money, even if Brooks won't pay up. Is that smart or even possible? How could I arrange it? Call my bank? I can see myself talking to my bank: "Hey, guess what? I'm kidnapped and need several hundred thousand dollars for my release. Will you forward it to a bank in Istanbul or wherever?" Oh, Christ! Am I losing it?*

She dropped her head in despair. After her short trip into humor, tears flowed. She lay down on the sleeping bag as a dark cloud shrouded the positive feeling she had experienced earlier. She remained supine on the sleeping bag, uncomfortable on the wooden floor, unable to wriggle into a position that would let her ease into sleep. It was early. She knew it would be hours before the men delivered the evening meal: some flat bread, a few pieces of chicken with hummus or rice.

The barn was washed in dim light. She didn't sense when evening arrived until the barn lights came on. Yet, no dinner or water was delivered. Her stomach growled. When the lights went out, she managed to nod off. In the morning, she got no breakfast. Through that day, the barn remained in semidarkness until the automatic lights came on in the evening. It was like that for two days. No one came in to empty her toilet pail, and the stench of her urine and feces offended every fiber of her being. Finally, the tall, thin man passed her a bottle of water through the wire mesh but nothing to eat.

"Where's the food? When will you take away the slops?"

The man walked away. He gave no answer. She guzzled the water. But then, not sure when the next bottle would be delivered, she slowed her drinking and only moistened her lips. For two more days, all she received was a bottle of water in the morning and one before the lights turned on. The slop pail continued to stink, but she stopped peeing because of the lack of water and food. She tried to maintain her exercise routine. That didn't work. She was starving and had no energy.

One day, she was so weak that she didn't hear when someone entered the stall, removed the slop bucket, and placed a clean pail in its place. Her physical and mental strength, which had rebounded from her first confinement, had dwindled. Most of the time, she lay on the sleeping bag, daydreaming and dozing fitfully. She thought about the helicopter flight. They had landed once in the middle of the trip to refuel, and Sarah had overheard Hamid.

"It's a good thing we don't have to worry about gate agents," he had said.

When the helicopter touched down near the barn, she was still blindfolded when a door opened. She felt the fresh air, leaned toward it, and yelled in the direction of the outside noise.

"Help!"

She wasn't sure her voice was noticed, but the lead man heard her and had hit her hard in the head again. She still had a lump on her skull where he'd banged her head into the metal wall next to her seat. He put tape on her mouth, and she remained gagged during the next leg of the journey. After refueling, she estimated that they flew for another hour. This helped her guess her their current location. She felt certain that they had reached the state of Washington, which was verified when she saw the snowcap on a mountain that had to be Mount Rainier.

But now, in this horse stall, the incident only led to her despair. The sense of being alone, the isolation of captivity, was driving her into a black cloud of fear—fear that she would not be found. She slipped into the sleeping bag, acknowledging that she was virtually hated by the men who had taken her. They had cut off her food and were keeping her alive with two bottles of water a day. Judging from the evening lights going on and off, Sarah calculated that it was the fourth day of being served only water with an occasional piece of bread. She tried to think of her total time in detention, but her mind was fuzzy. She couldn't seem to think through a single topic clearly. Finally, she concluded that she'd been detained in the Washington barn about a week.

Disguised in his ski mask, the chubby man arrived the next morning with a large shopping bag. It was plain beige with no lettering or markings on it. That surprised her.

"What's happening?" she asked.

He did not reply as he reached inside the bag, took out a cardboard package, and placed it on the floor. The top of the package was labeled Holsten's. He opened the top, revealing four food compartments. There were fried eggs, flat bread, hot cereal, and fruit juice. He watched Sarah scramble toward the steaming food, then tossed a smaller bag containing fresh underwear, a pair of pants, and a sweatshirt onto her sleeping bag.

"You stink," he said. "Put on these clean clothes and be ready to get out of here in fifteen minutes."

"We're leaving?"

She sniffed around her shoulders and arms.

It's not my normal odor but not too bad after several days without a shower or bath, she thought.

"Do you have a pail of water so I can clean up?"

"You heard me. We're leaving. Put on the clothes now."

He left her staring at the plate of food. She knew to be slow and careful in consuming the meal. She thought her stomach must have shrunk, so she consumed only the whites of the eggs and nibbled on the bread. She sat quietly, enjoying the sensation of the food rejuvenating her system. She changed her clothes and gathered her jacket with her penicillin pills in the pocket.

"I'm ready!" she yelled.

CHAPTER 22

Chopper Pilot

Palo Alto, California

B rooks panted heavily as he pushed up Old La Honda Road. He planned to cycle twenty-two miles over the La Honda Crest to Pescadores Beach, then back to Palo Alto. He wanted an exhausting ride to take a break from his anguish over Sarah's abduction. He lifted his body out of the saddle, inhaling the scent of redwoods that crowded both sides of the narrow road. The uphill pitch increased at each turn until he reached the crest at Skyline Boulevard. Sweat poured down his forehead when he felt the cell phone vibrate in the rear pocket of his jersey. He reached back and lifted the phone to his eyes. He saw *"Turner"* on the screen and pulled his bike to the side of the road.

"Bill! You caught me enjoying myself. What's up?"

"You're panting. Where the hell are you?"

Brooks laughed between gulps of air.

"I'm cycling on a tough uphill."

"I envy you, I think."

Turner paused a beat, then got to the point.

"Look—I'll be brief. Here's the scoop: This morning, a call came in from the sheriff in Humboldt County, near the Oregon border. A cousin of his drives a truck for a fuel company. He was servicing a helicopter in a private airport near Eureka when he thought he heard a call for help from the helicopter. The noise from the refueling garbled the sound, so he wasn't sure and didn't mention it to anyone. A couple of days later, at a family barbecue, he was talking to his cousin and mentioned it. The sheriff's department up there was on our alert list, and the officer thought we should know about this."

"Jesus! Do you think…?"

"I didn't think much about it at first until the sheriff reminded me that this airstrip has a reputation for being open to aircraft moving drugs and illegals."

Turner's voice rose.

"Get this—the trucker thought it was a woman's voice."

"Man, I'm listening," Brooks said. "Go on."

"We're still a long way from anything conclusive, but it does provide another link to my theory. The hostage takers may have moved Sarah north, and we may have spooked them into moving her to Canada."

"But Eureka? What happened after the guy heard the cry for help?"

"Nothing," Turner said. "He thought he heard that call, then listened some more. When he didn't hear a repeat, he let it go until he mentioned it to the sheriff."

"I'm curious: What's the sheriff's motivation here? Why did he call you? Isn't he likely to conclude this is a local issue?"

"We've been in touch with the sheriff before about this airstrip. We've asked him to keep tabs on the place because of drug shipments. We weren't getting much action until he called."

"This is a break if we can follow it up," Brooks said.

"That's why I called. The follow-up looks promising. First, a little background: Small planes and helicopters are able go in and out of this airstrip under the radar, so to speak. They can move illegal goods or undocumented workers unseen. Up there, nobody seems to ask questions as long as they pay in cash."

"I've seen private airstrips used in a similar way throughout the Middle East."

Turner chuckled.

"They're everywhere. I had an agent fly to the strip as soon as I got the news. He interviewed the employees there. They told him a chopper came in, got fuel, and left. No one recognized or knew the pilot. They paid cash, so no record there. But here's the good news: My agent took a sketch artist with him, and they talked to the truck driver. From him, we got a good facial description of the pilot. With this picture, we'll locate that pilot and squeeze the shit out of him."

"Can we find him in your database?" Brooks asked.

"Maybe. He'll also have a pilot's license and a driver's license. We'll send our picture to the FAA and State. Then we'll make the match. We *will* find him. Plus, we'll figure out who owns that chopper and start squeezing. We'll know in a day or two if this pilot and owner of the aircraft had anything to do with the movement of Sarah."

"I don't want to get too excited, but I am. Do you need me to come in?"

"I have several lines of inquiry I'd like to pursue with your contacts in Saudi Arabia," Turner said. "Yeah, it would be good if you came in."

"What if this chopper is en route, under the radar, to Canada? What can we do then?"

"I've put out an alert with a photo of Jabari Radwan to all air terminals and ports of entry in the state of Washington and to points in western Canada. I like the response. Everyone's on alert, including the Mounties. I worked with them recently on another case; they're damned good."

"Bill, you and your people have been unbelievable. I'll keep my fingers crossed. Call me when you want me to come in."

★ ★ ★

Two days later, Brooks was in his cramped Stanford office. He sat at his desk, reviewing data on cotton prices for his next book. He was delighted that the students had departed for the summer because that gave him more time to work on Sarah's case. If possible—if he could get his head clear of worries about her—he'd find additional time to work on the book. He pushed the graph of cotton prices aside, slid his chair away from the desk, hit the "save" command, and put his computer to sleep. The phone rang, and he pressed it to his ear. It was Bill Turner, bursting with energy.

"Brooks! Brooks! The net is closing on Sarah Pierce's abduction. I'm convinced this is an international case. I want to go over my questions for your friends in the Saudi Mukhabarat."

"Bill, don't leave me in suspense! What have you learned?"

"Pardon my excitement, but hear this: We found the pilot. He's a shady character and has ferried bad goods from drugs to people in low-flying aircraft. He's an expert with a chopper. When we lined up what we had against him, he started to sing for a deal. He told us who owned the aircraft and said he picked up four men with a blindfolded blond woman in Santa Rosa. He flew them to a ranch outside of Seattle. He stopped in Eureka to refuel, so the truck driver's mention to the sheriff was a mighty big break. When I showed him your photo of Sarah, he said, 'As they boarded the chopper, I had a quick glance at the five of them. That could be the woman.'"

Brooks practically yelled into the phone.

"Oh my God! Oh my God! Did he have the address of the location in Seattle?"

"He said it was quite remote, a ranch in horse country, but he had the longitude and latitude coordinates."

"That's fanta—!"

"Let me continue, Brooks—I'm on a roll. My guy Jim, with agents from our Seattle office, was there within the day. The ranch was empty, but the beds had been used. The sheets smelled. We checked an enormous barn, and there was a distinct smell of human shit in one of the stalls. Somebody was stashed there. We're pretty sure of that. We also found footprints in the dirt showing movement in and out of the barn. And get this: There was an imprint of helicopter wheels in the back meadow. Right now, we're looking for the owners of the property."

Brooks leaned back in his chair and let out a long sigh. This was the best news he'd heard in nearly a month. But still no Sarah. They were getting close—just not close enough.

Where would the kidnappers go next? Brooks wondered. *Where could they go?*

He put his left hand to his temple and figured there was an organizer who had contacts with wealthy individuals behind this caper. This someone knew people who owned helicopters and remote ranches and wineries, knew the right places to hide Sarah. There was a network of people involved. Someone with training and experience was running this. What was next?

"Bill, this is a sophisticated operation. Fast movements to

remote places. That's unusual. When I think of the ransom note, the reason for Sarah's abduction has to come from within one of those four countries. This is not some ragtag bunch. The source of their anger toward me absolutely stems from fanatics who know my work and hate it. This smells of radicals who are in government or have recently been pushed out. Somebody—some band of extremists—is totally pissed at me. The faster I can get to the Middle East and talk to my friends, the quicker we'll get to the bottom of this."

"When can you be at my office?"

"Does tomorrow morning at nine work for you?"

"See you then."

Brooks looked at the note on his desk. It was the kidnappers' cell phone number from the prior evening. He ran his finger across the ten digits, picked up the phone, and tapped the digits. It rang several times until a computerized voice said, "*Leave a message and time to reach you.*"

Brooks instead told the kidnappers what they had to do.

"Be smart. Get out while you can. Put Sarah Pierce in a taxi and send her to the nearest FBI office."

CHAPTER 23

Crossing to Canada

Cairo, Egypt

O mar Sayed had three primary contacts in the United States and Canada. As chairman of Egypt's Sovereign Investment Fund, he directed and approved the investment of Egyptian funds abroad. He had a strong preference for safe economies such as the U.S., Canada, England, and Germany. He placed funds with portfolio managers and business owners who had demonstrated above-market returns on capital. His three contacts in North America had performed exceptionally well and, importantly for him, they had family members connected with the Muslim Brotherhood. Although he didn't agree with Fathi Ashur, who claimed that he had these managers by the balls, Omar knew they owed him loyalty and appreciation. He had invested large amounts of capital in their enterprises. In addition, each of them had a high level of dislike for the past regime of Anwar Sadat and the current leadership of Hosni Mubarak.

Omar tapped the first of these contacts, Taha Jahin, for the initial hiding of Sarah Pierce in Santa Rosa. Omar expected that she would be ransomed and released within a week. When Davidson balked, Omar tapped his second contact, Youssef Al-Hariri, and moved the hostage to Al-Hariri's rarely used ranch outside Seattle. The need to move the woman angered him, and he spoke harshly to Jabari about being more demanding when dealing with Davidson. But he had prepared for this contingency and had required that Jahin and Al-Hariri have a plan to move her.

In the meantime, Omar's wife, Hasina, had noticed a change in his behavior. After several days of gentle inquiry, she pulled him aside before he left for work and queried him.

"Omar, are you healthy? Are you worried at the office? Is something wrong?"

"No, no. Nothing to be concerned about," he responded cautiously, studying her face to assess her degree of concern. She tugged at his arm.

"My dear one, in recent days you have been distracted, sometimes sullen. At other times, you have barked at the children for being noisy. That's not like you at all."

He placed a hand on her shoulder.

"Thank you. I'll be more thoughtful with the children."

That afternoon, he left his office early and sought out jewelers in the shops near his apartment building. He was looking for a stylish ring with semiprecious stones such as carnelian, jasper, or lapis lazuli. He liked the work of designer Seth Haddad, whose rings he'd seen in a newspaper article. He wanted to surprise Hasina and thank her for her concerns. His eyes were glued to an opal ring when he felt the vibration of his cell phone. He lifted it out of his coat pocket. Jabari Radwan was texting him from America. He mouthed a silent string of Arab curses and studied the message: *Must move hostage again urgent. Local man has helicopter ready. What destination?*

Omar glanced at the sales clerk standing nervously nearby, smiled at him, and pointed to the ring in the glass cabinet.

"I like this one and will return."

He turned quickly on his heel and left the store. On the sidewalk, he resumed his obscenities as he stopped and prepared two messages. To Jabari, he sent the address of a ranch outside of Vancouver, Canada. The ranch was about a hundred air miles from Seattle. He gave him the cell number of the owner, Hossan Beltagy. From a notepad in his pocket, he produced the geographic coordinates of the ranch for the pilot. To Beltagy, he tapped the message: *Hossan, my friend and colleague, as I mentioned in the past, I may need, at times, to depend on your friendship and skills. Please call me as soon as possible.*

Over the past four years, Omar had provided Hossan with hundreds of millions of Egyptian pounds from the Sovereign Investment Fund. Like Taha Jahin, who was successful in the United States in the rug and wine business, Youssef Al-Hariri made a fortune in seafood processing in Seattle. Beltagy was even wealthier than the other two. He had invested in building condominium complexes in Vancouver. He had recently purchased three Gulfstream jets, which he used to ferry his co-investors from Egypt, China, Japan, and Saudi Arabia to Vancouver to view his investment opportunities. While Jahin and Al-Hariri had access to helicopters to move their products, employees, and customers, Beltagy had a small fleet of aircraft. Pleased with his selection of investments abroad, Omar was confident he had power over the recipients of those funds to do his bidding. The three owed their success in no small part to him because of the capital he provided on very favorable terms.

Hossan was being driven to his office in the firm's black Mercedes 450S. He had the window between the driver and the rear seat elevated for privacy. On his route to work, Hossan liked to do business on the telephone. When he received Omar's text message, he punched in the code, and the phone rang immediately. Omar was walking back to the jewelry shop to purchase the ring for Hasina when the phone vibrated. He glanced at the screen.

"Hossan! Such a fast response! Where are you? How are you, my friend?"

Hossan glanced out the window as his car zoomed past a row of buildings. He was pleased by a handsome apartment complex and held the view while he spoke.

"I'm admiring one of our best investments on my way to the office."

"I must come to see the investments you've made. The cash flows from sales and rentals have been most impressive."

"We've done well together. And to what do I owe the pleasure of your call?"

"We have an enemy of Egypt in our hands and want to force his withdrawal from the country," Omar said. "Specifically, we must get this man away from Mubarak. To do that, we've taken a hostage to put pressure on him. That was fast. Are you with me?"

"Go ahead."

"I'd like you to hide the hostage for a few days at a remote location like your ranch outside the city. The one near that ski area—Whistler."

Hossan continued to view the passing scene along the busy street. He was troubled as he sought to maintain a calm tone in his voice.

"As you know, I'm sympathetic to actions that limit the rule of our corrupt leader. And I'll do just about anything to return to Egypt safely and without fear of prison. But I don't want to risk prison here. I'm wondering if this is safe from the Canadian authorities."

"I expect to have the arrangements concluded with this devious American in a few days," Omar said. "If he becomes more troublesome, which I do not expect, I might need you to move the hostage to Egypt on one of your jets."

Hossan moved the phone away from his mouth and let his breath out slowly.

Holy shit! he thought. *An American? Not smart.*

His mind raced to the thought that taking money from the Sovereign Fund might have been a mistake. He tightened his grip on the phone. A string of curse words flew through his mind.

They believe they own me, he thought. *And in a way, they do.*

"As I mentioned, Omar, I need to be careful in this country. I don't want the attention of the Mounties or any of their financial regulators. I have an upscale reputation here."

"I realize that. I can continue to help you sustain that reputation in Canada and help you get re-established in Egypt."

Hossan put the phone away from his mouth so Omar could not hear his labored breathing. He was trying to get it under control. Sweat creased his brow.

He's got me by the balls, Hossan thought.

"Look, Omar, I'm not trying to be difficult, but I must be smart. I want to help you in your war with Mubarak. I'm here because that son of a bitch doesn't want me in the country. I must not draw attention to myself."

"Don't worry. The hostage will be in and out in a few days. As I said, I may need to bring her to Egypt to really put the squeeze on this bastard Davidson."

"OK. I understand. Yes, I do have the ranch near Whistler. You've been there. You know what it's like—quiet, totally remote. That location could work for several days. I have a plane scheduled to return an investor to Qatar next week. I'm not sure of the actual date—my calendar is not at my fingertips. Your hostage could fly on that plane with the investor, but she'd have to fly as an invalid. She'd have to be totally drugged for the whole trip to avoid hard questions by my guest as well as by the customs people in Canada and in Iceland where we refuel. And you'll have to manage the agents in Egypt—"

"Do you have a physician who could administer that type of drug?" Omar interrupted. "We're talking twenty-plus hours of flight time."

"Yes, yes, you can trust me on that."

"I'm rethinking, Hossan. What if you dispatched another plane, and I'll pay for it? On this flight, my lead man—his name is Jabari Radwan—could be dressed like a successful businessman returning to Egypt after reviewing a deal with you. He'd have to have a prospectus of one of your investment opportunities, but it could be the same deal the Qatar investor has reviewed."

The line went quiet for a moment, then Hossan spoke.

"Let me look at the schedules of my long-flying aircraft and see if I have plane and a crew for this. It's possible. Can you wait a day for the response?"

"Yes, and let me reiterate: I may not need to fly the hostage to Egypt. We can come to terms before then. But I want to be ready to move her as needed."

Hossan wiped his brow.

Oh my God, dear Allah, this is a woman—and an American woman at that, he thought. *What has Omar done?*

"I can get back to you in a day. Same time tomorrow?"

"Of course," Omar said. "In the meantime, is it safe to deposit the hostage at the ranch near Whistler?"

"I'll have it ready for your people later today."

CHAPTER 24

Ashur's Ultimatum

Cairo, Egypt

President Mubarak waved Galal Murad and Fathi Ashur into his office. Instead of directing them to the comfortable chairs in the corner of the vast room, he stood in front of them, his hands clasped behind his back, his chin thrust forward.

"It's been more than a month with no results, General. Where the fuck is the American woman?"

"Your Excellency, if I may," Ashur answered with a nod toward General Murad. "I've conducted the search and given it my full attention. May I respond?"

The president waved a hand at Ashur indicating agreement, then turned toward Murad. "Galal, I want you to remain after Ashur speaks."

Mubarak swiveled his head toward Ashur and practically snarled.

"What do you know, and what's being done? The American ambassador is insistent that Egyptians are involved and is raising hell with me, threatening sanctions if we don't find the hostage."

"Your Excellency, we've identified a new faction, a rogue operation with few recruits. They're called al-Hura. They are focused on getting Western bankers out of the Middle East. Their first target—and not their only one—is this Dr. Brooks Davidson, who has been one of your advisors."

"So many questions, Ashur. First, are there Egyptians in this group?"

"Yes, unfortunately, they've recruited dissidents from several countries who are living in Western countries like France, England, and the U.S.—countries with banks active in Egypt, Saudi Arabia, Jordan, and other countries. We've found evidence that they've tried to recruit Egyptians."

Mubarak looked puzzled.

"Exiled Egyptians are associating with the scum in Al-Qaeda or the Muslim Brotherhood?"

"Exactly."

"Who has the woman, and where is she? Ambassador Ticonne pesters me every day with this question."

"That's the challenge," Ashur said. "It's been a month since we began our search. We do not know the leader's name, nor do we have the names of any members of his operation. We've interviewed several Egyptian individuals who admire the goals of al-Hura, but no one knows about this kidnapping."

"Really? And you've used your usual interrogation methods to elicit the truth?"

"Yes, and no concrete results."

"Where are the scum you interrogated?"

"In Tora Prison," Ashur said. "Some are new radicals. Some we've known for years. But all claim no knowledge of the abduction."

"Have you questioned any in the Brotherhood leadership?" Mubarak asked. "They've been quiet lately."

"We have, Excellency. They've been cooperative and offered some names while insisting it's not them. They made the point rather strongly that this is not the right way to get rid of the capitalists."

"And these names turned up what?"

"If I may use their rather crude language, Excellency, they said this was 'the dumbest fucking caper they ever heard of.' If they wanted Davidson gone, they should have taken him or killed him outright. Send a real clear message to the capitalist leeches in the banking world."

The president shifted his attention to Murad.

"General, what do you say to this?"

"Your Excellency, Deputy Minister Ashur is our best and will get to the bottom of the plot if there are Egyptians culpable. Personally, I believe that some rogue elements in our country may be part of this since the message was to get Davidson out of our country. You do have enemies, sir, and we know who they are. One of them will crack. Ashur knows how to crack them."

Mubarak let out a long sigh.

"This won't just go away."

He unleashed a burst of curses.

"Minister Ashur, keep the pressure on until you've found the woman and the bastards who kidnapped her—or until you're able to conclude no Egyptians were involved. You may go. Galal—stay with me."

Ashur exited through the imposing mahogany doors. An aide closed them as he left. He did not hear a word exchanged between Mubarak and Murad, but he could guess the first question, and it would be about him.

President Mubarak walked with the general to the chairs near his desk. He sat in a chair beside the general, a sign of the familiarity and trust that had developed between them over dozens of years.

"Galal, I know Ashur has been your top deputy for some time, but do you totally trust him? We know members of his family have been associated with the Muslim Brotherhood."

"That was long ago, Hosni, and that notorious uncle now builds boats. He's out of the Brotherhood business. As for Ashur, remember: He was the one that discovered the Russians were planning to blackmail you. Their scheme was to say you took bribes and had millions in foreign bank accounts. They wanted to force you to purchase Soviet weaponry. Ashur was the one that exposed the plot and got the entire crew deported. He's loyal."

"Yes, I remember and never forget a friend. But times change, Galal, and friends do have a tendency to come and go. We must keep our eyes open. The Muslim Brotherhood has been quiet for a while. We must be vigilant."

Mubarak rose. The conversation was over. He patted Murad on the back and gave him his unofficial orders.

"Keep an eye on Ashur's work. Let's talk of this every day. Right now, I'll telephone Ambassador Ticonne and tell him about al-Hura."

The general returned to his office and immediately picked up his telephone. He rarely called anyone directly, typically leaving that task to his secretary, who arranged all calls. He called Ashur and spoke quickly.

"Ashur, that was an unsettling meeting with the president. Come to my office at two o'clock today. I have concerns that there may be dissidents within our government who know about the abduction of the American woman."

"Did the president offer more information after I left?"

"No, but my instincts tell me this operation was designed to embarrass him. This is not about the Saudis or Jordanians. I'm worried that the attempt to discredit the president and the

American Davidson was undertaken by the Muslim Brotherhood. These Brotherhood sympathizers are in one of our departments. I want your thoughts on that."

Ashur placed the phone on the cradle.

"Double loads of camel shit!" he said to the empty room.

What had the American ambassador actually said to Mubarak or to the general? he wondered. *What have Sayed's hostage takers said to the American Davidson? Has Davidson called Ambassador Ticonne and been active with his contacts in the State Department, FBI, and CIA?*

He lifted the phone again and called Omar Sayed. He reached Sayed's assistant.

"Please tell the minister that I called, and we're to meet at our normal place tomorrow at noon," he told her. "Thank you."

★ ★ ★

Early summer heat was beginning to rise in Cairo; the next day was in the mid-eighties. Hot weather tended to make Fathi's left leg ache. He sat on a bench near the Nile and waited for his cousin. He pulled out a pack of Cleopatras, loosened his tie, pulled out a cigarette, and lit it. He puffed slowly, watching the smoke waft toward the river. He leaned back, organizing his thoughts for Omar, enjoying the quiet moment. He spotted his cousin walking down the path and waved.

"Omar, over here."

They stood and kissed each other on the cheek. Fathi spoke first.

"Let's sit here. My leg is killing me today."

Omar glanced around.

"You're not afraid that our conversation will be overheard?" he asked, smiling mischievously as he thought of his cousin's obsession with secrecy. "Or are you concerned with the gossip that occurs when two ministers are seen together in private conversation?"

Fathi ignored Omar's gibe. He waved a hand toward a bench.

"Time is precious," Fathi said. "Sit. We've been meeting here occasionally for a few years. Have we seen members of the government along this stretch of the river?"

"No, but that doesn't mean a government colleague won't wander by. And cousin, you must know my blood pressure rises every time you call. What is it this time?"

Omar's tone altered when he felt the serious intent of his cousin's reply. There was no playfulness in Fathi today—if there ever had been.

"You get right to the point, Omar, much like the Americans you despise."

Fathi dropped his cigarette and ground the butt into the dirt path with the heel of his shoe.

"I just came from a meeting with General Murad and the president. They want me to accelerate my search for the American woman. The pressure from the Americans is intense. I gather they're pushing the other countries too, but I don't know that for certain."

"That doesn't mean—"

Fathi held up his hand.

"Let me finish. This is getting too hot for me. I can't delay, fake, or fail in finding out if Egyptians are involved."

He paused, staring hard into the eyes of his cousin.

"Omar, by one week from today, if the woman has not been released—"

"What?!" exclaimed Omar, who was starting to rise from his seat.

Fathi placed a strong hand on Sayed's leg.

"Sit down, cousin, and I'll finish. If the arrangements you've orchestrated have been or have not been met—it doesn't matter— the woman must be released and your crew dispersed, disappeared."

He waved an arm as if sweeping the kidnappers into the Nile. Sayed pushed Fathi's hand off his leg and stood. His face was flush as he looked down at Fathi.

"This can't be rushed, Fathi. We're making progress with Davidson. He's considering the money, the conditions."

"It's been over three weeks, Omar. You're dreaming. The American ambassador intimated to President Mubarak and the foreign secretary that the FBI is on the trail of the kidnappers. This is unraveling. Close it down."

Sayed remained standing, his face getting redder. He pointed a finger at Fathi.

"You're losing heart, cousin. What about the Brotherhood's economic goals of ridding the country of foreign capitalists? What about—"

"I approve of the goals," Fathi interrupted, "but this action is not proving to be effective. You could be easily implicated if the Americans find the woman and your hostage takers. Everyone will talk. This is prison if you're lucky and, more likely, it's death."

"Allah, help him."

Omar raised his hands to the sky.

"I have a place to stash the hostage. They'll never find her, trust me. I know how to keep this away from me and you."

He pointed a finger at Fathi's chest. "You have nothing to be concerned about."

Fathi rubbed his sore leg and moved restlessly on the bench as if he could not find a comfortable position.

"I've run actions like this for years. They've never reached the top-level government awareness that this has. I see the risks clearly. I'm convinced you don't. I repeat. It's time to close it down."

He stood up.

"What? That's it?" Omar nearly yelled. "You're preparing to leave?"

As he rose and began to walk away from the bench, Fathi's features were dark and drawn. The white scar on his cheek was bright against the dark skin of his face. He faced Omar.

"You've heard my best thinking, cousin. If you persist, I cannot help you."

Omar rose beside him, his mouth wide in anger.

"Think more about that conclusion, cousin. It's not your best or most creative thinking."

They parted without a kiss on the cheek or a handshake. Omar waved goodbye. It was a useless gesture. Fathi never saw it. Omar sank back onto the bench, reached into his pocket, and pulled out two phones. He selected the recently purchased phone, the disposable one, and quickly punched in a text message to Jabari Radwan and Hossan Beltagy: *Bring the woman to Egypt within the week or sooner if there is pressure from Canadian authorities. Directions for landing location and the address of a safe house will follow.*

CHAPTER 25

Cell Number 3

Vancouver, British Columbia

Hossan stared at Omar's text message. His intuition told him that Omar was in trouble and that he should have contingency plans. In his mind, it was quite likely that he would have to fly the hostage out of Canada. Via private phone calls, he told his flight manager to hold one of the Gulfstreams in reserve and be ready to fly on short notice. His message to the Whistler ranch manager was to have the property ready for four employees and a fifth guest, who was to have a private room secured by locks. Hossan's plan was to have one of his helicopters fly to the Seattle ranch and pick up the hostage.

"Minister Sayed, my pilots fly to remote locales every day," Hossan said in his return call to Omar. "Seattle is only a hundred fifty miles away. We'll be in and out of this ranch quickly. It will look like another business trip to the air traffic people."

Omar spoke slowly.

"I want her moved without a trace? Isn't a car safer?"

"No. You have the border people to deal with. That's not a problem with my planes and crews. We fly right over the border and under their radar."

When the helicopter touched down on the pasture at the Seattle ranch, Sarah was marched toward the spinning blades. With her eyes blindfolded and her hands bound, she felt awkward and stumbled on the grass. Her captors barked at her in their accented English. One of them—she knew it had to be the tough one—pushed her hard up the steps and then into the cabin before shoving her into a seat. He fastened the seat belt tight across her waist.

"Sit tight!" he commanded. "Don't say a word. We'll be at our destination in under an hour."

"Why are we leaving?" Sarah queried. "Are we being chased? Are the police or FBI after you?"

She immediately ducked her head, aware that her taunting question might provoke a swat to the head. Jabari looked at her, shook his head, then sat across from Sarah.

"Don't try my patience, lady, or I'll put the gag back on."

The pilot shouted a few commands to the passengers. Sarah heard a different accent. She listened to him speak and concluded that the man was Canadian. She turned her head to speak, hoping it was in the direction of the leader.

"Are we flying to Canada?"

The thought of their frequent movements triggered her fears. *Oh, God!* she thought. *I'll never be found.*

She started a slow, sniffling cry at first. Then the tears rolled down her cheeks, and deeper sobs stopped her from asking her next question. Jabari frowned.

"Lady, you are one annoying bitch! When we get to our destination, I want you to send another message to Davidson."

She lifted her bound hands and pushed the blindfold against her eyes to dry her tears.

Davidson! Brooks Davidson! she thought. *He brought this horror upon me. What did I miss in his background?*

She recalled what her friend Jan had said about him and his reputation at Stanford. It was all secondhand, but Jan was usually reliable. She claimed that friends in Palo Alto said Brooks was commercially, rather than academically, oriented, and had little time for fellow faculty and students. Also, he had women at every stop on his travels. Sarah had dismissed these observations as uninformed stories. She had learned that Brooks had published six books. He had earned this position at Stanford. And how could he have women in every stop when he'd spent every weekend over the past few months with her? Yet this strange, horrible ordeal had come to her because of him. She turned her anger at Brooks toward the leader.

"I've asked this before, Mr. Bully who hits women: What has Brooks Davidson done that made you decide to kidnap me?"

Jabari bit his lip, then lifted his hands. He looked over at Sarah. The slender, blond bitch would not stop talking.

"Lady, I'll give it to you fast. After that, you shut up, or I'll whack you again. This Davidson, this very rich man who seduces the president of my country, is turning Egypt into a capitalist trophy in the Islamic world. That's what he's guilty of. We want him to pay for the curse he's placed on Egypt."

Sarah sat up straight and faced the voice.

"You know, Bully Man, you and whoever planned this are crazy. One man can't change the direction of a country. Our president can't do that. Why do you think Davidson can? I don't know where you get your information, but it's all wrong."

"Lady, I can throw you out of this chopper, and all my troubles would be over."

"Are you that stupid? Open the door, and you and your henchmen would fly out with me. Besides, if you left me alone or let me go, your troubles would disappear."

"I have other ways to deal with you."

"Touch me, and you'll get TB. You've seen the sores on my arms and wrists and heard the coughs. You didn't do your homework about my health, did you?"

"Shit, lady. One more word from you, and the gag goes back on."

Mustafa rose from his seat and walked up to Jabari. He leaned over and whispered in his ear.

"Don't let her get to you. Let's focus on Minister Sayed and get this done so we can release her. I know how to keep her quiet, and that's by not feeding her. We'll starve her for a few days in Vancouver. That will shut her up."

Jabari glanced up at Mustafa.

"I'd rather torture her, wouldn't you? Give her something to fear."

"Remember what Minister Sayed said: no physical abuse. It will wreck his plan, and we'll get no money."

Mustafa returned to his seat. Jabari leaned back and closed his eyes. He started to relax when the pilot told everyone to fasten their seat belts as the chopper descended.

They landed in a broad meadow. The door slid open. Sarah thought she heard the pounding gallop of horses. Jabari's crew pulled ski masks over their faces and let Sarah remove her blindfold. She spotted the horses and marveled at their beauty when they raced away from the roar of the helicopter. When she set foot on the grass, she heard the voices of the ground crew and knew she was in Canada, but she had no idea where. The air was cooler. She pulled her jacket closer to her chest as best she could with bound hands. She coughed.

Is the air thinner here? she wondered.

She touched her jacket pocket and relaxed as her fingers felt the penicillin bottle. They trudged across the meadow toward a large barn, its siding weather-beaten to a light gray color. The double-entry doors were vast: more than ten feet high and equally wide.

You could drive a large truck in here, she mused.

Her heart sank as she realized this barn was to be her next prison cell. The leader took her by the elbow and led her to the back of the building, past dozens of horse stalls, until they came to a door painted red. The man opened it with a key and led Sarah through it.

Sarah surveyed her new quarters. It was a single room without windows but had furniture, unlike her first two cells. Her eyes lit up at the sight of a bed topped with a thick blue-and-white patchwork quilt against the back wall. Nestled into one of the side walls was a desk with two spindle-back chairs. One was tucked under the desk; the other was beside it. On the desk were a ballpoint pen and a pad of paper. Her eyes brightened at the prospect that she would be able to record her experiences, and she hoped her captors would not see the paper and remove it. A dusty-brown, oval raglan rug covered the plank floor.

This is a real room, not a horse stall, Sarah thought.

She pinched herself. It actually had a degree of rustic charm. It crossed her mind that the room was probably designed for a jockey or stable master. The leader opened a door on the third wall and pointed to a sink, a toilet, and a shower stall. Sarah's shoulders dropped in relief; she realized that she could wash, shower, and clean herself. The leader motioned for her to extend her hands, and he cut the tape that bound her wrists.

"There's water for you in the sink," he said.

"Can you bring me any books or magazines to read? Something, please."

Jabari shook his head and moved toward the door. Sarah's next question stopped him.

"Can I go for a walk in the meadow and see the horses?"

Jabari motioned the other men out of the room. As he reached the door, he turned back to Sarah.

"I'll let someone else decide."

There was a plastic cup at the sink. Sarah filled it at the faucet, crossed to the bed, sat on the edge, and sipped the water slowly. It tasted delicious. She placed the empty cup on the rug, kicked up her legs, and lay down on the thick quilt. She drew her mind to the fact that she'd been moved three times.

Maybe the kidnappers were being chased, but by whom? she wondered. *If I were in Canada, how would American police find me?*

The confusion and uncertainty of this thought began to overwhelm her. She felt the black cloud of anxiety coming again. To fight off tears and despair, she turned her thoughts to Brooks and let the anger flow into her mind.

How could he have put me in this situation? He claimed to love me. Really? And what was this talk from the leader of a "very rich American?" Was Brooks really rich? Why wouldn't he mention it? That's unlike a man. They brag about their wealth or show it off. They all do, but he didn't. So he must not have it. On the other hand, we did travel first class to New York and stay at the Four Seasons. We always dined at the best restaurants in San Francisco and New York. Fergy said he was a member at the Bullion Club, a place for movers and shakers—everybody was rich in that club. Still, how could he, one man, be so important to a country that they wanted him removed? Damn! If he's so bad, how come they didn't just kill him?

She rolled over to her side and faced the door.

I can't wait to see him and read him the riot act! she thought. *The bastard was at minimum a liar as well as irresponsible for getting me, his friend—a loved one—into a horrendous situation. I vow that I will live! I will survive this some way and bring some of this hell right back to him!*

CHAPTER 26

Power Plays

Palo Alto, California

It had been four weeks to the day that Sarah had been kidnapped. Brooks tossed and turned in bed, his sleep restless, uneven. No one in the FBI, CIA, or local police had an idea of her whereabouts. Normally, Brooks thought of himself as the calm one in a storm, but he didn't feel calm today. He rose from bed, plagued with nightmares of Sarah being tortured, dumped in a remote forest without food or water, screaming for help. He walked into the bathroom and peered at his face in the mirror. He saw bloodshot eyes and dark pouches beneath them. His face was drawn and tired.

"Shit!" he said to the mirror. "I'm an old man!"

He walked to the kitchen and opened the refrigerator. It was empty except for a bottle of orange juice and a bowl of boiled eggs. He poured a glass of juice and cracked open an egg, sprinkling it with salt and pepper. He sat at the kitchen counter and munched the egg and sipped the juice. The food gave him a jolt of energy. More alert, he knew he had to break out of this no-results mode. He resolved to work his body hard today. As an athlete, a demanding workout always cleared his mind and helped him find the right path of action. He glanced out the window. The early-morning light was promising. It would be a sunny day. He'd get on the bike early before it got too hot. He finished the juice with a quick swallow and went to his bedroom for his cycling clothes.

In the garage of his condo, he pumped the tires of his Gunnar, sped out of the garage and across the parking lot, then headed up Sand Hill Road over Highway 101 and onto Woodside. He pedaled through the town at twenty miles per hour, pleased that there was no traffic on the main street. Then came La Honda Road, the route to the peak at Skyline Boulevard. He stood up from the saddle often, pushing more power onto the pedals. Sweat poured down his face. He wiped it away and pushed harder, driving to purge himself for his ineffectiveness in finding Sarah.

"It's been four weeks," he shouted to the redwoods he passed as he climbed and climbed. He reviewed what Bill Turner had told him he previous day.

"I'm as pissed and disappointed as you are, Brooks," Turner had said. "Every time we get close to Sarah, the sons of bitches seem to have a special warning of what we're doing, and they move her. We were close in Santa Rosa. I put holy hell on Jahin, threatening deportation, but he wouldn't break. He gave us nothing. It was the same with Youssef al Hariri in Seattle. Our agents pushed him hard and got zilch. Both men are Egyptian. Both were clearly uneasy and evasive when questioned. But…"

Turner had lifted his hand in despair.

"I didn't have the proof to hold them."

Brooks recalled his reply.

"Yeah, but where's she going next? If Egyptians are involved, is there some kind of secret Egyptian transportation group moving her around? Who's in charge of that? Who has the money to move her by aircraft? The pilot from Santa Rosa was paid in cash."

As he pedaled hard, Brooks returned to the disappointing realization that he, Turner, and Claude's CIA agents had not discovered the names of the kidnappers or their leadership. No organization from the Islamic world claimed they had Sarah in captivity.

Who was this group? he wondered. *What new ideas could be employed to find her?*

He decided to get off his bike, rest a while, and come up with at least one new idea. He pulled over to the side of La Honda Road, placed his bike against the trunk of a redwood, and sat against its massive base. He rested his back on the rough red bark and wiped the sweat from his brow. As he cooled down, one idea came to mind and began to dominate his considerations.

I'll offer the bastards money—say, $200,000—which is the going rate for captured journalists, he thought. *But I'll agree to remove myself from only four countries: Jordan, Israel, Iraq, and Qatar. If the captors don't agree to those conditions, it will indicate that they are either from Saudi Arabia or Egypt. That means Turner was right—the information he secured from the Santa Rosa pilot pointed toward the Egyptians.*

The Saudis were still a possibility, he knew. Brooks knew his trip to the kingdom could erase or prove that country's involvement. He had confidence that Ambassador Ticonne's pressure on Egypt could reveal if an Egyptian subgroup such as al-Hura or the Muslim Brotherhood were involved. He climbed back on his bike and played with that idea while he pedaled to the top of the hill. Reaching Skyline Boulevard, he rode toward a grove of trees and dismounted where the shade gave him respite from the sun. Again, he rested against a tree and sipped water from his bottle. He reviewed his planned message to the kidnappers. He went through the steps of the plan one by one.

This could work, he thought. *It might put the kidnappers in a box and reveal what country's behind this.*

He rose from the ground and swung onto his bike. He wanted to get these ideas on paper and review them before sending a text message to the kidnappers. He could not get to his condo fast enough. As he raced downhill at speeds over thirty miles per hour, his attention was divided between his plan and the potholes on the road. He batted around the idea of sending a copy of his message to Turner or to Anderson but ultimately decided against it. They would resist his course of action because it ran counter to U.S. policy that barred negotiating with terrorists.

On arrival at his condo, sweaty, but still satisfied with his decision, he went to his computer to type the message. He studied the text. He decided to shower and review the plan one more time before sending it. He stepped out of the shower as the phone rang. Hesitantly, he picked it up.

"Brooks, so glad to get you. It's Claude."

"Interesting, old man. You were on my mind as well. What's up?"

"First and foremost, I'm pestering you, and I know it. I want you in Saudi ASAP."

"Yeah, I know, I'm—"

"I admit I'm being super pushy and aggressive. I've booked you on a U.S. Air Force transport flight from Moffet Field to Jeddah tomorrow at seven a.m. I understand the field's near you in Mountainview. The flight—I want you to confirm that you'll be on it."

"Jesus, Claude, I'll get to Jeddah soon, but—"

"Sorry, Brooks, I can't wait. The White House is screaming about the oil embargo issue. It's gone from a worry to a priority. This concern ties into another issue. We want your ears and eyes on that too."

Brooks let out a long sigh.

"What's this all about? "

"OK. You know the oil issue, and you know how to handle that. But the need for speed has increased. The second issue may be related to oil—and to what's happened to Sarah. This issue is even bigger."

Claude took a breath to slow down, organize his thoughts, and up his chances for convincing Brooks.

"Our agents, while checking in with all types of informants across the Middle East, have found an abundance of unrest with the locals. The feeling our guys get is that something big, like an attack on an embassy or government base, is going to happen. The target is likely to be the U.S. or one of our allies. The expected timing is soon. Our informants have not been specific regarding who, what, or when. It's just that they are sensing tension in the radical militants. They claim there's a lot of nervous energy ready to explode."

"And you want me to check on these rumors too?"

"I know it sounds vague—a little weird—but some of our local people are scared. You have great connections with the Saudi intelligence structure and with Mubarak's people. Ask a few delicate questions. No one does this better than you. Let's hear what you learn. And get me the oil embargo info as fast as possible."

"Shit, man. I'm about to put some pressure on the kidnappers, but I guess that I can do that tonight."

He thought about the arrangements.

"Yeah, I can make a plane tomorrow morning. I'll get your info."

"Brooks, old man, that's terrific! But what are you doing with the kidnappers? No negotiating. We're all working to find Sarah. I know the FBI has some leads."

"I've got a squeeze play in mind. That's all you need to know."

"Nothing foolish or risky. I know you—be careful."

"I will. I'll be in touch once I reach Jeddah."

CHAPTER 27

Closing In

Cairo, Egypt

Omar Sayed pulled the burner phone from the drawer of his desk and opened to a message from the prior evening. Jabari had forwarded the American's response to his most recent demand for money and a signed agreement. Omar picked up his office phone and instructed his aide to hold all calls; he wanted no interruptions. He studied Davidson's message for the tenth time. He was certain that the American was trying to determine which country had sponsored the kidnapping so he could use his political connections to apply pressure. He thought about no response, then changed his mind. He decided to give Davidson a hint of possibility that the woman could be freed quickly. He typed a message to Jabari.

Respond to the American with this message: Pay 2.0 million U.S. dollars to the bank codes we supplied. When we see the deposit has been made, we can talk about conditions.

In the text message, he requested that Jabari call him in the early evening. It was time to heighten the pressure on the American by stopping the chase by the FBI. This was the moment to bring the hostage far away from her pursuers.

Omar arrived home as the sun was setting, giving a hint of relief from the heat of the day.

As he opened the door to their apartment, his daughter rushed to him.

"Can you help me with my essay? You're the best at writing."

Omar kissed his daughter, then stepped inside the apartment and kissed Hasina, who was standing nearby.

"Flattery wins every time," he said.

He placed his hand on his wife's shoulder and gave it a gentle squeeze.

"We'll be in my study until you call us for dinner," he said as he ushered his daughter into the room.

Seated in a stuffed leather chair, his legs extended, Omar faced his desk and listened to his daughter read her essay. As she finished, she placed the paper on the desk and looked expectantly at him.

"Well, Poppa?"

"Ah, your use of words and language is—"

A sound interrupted him.

"What's that buzz?" his daughter asked.

"Please, my dear, open the desk drawer and pass me the phone."

Pulling open the drawer, she glanced at the object inside.

"That's an odd-looking phone. There's no caller identity on the screen."

"Excuse me while I take this call."

Omar watched as she left the room, then pressed the screen to take the call. The phone was one of his burners. He had purchased several prepaid cell phones to handle his calls to and from Jabari. He spoke with urgency before Jabari could say hello.

"I have news for you, and I imagine you have news for me. You first."

"Minister Sayed, Mr. Beltagy told me the Mounties called him. Mr. Beltagy called his friends and found the Mounties also had called them. There is pressure in Canada on Egyptians like there was in Santa Rosa and Seattle. Mr. Beltagy said the Mounties showed him photographs of our hostage, and they were sending her photo to the police, airport people, port people, and customs officials. Somebody in our network must have talked. These police know the woman was captured by a radical Egyptian group."

"Relax, Radwan! I've checked with Jahin and Al-Hariri, and, yes, they have been questioned but have not talked. No one has confessed to knowledge of you or the hostage."

"Mr. Beltagy said that one of the pilots might have talked."

"The pilots know nothing. They have no names and no ability to recognize a photo shot of you or any of your crew. You're safe, believe me. I hear your concern. I'm wary of the attention the hostage is getting. Here's what we'll do. This is a big move. I realize it will be difficult for you and your men. I will add 50,000 U.S. dollars to your compensation for this move. My plan is for you to fly the hostage to Egypt. I'll have that special payment for you and your crew when you arrive. OK?"

"I...I..." Jabari stuttered.

Omar broke in with confidence.

"I've talked to Beltagy. He agrees and is securing a plane. You'll land in Cairo, then bring the hostage to Minya. That's where the bundle of money will await you. Do you have paper and pen?"

When Jabari was ready, Omar continued.

"OK, here's the list of actions you'll need to take: I want you to buy or borrow an abaya for the hostage to wear. She's to be covered from head to toe. Next, at a pharmacy in Vancouver, you will purchase dark green food dye and cover the woman's hands and face with it. Also, dye her hair with a black food dye. That will last a few weeks. The dye on her skin will last a couple of days. You'll need to move fast. Do you have all that?"

He didn't wait for an answer.

"Good. Now here's the big requirement. Beltagy will manage this. The woman is to be drugged and placed on a hospital stretcher in the plane. We need her to be unconscious when the customs official enters the plane in Vancouver and still be unconscious when customs enters the plane in Iceland. You'll land in Iceland to refuel. She'll be covered in blankets while on the plane and will be wearing that abaya. She'll be totally disguised. Beltagy's done this before— transported sick passengers so the customs officials won't be curious. They'll see her as an invalid who's been sedated and is being transported to a Cairo hospital. Beltagy will give you a passport for her. She'll be known as Ahura Beltagy, a niece of Beltagy. Do you have that so far?"

Jabari looked at his notes and sputtered.

"Yes, Minister. Shall I repeat what I have? We'll need passports as well?"

He recited the items on his notepad while Omar listened impatiently, then voiced satisfaction.

"Excellent. Beltagy will have passports for all of you. Other questions may arise, so call on your burner phone at any hour over the next few days. I have a couple of more details. The plane will land in Cairo and go through customs in the private-aircraft section of the airport. There will be no problems there. I control the customs personnel."

Then Jabari spoke with concern in his voice.

"Minister, it's a long flight from Vancouver to Cairo. Her drug will wear off. She'll start talking, and she talks all the time."

"I was coming to that, Jabari. To ensure the woman makes no trouble, she'll be given another dose of medicine after nine hours of flight time. You'll be near the coast of Europe around then. You'll offer her food and drink, and you'll have crushed drugs put into her food. That will keep her heavily sedated until after you land in Cairo. At the airport, a limousine will meet you and take you to a safe house in Minya. This house is a large compound that my people in the Muslim Brotherhood have used often."

He paused, giving Jabari time to write down the instructions.

"OK," Omar said. "That's a lot of information. Did you get it all? Please repeat it to me."

Jabari stopped scribbling on his notepad and read off the details to Omar.

"Is my entire crew to fly to Egypt too? Hamid wants to return to the U.S."

"No, no. I insist on this, Jabari. All payments to them will be made in Egypt. They are to stay with the hostage until I say leave."

"And my wife and children, Minister? My wife told me the FBI has visited her. What about my family?"

"I've made plans to move her and your children to Mexico until the job is done. Then we can move your family back to Egypt. I know you wanted that. Baligh, Mustafa, and Hamid have no family in the U.S. I only have to move your people."

"When will you send her to Mexico?"

"Tomorrow, if you and she agree."

"I think that's safest. Please do it. And I have your assurance that all of us can return to Egypt with no risk of imprisonment?"

"You have my word on that. Any other questions?"

"What about Davidson's offer to pay two hundred thousand and sign an agreement to not work in four countries?"

"I sent you my response. You haven't seen it?"

"It's been a rough day here. I'll look at it now and send it right off. You didn't mention the date for the flight to Cairo."

"Beltagy claims he can have a plane available in two days," Omar said. "He'll have a physician ready to inject the woman as soon as you board the plane. So buy the green and black food coloring today."

CHAPTER 28

Dyed and Drugged

Vancouver, British Columbia

Jabari stood over Sarah, a gray abaya in his hands. He had a stack of the long cloaks beside him draped over the back of a chair, all different sizes. He resented the work of shuttling the prisoner from place to place and was pleased with the decision to move her to Egypt. He'd held the hostage for six weeks and felt this should be the last stop, and then he'd better get his money. He looked at Sarah with a half-smile, quite sure she'd look Egyptian with her dyed-black hair and the abaya.

"Try this one on."

"I'm not wearing that ridiculous-looking thing! Ugh."

For Jabari, it had been a month and a half of guarding the hostage. His band of patience, never particularly wide, had long since evaporated.

"Goddammit, woman! Put the fucking thing on! You're going to need it where you're headed."

"Oh, God! Why must I wear this?"

Tears dripped down her cheeks as she lifted her arms to try on the garment. Jabari sighed in satisfaction.

"This one fits. Now keep it on. And here's a head scarf that goes with it."

Sarah ignored Jabari's hand holding the headscarf and choked out the words between sobs.

"Where are we going?"

"We're taking a little trip. You'll see when we arrive."

Sarah sank to the floor. Jabari turned to Mustafa and Hamid and spoke in Arabic.

"Put her on the fucking bed! Push up the abaya. Let's start painting her face, hands, arms, and legs with the green dye."

Hamid pinned her down slowly, giving him a free moment to squeeze her breasts. Mustafa, ever aware of Hamid's sadistic tendencies, pushed Hamid's hands to Sarah's shoulders then held her ankles in a firm grip. Sarah started to resist, thrashing her legs upward and pushing her hands toward Hamid's face, but to no avail. They were too strong. Jabari laughed at the squirming woman.

"Troublesome little bitch, aren't you?"

After a short stretch, Sarah stopped resisting. Jabari turned to his men, speaking again in Arabic.

"We'll do her hair last, and we'll have to tie her hands and feet to get that done."

He looked at Mustafa and Hamid, nearly prone on the bed holding Sarah down. He spoke with a hint of amusement in his voice.

"Unless you two want to hold her for the next thirty minutes."

When they had finished staining her hands and face and dyeing her hair, they untied her hands and feet. She rose from the bed and moved awkwardly in the abaya. Trying to avoid tripping over the hem of the long cloak, she went to the mirror in the bathroom.

"Ooooh," she cried as she studied her face and hair. "Sarah's disappeared! Who is this new person?"

She brought her hands to her face. The green food coloring had turned her skin a soft brown. She fluffed her hair with her hands, marveling at the effect that black hair had on her appearance. She was a different person. Tears rolled down her cheeks; the stain remained.

Mustafa yelled to her.

"Lady, come out. I want to see you."

She stepped from the bathroom and walked toward the chair at the desk to face him.

"Yes, you look like an Arab woman now, not like some pale Scandinavian. Much better."

Sarah's eyes turned cold.

"Why do I need to look like an Arab woman?"

Jabari stepped forward.

"Because you're going to live with some Arab women until your man pays us. Have you ever been to Egypt?"

"Oh my God, no! Egypt? Why Egypt?"

Jabari smiled.

"You'll love Egypt—warm weather, lots of sun. And the women can keep you better than we can. You'll be fine there until your husband pays."

Sarah shook her head.

Are they crazy? she wondered. *Egypt is thousands of miles away. We can't be going there. How will we get there?*

Her heart was beating rapidly. She started to perspire beneath the abaya.

"You can't move me that far. I'll be discovered by customs officials or airport people."

A knock on the door startled her. She watched Jabari open the door and give a warm greeting to a short, squat man in a brown suit. He carried a brown satchel in his right hand. He pointed to Sarah.

"A good job, boys," he said in Arabic. "She looks like an Egyptian woman. Now be ready to hold her if she resists."

He introduced himself to Sarah as a physician who specialized in the various shots one needed to travel safely to Third World countries. He opened the satchel and pulled out medicinal vials and syringes. He smiled at her.

"These shots won't hurt too much, and they'll protect you from what I call the 'Nile Nasties.' Will you allow me to inject you in your left arm?"

He looked at her expectantly.

"Please extend it."

She complied. The physician worked the needles expertly, gently inserting them into her arm below the elbow. He glanced at her face as he worked and sensed that she felt minor discomfort. She didn't complain, and he was pleased with the ease of the process. Sarah believed the shots were for her protection. The physician seemed competent and skilled. She had no idea that the drugs were meant to render her unconscious.

"You're a good patient," he said as he wiped a dot of blood off her arm and covered it with a Band-Aid.

He rose from his chair beside Sarah and whispered to Jabari.

"She'll get sleepy in about twenty minutes. You need to get moving to the plane."

The doctor motioned to Jabari to move even farther away from Sarah, well away from her ability to hear their conversation. He held Jabari's elbow.

"As I understand it, there will be a gurney at the terminal, and she'll be on it for most of the flight. She'll be unconscious when you arrive at the airport, so you'll be safe from local airport officials. They clear sick people without much attention. Be sure that you have all her documents to show the agents in Vancouver and later in Iceland, where, as I'm told, you'll land to refuel. Is that clear?"

Jabari nodded.

"We have a passport for her and all kinds of other documents that prove she's Egyptian going to Cairo for medical treatment."

"Right. Good. Now one last requirement: She'll become conscious after you've left Iceland. Put your masks on, and let her get off the gurney and walk around. Offer her some food and drink. She'll be hungry and very thirsty."

He extended his hand and gave Jabari a bottle.

"Grind three of these pills to a fine powder and put the drug into her drink. Do this about four hours prior to landing. These are slow-acting agents. She'll fall asleep about an hour later. That will keep her unconscious when you land in Cairo and have placed her in the vehicle that will drive you to Minya."

"You sound confident about the drugs and their duration, doc," said Jabari with a skeptical look.

"I am. I've done this many times with Hossan. The drugs will last. She'll be out for hours. With a sick and unconscious patient, we've never had a problem with the customs or any other airport agents in Vancouver or Iceland. And your Minister Sayed, I've been told, has taken care of all the landing procedures in Cairo. You should have no problems."

Jabari stood silently, gazing back at Sarah, then at the doctor.

"She better be out and not talkative. She's a pain in the ass. Talk, talk, talk—that's all she does, whether anyone's listening or not. I can imagine what she'd do if she was awake when agents come checking passports."

The doctor dropped his hand from Jabari's elbow and pointed a finger toward him. "Hossan and I have had many illegals shipped out of Canada. It's worked every time. Relax."

He motioned with his hand toward the door.

"The car's outside; the driver's waiting. You need to get to the plane."

At the private hangar, they put Sarah, now unconscious, onto a gurney, then folded its legs and placed the gurney's flat bed on top of the seats in rows one and two. Jabari, Baligh, Hamid, and Mustafa took seats across the aisle. Sarah slept in one position as the jet flew toward Iceland.

Hours later, when the customs agent in Reykjavik boarded the plane, she inspected the passports of the four Egyptians and gave a cursory look at the comatose "patient." Jabari gave the agent Sarah's fake passport. The agent pointed to her.

"This is Ahura Beltagy?"

"Yes. She's sedated due to a heart condition," Jabari said. "We're keeping her stable until we reach the hospital."

The agent nodded and gave Sarah's passport a glance.

"Your documents are in order. I hope she recovers rapidly in Cairo. Best of luck."

With Iceland behind them, the jet climbed over the Atlantic, finding smooth air at thirty thousand feet. When the seatbelt sign went off, Jabari and Hamid walked to the back of the plane and sat at a small table to play blackjack with chips. The stack was nearly even when Mustafa joined them and pointed to Sarah's gurney.

"She's begun to move. It started with a cough, then a groan. I saw her eyes blink. They closed again, but she'll wake up soon. We should put a mask on her or put on our balaclavas. I suggest we give her a chance to walk about. What do you think?"

Jabari leaned back and stretched his arms over his head.

"You've been the decent one, Mustafa, always giving her a break. OK, let's don our masks and have her walk around for an hour or so. Then we'll give her the magic cocktail, and she's off to sleep again."

They returned to the front of the plane and hovered over her body. Jabari tapped her shoulder.

"Lady, you awake?"

Sarah blinked, then closed her eyes again. She repeated this action several times. Finally, staring at the three masks looking down at her, she spoke.

"Who are you people? Are you new to me? Where are we? The masks—I can't tell anything from the masks."

"It's the same people," Mustafa said. "We're over the Atlantic. You've been sleeping."

Sarah rubbed her eyes and pushed her hands against her forehead.

"I feel fuzzy. I've been drugged, haven't I?"

Jabari looked down at her.

"Want to get up, walk around? You can."

Sarah swung her legs off the gurney and saw that she was still a foot or two above the floor.

"Can one of you help me down?"

Two of the men lifted her to the aisle. She wobbled and reached out to the tops of the seats to control her movement. Baligh laughed.

"Not too steady, are we?"

Sarah was dizzy and unstable. "Let me have a moment. What was given to me? I've never slept so deeply." She reached for the arms of the next seat, then the next as she staggered down the aisle. "Is the restroom this way?" she shouted over her shoulder.

The men took their seats and watched her totter toward the restroom. When she managed to get there, she washed her face with cold water. Looking into the mirror as she dried her face, she screamed.

"What the hell?"

Then she remembered that they had dyed her face and hair. She sat on the toilet and peed, then washed her face again and again with cold water. The brown face remained. But the water refreshed her. Her mind cleared.

As long as they let me, she told herself, *I'll walk the aisle, do some yoga, and look out the window. Where the deuce am I?*

She walked to the nearest window and gazed down. The sky was cloudless. Bright sunshine illuminated the water.

That's the sea, she thought as she studied it for a moment. *But what direction are we flying? Where is the sun? We're over the Atlantic, the friendly one had said. We must be heading toward Europe or Africa. Her mind raced with concerns that began to depress her. Are we really going to Egypt? Will I ever be found? Is Brooks making the payment? What's happening with that? Does he not care? How long has it been? It must be a month. Oh, God, what can I do?*

She turned from the window in despair, recognizing that the flight moved her farther and farther away from American police and help. She walked up and down the aisle, momentarily pleased to have movement. She saw four sets of brown eyes watching her. She looked around the cabin.

This is a private jet—very large and expensive, she thought. *Somebody has a lot of money and organizational wherewithal to arrange this plane, the helicopters, and the different hideouts. I'm a small fry, but I'm caught up in a much bigger game. What's this Brooks Davidson all about? Who is this man who caused me so much trouble?*

Suddenly, a look of annoyance crossed her face. To no one in particular, she spoke.

"Where are my regular clothes? My jacket has my TB pills. I need those, or you're all going to get the infection. And where are my good pants, shoes, and blouse?"

She moved closer to Mustafa.

"Do you have my clothes?"

He pointed to a small plastic bag tucked under the gurney.

"Everything's there. Check it out."

She looked under the gurney and saw the bag. Somewhat relaxed, she turned back to Mustafa.

"Can I ask you some questions?"

Jabari answered for Mustafa from the seat behind.

"No! And shut the fuck up! I'll bind and gag you if you talk!"

CHAPTER 29

The Kingdom

Saudi Arabia

Brooks had been to the Saudi Arabian oil fields before–in fact, many times. As he walked across the arrival bridge at King Fahd International Airport in Dammam, he could see the mid-July heat shimmering on the tarmac below, creating a mirage of water on the surface. Outside, he knew the temperature would be above one hundred degrees. He retrieved his luggage, went through passport control, and waved to the driver who was holding aloft the Aramco sign with his name on it.

"Welcome, Dr. Davidson," said the driver, in excellent English. "I understand I'm to take you to Abqaiq and the Euro Mansion Hotel."

"Yes," Brooks replied in Arabic. "I appreciate the courtesy of the car and your meeting me here."

The driver looked at Brooks, surprised, but then shifted his speech to Arabic.

"Aramco welcomes you, and I'm to tell you that Production Chief Ismail Al-Sahib will meet you in the lobby at six p.m. I understand he is an old friend. He will have two others from Aramco Production with him."

"Thank you."

Brooks gazed outside the terminal.

"How is the traffic on the road? I haven't been here for a few years. Is it still clogged with trucks, cars, and the occasional herd of goats or camels?"

The driver's face opened in a wide smile.

"Some things never change in the desert, Dr. Davidson—especially the heat. And the animals are always present. You remember the Pakistani drivers? They still drive their trucks like it's their last job. On every trip, they try to pass whoever's in the road. They are too willing to meet Allah."

Brooks laughed.

"It's always good to see familiar ways when I return."

As they drove from the airport, the urban setting gave way to the desert he knew so well. For miles and miles, the land was flat, endless stretches of sand. They passed the occasional Bedouins with their camels and clusters of goats, tended by herders with long, hooked staffs.

No matter how often he traveled to the Ghawar oil fields, the vast, barren landscape mesmerized him. He was fascinated by the fact that thousands of oil-field workers, many with families, lived in this flat area dominated by sand, dust, and oppressive heat. For him, the labor pool was not an economic force but a psychological phenomenon. People were willing to live in a harsh environment if there was work that paid well. It was Aramco and the Ghawar oil field, the largest and most productive in the world, that offered those jobs for workers willing to endure the conditions. And for him, the Ghawar and the gated Saudi Aramco community of Abqaiq represented the best location in Saudi Arabia to answer Claude Anderson's question: Were the Saudis preparing for another oil embargo? He knew a truthful answer rested in the minds and plans of the production chiefs in these fields.

Brooks showered in his room, feeling better after the heat and dust were washed from his body. He toweled off, donned tan slacks and an open-collar white shirt, and descended to the lobby to meet Ismail Al-Sahib. Al-Sahib and two strangers were waiting for him in the hotel lobby. Al-Sahib rose from his chair, opened his arms, and embraced Brooks.

"After three years, it's been too long, my friend. You look well."

"As do you, and I agree—too many years separate us."

Al-Sahib turned to his companions and addressed Brooks.

"Please meet Jamall Al-Yami. He is responsible for the drilling at many of the rigs in the Ghawar. I know you want to spend time with him on-site."

Al-Sahib touched the arm of his other companion.

"This French gentleman is Thomas Gilbert. He is with Schlumberger and has been essential in improving well maintenance and increasing the production in some of our older wells. He'll provide you with another perspective on our operation. From what the oil minister told me, we are to give you whatever information you need. I take it you know of a firm that has some new recovery technology for us?"

"I do, and there may be a fit. That's why I'm here."

Al-Sahib clapped Brooks on the back.

"Let us have dinner and get reacquainted."

★ ★ ★

The next morning, before the sun rose, Brooks was in the back seat of a Mercedes SUV tearing down the Ain Dar road toward the first production office in the Ghawar. There, Al-Sahib introduced him to the production engineers and left him to pore over drilling logs, production records, and well-output forecasts.

Brooks, at times with Al-Sahib in tow and always with Gilbert by his side, pored over current production data and forecasts. For a week, he visited various offices in the Ghawar, examining records and discussing production plans and detailed near- and long-term projections. At no point in the data or conversations with the production chief was there a hint of a slowdown or shutdown as prelude to an embargo. It was apparent from his earlier discussions with the oil minister in Riyadh and with the engineers in the field that Saudi Arabia needed the income, and any interruption to the flow of black gold would harm the kingdom more than it would distress the economies of its customers.

Each day as Brooks traveled to the offices in the Ghawar, he felt he was leaving Sarah's fate to others—to the FBI, CIA, and State Department. It gnawed at his heart and soul that he was not doing enough for her safe return. He was eager to get Claude Anderson's work done so he could meet with his friends in the Saudi Mukhabarat. On his mind every day was the question of what Saudi intelligence officers knew of the group that kidnapped Sarah. As the sixth day came to a close, he reviewed his notes and charts full of data.

I have enough, he thought.

He turned to Gilbert.

"The production is going full bore, with no sign of production problems or plans for a slowdown—not even for well repairs."

"It's been a pleasure to work with you over the past few days," Gilbert said. "You can see from the data that the firm you introduced to this field has been a great help in reducing well closures, fires, and other accidents. We at Schlumberger will be most interested in working with you when you bring new American technology to Saudi Arabia. On the point we discussed over the past few days, I agree with you—there's no foreseeable production slowdown needed or planned for whatever reason."

That evening, Brooks called Anderson.

"Claude! Sorry to bother you so early. I have reached a conclusion on the question of an embargo. I have two feet of data in my briefcase for backup if you need it, but my one-liner to you is the Saudis are not planning an embargo. They need the income, and there are many reasons for that. Also, production is going so well, it looks like they're attempting to increase output more consistently in order to improve their share of the global market."

"Jesus, Brooks, I nearly spit out my oatmeal. That's dammed good, dammed reassuring news. When can I get this in writing?"

"In a couple of days, I can give you a short version, which will include the fields I visited, a summary of the production records, and the forecasts from these fields. If you need a longer version, you'll have to wait until I get back to the U.S."

"And when is that?"

"As we talked about, I'm back on Sarah's case. My first stop is with my contacts in the Saudi Mukhabarat. Then I'm off to Egypt to see Mubarak. I don't know when I'll return, but I'll be in touch daily if you'd like."

"Yes. That would be good. Once I give your summary to the boys in the White House, they'll want to talk with you and probably see some of your data. I'll need to know how to reach you."

"I'm off to Riyadh and the Mukhabarat in the morning. You have my cell number. I always know how to find you."

★ ★ ★

In his years in the Middle East, Brooks had spent many days in the Saudi Mukhabarat headquarters, sharing information on threats to the kingdom and to the U.S. from Saudi radicals. As his plane touched down in Riyadh, his thoughts focused on Tariq Al-Outaibi. He was not at the top of the Mukhabarat, but he was always present in key meetings. Tall, slender, and taciturn, he spoke only when asked. His English was excellent, and his comments precise and astute. He never seemed friendly or unfriendly to Americans or foreigners in general. He did his work, and the results were excellent. Rarely did he participate in social gatherings after work, so Brooks had no personal interactions with the man. Although he did not know Al-Outaibi well, Brooks trusted him and thought he'd be honest in their discussions.

He spent the first day at the Mukhabarat with the people who held similar positions to his when he was with the CIA. They exchanged insights on American and Saudi policy as they affected each other. He delved into Sarah's situation and, in each conversation, received sympathy followed by convincing arguments that the Mukhabarat did not know the radicals behind Sarah's abduction. He knew he had to get deeper into the organization to agents who were closer to operations on the ground. In the evening, after he returned to his hotel, he showered and cooled down from the hot day. He was still adjusting to the heat in the country. He picked up the telephone and called Tariq Al-Outaibi. Al-Outaibi answered in Arabic.

"Who is calling? Brooks, answering in Arabic, identified himself and explained that Sarah's situation was the reason for his call. Al-Outaibi was careful in his response.

"I knew that you were in the country, but I'm surprised to hear from you. Who else have you talked to?"

"I've met with several of my old friends in the agency, and we talked U.S.-Saudi policy issues. Mostly, they wanted to know my thoughts on the Bush administration. Also, I had a very brief moment with King Fahd, who assured me that my advice and investment ideas were welcomed and desired in the kingdom."

"I understand," Al-Outaibi said. "I heard that the radicals wanted you out of the region, but I paid it little attention. You are valuable here. Everyone knows that."

"Thank you. May I call you Tariq? We've met several times."

"Of course. Yet I'm not sure why you want to talk with me."

Brooks had anticipated that question and had his reply ready.

"I have great respect for your skills, Tariq, and your honesty. As I mentioned, a close friend has been kidnapped by a group associated with dissidents in the region. I'd like to know if you, as a good friend of America, know anything about this."

Again, there was silence on the phone. Finally, Tariq spoke.

"I see. Let us meet at Café Z tomorrow afternoon at two o'clock. We'll speak in English so there's no chance that anyone will understand our conversation. I'll see you then."

* * *

The next day, Brooks arrived at a bustling Café Z. From a table against the back wall, Tariq rose and waved to him. Tariq spoke in English.

"Brooks, I offer my sorrow and sympathy for the unfortunate capture of your friend. You have many friends in our country who are distressed at what happened. We can talk freely here. The establishment is owned by a cousin of mine. Government officials, from my organization and other ministries, never come here."

"You know, Tariq, I'm a typical American; I like to be direct. May I ask if you or people within your group know anything or heard anything about this kidnapping?"

Tariq smiled and stroked his short beard.

"We've had discussions. There have been several scenarios, to use that American term, as to why this was done."

"Are there any that seem feasible to you?"

"Yes, and please remember: I'm just exploring a hypothesis."

He sipped his tea as he carefully arranged his thoughts.

"It seems to me—and I'm not saying this belief is widely held in the agency—that President Mubarak of Egypt is in deep trouble. Slowly, the Muslim Brotherhood has increased its legitimacy as a political force and now has over twenty percent of the seats in the parliament. The Brotherhood believes, as many do, that Mubarak is corrupt and bringing too many Western capitalist interests to Egypt. You know this, correct?"

"Yes, we agree on the interpretations."

"So, the Ford Motor deal, which all should praise, instead raised havoc with the Brotherhood. This we've heard at the agency. I believe it to be true. And I conclude, though others may not, that somewhere in the government agencies, enemies of Mubarak are using the Ford project to embarrass him. The implication was that he was paid off—bribed—to make this deal."

Brooks was not surprised by the rumors and responded calmly.

"There were no payoffs. But is that the chatter, so to speak, in the region?"

"Yes, and it conforms to information we share in the trade. It's a widespread belief that Mubarak favors Western culture such as music, dress, art, and films. It's also accepted as fact that he has bank accounts in the Cayman Islands like your millionaires, and so on. If you follow my logic, you were selected to be the victim by one of Mubarak's enemies because you are reputed to be close to him. You are seen as a representative of the influence the Brotherhood wishes to remove from the country."

Brooks pushed back in his chair and stared at Tariq.

"There were other countries mentioned in the ransom note. Do you dismiss their issues with capitalist projects?"

Tariq's response was immediate.

"I do. You've talked to King Fahd, so you know he values you and your ideas. I've heard King Hussein values your work as well. It seems to me this narrows it down to Egypt."

"You think this was a plot to embarrass President Mubarak?" Brooks asked as he studied Tariq's eyes. "You've reached important conclusions."

"I realize that, but I try to be honest and thorough," Tariq said. "Do my ideas seem logical to you?"

"They do. What I can't figure out is why they chose Mrs. Pierce and did not come directly for me."

"Oh, I think that's obvious. You have too many friends in the region and in your government. All hell would break loose if anything happened to you."

"My government, perhaps, but look at what happened to Dietrich Patz."

"You're not him. He was a journalist—antagonistic. He embarrassed our people with his insights on our religion and lifestyle. He was a pain in the ass, as you say in America. You've brought thousands of jobs to Saudi Arabia, Jordan, and other nations. Very different from what journalists do. And we don't forget our friends."

"So you think the idea of this kidnapping arose from the

Egyptian bureaucracy? Perhaps an agency where there is a quiet cell of members in the Muslim Brotherhood?"

"That's a strong possibility. There may be more of these events in the coming months to show the country that Mubarak is corrupt and should be removed."

Under the table, Brooks stretched out his legs, relaxing. He was pleased with Tariq's insights.

"Our waiter's hovering," Brooks said. "We should pay attention to the menu. One last comment: You've put the pieces together brilliantly, as always. Now the challenge is to find the agents within the government who initiated this."

Tariq looked up from his menu.

"If we turn up any useful information, we'll get it to you. That's all we can do. I know you understand that."

"I've received more than I expected. I appreciate the offer. I know what I must do."

He glanced down at the menu, then raised his eyes to Tariq.

"If the time arises when I can help you, I want you to call."

"I may do that sooner than you think," Tariq said. "My wife wants to visit America and especially see the golden city of San Francisco."

Brooks smiled a warm, welcoming smile.

"Anytime. I hope you'll allow me the privilege of being your host."

Tariq beckoned the waiter.

"Let us order and talk of other things. You might like the kultra with chicken or lamb. It's very good here."

CHAPTER 30

Safe House

Minya, Egypt

The bump in the road jolted Sarah. A sharp pain shot through her head. Her eyes flickered. She saw the back of two heads and noticed that one man sat beside her in a big car. She rubbed her eyes. All she could see out the window were sand dunes and bare hills. The last thing she remembered was eating hummus and flat bread on a plane. She shook her head to clear the cobwebs.

Is this a dream? she wondered.

She looked again. The desolate view was real. Occasionally, a brace of palm trees surrounding a large adobe structure punctured the empty landscape.

God, they must have drugged me again, Sarah thought.

Her mouth was dry. She found it hard to talk.

"Where...?" she began.

The word didn't sound right. She tried again.

"Where are we?"

"Sleeping beauty awakes," the chubby man said with a smile.

Sarah was startled. Neither he nor the other men wore masks. From the rear-view mirror, she recognized the stone-cold eyes and thin shoulders of the driver. The wicked scar down the side of his face was new to her. The chubby man had a round, soft face. His smile relaxed her for a second until a medium-sized man with the compact build yelled sharply.

"Put the fucking balaclavas on!"

The faces disappeared, but not before Sarah had a good look at the lead man—the man they called Jabari. He had wide brown eyes, high cheekbones, thick black hair, and thin lips. He was handsome, but his face was hard and unfriendly—a face she would not forget. Jabari, seated next to the driver in the front seat, turned to Sarah.

"If you saw any faces, forget them for your own safety. If you ever get free, you never saw any of us. Clear?"

He didn't wait for an answer.

"You're in our world now. You're in Egypt. Our rules apply. If your Dr. Davidson doesn't pay soon and sign the agreement, I will personally drop you in the Nile, where you can swim with the crocodiles."

He turned to the front and spoke to the driver in Arabic.

"We're a mile away," Jabari said. "It will be a long driveway marked by two tall palm trees at the entrance."

"You've been here before?" the driver asked.

"Yes, it's a big house—many rooms—and has been in my family for a century. It has been a home and refuge for the brothers who fight the good fight against the foreign devils."

"We will stay here?"

"For a while, until the boss in Cairo says we can leave, and he pays us."

"Will we have to watch her all day like we did in the U.S. and Canada?" the driver asked. "I'm sick of watching the bitch, as are Mustafa and Baligh."

"No—this is the good part," Jabari said. "Most of the people in the compound are women, the wives of Muslim Brotherhood warriors who are working elsewhere or are in jail. Our hostage will be guarded by the women. They have done this often over the years. They surround our captives like loving sisters, but actually it's a form of total control. This one will never get away from them—if she even knew where to go."

He let out a hearty laugh.

"Can you imagine her trying to escape in Minya?"

He laughed again.

"So we will be free to go to the city, have some time to ourselves?" the driver asked.

"Yes. There will be times we can visit friends, go to a café in Minya. But we will keep a close watch on her too."

Sarah dropped her head in dismay. The lead man had shifted back to his language, and she had no clue of what was discussed. Tears filled her eyes. She delicately wiped them away.

I'm in Egypt, she thought. *I'll never be found. What can I do? It's taken too long to settle the terms of my release. I've got to do something. Escape?*

The word formed in her mind, but how would she do it? She was bound and gagged and always in a locked room after every move.

Would it be the same here? she wondered.

She looked at the tear stains on her hands and marveled at the brown color of her fingers.

I'm beginning to look like them, she thought. *That may help me get away if I'm not locked in.*

She toyed with the idea.

It's been over a month, she estimated, *and they've been on the run. Something is happening out there. As time goes on, they may get careless.*

She leaned forward in her seat, straining the shoulder straps on her safety harness, and tapped the lead man's shoulder. "I'm thirsty," she said. "I'd like some water."

"So would I. We'll get to water soon."

A few minutes later, the driver braked hard, turned the SUV between two tall palm trees, and entered a long gravel drive. Palm trees provided shade to the drive as it wove toward a metal gate at the end. Dust flew as the gate swung open. The SUV slowed down in the middle of a courtyard, then pulled up to a circular fountain of blue ceramic tile. Two scruffy dogs lapped at the water in the fountain, lifted their heads to survey the vehicle, then returned to their drink.

The courtyard was so hot that Sarah wanted to stick her head in the water, but two of her captors ushered her into a house. The air was cool in the entry hall. Children scrambled toward Sarah, and the men shooed them away. Sarah was brought into the middle of a spacious living area where several women sat on cushions, some sewing, some reading, some talking in hushed voices. There were many of them. Sarah tried to determine the number but lost track as the children circled around her, speaking to her, seeking her attention. Sarah's eyes left the children, and she looked at the women again. In their abayas, some with their faces fully covered in niqabs, the women stared at her. Their quiet demeanor, the steadiness of their gaze, unnerved her. She looked away.

Only one man was in the room. He wore baggy clothes and sandals with no socks. His bronze face was deeply lined, and he had a stringy beard of gray. His eyes studied Sarah for a moment. Then he returned to smoking his pipe. The woman beside him rose from her cushion. She approached Sarah and spoke in broken English.

"You will stay with us. I show you your room. Do you like some tea or water?"

Sarah wanted to say she'd love a dry martini.

"I'd like a glass of water," she replied. "Thank you. You speak English, yes?"

The woman smiled. Her teeth were white. "I speak a little," she said. "My daughter—she come often. She speak good English."

"Who are these people?" Sarah asked as they walked down a long corridor.

"You are American, I understand. We live differently here. This is my family—my sisters, my cousins, their children—always welcome. Some stay a few days, some years if the men are away."

After walking down several halls, the woman opened a door and ushered Sarah in.

"This is your room. The bath is down the hall."

She pointed with a crooked finger. Sarah surveyed the room. It had one bed with a woven blanket on top and white sheets underneath it. A small wooden desk and an old chair stood in a corner. A lamp was on the desk, and another one was on a table next to the bed. A single window near the ceiling was blocked on the outside with iron bars. A three-blade fan purred overhead, providing a cooling breeze. Sarah was tired. She pulled out the desk chair and sat down. The woman entered the room after Sarah and sat on the bed.

"I am Ani," she said. "Forgive my English. My daughter will help in a few days. For now, for today, I say I will protect you. I will make sure the men don't hurt you. I don't know about these politics, but I honor what the men want. Do you understand?"

"Yes, a little. I want to be free. Can you help?"

Ani sat up and straightened her back.

"That is men's business. Politics not me. I protect you. That's all. Come."

She rose.

"Follow me to kitchen. You will eat there."

Ani showed Sarah the kitchen, where three women were cutting vegetables. "You may come here anytime for tea or bread—anytime."

Sarah brightened at the thought.

"Can I help with the vegetables, with the cooking?" she asked. "Do you have any books in English that I can read?"

"Lady very busy. I think about it. You have small bag of clothes. Do you want them washed? Do you want to rest now? It is common this time of day to rest."

Sarah went back to her room, thinking she'd never find her way through the maze of rooms and halls darting one way, then another. Complicating the arrangement of rooms for her were dozens of women walking and running in and out of the rooms. When she walked from hers to the front living area, she realized she was not locked in her room, but many eyes were always watching her. As she moved toward the front door, one of the women rose from her seat and accompanied her out to the courtyard. Sarah made a motion with her hand, beckoning the woman to walk with her, and they strolled around it in the bright sun. Sarah stared at the ten-foot-tall adobe walls and the massive metal gate at the entrance. She knew an electronic device activated it. She quickly surmised escape would not be easy unless she could find the device.

Jabari, covered by a balaclava, walked out to the courtyard and confronted Sarah.

"You can see this is a different type of prison," he said. "You are still our prisoner and guarded, not only by us, but also by a dozen women. Believe me, they'll control you far more actively than we did. Escaping is impossible. You're miles from a city, you don't know where you are, and you don't speak our language. If you ever got out of this compound, my men and I would quickly find you."

Ani waved a finger at Jabari and spoke Arabic. "Take off that mask while you're in my house."

"Auntie, I can't do that."

CHAPTER 31

Mounting Pressure

Riyadh, Saudi Arabia

B rooks opened the curtains of his room at the Four Seasons. From the forty-eighth floor, he stared down at the city and out to the desert in the distance. The view was spellbinding. He stretched his arms over his head, bent his trunk left and right, and, feeling a bit more relaxed, returned to the desk and his computer. He was putting the finishing touches on his initial report to Claude Anderson. Brooks reread the summary and felt his conclusion was clear: There was no immediate threat of an embargo led by Saudi Arabia. He sorted carefully through the ensuing sections of the interviews with all the production engineers as well as with the oil minister. He felt the appendix at the back of the report was filled with too much detail. He had sections on current production from each field, along with their individual forecasts as well as prices now and expected over the next three years. But that was what Anderson wanted: detailed backup. Brooks saved the document in a file and stored it in the separate account that Anderson had given him. He downloaded the document onto a flash drive and planned to bring it to the American Embassy the next day. Anderson was explicit: Don't send it via email. It would go to Anderson in a diplomatic pouch. It was late afternoon in Riyadh and early morning in Washington when he called Anderson at home.

"Claude, sorry to bother your breakfast. The report's done and will be on its way in the morning via secure diplomatic pouch."

He could hear Claude munching some kind of cold cereal.

"Again, sorry about the time."

"No problem, old man. I want to talk with you. New developments here."

"I'd like to get to those, but remember—you asked me a question about threats to America? You requested that I check with my contacts in all four countries."

"Yeah, of course," Anderson said. "I was coming to that. Is that in your report?"

"No, it's too speculative and too sensitive. I prefer to give it to you verbally. You can do with it as you wish."

"OK, what's up?"

"This is quite vague," Brooks said. "The people I met—and they are all listed in the appendix of the report—sense that one of the radical groups in the region is planning a major attack on an American site. No one seems to know who will do this or what the target or targets will be, but the message is clear: An attack is in the offing, this year – 2001. This is late July, and I'm guessing from what I've heard that there will be an attack in September or October. Get all the agents you can to dig into their contacts to see who'll talk. The people I spoke with all agreed—independently, of course—that a strong dose of preventive action is needed at this time."

"So the natives are getting more and more restless?"

"That's what I'm hearing."

"Anything more specific?" Anderson asked.

"The only odd comment I heard—and this from a high intelligence source—thought the attack will be on American soil. How about that?"

"Like Yousef at the World Trade Center in February of '93?"

"That's what I was led to believe," Brooks said.

"Well…Shit! Shit! Shit! Thank you, old friend, for ruining my breakfast."

"You wanted my views. Now what do you have for me?"

"Nice transition, old boy, and I want to keep talking with you about the rumors of an attack," Anderson said. "Now back to Sarah's situation. Apparently, the FBI has turned up more evidence that Egyptians were involved in the snatch of Sarah. Bill Turner has called Frank Ticonne at the embassy in Cairo."

"I need to know what Turner learned."

"I know Frank used Turner's information with Egyptian officials and has been trying to reach you. Is your phone dead?"

"It's been misbehaving in the desert," Brooks said. "I'll call him."

"When you finish with him, let's put our heads together and see how we can squeeze the Egyptians."

As soon as Brooks hit the end-call button, he placed a call to Ticonne and was patched through to the ambassador.

"Brooks," Ticonne boomed into the phone. "How are you, and where the hell are you?"

"Fine. I'm in Riyadh."

"Oh, good—nearby. When can you get here? Never mind. Let me get right to it. Your FBI man, Turner, sent me some very useful information. With his insights in hand, I met with Mubarak, Foreign Minister Hamdi, the head of the Egyptian Mukhabarat, General Murad, and a man named Fathi Ashur, also of the Mukhabarat.

As you know, Turner has focused on this Jabari Radwan. Let me tell you what I got from Turner. Radwan has gone missing from his job. He fits the description given by a pilot who flew him, three other men and—get this—a woman to Seattle. Turner's information indicated that this Radwan was a former Egyptian Mukhabarat agent. I told Mubarak and the others what the FBI found."

"What was Mubarak's reaction?"

"First off, Mubarak emphasized how valuable you are to the country. Then Ashur spoke up and said Radwan had been expelled from Egypt and probably had joined a rogue group, a radical band from the Muslim Brotherhood. At this point, Mubarak silenced Ashur with a flash of his hand and emphasized there were dissidents in the country trying to embarrass him. He expressed that theme off and on through the entire meeting."

"He's claimed that in your prior conversation too, right?"

"Correct, but here's where it got interesting," Ticonne continued. "I said that a computer programmer in San Francisco would never have the money or organizational skills to pull off a caper like this. He had to have support from a group like Al-Qaeda or the Brotherhood. And since he was Egyptian and unlikely to have contacts in the other countries for the capital or skills needed for this job, his help most likely came from Egypt. Then I stared hard at General Murad and asked, 'What do you know about this?'"

"Jesus, Frank, that's stunning and aggressive," Brooks said. "You seem prepared to test American-Egyptian relations. What happened next?"

"The room got quiet. Mubarak seemed nervous and looked at General Murad. Then this Fathi Ashur spoke again, repeating what he told us earlier. He said, 'Jabari Radwan was expelled from Egypt as a criminal five years ago. You, in America, accepted him, employed him. If he's involved in this plot, he's your problem, not ours.'"

Brooks felt a jolt of optimism lifting his spirits. It seemed like Tariq of the Saudis and Turner of the FBI were reaching the same conclusion.

"That's very interesting, Frank. Was Ashur trying to deflect your attention, and Mubarak's, away from the Mukhabarat?"

"I let the comment sit there, then said, 'Your problem is that some person and some group in Egypt wants Brooks Davidson out of the country. Instead of asking him to leave, that group has committed a serious international crime. Since the leader is Egyptian, I believe this is your problem as well as mine.'"

There was silence on the line. Then Ticonne spoke again.

"Mubarak attempted to calm the waters, saying, 'Does your FBI have any proof that the criminals, other than this one Egyptian, are from Egypt? Are the others from the countries mentioned in the ransom note?'"

Brooks interjected.

"Did you mention that I talked to the leaders in each country and staff from their intelligence agencies as well? It was unanimous—all were astounded by the act."

Ticonne continued.

"I wanted to keep the air in the room pleasant. I noted that we had no identity of the other assailants, but the FBI was making progress on the faces recognized by the pilot. I said our information indicates there is a move in this country by the Muslim Brotherhood to remove capitalist influence. Was it possible that Radwan was part of an Egyptian Brotherhood plot to remove a capitalist? I paused to watch their faces. Then I told them that is not the case in the other countries."

"Where did you get that info, Frank?"

"Our boys in the CIA, as you would expect. They've found some info on an anticapitalist memo circulating among the Brotherhood leaders. Let me go back to Ashur's response to my last comment. His face showed a degree of controlled anger when he said, 'How do you know the Brotherhood has that agenda? How do you know that Radwan was recruited by the Brotherhood and not by Al Muharib, Al-Qaeda, or other radicals?'"

Brooks voiced his thought.

"Ashur is protecting someone or something—possibly his job. Maybe he realizes that a group is trying to embarrass or dislodge Mubarak, and he doesn't want to find the source."

"I agree. Something is going on in Egypt that is not happening in the other countries on the ransom list. When can you get here to increase the pressure on Mubarak?"

Brooks nodded, pleased with what he heard.

"I have a few more details to wrap up in the other countries. I'll email you on my arrival."

"Excellent! Make it fast, will you? Until then."

Brooks sighed. He had one more difficult task to complete. He had to make his weekly call to Sarah's girls and give them the status of the search. He'd told them in prior calls that he'd offered ransom money and an agreement to stop work in certain countries. He would confirm with them tonight that those offers had been refused, but at least the kidnappers were negotiating. He had one piece of good news: A video of Sarah had been sent to his cell phone. He would forward that to them. Sarah looked thinner and distraught, but she was able to communicate clearly. She did not appear to be abused or injured.

CHAPTER 32

A Miracle

Minya, Egypt

While Sarah was confined to the Minya compound, she found her door unlatched and realized she was free to wander around the maze of halls and rooms. Her initial focus was to find a bathroom, and, in that process, she also located the kitchen. As the days went on, she would meet one of the women or one of the many men who seemed to come and go. They would gesture her toward one room or another depending on their understanding of her question. Following their finger pointing and their odd pantomime gestures, she'd discovered new rooms that had books or couches or more beds or storage boxes. After a few days, she could find her way around the complex with ease. The women, and her captors when they were present, let her walk throughout the house, but she had to be guided and guarded when she wanted to walk in the courtyard.

In her exploration of the maze of hallways, her most satisfying discovery was the kitchen. Here, through her gestures, she indicated she'd like to help and offered to wash the vegetables. Eventually, Ani allowed her to use a knife to cut vegetables as long as Sarah returned it when the work was done. After a few days, she was allowed to do some basic cooking with a large frying pan. Ani, who seemed to be the owner of the house and bossed around the other women with constant commands, taught her several basic Arabic phrases. After a few days, Sarah could converse with simple requests and questions in Arabic. Children scampered around Sarah, touching her wrists and hands, apparently fascinated that her slender arms and substantial height were different from theirs or their mothers'. The women laughed and shooed the children away.

While several of the men in the compound did not wear masks, her captors continued to do so, but they weren't as disciplined as at first. Occasionally, they would forget their masks and hastily put them on when Sarah entered a room. It didn't matter to her. She remembered their faces from her brief glimpse of them on the flight to Egypt and on the drive to the compound. She'd never forget those faces. If she were ever freed, she knew she'd recognize the four men in photos. Of that, she was certain. After a few days, the compound was at times a relaxed environment for her. That changed whenever she saw the men who kidnapped her. Her mouth would tighten, a shiver would crawl up her spine, and the anxiety of the first days of captivity returned. Often, she would turn away and scamper to her room. One day, the lead man, whom Ani called Jabari, walked Sarah back to her room.

"Sit!" he commanded, pointing to the chair near the desk.

She glanced up at him.

"I've been here several days, and you've been away. When will this be over? It's been so long."

"I've been working on your situation. Progress is slow, but I want to enforce this message to you. I know it's easier for you here, but make no mistake: You'll never escape from this compound.

I'm repeating what I said earlier. You have no idea where you are or where to go for help. You do not speak our language. The women are sworn guardians to our cause and are as good a set of guards as my men—maybe better. I hear Ani has given you the rules, and you are following them. Good! You can walk around the house, walk in the courtyard with a guard, and, if you need any products or fresh clothes, tell Ani. She will get them for you."

"If you're making progress, why won't you tell me?"

Jabari snarled.

"It's not up to me. Powerful people want this done, but your man has gone and gotten your government involved. This would have been over weeks ago if he'd done what we demanded."

Sarah knew deep down that she was feeling stronger, more resourceful about getting out of this prison. But each time she saw the lead man, her confidence ebbed. He frightened her. She placed her fingers over her eyes, not wanting him to see the tears she fought to control. It didn't matter. He had stepped out of the room. She walked over to her bed and lay down.

"What can I do?" she intoned quietly. "When will this be over?"

A soft knock on the door disturbed her reverie. She looked up as Ani entered. Ani joined her hands in the form of a prayer.

"Missy, can you come and look at baby?"

The two women walked to the open living room. Next to a low table that held a carafe of tea was a young woman in an abaya with no headscarf. Seated on bright cushions with geometric designs, she was cradling an infant in her arms. The woman's hair was a luminous black and lush in texture. Her face was thin. Her eyes were dark and oval. Sarah thought she was quite beautiful, but what caught her attention was the little girl. She was coughing in spasmodic fits. Sarah looked at Ani.

"What's wrong with the child?" Sarah asked.

"We don't know. She keeps kicking, screaming, and coughing up bad things."

Ani made a crude gesture of regurgitation with her hand touching her mouth and extending it out toward Sarah. "Have you seen this, missy? Can you help us?"

Sarah glanced around the room. The seven women who had been sewing and talking were silent as they watched Sarah talk with Ani.

"Has the baby seen a doctor?"

"My youngest daughter—she's the smart one, a doctor—she comes soon. Finally, she comes to see the baby."

Sarah moved closer to the child, who was bent over the mother, and gestured with her hands. Sarah studied the infant's size and guessed her to be about a year old.

"May I touch the baby?"

Sensing agreement, Sarah touched the baby's forehead and cheeks with the tips of her fingers. She looked up at Ani.

"This child needs a doctor now. You must call a local doctor."

"No, not smart—her husband," said Ani, pointing to the mother. "My husband and her husband no trust doctors. He only trusts Akila."

"Akila?"

"Akila is one of my daughters. Other daughter…"

Ani pointed to the young lady holding the infant.

"…is Anit, baby's mother."

"Akila—does she live in this city?" Sarah asked.

"No, many miles by train or car. She's at famous hospital in Cairo."

"May I touch the baby again? I'll be gentle."

Ani explained to Anit what Sarah intended. The mother rose and lifted her daughter toward Sarah. She placed her hand on the child's chest. It was hot to the touch. Her legs started to jerk.

"The baby is very sick," Sarah said. "I believe she is beginning to have convulsions, which are dangerous. You should call a doctor now."

Ani wiped her brow.

"No, no. My husband says no—only Akila."

"I believe the baby has pneumonia because I had the disease, and I coughed like that. I had the high fever too. Do you understand, Ani?"

"Yes, but what can we do? Cold cloth not work—no doctor."

"Let's put the baby in a cool bath—see if that helps. Please call Akila to come as soon as possible."

The bath helped the child calm down, and soon she drifted off to sleep. Anit and the women around her smiled at Sarah. They offered her a sticky sweet pastry. Their eyes twinkled. Their heads nodded in recognition of her help.

★ ★ ★

In the morning, Sarah looked for Anit and found her with the child back in her arms. She was listless. Sarah placed the back of her hand on the baby's cheek and gave Anit a weak smile. She whispered the word "better," but she knew that was not true.

Akila arrived mid-morning in a car driven by a uniformed man. She wore a summer suit with a knee-length skirt and low-heeled black pumps. Her jet-black hair was cut short. Her scarf covered the top of her head and fell away from her round face. Ani greeted her enthusiastically and brought her immediately to Anit and the child. Akila reached into her physician's bag, retrieved a stethoscope, placed it on the child's chest and listened to her breathing. Sarah, who had been standing nearby, spoke to Akila.

"Do you speak English?"

Startled, Akila lifted her head abruptly upon hearing the question, then, recovering, asked one of her own.

"Who are you?"

"I can say more later, but right now, I believe the child has pneumonia, and in late stages at that," Sarah said. "Do you agree?"

"How do you know that?" asked Akila, staring up at Sarah.

"The child had convulsions last night. I'm familiar with the symptoms of pneumonia."

Akila's eyes were wide, her mouth askew.

"Who are you? Why are you here?"

"I'm a prisoner, an American."

"Mama," Akila turned to her mother, speaking in Arabic. "What are we doing with a prisoner in this house? Is this more of the Brotherhood's stupidity?"

Akila cursed as she looked at her mother and the other women, who ducked their heads, avoiding Akila's penetrating stare.

"The baby first," Ani said. "Then we talk about the other."

Akila nodded to her mother and turned to Sarah.

"When you had pneumonia, what was prescribed in America?"

Sarah motioned for Akila to follow and went to her room. She rummaged in her plastic clothing bag and pulled out her jacket. In the pocket, she grabbed the bottle of pills and read the chemical definition to Akila. Akila raised her hands in the air.

"Wonderful! You have the right antibiotic. It would take days to get that medicine here. The child would likely die."

"Do you think we can cut the pill size and dosage down to the correct amount so it will not harm the child?" Sarah asked.

Akila studied the bottle.

"Yes, I see the dosage. I can adjust it."

She looked at Sarah.

"It's a miracle you're here. You're going to save a life. Work with me to cut the pill down to size and dilute it."

"You don't have this medicine with you?"

"No, I'm a surgeon," Akila said. "I don't carry antibiotics. Let's get to work."

As they ground the capsules to the right proportions, Sarah spoke.

"Your English is without accent. You sound like you came from somewhere in the U.S."

"I studied medicine at Boston University. I liked Boston, but I'm needed here. Where are you from?"

"California—the San Francisco area."

"You must tell me how you got here when we're finished, yes?"

"Definitely."

Akila deftly placed a tube in the baby's mouth, and she swallowed the medicine.

"Let's see how she does. First, let's get her back to bed and let my sister rest."

With the baby asleep, the women gathered in the sitting room to resume their sewing. Several placed needlework in their laps and gazed at Sarah, a smile on their lips. Anit, with her hands joined together near her face, displayed the Arab symbol of prayer and thankfulness. She bowed to Sarah with tears streaming down her cheeks. The smiles of the younger women revealed lovely white teeth. The older women's smiles were equally warm, but their teeth were crooked and gray. They all hugged Akila and greeted her with many different Arabic expressions while Sarah, also smiling, looked on.

Akila received the praise with a sense of calm, then sat next to Sarah.

"OK, miracle woman, please tell me how you happened to be here at this particular moment."

CHAPTER 33

Plan B

Cairo, Egypt

Omar was in Abu Dhabi. Frequently, he traveled to other countries to attract new businesses to Egypt and to secure investors for his projects. On this trip, his objective was to confirm an investment in three new cotton mills with the National Bank of Abu Dhabi. His cell phone rang constantly with calls from Fathi. He left messages for Fathi, but they could not find a suitable time to talk. In his last call, Omar had left a message for Fathi: "*Let's meet at our normal point along the Nile on the 26th when I'm back in Egypt.*"

When the day arrived, Fathi went early to the meeting place. He wanted to settle his mind and reflect on exactly what he wanted to say to Omar, but he found it hard to be calm. He puffed on his cigarette, seeking calm from the nicotine, letting the smoke flow from his mouth in a thin stream.

"Where the fuck is Omar?" he cursed as he paced back and forth. "I haven't got all fucking day."

He stubbed out the cigarette on the ground and drew another from the pack. Feeling the heat, he took off his jacket, placed it on the bench, then lit the fresh cigarette. Omar appeared in the distance and waved. As he approached with open arms, his cousin took a step back. Ignoring the insult, Omar spoke.

"What's going on? You sounded rattled in your messages."

"I've been meeting with the foreign minister and General Murad, along with others too," Fathi said. "This caper of yours has exploded into an international incident. The Americans are batshit. So is the president."

"Calm down, cousin. Radwan tells me the American is beginning to negotiate. He'll fold soon. I'll have him out of Egypt. That's what we want, right?"

"Wake up, Omar. This is failing. The American ambassador, Ticonne, told President Mubarak they knew the leader of the plot was Jabari Radwan, a man who worked in my organization. The Americans claim they have evidence from the pilot who transported Jabari's men and the woman to a location in Seattle. The Americans know this is Egyptian-sponsored."

"Take a step back, cousin. Radwan was expelled from this country. He could be recruited by any of the radical groups in the region that want to hurt the U.S. The Americans are guessing. There's no proof, no evidence, that this is an Egyptian operation."

"Maybe, but Ambassador Ticonne hinted at sanctions in aid, meaning a halt to arms supplies, unless Mubarak gets aggressive in pursuit of the kidnappers."

Fathi looked sternly at Omar and pushed a finger into his chest.

"And that means me. I've been shifted from the background to the hot seat. I've got to find this Radwan and pretend I don't know what the hell he's doing."

"Why should you find him? That makes no sense."

"Of course it does," Fathi said. "Mine is the top ops unit in the country. The president trusts me to find out what's going on."

"Fine. Round up some of Mubarak's old enemies. Get them

to talk. You know how to do this. Get a confession or two that they want American capitalists out of Egypt. You can lead them down that path."

"I can't fake this anymore, Omar. That's what I've come to tell you."

"What exactly do you mean by that?"

"I want Radwan and his crew. Where are they?"

Omar recoiled and took several steps away from his cousin. His face expressed surprise.

"No, no, no, Fathi. Absolutely not. Think about it. If you capture Radwan, free the woman, three very bad things happen."

Despite his agitation, Omar put up his fingers in front of his chest and counted in a slow cadence.

"One, we don't stop the capitalism virus in Egypt. Two, we don't expose Mubarak's corrupt practices with the capitalists. And three, Radwan will talk, and you and I will be in Tora prison or worse. Is that what you want?"

Fathi stepped closer to Omar's face. They stood a foot apart as he spoke.

"Listen to me closely. I won't ask twice. Where is Radwan? I'll erase him and his men. It won't touch you."

Omar backed away from Fathi, giving himself some space.

"You're panicking, cousin. Listen to me: Get active with Mubarak's known enemies and hold a news conference in support of the Americans. You know how to do this. Show Mubarak and the Americans that Egypt is aggressive on this, but don't point your investigation in my direction. Meanwhile, I'll keep squeezing the American Davidson. I believe he's ready to break."

Fathi clenched his fists, lifted a hand to his mouth, and threw his cigarette down the path. Its tip sparked as it hit the ground three feet away. He watched it for a second. Without looking at Omar, he spoke. "You're not listening. I can't believe I'm violating my own rules. I'm asking you twice. Where's Radwan?"

Omar reached out toward Fathi, pleading.

"That I cannot tell you, cousin. It would only implicate you further if this falls apart. I'm protecting you. No more questions."

Fathi let his hands fall to his side. He faced Omar. The pale scar on his cheek had turned red. His eyes were somber.

"I've done my best for you," Fathi said. "I suggest you, your dear wife, and children leave Egypt."

He turned from Omar and walked away as fast as his gimpy leg would permit. When he reached his office, he was in a lather. He mopped his brow and called his assistant to summon his top staff. When they arrived at the conference room, he stood at the end of the table and asked them all to sit. He remained standing as he outlined his plan to find the men who kidnapped the American Sarah Pierce. He placed a photo of Jabari Radwan on the table for all to see.

"The leader of the kidnap team is Egyptian. Our president wants him found immediately."

★ ★ ★

After Fathi had walked away from him, Omar had remained seated at the bench near the river for an hour thinking through what his cousin had said. He knew Fathi to be a tough man— determined and thorough. He always did what he said, and that troubled Omar. He knew, or believed it to be true, that no one would think that Jabari Radwan and the woman were in Minya. He thought his idea to bring her to Egypt was brilliant and error-free. No one in the Muslim Brotherhood or anyone in Egypt knew the location of Sarah Pierce. Omar was secure, safe with that knowledge, and so was Jabari Radwan. He had forwarded one hundred thousand dollars to Jabari with the instructions to give each man in his crew fourteen thousand and to keep fifty-eight thousand for himself. He was confident that that would keep the men happy and quiet until the American Davidson paid the big money. He rose from the bench, picked up a few pebbles, and threw them into the river.

Maybe Fathi is right, he thought as he walked, head down, back to his office. *I should be cautious with my family. School is out. We were planning a vacation to a cooler climate. I'll send Hasina and the children to our villa. They love it there. It's the right time of year for swimming, hiking, and getting away from the suffocating heat of Cairo. I'll have her bring all the codes to our Swiss bank accounts. In case anything blows up, she'll be safe in Switzerland with access to tons of money.*

Omar had been pleased with the purchase of the villa in Brissago, located on Lake Maggiore, back when he was working in London. The price was right. The villa was on a hill overlooking the lake and minutes from the town. In the winter, it was a short drive to Ascona and excellent skiing. The children loved it. He had parked most of his savings from his work in London to a bank in Zurich, then added substantially to that private numbered account while at the Ministry of Trade and Industry. The construction and manufacturing companies paid him generous commissions to secure licenses to build their projects in Egypt. By his reckoning—though he hadn't looked at the bank account in several months—he had more than twenty million euros in the account. Hasina and the children would have a comfortable life there if they needed to stay in Switzerland.

When he reached his office, his assistant badgered him with messages. He walked past her, ignoring the conversation with a wide smile.

"Later. First I must make a couple of phone calls."

His assistant nodded in agreement. He proceeded into his office, closed the door, went to his desk, took a key from his pocket, opened a locked drawer, pulled out his private cell phone, and made a call. After three rings, Hasina picked up.

"You rarely use this phone, Omar. Is there trouble?"

"Not really, but I want to be careful. I'd like to take our vacation in Brissago a few weeks early. You and the children should go as soon as possible. I'll follow in a few days."

"That's a change," Hasina said. "Do you want to talk about it tonight?"

"Only if you don't like the idea. It's been so hot lately. I thought you might like to go to the lake a few weeks sooner than usual and stay longer."

"Actually, it's a great idea. I'll have to cancel several other obligations. Let's talk tonight."

"In the meantime, organize the passports for all of us, check on the flights to Milano and the availability of a Mercedes at the car rental. I would love to be out of here in the next day or two."

Omar placed the phone on his desk.

I've got to push her hard tonight, even if I have to tell her it's for our safety, he thought. He pondered how to phrase the request for an early departure to Switzerland without alarming Hasina. Several ideas came to mind. He picked up the cell phone and walked past his assistant.

"Sorry, an emergency," he said, holding up a hand. "I'll be back in fifteen minutes."

Omar left the building looking for a quiet space to make another call. On a quiet street several blocks away, he called Begat Othman. He'd met with the Muslim Brotherhood leader occasionally, briefing him on the progress to get Brooks Davidson to pay the ransom and sign the agreement to remove his services from Egypt. The call was met with a curt query.

"Who is Amon Re?"

The voice was unfamiliar to Omar, but he satisfied the request with a private code.

"Amon Re is Omar Sayed. My phone's untraceable. I'm calling for Begat Othman."

"One moment."

Othman came on the line.

"I hear no news of the American agreeing to leave Egypt. I don't like no news."

"Forgive me," Omar began. "The American has been difficult, but finally we are making progress with him. I call because we are approaching closure. We may have to protect our Muslim Brothers who have conducted the abduction. I want to have a plan in place for them if needed."

"I agree. Continue."

"Do you have people who can move them or guide them to a safe location in Sudan or another African country?" Omar asked.

"We've done this before. Khartoum is the safest city. The more advance notice I get, the better. Who is your lead man? I forget."

"Jabari Radwan."

"Have him call this number when he needs help."

Othman rattled off the number.

"Act fast when this is over—and faster if it looks like it could blow up."

"That's why I called."

After hanging up, Omar wiped his brow, feeling a dose of relief. The men could disappear if necessary. That would keep them safe from Fathi's agents and protect his career as well. He placed the phone in his pocket and walked a few blocks to a café. He stepped inside to cooler air, stretched his shoulders back, and took a couple of deep breaths. A waitress pointed to a table. He sat and ordered a Turkish-style coffee. The café was quiet at this hour. He placed his hands on the table and thought about his next call.

He felt more relaxed after the coffee. He paid the bill and walked out into the hot, late- morning air. The street, normally packed with cars, buses, and bicycles, was quiet. Omar glanced around and sensed adequate privacy for a call. He pulled the phone from his pocket and called Jabari Radwan. There was no answer, so he left a long message that described the next communication with Brooks Davidson and told Jabari to include the video of Sarah Pierce walking in a meadow with a snow-capped mountain in the background. He emphasized the urgency of getting Davidson to agree to terms.

"As always," he added, "there is the need for a contingency plan. I'm certain that no authorities, no agency, will ever discover that we have the captive in Egypt. However, if you suspect that Egyptian authorities or American agents are getting close, you are to dump the woman in central Minya and telephone the following number."

He recited the number and concluded his message.

"The people you contact will guide you to safety."

CHAPTER 34

Brooks Davidson

Riyadh, Saudi Arabia

Brooks stepped out of the shower in his hotel room, impatient with the morning ritual of shaving, brushing, dressing. He was eager to act. His mind churned over the news from Tariq Al-Outaibi. It pointed directly to Hosni Mubarak. It had consumed his waking hours and interfered with his sleep. Absently, he picked out his clothes for the day and dropped them on the bed. Satisfied with the outfit he selected, he returned to his thoughts about Al-Outaibi. The Saudi Mukhabarat agent had insights and pieces of supporting evidence that pointed toward the Egyptians. The news from Frank Ticonne that a suspect had been identified as Egyptian encouraged him, and it confirmed Al-Outaibi's analysis. Brooks was determined to get to Egypt and Mubarak as soon as the president would see him. He knew Mubarak would be furious at the possible embarrassment to him and his country.

Brooks had spoken with leaders in the five other countries, and their information all pointed toward Egypt. He knew talking with Mubarak would prove beneficial. They had a long association, beginning with his days as the top CIA officer in Egypt and continuing with his work bringing commercial projects to the country.

The idea that the president wanted him banished seemed absurd.

What was the reality? he wondered. *What did Mubarak know about this horrible plot?*

The more he thought about Sarah's abduction, the more preposterous it appeared.

Why would the Egyptians, or any of the other countries, want to exclude my advice on job creation and economic development projects? And why Sarah? She's a friend, not family. It made no sense.

He finished dressing and checked his outfit in the full-length mirror in the bathroom. He looked at his watch: it was seven a.m. in Riyadh and late evening in Dallas and Chicago. It was not a good time to call Sarah's daughters, but they'd said to call at any hour. He went to the house phone on the bedside table when he heard a ping. He crossed to the bureau, where his cell phone rested on the black enamel top. He spotted the Arab crescent and knew the message was coming from Sarah's captors. He opened the message. It read:

You have forced my hand. Time is running out. If payment of 1.5 million dollars is not in the bank, if the agreement is not signed by August 1, Sarah Pierce will disappear from earth. See attached video of her good health.

Sarah's video was just a few seconds long, showing her in baggy clothes and saying in a subdued voice, "Brooks, do what they say and free me."

The sight of her sent shivers down his spine. He gritted his teeth and thought, as he had every day since Sarah's abduction, *This is my fault.* He felt the anger rise in him.

They're all talk now, he thought, *but at some point, they'll tire of trying to get the ransom. When that happens, they'll abandon her or perhaps kill her.*

He paced around the room, feeling he must act, put more pressure on Ticonne, Claude, and Turner, and especially on Mubarak. He studied the video again and noted an interesting feature. In the background, behind her head, was a snow-capped mountain. Did her captors miss the significance of the mountain? He'd get the evidence to the FBI immediately. They would be able to identify the peak. His mood lifted with this piece of location evidence. From the video, and the fact that the FBI might be able to locate Sarah, his mind soared. But he also realized this could be disinformation to distract him and the agents he'd involve. His heart sank as he now feared they probably had moved her right after the video. Regardless, he'd send it to Turner.

He sat on the edge of the bed. His eyes lingered on the image of Sarah. She was thinner. Her cheekbones were too prominent. Her neck was too long. It seemed like her eyes were huge in her thin face. Otherwise, she appeared to be OK. She no longer had that deer-in-the-headlights look that characterized earlier videos. Her voice, eye movements, and general demeanor that radiated fear had subsided. He was heartened by this message and decided to call her daughters with the news.

He decided to call Lynne first. She was the more forthcoming and chatty of the daughters, although both girls, once over the shock of what happened to their mother, were decent and polite. As he looked for Lynne's telephone number, he recalled his first conversation with her. Apparently, Sarah had not talked too much about her dating Brooks or how their relationship was developing because Lynne had difficulty remembering him. Adrienne was the same. It made him wonder if their evolving relationship was important to Sarah. What did he really mean to her? This information perplexed him at first, and now he surmised that

Sarah was not interested in a long-term commitment. They had not broached the topic of formalizing their love affair. They expressed love and appreciation for each other, but marriage had never come up. Perhaps that's why the girls were not fully informed about his presence in their mother's life.

As he talked with the girls, he began to appreciate them—their maturity, thoughtfulness, and care for their mother. Because of his steady growth of feelings for Sarah, he wanted to forge a relationship with her girls, yet he knew he was struggling. They hadn't met him. They'd never spent time with him on vacations or weekends, hiked a mountain, played tennis, or shared so many other activities that are common in families. To them, he was a stranger who had brought a crisis to their lives. Still seated on the edge of the bed, he pushed those thoughts aside and called Lynne's number.

She's always busy—perhaps in bed by now, he thought.

As expected, the call went to voicemail. He left a message to call at any time, then summarized his latest efforts to free her mother. He attempted to inject enthusiasm over the actions of Ambassador Ticonne and the FBI. He concluded with a promise to send her the video clip of her mother from his latest communications with the kidnappers. In signing off, he mentioned that he was headed to Cairo and would call from there. Next, he called Adrienne. That call too went to voicemail. He left the same message.

He knew he had maintained an optimistic perspective: *We'll find her, get her back safely.* That was his commitment. Deep down, his history had provided other lessons. CIA agents, journalists, corporate executives, and wealthy tourists had been abducted, tortured, and killed. He knew Sarah's captivity could end badly. He wondered if she'd seen the faces of her captors. If so, they'd have to kill her, whether she was ransomed or not.

If they had remained faceless, and the ransom wasn't paid, would they dump her eventually? he wondered. *I've held them off for six weeks, but how much longer can I string them along? The next deadline, August 1, may have significance to them, but why?*

He thought about placating them with a down payment of $100,000, which could be collected at a location under FBI surveillance. He thought about a locker in the bus terminal in San Francisco or a hotel fitness center in any American city.

What if they cut her loose with the realization that he wasn't going to pay or sign the agreement? he wondered. *Where would they let her go? In the snow-capped mountains in the video? She'd freeze at night, even in the summertime. If they transported her to the Middle East, would they leave her in the desert? Oh, God! She'd never survive that environment unless some nomadic tribe found her. And then what—would she become a slave to be used or sold?*

Brooks decided that he needed a walk. He left the lobby and stepped out into one hundred-and-five-degree heat. He put on an old Panama hat to shield him from the sun and walked around the boundary of the hotel. He gazed at the rolling hills in the distance.

The endless desert, he thought, *has its own fierce beauty and its unique features. It breeds a special type of person. Strong, independent people live here. Their lives are shaped by the harsh terrain. It was no wonder that many of the desert people chose simple, ascetic lives and found the opulence and conspicuous consumption of the people and governments of the West intolerable.*

He walked toward the open spaces seeking an answer to a question that had bothered him since he read the ransom note.

What was it in the minds of the Muslim Brotherhood or any of the radical Islamic groups that drove this hatred of capitalism? he wondered. *Why had he become the symbol, the face, of capitalism?*

He thought about the economic data he knew so well: The average unemployment rate throughout the Middle East was more than twenty percent, even higher for people under thirty. No economic system employed by any of the countries in the region addressed this problem. His vision and projects with international companies and local organizations were effective. Jobs had been created. A higher standard of living had emerged for those who secured these opportunities. The countries' leaders seemed to agree with his vision. His deepest worry was Egypt.

What happened there? he wondered.

He turned from the edge of the desert and walked back to the hotel. In his room, he gazed out across the city lights until he was certain of his next course of action. He went to the phone, telephoned Saudi Airlines, and booked a seat for the following morning on the first flight to Cairo.

CHAPTER 35

Sarah's Ally

Minya, Egypt

Sarah's bedroom door was open. As Akila knocked gently and walked in, she saw Sarah resting on the bed. Akila pointed to the chair in the corner.

"May I sit here?" she asked.

Sarah nodded, swung her legs to the floor, sat on the edge of the bed, and looked expectantly at her visitor. The young physician opened her hands.

"I'm sorry about the interruption yesterday. Ani needed me when I was about to ask this question: When did you arrive here? So may we start there?"

Sarah wasn't puzzled by the question, but her sense of days, weeks, and time of day had become a blur.

"To the best of my ability, I believe I've been here for ten days. I'm not certain."

Akila let off a stream of harsh Arabic phrases.

"Pardon my curses. You don't need to hear what I said. I'm most curious: Why are you here?"

Sarah took in the short, stocky woman seated in front of her. Akila was educated in the United States and obviously intelligent, but could she trust this person? Because she was one of Ani's daughters, she was related to one or all of the kidnappers.

What do I have to lose? Sarah thought. *I'll tell her story my story and see what—if anything—happens.*

"It's so complicated and confusing. I hardly know where to start. Forgive me if I ramble and confuse you. Please ask questions as I go along."

Sarah then proceeded to relate the story of her arrival at home on that fateful night and being captured by four men. When she listed the names of Jabari, Mustafa, Baligh, and Hamid, she saw Akila's jaw drop.

"No, no, Sarah. You mentioned Jabari. How did you learn that name?"

"I was with these men for many weeks. I could not see their faces because they wore masks, but I could tell them apart by voice, size, and shape. On the flight to Egypt, they had drugged me. When I woke up, their masks were off. They went back on quickly, but I'll never forget their four faces. I could draw a portrait of each one right now. And their voices matched my expectations of their faces."

"OK, Sarah—back to Jabari. It can't be him. Jabari Radwan is my cousin and living in America. In fact, he was deported from Egypt for criminal activity. The same for the other men you mentioned. They were associated with a group called the Muslim Brotherhood and fled Egypt to avoid jail. It would be most dangerous for them to be in Egypt. You must have the names wrong."

Sarah's brow wrinkled, and her mouth tightened in a grimace as she shook her head, confused. She looked at Akila.

"The group has a lead man," Sarah said. "He has a hard voice and was harsh to me. Your mother, Ani, calls him Jabari. I think the name is right."

Akila stood up.

"Wait here. I'll be right back."

She returned in a minute with Ani in tow.

"Mama, Sarah tells me that cousin Jabari Radwan is here and brought this woman with him. That can't be true. Jabari's in San Francisco, in the U.S."

Ani stared at her daughter.

"Yes, it is true," Ani said as tears formed in her eyes. "Jabari is back, risking his life by bringing this woman here. My brother's son has brought the family nothing but trouble."

Akila patted her mother on the arm and led her from the room. When she returned, she spoke.

"Mama has confirmed what you told me. All the men you mentioned have had problems with our government. You have the names right. I'd like you to continue with what happened and why."

Sarah wiped away her own tears.

"I'm sorry, but retelling brings back harsh memories. The men kidnapped me, took me to a place nearby. Then we kept moving every few days. The lead man, Jabari, said that a man I know is an enemy of Egypt. He said important powers in government want him out of the country, and they also want money to release me."

"May I say this in my own words?" Akila began. "You were kidnapped and held for ransom. That was done to get a man you know to stop doing something in Egypt. That sounds kind of crazy, doesn't it?"

"Yes. What good am I to them? I'm a widow, living alone with a nice, small practice in psychology. I'm a nobody."

"I'm confused," Akila said. "Who is this man you know? He must be famous, rich, and very closely linked to you."

"That's the part that's crazy, Akila! Jabari said this man was my husband. But he's not. He's a friend. My husband's been dead for five years. This man and I have been dating for a few months—that's all."

"But he must be famous and rich, yes?"

"Not to my knowledge. He's a university professor. He's retired from our State Department, and he does consulting work in the Middle East. Since he's a professor, I don't see how he has the time to become an enemy of this country or any country."

"I want to come back to this man, but how did you get here?"

"We flew on a private plane from Canada. I believe it was from British Columbia, in western Canada. I was drugged most of the way. Finally, when I was awake, we were in a big SUV driving toward this house."

"You flew into Cairo or a private airport?"

"I don't know," Sarah said. "I was barely awake. I remember an official of some kind looking at papers and laughing in a big shed. That's all."

Akila stood up and paced with her head down across the tattered carpet. The room was small, so her steps were few.

"Sorry. I'm thinking."

Sarah watched her for a moment.

"I don't understand Jabari," Sarah said. "How can a man who is the enemy of your government be involved in a plot to remove my friend, who is also an enemy of your government? If they both are enemies of Egypt, they should be allies—yes?"

"Sarah, Sarah," Akila said as she smiled at her.

She returned to the wooden chair and sat down, trying to find comfort in the hard seat.

"This is quite complicated. I was thinking the same thing. Here's what I've concluded: Jabari and his friends are with the Muslim Brotherhood, as are many members of my family."

She saw Sarah begin to ask a question.

"No, Sarah, not me. I'm not involved with that political movement at all. The Muslim Brotherhood could have designed this crazy plot to embarrass a top government official, possibly President Mubarak. The Brotherhood dislikes Mubarak for his reliance on American aid and his corruption with payoffs for other projects."

Sarah sat straight up on the edge of the bed. There was new energy in her.

"May I comment? It makes no sense to me why I'm involved, but is it possible that Brooks Davidson—that's my friend—was chosen to send a message to people like him? I guess their message is if Americans want to work in Egypt, they put their families at risk? Does that make sense? I mean, why not kidnap him and force him directly to agree to their demands?"

"We're headed toward the same conclusion, Sarah. It's a strange plan, but I can state one fact for certain: Jabari didn't design this plan. It had to come from a top Muslim Brotherhood figure or from a top government official—one who dislikes what is happening in the country."

"But Jabari seems very certain—very much a leader and in control."

"That's true, Sarah. Jabari's smart, but he's not clever enough to design this plot. Trust me–I'm his cousin."

"I'm still confused, Akila. What is it about Brooks Davidson they don't like? He gives advice to government officials; they can take it or leave it. Is that worth kidnapping me to get at him?"

Akila rose from the chair, walked over to the bed, and patted Sarah on the shoulder.

"Only Allah knows right now, but I intend to find out."

She turned to leave the room.

"I'll be back soon and hopefully have some answers for you."

"Oh…"

Sarah stood up.

"Really? You'll try to help me?"

Akila moved closer to Sarah and lowered her voice.

"I don't want the others to hear this."

She put a finger to her lips.

"As I said, Jabari is a workman, a man who takes orders. I need to find out who is giving the orders and the real reason you're here."

Sarah studied the kind, yet unrevealing, face of Akila.

She didn't answer my question, Sarah thought. *She may not help me. Or maybe she cannot. Could the issues with Brooks come from his years in the State Department, or could he be doing something illegal that is beyond his consulting? There could be issues to address that are well beyond Akila's knowledge.*

"Anything you can do, I appreciate," Sarah said.

Akila tapped her on the wrist.

"I'll be back."

Akila left the room and wandered through the halls of the compound in search of her mother. She found her in the kitchen.

"Mama, where is Jabari?" Akila asked.

"He and his boys—they're out hunting ducks. He told me he'd be back soon, so we'll see him shortly."

Akila left her mother and went to her sister to check on the baby. Seeing her in her crib kicking her legs, moving her arms, gurgling, and smiling, Akila knew the crisis with the child's infection was over. Hearing the noise of an engine in the courtyard, she walked out to see a black SUV park beneath a palm tree. Jabari opened the driver's door and saw Akila and waved.

"Cousin, it's been so long," Jabari said as he stepped from the car. "It's good to see you. Mama told me you were coming for the baby."

Just then, his cell phone rang, and Jabari stopped. He placed the phone against his ear and listened. He made a gesture to Akila, signaling for her to wait. He began to talk excitedly. Akila approached him with a cutting motion across her throat.

"Stop the call," she whispered.

Jabari waved her away. Akila spoke louder.

"If you don't talk to me now, I'll take the American woman to Cairo and drop her off at the American Embassy."

He cut the call short and stared at her. Finally, he hissed.

"Akila, stay out of this. You don't know what you're doing."

"Do you know what you're doing, Jabari? You're in serious danger being back in Egypt. You know that, right?"

She looked hard into his eyes.

"Once you were smart, Jabari. What's happened to you? You've kidnapped an American woman. Their covert services are good. They will find you, kill you and your associates."

"Stop, Akila; you talk crazy. You have no idea how politics work. We're trading the woman for concessions, that's all."

"You're not that dumb. Who convinced you that this was a good idea? You're brave. No one in the family ever questioned that. But this? Does someone high up have something on you. Are you being blackmailed?"

Jabari placed his cell phone back in his pocket.

"Stay out of this, cousin. The whole plan comes from on high."

Akila stepped closer to Jabari and tugged on the sleeve of his shirt.

"OK, I get it. Someone on high has a big plan in mind. But this is the Americans, Jabari. They're like the Russians—they don't like it when their people get kidnapped, hurt. This will unravel. And where will the blame be placed?"

She took her hand off his shirt and pointed a finger at him.

"On you! I don't doubt your commitment to grandfather's Brotherhood cause. You were a pawn in the big game before. Look what happened. It will happen again. You do realize that, don't you? Remember, that's why you fled to America."

Jabari flicked his hand at her dismissively.

"Cousin, stay out of it. It's much bigger than you. Despite your fancy education and your position at the medical school, you don't understand politics."

Akila left him and went in search of Sarah. Jabari watched her leave, took out his cell phone, and called Omar Sayed's daily throwaway phone. It went to voicemail, so he sent a text:

Received your message. Will place woman in desert at midday. Take video of her alone in an unknown desert, send to Davidson. That's where she'll be if he doesn't pay/sign in five days. Contingency plan received.

He walked into the house. He thought of Akila and shook his head. She was wearing a short skirt with no headscarf and had those aggressive female attitudes.

She's not a Muslim woman anymore—not to me, he thought. *She's been corrupted by the American lifestyle during medical school in Boston. But if she wants to cause me trouble, I know how to keep her quiet.*

CHAPTER 36

His Excellency

Cairo, Egypt

Earlier in the week, Frank Ticonne had told Brooks that he had secured meetings with General Murad and President Mubarak for July 25. Brooks used the time on his flight from Riyadh to Cairo to plan what he would ask the two men. He had prepared questions for top officials on more occasions than he could count. This time, a life was at stake—a life extremely important to him. He thought about how to frame the discussion in a manner that would not offend either man. He was convinced from the emerging evidence that Egyptians were involved in Sarah's kidnapping, and he worked on a line of thought that would persuade them not only to pursue Jabari Radwan but, more importantly, to determine who designed the plot.

When the plane landed at Cairo International, an embassy driver escorted Brooks through customs and out to a limousine. He knew the traffic snarl on Cairo streets tested the patience of all motorists, but today the car moved steadily toward the embassy. The guards waved them through the entry gate in the tall, sand-colored wall, and the driver parked the limo next to a bevy of embassy vehicles. Brooks gathered his travel bag from the trunk of the car and walked to the reception room with its lofty eggshell-white walls, warm desert-colored rugs, and plush red-leather chairs and couches. Ticonne stood as Brooks entered and extended his hand.

"At long last, old friend. How was the journey?"

"Fast and easy, Frank. Thank you for the car and driver—and for clearing time on your schedule."

"You and I have been in this territory for many years. Kidnapping is infrequent out here, so it's especially horrific. It's created a special kind of hell for you, hasn't it?"

For the first time in more than six weeks Brooks heard a personal note of anguish, a note of compassion and understanding of what he was going through. A surge of release flowed through him. He wanted to hug Ticonne for the empathy offered but felt it would be inappropriate. Instead, he shook his hand enthusiastically and held it an extra second.

"You, more than most, know what this is like," Brooks said. "It's been a real hell for me."

Ticonne grasped Brooks by the elbow.

"Let's get to my office and chat a bit. I want to compare notes and agree on our agenda for the meetings tomorrow."

Brooks had been in the ambassador's office on many occasions. Ticonne gestured to two chairs facing the front of his wide mahogany desk. As they sat, Brooks' eyes swept the room. He found familiar photos on every wall. There was Ticonne greeting President Carter, sitting with President Ford, talking with President Reagan. There were photos of both Bushes, both Clintons, and dignitaries from every country in the Middle East. The man's career was documented in photos. Brooks wanted to avoid the inclination to engage in small talk with an old colleague.

"I'd love to catch up with you, but your schedule is jammed. Let's get right at it. I understand we see Murad first, then Mubarak late in the day."

"I agree there's much to talk about," Ticonne said. "Maybe a drink at the end of the day? I'll find you a desk and pick you up about five. And yes, back to business. We're about to accuse this government of encouraging or, worse, orchestrating the abduction of one of our citizens. We need to frame this carefully so they won't throw us out."

"I know you visited with Mubarak and discussed the ransom note and the mention of Egypt," Brooks said. "As I recall, you thought he seemed defensive."

"He became quite disturbed when I mentioned that we had evidence of an Egyptian in the hostage-taking crew."

Brooks laughed.

"I would love to have been there when you mentioned the FBI's evidence. I can see his face now. When we meet Mubarak, let's start by asking what they've learned since you last met. Start with an open question."

"I agree," Ticonne said. "I'd like to ask if they've found that radicals from other countries were involved. We know from your sources that's unlikely—yes?"

"So far, I agree. The Saudi and Jordanian intelligence services knew nothing about this plot and were confident the people they worry about were not in the U.S. I've prepared a set of questions we could use if the conversation heads where I think it will go."

He handed Ticonne a typed sheet of questions. For the next hour, they discussed their strategy for the first meeting with General Murad and then the next with Mubarak.

★ ★ ★

When Brooks and Ticonne entered General Murad's office the next day, the old soldier greeted Brooks with enthusiasm.

"It is grand to see you again, although the topic is not one we'd choose. I've always thought of you as a true friend of Egypt. I express deepest sympathies for the abduction of your fiancée."

"Thank you, General, but, no—Sarah's a close friend, not yet a fiancée."

Murad greeted Ticonne, and they turned their attention to Fathi Ashur. Murad spoke.

"May I introduce the director of our Internal Operations, who has the responsibility to follow through on the information that the ambassador supplied to us."

Ashur, who had been standing next to the general, extended his hand to the Americans. His face was stern as he spoke in sharp, precise English.

"Gentlemen, I've reviewed the information you supplied to General Murad. I must say your supposition that this is an Egyptian plot is unfounded. The man you cite was, as you said, Egyptian and formerly of the Mukhabarat. But..."

He pointed a long, slim finger forward.

"Radwan had been expelled from Egypt for illegal wiretaps on our citizens. He's no longer Egyptian."

Brooks studied the cool demeanor of Ashur and directed a comment to him.

"I'm not interested in whether he's Egyptian or a Martian. I'm interested in who he knows in Egypt because Egypt is where he knows people."

Brooks stopped to stare at Ashur, then at the general.

"This Radwan who worked in your organization is a pawn

not capable of a grand abduction scheme. He was a computer programmer in America. He has no money or skills to pull off a caper like this. We want to know who planned this. It's natural to think the source of the idea and the money needed for this elaborate conspiracy came from this country."

Ashur remained cool as he gazed at Brooks and Ticonne.

"Both of you know the Middle East. These days, there are many active radical organizations throughout the region. Since he was expelled from our country, I expect Radwan was a natural recruiting target for Al-Qaeda, Al Muharib, and several others who want to cause your country trouble. He was available in your country to do harm."

Ticonne interjected, addressing Murad.

"General, since this man is Egyptian, who would be supporting him if such support were to come from Egypt?"

Murad decided to lighten the mood.

"Gentlemen, we've been standing. Let us sit and discuss this in a more comfortable manner."

He directed them to a set of chairs near his desk.

"Back to your question, ambassador. A long-standing problem for us has been the Muslim Brotherhood. They're a natural group to question. We're doing that, and Director Ashur can cover it better than I. My opinion is that the planning and money you mentioned are not coming from this country but from one of the radical groups out of Iran or possibly Iraq. I agree with one of your statements."

He looked at Brooks.

"I did not know this Radwan when he was employed here, but I'm certain he would not have the skills to organize this abduction. It had to come from a well-financed, sophisticated group."

Brooks turned to Fathi Ashur.

"Director, my impression of the Muslim Brotherhood in Egypt is that they are trying to become a legitimate political force. Are they likely to be behind a plot like this? It would seem this action would undermine their image of political respectability, no?"

Ashur moistened his lips before replying.

"I agree they've not been a problem in the last few years. But they dislike President Mubarak and, from time to time, seek to embarrass him. My people are questioning several of their activists to determine what they know about this plot."

"And where are these activists?" Ticonne asked.

"Some are in jail, and some have been recently released," Ashur replied. "These interrogations are ongoing."

Brooks spoke next.

"Director, are you investigating any of the other groups you mentioned, like Al-Qaeda or Al-Hura? Are they active, troublesome, these days?"

"Yes, Dr. Davidson, we have our eyes on several groups and have access to them. They are being interrogated as well."

The four men talked for another thirty minutes, but little of consequence came of it. Ticonne signaled to Brooks, and both men rose. Ticonne spoke next.

"You'll let us know if any information on the location of Sarah Pierce emerges from your investigations? We appreciate your efforts."

Brooks faced the general.

"Before we depart, one last question."

"Certainly, Brooks. Go ahead."

"I'm curious why I was singled out in the ransom note. I'm one investment advisor and can cover only a few projects. Why weren't Goldman Sachs or the investment banks in London,

Paris, Frankfort mentioned? The big banks offer so much more in services and capital. Do you have any thoughts on that?"

Ashur and Murad looked at each other and shook their heads.

"No, but let us think about that," the general said.

Later in the day, Brooks and Ticonne traveled to the Heliopolis Palace to meet with President Mubarak. His office was wide and deep. Tall windows amplified the effect of size in the room. The polished marble floor added to the grandeur of the office of the head of state. Mubarak welcomed them as they sat on couches far from the president's working desk. Mubarak, joined by Foreign Minister Hamdi, opened the conversation while placing a hand on Brooks' arm.

"I can understand your distress, my friend. It must be severe. I am so sad for you. I hope the general and his staff gave you confidence that our Mukhabarat and police will do everything in their power to find Mrs. Pierce. I have emphasized this."

"Excellency, I appreciate your interest in my case," Brooks said. "It is most reassuring. If I may, I have a couple of questions for you, as does Ambassador Ticonne."

"Of course," Mubarak replied with a wave of his hand as he removed it from Brooks' arm. "Who goes first?"

He let out a short laugh.

"I'll be brief, Excellency," Ticonne said, "but I ask that if your police or Mukhabarat discover who organized this plot and recover Mrs. Pierce that we at the embassy are notified immediately. We seek to determine the proper procedures for recovery and prosecution."

"Certainly, Mr. Ambassador," Mubarak replied. "We have working procedures in place and will follow them as we have in the past."

"My questions," Brooks said with a smile, "are brief. First, Excellency, I want to assure you that I do not want to create difficulties for you. If you wish me to stop bringing investment ideas to you, I will do that. And I thank you for the opportunities we pursued in the past."

"Dr. Davidson… Brooks—you are so different than the bankers who only bring me deals. They say, 'Buy this; buy that,' and their proposals never fit the skills of my people nor the needs of the country. It is true, I see you less often than the bankers, but when you come, your ideas fit our needs. I want more of you, not less. This ransom note that the ambassador showed me is the exact opposite of what I want. I want you to believe that."

Brooks nodded and smiled at the president's statement of support.

"My second question, Excellency, is about the ransom note. I mentioned this fact earlier to General Murad. Why am I the only advisor the kidnappers want removed from Egypt, Saudi Arabia, and so on? What about the bankers from London or Paris? So I was thinking: Who benefits from my leaving Egypt or any of these countries? It must be personal. Someone, some individual, must benefit. Or possibly someone or some dissidents in the country are using your ties to the West to embarrass you."

"Do you know who that might be in Saudi Arabia, Jordan, the other countries?" Mubarak asked.

"I've visited these countries, talked to your counterparts, like King Fahd. We haven't found anyone yet."

"And here?"

"I think your Mukhabarat or police might want to talk with your minister of Trade and Industry, Omar Sayed," Brooks said. "There may be others in your government who are hostile to this regime, as I mentioned previously."

"Others—they do exist, Brooks. There are those who want to expose me, embarrass me, but we know who they are. But Sayed? Oh, no. He's been ineffective—that, I realize. He brings little ideas that employ hundreds, not the millions of jobs we need. He's still an academic. No, not him."`

"Excellency, he's a cabinet minister and, as you've said, he's not pulling his weight. That may be a source of great frustration to him."

Mubarak turned to Hamdi.

"What do you think? Should we have Sayed interrogated?

CHAPTER 37

Akila's Plan

Minya, Egypt

Since she arrived in Minya, Akila had spent time visiting with her mother and ensuring that her sister's child recovered from pneumonia. She also spent hours talking to Sarah. Fascinated by Sarah's ordeal, Akila thought hard about Jabari's plan, seeking to understand its logic. She could not grasp who would benefit from the abduction of this gentle, lovely woman. The plan sounded weird. The idea that Sarah's friend, Brooks Davidson, would pay substantial dollars to free her and agree to stop all work in Egypt seemed to be devoid of good thinking. Reluctantly, she realized, she might be missing something. She simply could not deduce anything clever about the plan. She concluded that this was a crazy, impulsive act by a madman. To her, it was morally wrong in the eyes of Allah, and it was her duty to correct the sin. She searched for her mother and found her in the kitchen peeling vegetables.

"Mama, do you have a valise or small suitcase I can borrow?"

"Yes, my dear. It's old and battered. You can keep it. Are you leaving so soon?"

"I'll be back, Mama. The suitcase is for the woman. She's going to travel. I want her to look like an Egyptian with an old suitcase, headscarf, and abaya."

"She's leaving with cousin Jabari and his men?"

"No, Mama, you must tell no one, especially Jabari, that the woman is traveling. This is our bond—our love bond. The men have done wrong—a wrong against Allah, Mama."

Ani went to her room and pulled out a battered brown suitcase the size of an overnight traveling kit and placed it at Akila's feet.

"You are right, my love. I've been most uncomfortable with Jabari and his men. It's God's will that I help. I promise silence. The woman saved the life of Anit's little one. If this will help her, I want to do it."

Akila carried the suitcase to Sarah's room. Gently, she knocked on the door and entered. "Sarah?"

Resting in the afternoon heat, Sarah lay on her bed, her eyes focused on the ceiling fan that kept the air moving. She had been attempting to meditate, seeking the zone within that gave her the greatest sense of peace, but her concentration was fleeting. When the door opened, she was startled. No one came to her room in the afternoon. It was quiet time in the house. Jabari and his men were out hunting birds. The women were resting, sewing, or preparing food. The greeting frightened her. She thought it might be the lecherous kidnapper, Hamid. She rose from the bed ready to fight and scream. Seeing Akila with the piece of luggage, she flopped back on the bed.

"Are you leaving?"

Akila put a finger to her lips. She spoke quietly.

"You're leaving. I have an idea, if you're willing."

Sarah sat up with a puzzled feeling inside.

"What? Leave? How is that possible? Or is it to another prison?"

Akila's mouth opened wide. She had guessed right about the American woman. Sarah was still very frightened—a selfless, decent, gentle lamb in the clutches of wolves.

"Patience, Sarah," she said as she sketched out her plan.

At the end of it, Sarah placed her Sunset Cove clothes in the suitcase while Akila went in search of her driver. He was in the kitchen, dining on a falafel and tea. He listened to Akila's instructions, finished his meal, then walked to the car in the courtyard. He turned on the ignition to set the air conditioning on high and waited behind the wheel for Sarah and Akila. With Jabari and his men away from the compound, the two women walked quickly out the entryway to avoid detection from the others in the house. Two steps into the midday heat had Sarah sweating under the abaya and headscarf. Getting into the back seat, Akila advised Sarah to lie down on the floor behind the seats until they were past the guards at the gate. Akila spoke to her driver.

"Ahmed, leave the courtyard slowly. Make it evident we're in no rush. Then drive us to the train station in Minya."

Sarah, still prone behind the back seats, spoke up.

"Akila, you told me your plan, but I've been thinking: I can't go on a train. I don't know where to go, and a woman cannot travel without a man in this country. I've learned that much about your culture."

"Here, we got lucky, Sarah. In one of those wonderful coincidences, my medical technician at the hospital—his name's Masudi; remember that name, Sarah—is returning to Cairo after a short visit with his parents in Minya. I've talked with him. He's willing to escort you to Cairo."

"I don't understand."

"He'll purchase the tickets, be your escort to the platform and the train, and accompany you to Cairo. Once you arrive, he'll get you a taxi either to a hotel or the U.S. embassy—your choice."

Akila paused, scanning Sarah's face.

"You look confused. Do you remember our plan?"

Akila's fast flow of directions caused Sarah distress. She sat up and faced Akila. "I'm sorry. I do remember your plan, but this is moving very rapidly. I don't have money to buy a train ticket or a cab ride. And I don't want to get you in trouble."

"I've given this a lot of thought, Sarah. On the money, I've taken several Egyptian pounds from Ani's purse. When she discovers it's gone, she'll think you stole it. I did that as a way to fool Jabari into thinking you escaped on your own. You'll give the money to my tech. He'll use it to purchase the tickets and give you back the rest for cab fare. Once you're on the train, you'll not be detected as no one knows you're missing. Your headscarf and abaya protect you. No one will recognize you or give you a second look. Besides, you're safe traveling with a man."

"I don't know the language except for a few phrases. What if the conductor asks me questions, wants to see a passport?"

"Good questions, Sarah. Masudi will say you're visiting from Russia and don't speak our language. Your passport? Rarely do they ask, but if it happens, he'll say it's in your hotel in Cairo."

"And the men, Akila. They'll be after me."

"They're not that bright, Sarah. By the time they've returned from hunting, you'll be on the train to Cairo. Ani and I will say we saw you sleeping in your room before we went to rest. We'll act very surprised you're not in your room and suggest you must have left the compound for a walk. They'll spend too much time grilling me and asking Ani and my cousins endless questions. Then they'll start driving through the neighborhood asking people if they saw someone with your description. They'll never figure out where you've gone. Even if they do conclude you left by boat or train, by that time you'll be in Cairo."

"What about Masudi? He won't squeal?"

"He's a very good man, fully devoted to the same ideals for living and for honest government that I have. He was astounded when he heard your story. He wants to help. You'll go to your embassy, right? Once there, the men and the brains behind this can't touch you."

She looked over at Sarah expectantly. Sarah's mouth pulled back in a self-effacing wince.

"Sorry, I'm a little slow and stunned at the prospect of getting free. Thank you for your help, your patience. I'm beginning to visualize how this plan could work."

She looked at Akila, surprise on her face.

"Oh my God—you're totally amazing. But why are you doing this when it can only bring you trouble?"

"It's a long story. Quite simply, I agree with my family's issues about our previous dictators, corrupt governments, and particularly with past foreign domination. I don't like Mubarak's regime. That's a longer story. However, I do believe in decency and fair treatment of people who disagree with government policies. What my cousin has done, by kidnapping you, is morally wrong even if he believes this addresses some evil Mubarak has done. If they had kidnapped the real enemy of the state, that would make sense to me. But going after you? It boggles the mind and is totally wrong. I had to do something."

"How can I thank you?"

"You're not free and clear yet. Wait for that. When you get free, I want to hear from you to make certain you're safe. You must be careful when you contact me. I'll give you a safe way to do that."

She took a notepad from her pocket book and scribbled a message on a scrap of prescription paper.

"Follow these directions. We'll find a way to talk."

When they reached the doors to the train station, Akila guided Sarah to the bustling interior and the kiosk where her technician waited. He greeted Akila with a kiss on each cheek, then faced Sarah.

"I'm Masudi, and you're the brave American?" he said in whispered tones.

Sarah bowed to him in acknowledgement and turned back to Akila. Awkwardly, with the abaya compromising her movements, Sarah reached to hug Akila. Akila did likewise.

"This is not a custom of mine, but, for some reason, I like the gesture from you," Akila said. "You're very forgiving, aren't you?"

"Forgiving?" asked Sarah, surprise in her eyes. "There's nothing to forgive here. You've helped me from the moment you arrived. I thank God for you. You're a miracle."

She thought this stranger had done more for her than Brooks, her government, or anyone else. Akila watched Sarah and Masudi turn and head to the ticket counter.

Don't linger, she silently advised Sarah. *Don't give any Egyptian police officer an ounce of time for recognition.*

As Ahmed drove her from the train station, Akila said a quiet prayer for Sarah's safe passage. When they arrived at the compound, she told Ahmed to drive back to Cairo and that she'd return by train in a day or two. She noticed, with relief, that Jabari's SUV was not in the courtyard and went straight to her room. As she rested, she worried about Jabari's rage on Ani and her cousins when he discovered that Sarah was gone. She thought she had a convincing story and went over it again and again. She believed he'd never deduce where Sarah was or her role in it. He might suspect her but would never have proof. She was protected by the normal behavior of her family in the afternoons and the ironclad silence promised by her mother and her driver.

CHAPTER 38

Concerted Actions

Minya and Cairo, Egypt

Jabari and his men had stopped tracking birds at the edge of the desert. In the tent they had pitched earlier on the sun-baked sand, they sat in its shade, drinking pomegranate juice.

"Let's wait till dusk," Baligh suggested. "There'll be more birds when it's cooler."

Jabari stood up and dusted off his pants.

"No, I think not. I'm ready for a smoke and a drink. Time to cool down in a café. Then we'll get back to the compound and look in on the hostage."

He rubbed his hands together, wiped the light oil off the barrel of his rifle, and faced his men.

"I want to talk with Minister Sayed. The fucking American has offered more money, but he's still insistent on staying in Egypt. We've got to get this shit straightened out and be done. Get all our cash."

Mustafa began to take down the tent poles and roll up the canopy.

"Jabari, I want this over. I want to get back to the U.S. for work. I can't last much longer."

Jabari gave him a short glance and walked toward the SUV. "Yeah, yeah—let's get going. I'll talk to the minister."

★ ★ ★

Akila was resting in her room reading a medical journal when she heard the crunch of gravel in the courtyard and knew it was Jabari's SUV. She stiffened in her bed, awaiting the raucous scream from Jabari when he learned that the hostage was missing.

Jabari left the men to collect the rifles and carry the cooler filled with guinea fowl into the house. A dark premonition clouded his mind and startled him. He had been out hunting longer than usual. His intuition told him to check on the hostage straight away. He went directly to Sarah's room and entered without knocking. Stunned, he swept the empty room with his eyes. Momentarily confused and thinking she normally rests at this hour, he stared at the empty bed. Scratching his head, he walked slowly toward the kitchen. He looked left, then right, thinking Sarah might have risen earlier than normal and would appear momentarily in one of the hallways. Reaching the kitchen, he saw Ani.

"Where's the American?"

Ani looked up from her pile of vegetables.

"In her room, resting. I haven't seen her since midday meal."

Jabari walked throughout the rambling house, asking the women in different rooms if they'd seen the American. They stopped talking, put their sewing down, and shook their heads—no. Jabari went back to the courtyard, told his men to search every room for the hostage, and asked the guard at the gate if he let two women out for a walk. The gatekeeper looked up from his magazine and shook his head.

"Not much activity all day. Your SUV left, and the doctor's SUV left. The doctor came back. Then her SUV left again. Just the driver and the doctor—that's all."

Back inside, Jabari and his men convened in the main living area.

"She's not in any of the rooms," Mustafa said.

Jabari pulled the cell phone from his cargo pants pocket and called Omar Sayed. Sayed was in his office and alone at his desk. He fumbled in the desk drawer to find the throwaway phone. Seeing Radwan's code on the face of the phone, he frowned.

"What is it, Radwan? I'm busy."

"Minister, have you moved the woman and not told me?"

Sayed's voice rose.

"What … what kind of stupid question is that? Of course I've not moved the woman."

A string of Arabic curses followed.

"Why?"

Jabari spoke slowly.

"We've searched the house, the grounds. She's not here."

Jabari pulled the phone away from his ear. Hamid standing nearby heard the minister screaming into the phone. Jabari kept his voice calm.

"She probably went for a walk with one of the women. We'll find her."

When objections from Sayed mounted, he spoke again.

"Minister, in the heat of the day, she'll not go far. She does not know where she is. She has no money, no language ability. We'll find her quickly."

He promised to call as soon as they found her. As soon as he ended the call, he barked at his men.

"Search the rooms again and start looking on the streets outside the compound!"

He stormed back into the kitchen and faced Ani.

"She's not in her room or in the courtyard. Where is she?"

Ani appeared confused.

"What...what do you mean? She's not with me."

Jabari walked over to another aunt in the kitchen. He towered over her and raised his hand. The woman cowered and shrieked.

"I have not seen her since the meal," she wailed.

Jabari walked through the other rooms and quizzed all the women again. They claimed no knowledge of Sarah's movements. They had heard no cars coming or going from the courtyard, and no visitors had arrived. It had been a quiet day. Ani followed him around the house.

"It's too hot to walk outside, Jabari, but she must have done that while the guards were having their lunch."

Akila, aroused by the noise, appeared from her room.

"What's all the commotion about?"

Jabari glared at her.

"The woman's gone. What do you know about this?"

Akila faced him, her eyes and face a picture of total calm.

"I've been sleeping, but I imagine she got restless and went for a walk."

Jabari turned to his men, who had gathered around him. He snarled at Baligh.

"Get the SUV and search the road to central Minya!"

Then he turned to Mustafa and Hamid.

"Search the neighborhoods," he ordered. "Go door to door. See if she asked for help or is hiding in another house."

He watched them run out the door, then turned toward Akila. "We must talk."

As Akila walked away, Jabari reached for his cell phone and stomped out to the courtyard. He called Minister Sayed. After six rings, it went to voicemail. He left a message: *"Minister, the search is on by foot in neighborhoods, by car on nearby roads, and eventually we'll check all transport stations in Minya."*

He went back into the house and found Akila alone in her bedroom. She was bent over the desk, typing on her computer.

"Stop!" Jabari commanded. "I want to talk."

Akila didn't look up.

"I'm busy. Later."

"Now, woman!"

Her fingers continue to fly on the keyboard, her eyes focused on the screen.

"No! Are you hard of hearing?"

He slapped the wall and left her room. Akila called after him.

"Have you informed your bosses that you've lost the hostage?"

He turned back toward her doorway and yelled.

"Akila, you know more about this than you're saying. I'll get to the bottom of this."

Just then, his phone rang. Omar Sayed was abrupt.

"Have you found the woman?"

Jabari went into the courtyard. He paced while talking, staying away from the house and the gatekeeper's post so no other ears could hear.

"As I said in my voicemail, we have an aggressive search. I've broadened it out to include all Christian churches in the area."

Sayed demanded an answer.

"How can she get away when she has no money, no knowledge of where she is, and no language skills to ask for directions or call a taxi? Someone must have helped her. What about the people in your safe house? Are they all related to the Muslim Brotherhood?"

"Yes, Minister. The wives of many Brotherhood men are here.

They've been loyal guardians of the hostage, although there is one I should question aggressively."

"Do it and get back to me fast," Sayed ordered. "In the meantime, I'll have my personnel guarding all the boat docks, the train station, and the entrance to the American embassy in case she found a way to get to Cairo."

He stopped for a second.

"Describe what she was wearing, color of her eyes, her hair. I'll get my people moving."

"I believe she was wearing a gray abaya this morning. Her eyes are green, and her hair's been dyed black and is covered by a headscarf. She's very tall, nearly as tall as me."

A string of Arab curses stung Jabari's ear.

"Listen, Jabari, a tall woman wearing a gray abaya describes a million or more women in Cairo every day. That's no help. Get to all the transport stations fast. Find her. You know the consequences of failure."

Jabari wanted to tell the minister to go fuck himself but knew his future was dependent on the minister's goodwill.

"We're on it here. I know how to scare the women in the compound if any of them helped her."

"Call me in an hour."

Sayed ended the call. He was back on the phone immediately, calling his chief of staff.

"Taha, I need you to activate a team of inspectors. I've been told by our field agent in Minya there is a radical woman who left a message online that she intends to disrupt port activities or trains into Cairo. She may be carrying a bomb. Post men at each transport center. I'll send you her description. Also, place two agents near the entrance to the American, British, and French embassies in case the woman seeks asylum in one of those countries."

Next, he called Fathi Ashur.

"*It's urgent, cousin,*" he said in his message. "*Same place, same time, late this afternoon.*"

★ ★ ★

When Omar arrived, Fathi was already there, as usual, smoking a cigarette, his troublesome left leg protruding out to the path. Omar stepped over the leg and sat next to Fathi.

"Fathi, you've been so quiet, so remote in recent days. Are you all right?"

Fathi puffed on his cigarette and released a billow of smoke.

"Basically, I'm OK, but I'm meeting with you for the last time. In our prior meeting, I gave you some advice, and you ignored it. You're becoming toxic, cousin. I warned you a week or so ago."

"I didn't ignore what you told me, Fathi. I said it was premature. Now it may be time to take your advice."

Fathi took a long drag from the cigarette and became quiet, organizing his thoughts. He felt a familial responsibility for his cousin, but he worried it had become a stretch too far.

"Omar, I was with the president yesterday. General Murad was there, as was the foreign secretary. As you know, the Americans are livid and very active in their search for the woman who's been kidnapped, and—."

"She's escaped," Omar interrupted. "That's why I wanted to meet. She disappeared this afternoon."

Fathi brushed the smoke away from his face. He glared at Omar with disdain.

"After two months, you've lost the hostage? This is one fucking disaster after another." He sucked again on his cigarette.

"It strengthens what I want to say, and why I want to say it."

He waved the cigarette at Omar.

"Sorry. I interrupted you. Did you want to say more about her escape?"

"Yes, I'm asking for your help. Can you supply some agents and use your network of contacts to help find her?"

When Fathi looked over at Omar, his face was sad.

"First let me tell you why I agreed to meet."

Omar nodded.

"As I started to say," Fathi began, "the meeting with the top brass was all about your plot. Dr. Davidson and the American ambassador were there as well. The Americans were not polite. In fact, Davidson was downright insulting. The Americans have evidence that Jabari Radwan was the leader of your plot. They knew he worked in the Mukhabarat. They laid that observation rather heavily on me. Then Davidson made the aggressive assertion that our president has problems in his own government. Davidson and the ambassador made it quite clear that a sophisticated Egyptian is likely to have organized the kidnapping to expose and embarrass the president. Davidson went on to say the president ought to look within his own administration for people who might want to embarrass or expose him for accepting too much Western technology and capital. Davidson implied that the manager of this plot was likely to have a vendetta against him as well as issues with the president. He suggested the president have his interior police, meaning me, interrogate administrators who might have Brotherhood or other groups' radical interests. Then Davison mentioned you by name."

"What?"

"Yes—you."

"What did the president say?"

"Actually, he saw you as an unlikely candidate. However, not for reasons you'd find complimentary."

"Fuck! Fuck! Fuck! What did he say to you?"

"He and General Murad want me and my internal ops unit to conduct the interrogations. The general and I went over the president's list of his most vocal enemies. I have my marching orders."

"So do it. It's a good smokescreen until I find the hostage and get this sorted out with Davidson."

"There's no time for that, Omar. You're on the list. Here's what you'll do: Prepare a letter of resignation, conveying to the president that you want to return to academia, and you appreciated the opportunity to work as a top administrator in his government. Then you, Hasina, and the children will leave the country with no forwarding address."

Omar was momentarily stunned to silence. He began to wring his hands, and drops of sweat appeared on his brow.

"There's no way they can trace this to me. They'll never find the kidnappers or ever find the woman."

Fathi finished his cigarette, stared at the red-hot tip, and flicked it onto the pathway. He stood up, brushed off his pants, and straightened his jacket. He looked down at Omar.

"Do as I say. Leave or be prepared for interrogation by my people."

He kicked the dying ember of his cigarette down the path as he walked away.

CHAPTER 39

Identified

Cairo, Egypt

On the train, Sarah whispered to Masudi.

"I know we shouldn't talk—someone might hear our English—but I want to thank you from the bottom of my heart."

He patted her gently on the arm.

"My English is simple, basic, and I understand," Masudi said. "You're welcome. It's OK. Pretend to sleep. I'll keep the conductors away."

She closed her eyes and sought to subdue the anxiety that coursed through her body like an electric current. Sarah placed her head against the back of the seat and tried to meditate. She worked on her mantra: *Free me. Free me.* She repeated it again and again in a soft drone, yet she could not stop the flashing images in her mind's eye. The masked faces of her captors jumped into her consciousness, breaking the soothing rhythm of the mantra and pounding her with the fear of getting caught. She realized her captors hated Americans and worried she would confront that hostility once Masudi placed her in a taxi. She tried to find a comfortable position in the seat, yet the long abaya constrained her movements, making comfort nearly impossible. Masudi could see her unrest and reached over to touch her arm.

"You're going to be safe; don't worry."

"May I take your hand?" she whispered.

Masudi nodded, and she placed her thin hand in his large, warm palm. It soothed her for a moment before she felt it was an inappropriate gesture in their culture and pulled her hand away.

"Thank you," she said shyly.

Again, she rested against the back of the seat and tried meditation. After a few minutes, she grew restless.

"What time is it?" she asked.

Masudi showed her his watch and pointed to the hour of their arrival.

"We have another hour to go."

Every few minutes, she would grasp his wrist and check on the time. It felt like the train was on an endless journey. With each mile, the Cairo station seemed to step farther and farther away. She tried breathing exercises to calm her nerves. Nothing worked. When the train slowed to enter the station, she jumped from the seat and reached overhead to get the small suitcase she had brought. Masudi calmly restrained her.

"Easy, Sarah. Slow down. We've made it. We'll walk slowly to the taxi station. Just follow me. Do as I do."

She wanted to bolt from the train and sprint to the waiting taxis but followed his directions. When they reached the taxi stand, she stood behind Masudi as he provided the address to the driver, then gave Sarah two hundred fifty Egyptian pounds for the trip. Because she didn't know the proper gesture to thank a Muslim man, she bowed her head toward him and joined her hands in a prayer gesture at her chest.

"Thank you so much," she said. "You have no idea how grateful

I am. I will find some way to repay your kindness and courage. I have a way to contact Akila. I will find you again."

Masudi extended his hand to her.

"You're the one with courage. May you get safely home. I'm honored to help."

She took his hand and wrapped it in both of hers, tears welling in her eyes. She reached for the door of the taxi that Masudi had opened. She dropped into the seat, gathered the abaya around her, and placed the suitcase on her lap. The driver turned his head to her, then spoke in perfect English.

"Your escort said it's the U.S. embassy, ma'am."

"Yes, sir," she replied in perfect Arabic.

She waved goodbye to Masudi as the taxi pulled away from the curb. A short while later, when she spotted the American flag at the embassy entrance, she was nearly dizzy with delight.

"Oh my God!" she said half-audibly to herself. "Have I really made it? I'm here. I've escaped. I'm free."

The driver heard some words but didn't understand what she said. He turned to her. "Ma'am?"

She felt like crying, but no tears would come.

"Sorry. I'm excited!"

She jumped from the taxi, dumping her suitcase onto the pavement. She kicked it aside and reached into the front window of the taxi and gave the driver all the Egyptian pounds Masudi had given her.

"Ma'am, too much," the driver protested.

"I don't care. I'm free," she exulted. "Thank you. Thank you."

As she picked up her suitcase, she looked at the driver with tears forming. She brushed them away, hurried to the Marine guard station, and stripped the scarf from her head, revealing black hair that showed touches of blond roots. She looked at the ramrod-straight Marine and made an announcement.

"I'm Sarah Pierce, an American seeking safety. I've been a hostage of terrorists for the past two months."

Polite but firm, the Marine studied her up and down.

"I can help, ma'am, but first I must check for explosives on your body and in your luggage. Put down the case, ma'am, and extend your arms. I'll pat you down."

Seconds later, he was satisfied that she carried no bombs under the abaya or in the suitcase.

"Follow me," he instructed.

As he left his post to take Sarah to a room at the rear of the guard station, he instructed a fellow Marine.

"Cover the front, call for reserves, and call reception for this visitor. She claims to be an American and an escaped hostage. Her name is Sarah Pierce."

In the small room, the Marine corporal spoke.

"Ma'am, I will have to body search you again from head to toe."

He watched as Sarah stared at the one chair in the room, collapsed on it, and placed her head in her hands. He gazed down at her.

"Are you all right, ma'am? Do you understand? I must search for weapons."

"Sorry, I can't get over it. I'm free."

She looked up at him, seeking some form of recognition that he understood her ordeal. Her hands fluttered in a nervous gesture.

"Do you want the abaya off? I don't know what to do."

The corporal was quite serious.

"Ma'am, just take off your sandals, then lift your arms out to the wall."

The Marine conducted the search more thoroughly this time. He used an electronic wand, sweeping it inch by inch up and down the abaya. Then he checked her over with his hands. He left nothing to chance. Sarah was delighted to be in American custody, but expressing her thoughts was difficult. She couldn't find the words to explain her questions or to offer him appreciation.

"What's next?" was all she could manage.

"I'll be through in a minute. Then you'll be taken to people who can answer your questions."

She pushed long strands of hair off her forehead. The movement was jerky, and she poked a fingernail into her scalp.

"Ouch! Damn! Sorry, but I want to be protected from the kidnappers who, I know, are looking for me."

"Yes, ma'am. You're safe now. Here's your escort."

Two Marine guards appeared, then took Sarah to an office that, to her, looked like a large reception room. The lead guard, a sergeant, asked her for identification.

"Passport, ma'am?"

Sarah shook her head.

"Anything? We need to prove you are who you claim to be."

Desperate to prove she was a legitimate hostage and an American citizen, Sarah rattled off her story so fast that it became a flood of details and baffled her Marine guards.

"With no passport or other identification, ma'am, it's not us you must convince," the sergeant said. "Think how best to tell your story to one of the diplomats."

The two Marines assumed positions on either side of the exit door and asked Sarah to sit and wait. Sarah sat on a cushioned chair, fidgeting with her hands, glancing at the pictures on the wall: large photos of American landscapes. Her eyes rested on a mountain peak that looked like Mount Baker in Wyoming. She and her late husband had hiked there. The memory and familiarity of the mountain calmed her. She began to relax and feel more secure. The minutes seemed like hours before a young man entered the room. Sarah studied him. He was short and handsome, with closely cropped light brown hair and warm brown eyes.

He's too young to be of much help, she thought.

His manner was curt.

"I'm Samuel Barstow. I'm here to understand your situation. Please—your name and address."

Sarah responded quickly, then launched into her story. His eyes widened.

"You're the Sarah Pierce who was kidnapped in Northern California about two months ago? You're *that* Sarah Pierce?"

He studied her carefully, looking for a break in her composure.

"I have a thousand questions for you," he continued, "but first, do you have any proof of identity?"

She bit her lip.

"No."

She paused for a second.

"Wait a minute. Will a prescription bottle be helpful? I have one in my suitcase."

"Sure; that could be a start. The guards found pills when they checked your suitcase but didn't tell me where. Go ahead, get the prescription bottle. Then I'll ask questions that will help us confirm your identity."

"The bottle's in the pocket of my jacket."

She handed the bottle to Barstow, who scanned the bottle and noticed her name on it.

She could have picked this up from the real Sarah Pierce, he thought.

His eyes swept her from head to toe, taking in the streaky black-blond hair, the tanned face, and the ill-fitting abaya.

"Look, you must understand that we've had many false leads in this case. Hundreds of people have called the State Department saying they saw you in Las Vegas, Portland, Seattle, Geneva, and Brussels. Others have claimed to be you and said they had escaped the captors in Sacramento, Los Angeles, even Lake Tahoe. They all want restitution. If you're the real Sarah Pierce, help me so I can help you."

"Who are you?" Sarah asked. "What do you do here?"

"I'm the chief political/economic officer in the embassy and generally the first stop to provide authentication of Americans who need our help. I'd like to start with the basics: your fingerprints and a photo."

He pointed to a tall, angular woman who had accompanied him into the room.

"This fine lady will take your prints and picture. We'll send them to your Department of Motor Vehicles in California to identify you and confirm your address. OK?"

A short while later, as Sarah's fingerprints were taken, Barstow plowed through questions that she found tiresome—until he asked one in particular.

"Do you know a Brooks Davidson?"

She corrected her posture and sat straight up in her chair. Absently, she touched her face with her stained fingers.

"Know him? Of course I know him. Or, at least, I thought I knew him. He got me into this mess, according to Jabari and my other jailors."

"You know the names of your captors?"

"Yes. I heard them speaking to each other from time to time

and, for one short instance, I saw their faces on the flight to Egypt. The leader was this Jabari. He was cold and difficult. He hit me on occasion. Mustafa was nice and would stop him. Hamid was weird, scary. His hands were always twitching by his sides. Baligh was quiet—never said much. I escaped from a large house in Minya with many halls and rooms. Women and children live there, but I didn't get any of the women's names."

"Describe Davidson and how you knew him."

"He's in his early sixties, a professor at Stanford. He's tall, over six feet, medium build, with a mix of brown and gray hair, though mostly gray. He worked in your department for many years, then retired to teach. He has a large condo in Palo Alto and drives a huge Lexus SUV. Do you need more?"

"I do. We'll send a copy of the photo to Davidson as well, OK?"

Barstow spent the next hour asking Sarah questions about her work, telephone numbers, and names of colleagues, children, siblings, and friends. He asked for data on the vehicles she owned. The questions rolled nonstop until her jaws began to ache from talking. She realized that she had not had a lengthy conversation in nearly two months. Barstow gave the information to the woman who had taken Sarah's fingerprints. As she raced off, he called after her.

"Get Ms. Pierce's photo, the vehicle data, and fingerprints to the Cal DMV first."

He turned to Sarah and offered his first smile.

"Sorry about all the questions, but we need to make certain you are the real Sarah Pierce. To find you in Egypt is a major surprise."

"They moved me a lot. I never knew why."

"As I understand it from Ambassador Ticonne, there were dozens of FBI and CIA agents looking for you. Your captors were on the run."

"So much is confusing," Sarah admitted. "I'm overwhelmed at the moment."

Barstow smiled again.

"I'm not surprised. I'll bet you'd like to get out of the abaya, take a nice long, shower, and put on some fresh American clothes."

She studied his face, not quite certain of his sincerity. She felt uneasy with him. She was convinced that he didn't believe her story and wouldn't until the California DMV confirmed the information.

"Are you going to send it to Brooks Davidson too? I know his email address."

"No need, Ms. Pierce. He's in the country somewhere. We'll get him here."

Sarah's shock was evident. Her mouth dropped wide open.

"In Egypt?"

"Yes, ma'am," Barstow said. "I believe he's with Ambassador Ticonne meeting right now with Egyptian officials."

"Oh, God," she moaned. "So much has happened."

I don't know what to think, she thought. *How can I talk to him? I'm not ready. What will I say?*

"When will he be here?" she asked, in a barely audible voice.

Barstow pulled a cell phone from his pocket and punched in a set of numbers.

"Caroline, can you join us?"

A young woman entered the room and introduced herself as Caroline Bates.

"I'll take you to a guest room for a shower and change of clothes. Would you like that?" Sarah nodded.

"Please follow me," Caroline said.

As Sarah left the room, she looked back at Barstow.

"When will Brooks Davidson arrive?"

"Ma'am, I don't know, but I'll find out," Barstow said. "I'll call your room or tell Caroline as soon as we know."

As they walked toward the guest room, Sarah thought about what she would say to Brooks.

How do I deal with what he did to me?

CHAPTER 40

Late-Night Flight

Cairo, Egypt

Omar Sayed walked back to his office, distressed from the conversation with Fathi Ashur. He thought Fathi had lost respect for him. That hurt him deeply. He was certain that his plot to abduct the American woman was foolproof. It could never be linked to him. His agents or Jabari would find the woman. She would have no idea where to go to get free. But as he thought about it, interrogation by his cousin's ops staff was a process he wanted to avoid. They could reveal his culpability. Fathi's staff, he knew, was excellent. It was considered by officials in other countries as one of the best intelligence agencies in the Middle East.

Could they break me? he wondered. *Do I have the strength to resist?*

He plunked down in the comfortable leather chair behind his desk. He scrolled through the messages on his computer, then closed the screen. He had no desire to work. He wondered if his wife and children had reached their villa in Brissago on Lake Maggiore. They would be safe there, no matter what happened to him. He had made a vow with Hasina to keep their villa in the hills above the lake a secret from family and friends. He felt that someday he might need a hideaway. Now he was pleased with his planning. Feeling restless, he pushed the button on his desk to activate the wide-screen television on the opposite wall. Each evening, he watched the BBC World News broadcast. The first few announcements passed his eyes as uninteresting. Then came a bombshell announcement by the show's host:

"We have shocking news tonight. The American woman who was abducted several months ago from her seaside home in California has apparently escaped her captors. We have unconfirmed reports that Sarah Pierce, who was kidnapped on June ninth, walked into the American Embassy in Cairo today, undernourished but otherwise healthy. The motive behind the abduction remains unclear. At this time, there is no official word on why she was targeted, how she ended up in Egypt, or how she escaped her captors, though multiple sources indicate that a terrorist group from Egypt is a prime suspect. Egyptian officials had no comment."

Omar nearly fell out of his chair.

"What?" he screamed at the television. "The woman got to the U.S. embassy? No fucking way!"

He picked up his desk phone and called the BBC office in London, seeking authenticity and clarification of the announcement. The lines were busy. He went to his cell phone and called a friend in London who worked at the BBC.

"Ashton, I just heard the news about the American woman. Can you verify?"

"Omar, it's been an age since we last talked. Are you thriving in the bureaucratic world? And, yes, we have the scoop. It's dazzling news. The woman's story is amazing. We'll be playing it more fully tomorrow. You must have egg on your faces in Egypt. It appears the entire crew of kidnappers was Egyptian. What is Mubarak saying? Can I quote you on any of this?"

"No, no. I know nothing. The foreign secretary would be the best source for you."

"I'll get to him straight away. Thanks for that suggestion, and good to hear from you. Let's talk again—soon."

Omar shook his head, reeling from the news. Sweat appeared on his forehead and dropped on the notepad in front of him. He put down the phone and made a list of essential calls and messages. He reached into the drawer on his desk for the latest throwaway phone and pressed the buttons. His first call, to Jabari Radwan, went to voicemail, and he messaged: "*Radwan enact Contingency Plan immediately. Drive the men to Kom Ombo tonight and call the number I gave you yesterday. The men in Kom will house you and provide you with new identity papers. They'll set up your next location in another country—probably Sudan. A plan for your wife and children to join you will be developed.*"

He called his wife. No answer. He left a message: "*Hasina, God willing, I'll join you in the next day or two. I plan to fly to Milan as soon as possible.*"

He took a moment away from his phone calls to type a letter of resignation to President Mubarak. He phrased it carefully to emphasize his pleasure at working in the president's government but stated that he missed the academic life and wished to return to it. He selected a long envelope to enclose the letter, sealed it, and left a message on his secretary's desk to hand-deliver the letter to the president's office as soon as she arrived in the morning. He called his driver and left the building, careful to avoid any goodbyes or "see you tomorrows" to his staff. Reaching his apartment, he went to his bedroom, dropped momentarily on the bed, then rose to pack clothes for the trip to Brissago. He placed the suitcase, stuffed with his leisure clothes, on the floor of the entry hall. Glancing down the hall, he saw a stack of bills neatly organized on the hall table.

I need to make arrangements, he thought. *There is a chance I will not see this apartment again.*

He assembled the bills and walked back to his study. From his briefcase, he pulled a checkbook and prepaid his apartment rental, apartment maintenance, and utility bills for six months. He opened a drawer in the desk and retrieved a pad of paper and prepared a note to the post office to cancel all mail deliveries. He left no forwarding address. Next, he crafted a note for the building manager to sublet the apartment in October for a year unless the Sayed family notified him otherwise. He went back to his bedroom and checked the closets and armoire to be sure he would have all the clothes he needed. Satisfied, with his suitcase in one hand and the stack of bills in the other, he took the elevator to the lobby. He placed the envelopes in the outgoing mail slot, then descended the stairs to the garage. He changed his mind and climbed the stairs back to the lobby, leaving his car in the garage. He left by the front door of the building and took a taxi to the airport. An hour later, he boarded the last flight to Milan.

★ ★ ★

Late morning the next day, Omar stood at the entrance to the Sheraton Hotel at Milan's Malpensa Airport. With his suitcase and briefcase beside him, he waited for Hasina. She was always punctual, he noted, and the Mercedes arrived exactly as she had promised. He smiled as he watched her park the car at the curb a few feet from him. An attendant opened the door for her. She stepped from the car and waved him away.

"I'm picking up my husband. He's right there."

She pointed to Omar. Omar smiled, opened his arms, and hugged Hasina.

"My dear, your timing is perfect. How was the traffic?"

"Oh, not so bad, but, Omar—have you heard the news? It's everywhere. An American was kidnapped by Egyptians and escaped. It's all over the news. What's Mubarak saying to the Americans? What will he do?"

Omar signaled to Hasina to hand him the car keys, and he proceeded to open the trunk and place his suitcase and briefcase inside. He gave the keys back to Hasina, who got back into the driver's seat. Omar got into the passenger seat and looked over at Hasina.

"My dear, we have much to talk about."

CHAPTER 41

Safe and Sound

Cairo

Brooks and Ticonne had separated after their meeting with President Mubarak, General Murad, and Fathi Ashur. Brooks settled into a taxi and directed the driver to the Hilton Hotel. He looked at his watch and frowned because he knew he would miss the early evening news. He pulled a date book from his briefcase and turned to July 28 to confirm his meeting today with a Saudi agent at the cocktail hour. He then reached into his pocket to turn off his cell phone. He wanted no interruptions while meeting with an old friend.

Twenty blocks across the city, Frank Ticonne sat in the rear seat of the embassy car as his driver weaved through the dense Cairo traffic. He thought about the meeting with Mubarak and his two intelligence chiefs. He was dissatisfied with the meeting and knew Brooks was certain that Ashur was hiding important information. Slowed by a traffic jam, Ticonne leaned forward to ask his driver a question when his cell phone rang.

"Ambassador Ticonne. This is Sam. I have big news. I believe we have the American hostage, Sarah Pierce, at the embassy. She's safe and sound."

Ticonne sat bolt upright in the back seat.

"What? Say again?"

"Yes, sir. She walked right up to the guard gate. At midday, a taxi dropped her off.

We've been working to get her identification verified. That's almost done. It looks like this is the real Sarah Pierce."

"She's in Egypt? Cairo? How did this happen. Has she explained?"

"What we've learned so far is that she was abducted from her home in California, as we knew, then was flown from place to place as the FBI closed in on the kidnappers. In the end, she was in a compound in Minya and escaped from there."

"Minya? Good God! How bizarre! I agree—this group spent a fortune hiding her. It's astounding. How did she escape?"

Barstow sighed.

"That's not clear just yet. She had help but won't talk about it. From her comments thus far, this appears to a large and sophisticated conspiracy. Clearly, there's more to be determined. Will you be back in the office soon?"

"I'm on my way," Ticonne said. "I'll be there in thirty minutes. Give Ms. Pierce whatever she wants in food, clothes, shower, rest. You know the drill."

"It's being done as we speak, Mr. Ambassador. Caroline Bates is on it."

"This is good work, Sam. Excellent."

He hung up and immediately called Brooks Davidson. The call went directly to voicemail.

★ ★ ★

At the embassy, Caroline took an unsteady Sarah Pierce by the arm and led her to a modest-sized guest suite. Sarah walked in,

317

her eyes sweeping the room, absorbing the comfort of a Western interior, and immediately flopped on the bed.

"This feels so good."

Caroline laughed.

"Ms. Pierce, let me show you the bath, the shower, the robes— and tell me your size. I'll find some fresh clothes. Will a pantsuit and blouse be OK? I think we have your size in storage."

Sarah wanted to stay on the bed and submerge into its quiet comfort, yet she was consumed by a need to act. She wanted to call her daughters and tell them she was free and safe. She knew assisting the embassy staff would prove her identity, and she had to take time and think about Brooks.

After Caroline departed, Sarah shed the abaya and stepped into the shower relaxing under a hot stream of water. She thought, *What had happened to me and why?* she wondered. *What was it in his background that made terrorists want to punish him by kidnapping me?*

It made no sense, but it was becoming clear there was much about Brooks Davidson she didn't know.

I'm confused, my mind's a mess she thought *and considered, How should I think about the man I'd grown to love?* These thoughts dominated her thinking as she toweled off.

Caroline's return with a set of clothes interrupted her reverie. Fully dressed, Sarah studied herself in the mirror and was shocked at how skinny she'd become.

Oh, God! she thought. *I've got so much to recover—mind and body.*

"You look grand in that outfit," Caroline said. "It was made for you."

She walked around Sarah, assessing every angle.

"Yes, a perfect fit. Now, I have other news: The ambassador has arrived and would like to meet with you as soon as you feel ready. He'll talk to you about a debriefing and about the availability of counseling, which is pretty normal when someone goes through an ordeal like yours."

Sarah was still gazing at her image in the mirror.

"God," she muttered. "I look like a skinny old witch."

She turned from the mirror to face Caroline.

"I'm a psychologist, so I know the value of counseling, but I want to get back to the U.S. as soon as possible—like tomorrow. In the meantime, I'd like to call my daughters. How do I do that?"

Caroline went to the phone.

"Give me a number, and I'll connect you to both girls at once for direct conversation or voicemail."

Caroline tapped in the number and handed the phone to Sarah.

"I'll be back in about twenty minutes to take you to the ambassador," Caroline said. "Is that enough time?"

Sarah nodded. The phone call to her daughters was emotional: full of warmth, love, and release of fears. She came away from the conversation feeling elated—full of joy and thrilled to have a conversation with a family member. It seemed like a first step back to civilization.

When Caroline returned, she led Sarah to the ambassador's office, past a phalanx of secretaries who eyed Sarah cautiously and smiled when she met their eyes. Caroline knocked twice on the door, then entered the office. Frank Ticonne stepped out from behind a massive mahogany desk and extended his hand to Sarah.

"The amazing and brave Sarah Pierce. A pleasure to meet you. I'm honored to be in the presence of one courageous enough to escape from the hands of terrorists."

Sarah was unsure how to greet an ambassador, so she accepted his outstretched hand and smiled.

"You seem to accept that I'm actually me. Is that true?"

"I'll say more about that in a minute, but I'm delighted you're free."

"It's an immense relief to be in American hands," Sarah said. "You have no idea. One of your assistants said that you needed proof that I'm Sarah Pierce. Do you actually believe I'm Sarah?"

"Of course," he said with a laugh. "That's been proven. Modern technology is a big help here. Your California DMV thumbprint and photo match the prints and photo we took. Your photo also matches your passport photo on file at the State Department. It's all been validated while you were cleaning up."

"Well," she sighed, "thank God! I have never been so frightened in my life. It was terrifying when they first captured me, but the escape from that town brought my anxiety right back up. My needs are simple: I want know what it means to feel safe again."

Ticonne walked closer to Sarah. He gestured to a chair. They both sat down, and he shook his head in wonderment.

"I can't imagine how you managed to escape the clutches of these terrorists! I know we'll learn more about that later, and Brooks Davidson said that you were very athletic and strong. That must have helped you."

"I think so. Do you know Brooks?"

"Yes, quite well. We worked together in this part of the world on several occasions."

"Well, Brooks Davidson has some explaining to do."

Ticonne studied her and thought she had to be extremely angry with Davidson—and that would be difficult for him.

"Our allies in Egypt have some explaining to do as well. As for Brooks, you'll be able to query him to your heart's content. I believe Sam Barstow told you Brooks is in Cairo. I was with him an hour ago."

"I still can't believe he's here."

Sarah's head lifted abruptly as she stared at Ticonne.

"When is he coming to the embassy?"

"I left him after a meeting, and he went back to his hotel. I've been trying to reach him, but his phone goes to voicemail. He'll be in touch. He knows I have an urgent message."

Her eyes drifted off, and she ran a finger across her dry lips.

What's it going to be like to see him? she wondered.

She turned to the ambassador.

"When will he get your message?"

"Most likely around dinnertime," Ticonne said. "As soon as he calls, I'll patch the call to you. And one more item, Sarah, if I may. I know you want to get home as soon as possible, but we need to do a debriefing so we can find the criminals and bring them to justice. Also, I want to make sure you have counseling right away to address any PTSD symptoms that may occur after such an ordeal."

"As a psychologist, I understand the role of counseling, but I do want to get home," Sarah said. "How long will this debrief and counseling take?"

"A few days. Does that seem reasonable?"

"I don't know. This new sense of freedom is wonderful yet unsettling. I've been away from their prison only a few hours and already I have some residual fears and anxieties that bother me. My clinical experience tells me this is a typical PTSD response. And Brooks here—that's another complicating detail."

I don't know how to think of him right now, she thought.

A secretary opened the ambassador's door, but only her head protruded through the opening.

"Excuse me, sir," she said nervously. "Brooks Davidson is on the line, returning your urgent call. What should I tell him?"

CHAPTER 42

Awkward Moments

Cairo

Ticonne frowned at the secretary, annoyed at the interruption. Slowly, the scowl on his face disappeared as he fully digested her message.

"I'll get it Grace. Thank you," Ticonne said as he picked up the phone.

"Brooks! Are you sitting down? I have someone in the office who wants to talk with you."

He handed Sarah the phone.

"What? What?" Brooks wanted to know. "Frank—what's urgent? What's going on?"

Softly, her voice rising barely above a whisper, Sarah spoke.

"Brooks, it's me. I escaped."

For a second, there was silence.

"Sarah! My God, Sarah! Is it really you? You escaped—how? You're in Cairo? How'd you get there? You're at the embassy? Oh my God—this is a miracle. You're OK? I mean, how are you?"

Sarah shrugged her shoulders toward Caroline and Ticonne and, holding her hand over the phone, spoke to them.

"I think he's a little rattled."

Then she addressed Brooks.

"Where are you, and can you get here soon? I'm doing all I can to hold myself together with all these fast-changing realities."

"I'm trying to calm down and accept the amazing miracle that you're free, somehow in Cairo. Good God, I can't believe that I'll see you in a few minutes. I just finished dinner with an old friend at the Hilton. I'm flagging a taxi as we speak. Oh, so much to say, so much to be thankful for. Here's a cab! I'm on my way."

When Brooks arrived at the embassy, he was quickly escorted to the ambassador's office. As he entered the door, he opened his arms to greet Sarah and pull her close to him.

"Oh, Sarah! I'm lost for words. You're free, you're a sight for sore eyes, and you're here!"

He hugged her tightly, nearly crushing her thin body. Sarah grabbed onto him, burying her head into his chest.

"It's been so long," Sarah said. "I thought I'd never see you or my girls again."

"I know. I know."

Brooks then whispered in her ear.

"My beautiful Sarah—there are no words to this horror. Can you tell me how you feel? Are you beginning to believe you're safe?"

"It's all a muddle. At times I'm confused as to where I am."

She turned away from Brooks to look at Caroline.

"Caroline's been wonderful. She's helped me feel secure. So has the ambassador."

Brooks thanked them, then placed his hands on Sarah's shoulders, slowly easing her away from his body.

"Let me have a full look at you. I'm amazed, delighted. Look at you—still strong."

"Oh, Brooks," Sarah protested. "I'm an emaciated wreck, but

thank you. I see you all robust and healthy, and that's what I want."

She looked up at him. Her eyes asked the questions before she said them.

"How soon can we leave here? When can I get back to my normal life?"

Brooks dropped his arms from Sarah and turned to Ticonne.

"I know that Frank has spoken to you about a debriefing. It's important, Sarah. We want to capture these idiots and bring them to justice. And we want to give you access to some counseling before we leave. And I have an idea for you on a special type of counseling. It's a clinic in Zurich that I've used in the past when my colleagues and I have had a trauma like yours."

"I know. The ambassador mentioned that to me."

She looked over at Ticonne.

"You said three to four days, right? I was hoping…"

Ticonne nodded.

"Sarah, Brooks and I as well as my staff have done more debriefs than I can count, and each one is special. We'll take your debrief at the speed you can handle. There's no perfect formula. Everyone digests a trauma like this differently. If it's OK with you, I want to start in the morning. Brooks and I meet with President Mubarak tomorrow. I'd love to have a few observations from your experience that we can use in the meeting. Any tidbit of information that points toward the Egyptians will help us in this session. Back to my first point: We don't want to rush or put unnecessary pressure on you. This will go only as fast as you're comfortable. So, is a tomorrow start to the debriefing OK with you?"

Sarah shrugged her shoulders.

"Why not? I know I can rattle off a few names and places. And Brooks—I'll need to hear more about this clinic as I do want to get home as soon as possible."

Ticonne smiled at her.

"You're an international phenomenon, Sarah, and the U.S. government needs to know what happened and by whom. This is serious criminal activity. Consequences will be levied hard and fast on the kidnappers and on the government of Egypt if we find it complicit. We need the best facts you're able to recall."

Brooks stepped closer to Sarah. He placed his arm around her shoulders, still stunned at the lack of flesh on her bones beneath the white blouse. He gave her shoulder a gentle, reassuring squeeze.

"Sarah, as you can see, I'm struggling with your escape and arrival here, but a few thoughts come to mind. You'll need a little time to get a passport, a wardrobe, travel goods like toiletries, airline arrangements—things like that. These services will help you transition to normal life. Please bear with me and with Frank's program. All this will take a few days."

Sarah's face had become somber. Her moist eyes bore in on Brooks, and she gently wiped them away with the knuckle of her forefinger.

"I want to know why I was kidnapped, Brooks. I know what Jabari Radwan told me. I want to hear your side of the story."

Ticonne raised his head. He straightened his back in a pure diplomatic motion, his right hand pointed toward Sarah.

"You know the names of the kidnappers?"

"Yes. I gave the names to Mr. Barstow. I told him they were from the Muslim Brotherhood. I heard the women in the compound in Minya talk about the Muslim Brotherhood, sometimes in anger, even disgust."

"Sarah, this is outstanding information already," Ticonne said. "We can complete more of this tomorrow. There's no question your information will be very helpful in our meeting with President Mubarak."

He smiled at her, sensing her need to withdraw from the department's bevy of questions.

"I imagine you're exhausted and might like a few moments with Brooks before you retire."

"Yes, I'd like that."

Sarah turned to Caroline.

"Is it possible for me to get a couple of sleeping tablets for tonight? This is my first night away from captivity in what—two months? I feel kind of lost—out of control. My mind is spinning at high speed. I'll never sleep."

"Please follow me." Caroline said. "I'll lead you and Dr. Davidson back to the guest quarters."

"Brooks, after you and Sarah visit for a bit," Ticonne began, "please drop by my residence. We can have a drink and talk about tomorrow's meeting with Mubarak."

"Will do, Frank."

Brooks turned to Sarah and put his hand lightly on her elbow.

"Let's have a few minutes together, if that's OK."

He paused to watch her reaction. There was none. Her eyes had become flat, expressionless. He wanted to understand her silence. *Having seen me,* he thought, *she's reminded of the abduction and is probably resentful.* He did not question her quiet mood and sought to find a way to gently bring her back to him. He smiled, conveying a message of concern and love.

"Then you can have a good rest on your first night of freedom."

Sarah slowly raised her eyes to him.

"You have no idea how much I'd like that."

He speaks of rest, yet who is this man that put me into such a terrible situation? she thought.

"Come on," she beckoned to him. "Let's walk along with Caroline."

When they reached the guest quarters, Sarah took the sleeping pills from Caroline and stared at them.

"Good God!" she said to Brooks as she rolled them around in her hand.

"I never use these, but I'll need these tonight. I'm ready to jump out of my skin. Now..."

She looked at Brooks expectantly.

"I'm torn with conflicting emotions," she told him. "I admit I'm a mess and confused right now. Too much has happened too fast."

She extended her arms, welcoming him.

"Will you hold me for a few minutes? I need some warmth. I need to feel that I'm safe and secure again."

He held her for several minutes. She shivered at first. He could feel the tension in her upper body, especially the tight muscles along the top of her shoulders. Eventually, she was quiet, resting peacefully in his arms. He moved his head down to her and brushed her lips with his in a soft kiss. Her lips were dry. Her response was lifeless. He pulled his head away.

"I guess that was too aggressive—sorry."

"I'm not myself," she said, staring into his eyes. "I wonder if I'll ever get *me* back."

She hesitated for a second.

"When I think of this entire situation, it reminds me of a chess match. You play the big pieces—the knights, the rooks, the queen—with other big players in a world that's different than mine. You make your moves with rules and strategies that most people, especially me, never experience. As Jabari said, 'I'm just a little pawn in this big game of yours.' They took me to get at you."

"You'll get the Sarah back that I know and love," Brooks said. "Trust me, please. I've been there. It takes time. And to clarify—yes, they took you to get me to pay a ransom and to force me to back off my work. It was a crazy idea done by some madman. Don't think of yourself as a pawn or small player."

He thought he'd like to give her more details of what he did, possibly filling in the gaps of his business activities beyond what she understood. He couldn't. The government's national security laws prevented it. But he had withheld parts of what he did that weren't state secrets. These activities were not big deals to him, such as where he banked or the fact that some of his economic ideas faced resistance, even animosity.

Will she understand me better, accept me fully, when I reveal more of my background? he wondered. *Or will she develop a lack of trust in me that will spoil our wonderful relationship? Clary had no problems with secrets in our respective professions. Why should Sarah?*

He broke from his thoughts, watching for her reactions.

Did she follow my line of logic that a madman concocted this terrorist act, or was she too traumatized to absorb the message?

With patience and kindness in his voice, he spoke again to her.

"It's one of those things we'll talk about when you feel ready—all in good time. Now might be the time for you to take those pills and get a good night's sleep."

"Yes, I think that's best," she said. "You're not disappointed, are you?"

He shook his head. She liked the warmth of his hug, his strong physical presence that radiated confidence, and his assurance that all would be well. Yet, she was ready for him to leave. She had too many conflicting feelings. She needed to sleep and to be alone with her thoughts.

Brooks studied her face and watched her changing expressions fly across those oval eyes and sensuous mouth. She did this when she processed hard thoughts. She was troubled—he could see that—and she glanced at him like he was a stranger. He wanted to bring her back, calm her down.

"I'm so grateful you're here," he said. "There are no words for my gratitude right now. And on the abduction, I can't adequately express the pain I feel. I'm so sorry for my role in this. I know what the ransom note said. I know this is on me and, for what's it's worth, I'm not doing too well with it. When we have time, either during the debriefing or after it, I can tell you more about the factors that may have motivated these terrorists to choose me and therefore you."

She leaned up to kiss him.

"That will help me, I'm sure. Until tomorrow."

"Yes, tomorrow. Rest well, my love."

He turned toward the door, sensing that a degree of awkwardness had risen between them.

CHAPTER 43

Under Pressure

Cairo, Egypt

President Hosni Mubarak sat behind his desk, hands folded in front of him. Across from him and seated in two hardback chairs were Galal Murad and Fathi Ashur. Mubarak clenched his hands, rubbing them back and forth, and moistened his lips.

"Yesterday's meeting with Dr. Davidson and Ambassador Ticonne was embarrassing. The goddamn Americans have us by the balls again. What the fuck is going on, Murad?"

"Are you referring to the kidnap leader? His prior association with my organization?" the general responded.

"Don't be dense, Murad. We've got four Egyptians, fully identified by the Americans, who captured an American woman. You're telling me that you know nothing about it?"

Mubarak paused, his eyes flashing with anger.

"How can the Americans know more about this than we do? Dr. Davidson all but accused one of my cabinet ministers of being part of this plot. There is some kind of cover-up going on. If you can't find who's trying to embarrass me, then I'll find someone who can."

Before Murad could respond, Ashur spoke.

"Mr. President, we've interrogated several well-known opponents of the National Democratic Party. We've visited several of the top tier in the Muslim Brotherhood, active and retired, and no one knows about this plot. Jabari Radwan, the leader, as I said in previous meetings, may well have been recruited by a rogue group inside Egypt or even outside the country."

Mubarak rose from his chair as if shot by a cannon.

"Goddammit, Ashur! If you give me that crock of shit one more time about Al-Qaeda or other outsiders, I'll send you and your entire ops department to Tora!"

Mubarak paced around the large room. As General Murad began to rise from his chair, Mubarak shouted.

"I'll tell you when to get up, Murad! Stay there while I think!"

He paced with his head down, staring at the carpet. He circled the room a few times, then pointed to the two men.

"You two need to think better. I have an enemy out there, and I want that son of a shit-smelling camel found! I know this much: Some scum of the earth wants to remove the best economic ideas that have come to Egypt in decades in order to do what—to embarrass me? This traitor wants to show that I can't create a solid economy? The son of a whore wants to insinuate that I accept paybacks and kickbacks from capitalists? Yes, that dung heap that sucks dog's dicks wants to expose me, embarrass me to my people and to the world? I don't give a flying duck fuck about this Radwan. I want the person who created this mess!"

Murad and Ashur watched as the president strode around the room. He went back behind his desk but remained standing.

"Get up!" he shouted.

The two men rose, facing him. Mubarak looked at one, then the other.

"Tell me your prime suspect!" Mubarak demanded. "If you have no suspects, tell me what you're going to do to find this snake!"

Ashur turned toward Murad.

"May I comment, General?"

Murad flicked his right hand toward Ashur, signaling him to proceed.

"At our last meeting, Mr. President, you and the general asked me to find the kidnappers and the person who's responsible for the plot," Ashur said. "I've done the first part. I identified the kidnappers. Regarding the person responsible, I have one comment I'd like to make."

"Go on! Go on!" Mubarak urged.

"In our last meeting, the American Davidson said the person behind the abduction most likely had a personal vendetta against him and possibly wanted to embarrass you in the process," Ashur said. "He mentioned the name Omar Sayed, and, as I recall, Mr. President, you dismissed Minister Sayed as too ineffectual to be at the center of such a plot."

Mubarak sat in his chair, his eyes riveted on Fathi Ashur.

"I did indeed, and you agree, don't agree—what?"

"At first, Mr. President, I agreed totally. But as I thought more about Minister Sayed and how Dr. Davidson bypassed him on recent commercial projects, I could understand if he became motivated to harm the American. I could see that he would want Davidson out of the country forever."

Mubarak rubbed his jaw and turned his attention to General Murad.

"Galal, what are your thoughts? You know Minister Sayed. Is he capable of this type of subterfuge?"

"Hosni, I've known you for years. We've seen crazy plots to

332

remove you, expose you, and embarrass you."

Murad placed a hand to his mouth to wipe his lips.

"But this plot is more indirect than those of the past," he continued. "In a way, it's clever. As I think of what Director Ashur said about Minister Sayed, I'm inclined to agree. Sayed's an academic at heart, and those people think differently than you and me. As I watched him over the past few years, he's not like your most troublesome opponents. He has that populist view that I see as Muslim Brotherhood-type of thinking. I think Minister Sayed should be interrogated."

Mubarak mused aloud.

"If Sayed is Brotherhood, that is a real basis for motivation."

He turned to Ashur.

"Director, can you get to Sayed today?"

Ashur's lips twisted up in a cruel smile.

"Mr. President, General—I personally went to Minister Sayed's home last evening. What I found was surprising. That's why I mentioned him today. Neither he nor his wife and children were there. The building manager told me they were off on a long vacation and that he was to rent their unit if he didn't return by October. This is odd behavior."

Mubarak returned to his chair, leaned back and slapped his forehead.

"Allah on high. My assistant put this letter on my desk this morning, but I ignored it. It's from Sayed. Give me a moment. I'll read it."

He pulled a letter opener from his desk drawer, slit the envelope, and stared at Sayed's letter.

"I'll be..."

He waved the paper to Ashur and Murad.

"The piece of camel dung has resigned, wants to return to academia," Mubarak said. "Highly suspicious, gentlemen."

"That ties with leaving his apartment," Ashur said. "I will check with his deputy and determine what he knows."

Mubarak, still staring at the letter from Sayed, spoke.

"There may be other leads to follow, Director Ashur, but I want you to make this one your top priority. Get on it right now."

Ashur rose to shake the president's hand and left the room. General Murad also prepared to leave. Mubarak placed the letter back on his desk and shifted his attention to the general.

"Stay a moment, Galal."

He watched Ashur as he left the room. Once the door closed, he spoke.

"How much do you trust this Ashur? Is he on to something or just delaying action while he protects someone else?"

Mubarak's shift in attitude appeared to relax Murad.

"Fathi Ashur has proven himself again and again to be a loyal, dedicated warrior for Egypt," Murad said. "His instincts and intelligence have always been on the mark. I think he might be on the right track here. I'll watch him closely, but I'll be surprised if I'm wrong."

The president walked over and placed an arm on the general as he escorted him from the room.

"Keep me posted, and let's see if we can bring this to a good conclusion for us and for the Americans."

★ ★ ★

Ashur met his driver at the front of the Heliopolis Palace, and they sped back to his building in central Cairo. Instead of going directly to his office, he went to the floor for the Mukhabarat's

Center for Research. Ashur turned to face a secretary.

"I want to see the director now."

Flustered, the secretary rose and pointed at the office behind him.

"Busy, sir. I'll tell the director you're here."

The wall behind the secretary was all glass, and Ashur could see a group of men meeting in the room. He saw the research center's director, waved, and caught his attention. Dark, mid-sized, and dressed in tan slacks and an open-collar white shirt, the director rose from the small conference table. He waved Ashur to enter and dismissed the staff gathered around him. As they passed Ashur in the doorway, they greeted him with bowed heads. He appreciated the sign of respect and offered a soft "thank you" to each of them and to the secretary. He extended his hand to the director.

"May I have a minute?"

"Of course, Director Ashur. What's on your mind?"

"Disturbing times, my colleague—very unusual indeed. I'm getting more aggressive with some of our agents who have infiltrated radical terrorist organizations. I've asked a few of our agents to take extraordinary risks to secure information."

The research director studied Ashur's face, trying to anticipate the request.

"I see. You need our newest cameras or recording technology?"

"No, actually something more of a last resort," Ashur said. "If any of our agents gets caught or compromised, I want them to take a pill rather than get captured. I want zero risk that they'll reveal a plan when under duress. I know how convincing a rough interrogation can be."

"Of course, and we've always provided the most up-to-date capsules for your field personnel. Are these not effective in some way?"

"Not at all," Ashur said. "Your potassium cyanide capsule has been used and found to be very effective. I'd like to know if your research has found a better way, a smaller and easier-to-disguise capsule than the one that agent Pillis used last year. Also, I wonder: Do you have a capsule that would imitate the sensations of a heart attack?"

"I recall agent Pillis—a good man. It was a sad moment when he was forced to use that exit. And to your question, we do have a compound that works like a heart attack. Under a skilled autopsy, it would not be convincing, but to a less-informed observer, the death could look like a cardiac arrest."

"That's exactly what I need. I'd like two heart-attack capsules for an agent located in a special destination. I've placed this agent myself."

"I can get the capsules for you right now, Director, if you can wait. You'll sign as usual?"

"Of course, and I'll wait, if that's not too inconvenient for you."

"I'll be back in five minutes."

CHAPTER 44

Cornered

Brissago, Switzerland

Golden sunlight filled the master bedroom in Omar's Brissago villa. Resting on a pillow, he lifted his head and shielded his eyes, looking at Hasina, who had thrown open the curtains. She cast a shadow in the bright light. Past her shoulder, he could see the water sparkling on the lake below.

"What are you doing?" he asked, wiping the cobwebs from his eyes.

"You're lazy already. One day away from work, and you want to sleep forever."

She watched him move slowly out of bed.

"Omar, there's breakfast on the kitchen counter. I must be going. I want to be in Locarno when the shops open. The children will be with me. They need some new clothes."

She pointed to him, adjusting the accusation into a gentler observation.

"We had to leave the apartment in such a rush. They didn't pack too well."

He rubbed his eyes. Last night's wine was working its way out of his brain, but a little too slowly.

"Sorry. I'm not focusing too quickly. Why are you and the

children leaving on a day when we could go sailing?"

He shielded his eyes again.

"Just look at the sunshine."

"We can sail anytime," Hasina said. "This is the day for special bargains in Ascona and Locarno. Act fast—you taught me that."

She studied his face.

"I'll see you around six tonight."

She walked from the window to his bed, bent over, and kissed him.

"As you walk the village today, would you buy some fresh fish for dinner?" she asked.

She exited the room quickly. Moments later, Omar heard an engine rumble and wheels spinning on the gravel of the drive as the car drove off.

Alone, he thought. *What to do today?*

He'd left Cairo, resigned from his prestigious post as Minister of Trade and Industry, an officer in the president's cabinet. An important piece of his life, his work in government was over.

It was yesterday, or the day before, he mused, *and already I feel lost.*

He shook his head.

It had gone wrong, but how? he wondered. *How did that woman escape? Why had Davidson ignored the ransom demands? Why had he been so devious with his delays, lies, and lack of fear from Jabari Radwan's threats? Did he not care about the woman? It didn't matter,* he sighed, shaking his head. *She'd escaped.*

He swung his feet out of bed. He'd stay hidden until he heard from Fathi that it was safe for him to resurface and perhaps return to Egypt. His mind began to spin over what had happened in the past few days.

Was Fathi serious about Mubarak's threat? he wondered. *Did the president actually want him questioned regarding the abduction?*

No, he told himself. *This will quiet down in a few months when the woman is safe and back in the U.S. The Americans' interest in the case and Mubarak's secret police investigation will gradually disappear. My team of kidnappers will have disappeared into Brotherhood activities in other countries. If they bother me for more money, I'll buy them off or have Fathi's Mukhabarat take care of them.*

He felt safe for now. No one, except his mother, knew about his villa in the hills of this remote Swiss village. His bank accounts, cash machines, and telephones were all listed with Swiss companies. His mind spun. He mumbled out loud as he descended the back staircase to the kitchen.

"Slow down, Omar! Stop worrying."

On the counter, a tall glass of juice next to a plate of pita stuffed with mashed fava beans lifted his spirits. He sat on a stool at the counter and ate hungrily. When he finished, he wiped his mouth with a cotton napkin, sat back, and reflected on yesterday's flight to Milan. He'd left Cairo without attracting attention, without being followed. He was certain he was safe from anyone discovering his hiding place.

Time to think ahead, he thought. *How long should I hide before seeking teaching positions at Swiss, French, or English universities? It's August First; the coming academic year will be staffed, but next year is possible. I'll stay in Brissago and devote my time to writing my next book.*

But he was not ready to start that project. The sharp change from his heavy schedule at the ministry to no responsibilities left him unclear about filling the coming days and weeks ahead. Today was made difficult with his wife and children off to Locarno. He had thought the first few days of his new freedom would be consumed with family activities. Now they'd left him to fend for himself. He ate the pita slowly.

I'll settle down, he thought. *Give it some time.*

He finished the juice, rinsed the dishes, and decided to go for a sail. He returned to his bedroom and put on white boat shoes with no socks, white cotton slacks, and a blue shirt. He left the villa and walked down the hill, through the narrow streets, onto a pier at the lake. He looked for Karl, who, for years, rented sailboats roped to cleats on the pier. He caught a light morning breeze and sailed out between the islands on the vast lake.

★ ★ ★

It was mid-morning when Fathi Ashur arrived in Brissago. The prior evening, he had charmed his aunt, Omar's mother, into providing the address of the Brissago villa. Early this morning, a Mukhabarat driver had met him at Milan's Malpensa Airport for the drive to the lakeside town across the border into Switzerland. The driver parked the Range Rover in the car park near the waterfront. Both men stepped out, stretched their arms and legs, and inhaled the fresh air. Fathi pointed to a café across the street.

"Let's have an espresso while I get directions to Viale Collina. You can stay at the café or wander the streets—whatever you please. Again, I'll be gone an hour or two and will call if it's going to be longer."

They sat in the café. When not distracted by the flirtations of the waitress, the driver's conversational interest focused on the traffic they'd face when they returned to the airport.

"Minister Ashur, as you plan your day, there is no need to rush. If you get done early, we can beat the traffic into Milan. If you need more time, we can go after the rush hour."

Fathi interrupted the driver's conversation to ask the waitress for directions to Viale Collina. He finished his espresso, paid the bill with a generous tip, and left the driver for the uphill trek to Omar's villa. When he found number forty-two, he walked up a stone path bordered by bright flowers and knocked three times on a bright, blue door. After a few seconds, he knocked again. No answer. He tried the door handle. It was locked. He opened his briefcase and removed his small leather sack containing his lock-picking tools. He selected one that fit the front lock and quickly opened the door. Once inside, he called to ensure no one was home. Satisfied the villa was empty, he took a look at the rooms downstairs and upstairs, then sat on the living-room couch facing an ornate tile fireplace. He settled back against the cushions, checked his cell phone and saw he'd received no urgent messages. He removed a small, metal pillbox from his briefcase and placed it in his pants pocket. He took a book from his briefcase and began to read. When two hours had passed, he called the driver.

The driver, cell phone in hand, and the waitress were en route to her apartment when his phone rang. He nudged the waitress with his shoulder as Fathi spoke.

"My work has not started. Keep yourself amused and keep your phone on."

"Be assured, Minister Ashur, the phone is on."

Fathi placed the book in his lap, checked his cell phone again, and tapped out replies to several messages he had received. He leaned back on the couch as his eyes began to close when he heard a rattling of keys at the front door. He brushed the legs of his pants and stood up. When Omar entered the living room, he stopped. His head and hands started shaking.

"What...? Who...? What do...?"

He then let out a string of Arab curses.

"Fathi, you scared the shit out of me! What brings you here? How did you find me?"

He let out a long breath and stood staring at his cousin.

"This can't be good."

"Omar, I'll be direct and to the point," Fathi said. "It will be easier that way."

He waited for Omar to reply, but his cousin remained stunned. Standing tall, his voice calm and exuding confidence, Fathi continued. "President Mubarak has directed me to bring you in for interrogation. I think you know what that means. I have another plan. Would you like to hear it?"

Omar finally spoke.

"I need a glass of water. Will you excuse me?"

"Actually, no," Fathi replied. "But I'll accompany you to the kitchen. I'd like some water as well."

"You don't trust me? You think I'll run?"

Fathi gazed squarely into Omar's eyes.

"That's just what you've done. You left Cairo. You told no one. Do you actually think you can run from the Egyptian government?"

"I would have been in contact with you as soon as the Americans had left the country. I'd claim I was on a long trip."

"That would never convince or satisfy the president," Fathi said. "You know that. There are only two solutions to your situation: you come back to Cairo with me and face interrogation, or you accept my idea of an honorable exit."

"What the fuck's that?"

Fathi pulled the metal box from his pocket and opened it. Omar saw two small capsules, and his eyes bugged out.

"Are they what I think they are?"

"Yes, they're cyanide capsules, the newest design to imitate a heart attack. It's over in a second. You'll be treated as a hero of the country. Your sudden death will be regarded as a severe loss to Egypt. If you come back with me for interrogation, you will go down as a traitor."

"I can implicate you, Fathi!" Omar shouted.

Fathi's voice was calm.

"No, you can't. When Davidson raised your name as a possible master of the plot, the president said 'Interrogate Sayed.' I'll tell him and General Murad that I went to you that day and recommended you avail yourself for questioning. Instead of following my advice, you ran to your secret villa. It's your word against mine. You'll never win that contest."

"You bastard! You're a traitor to the family. Wait till I tell Gehad and others in the Brotherhood what you've done. You're finished too."

"You're not thinking clearly, Omar. Gehad doesn't know about our conversations. I'll tell him what I told you. I was not in favor of your kidnapping plot. What's more, my father, Gehad's brother, knows I wanted to stop this plot. You're on your own, as I told you from the start."

"You want me to kill myself?"

"Sit down, Omar. Let's go over this slowly and address your legacy to your wife and children and to Egypt."

Omar sank on the couch and put his head in his hands. He and Fathi talked for an hour, with Omar vacillating from rage to tears. Then he summarized Fathi's proposal.

"Here's what I understand: You want me to change into a bathing suit, and we walk to the lake. I go out to the end of the pier and put the capsule in my mouth. Just before I dive into the water, I bite the capsule, and I'm dead as soon as I hit the water."

"Basically, you've got it. You may wind up taking one or two strokes when you hit the water. Then it's over."

"You're a fucking bastard! You know that, don't you?"

"I've heard that before, but it doesn't apply in your case. Listen, Omar—do you realize what I'm doing for you? I'm saving your reputation for Hasina, your children, and your country. This way, you go out as a hero. The other way, you go out as a prisoner to be hanged or shot for treason."

Omar took a deep breath. Then he was quiet. Seconds passed, and then he stood up.

"OK, I'll change. We'll walk to the pier. Should I leave a message for Hasina?"

"No. Remember: You'll be diagnosed as having a heart attack while swimming. This is totally unexpected, a shock. You've been fairly healthy. I'll contact Hasina tomorrow and offer help, although I know your large family will know what to do."

"You're a cold, distant fucking bastard."

"Let's get moving, Omar."

They walked down the narrow streets to the lake and onto the pier. Then Fathi stopped.

"I'll watch from here," he said. "There are several people in the water to see that you're unable—"

"Shut up!" Omar blurted.

Staring at Fathi, Omar understood for the first time in his life the real character of his cousin—his ruthlessness. Fathi had not offered a farewell gesture—no handshake, no embrace, no wave of the arm.

"I'll see you in hell!" shouted Omar, his mouth twisted downward, bristling with disgust.

"Probably," Fathi replied, his face stone cold.

He watched Omar walk to the end of the pier and dive into the water. When Omar surfaced face down, his arms flopping listlessly at his sides, Fathi turned from the pier and walked slowly toward his car.

CHAPTER 45

Brooks

Cairo

After learning of Sayed's death, Brooks had an urgent desire to confer with President Mubarak. Brooks' meeting with the president had been rescheduled three times. Instead of meeting on August 6, they finally met on August 14. By that date, Brooks knew from Frank Ticonne and from Claude Anderson that the Egyptian Mukhabarat had chased the four kidnappers into Sudan, where they had vanished. Some agents thought they had gone to Iraq, while others said Syria, but it was clear the Muslim Brotherhood had closed ranks behind the four men and protected them.

On the eve of his meeting with Mubarak, Brooks was in his hotel room preparing for the session when the telephone rang. The caller spoke immediately, without identification.

"Dr. Davidson, I've deposited a message in your mailbox at the hotel. I send it to you as a friend of Egypt. The note will explain all. If you attempt to identify the author, it will be a waste of your time. Your guesses will be met with denial. It will be your word versus the words of Egyptian officials. You know how that will go. Good evening to you."

"One sec—" Brooks replied before the caller hung up.

Brooks stared at the phone for a second before placing it back on the receiver.

Who could this be? he wondered. *The caller had to be someone high in the bureaucracy. It's not Hagazi, Mubarak's assistant, or Hamdi, the foreign minister, or General Murad. I know their voices. Could the caller have been Fathi Ashur, the ops man in the Mukhabarat? No; that's unlikely. Ashur was too careful and reserved to contact an American outside normal diplomatic channels.*

Brooks reached for the phone and called the front desk.

"Is there a message in my mail slot for Brooks Davidson, Room 1432?"

He waited while the clerk searched for it. Seconds later, the clerk replied affirmatively.

"Excellent," Brooks said. "Would you have it sent to my room? Thank you."

When he received the envelope from the bellman, he tore it open, noting the script written in Arabic.

The caller knows me—knows I speak and write their language, he thought.

It said: "Dr. Davidson – You are a friend of Egypt. Your enemy is our enemy. The organizer and leader of the plot to kidnap Sarah Pierce is dead. You've seen the notice in the papers. The rest of his team members will be found and dealt with in a similar manner. You and Ms. Pierce are safe. Consider it done. Justice is served. Allahu Akbar."

His eyes lingered on the note. The author, whoever it was, confirmed that Omar Sayed was the brains behind the plot. Brooks looked at the obituaries in the paper. There were no obituaries of other well-known men or women. He returned the note to the envelope and placed it in his briefcase. He'd show it to President

Mubarak at their meeting. He wanted the president's impression of the authenticity of the information.

Would Mubarak finally believe that Minister Sayed was the master-mind behind the plot to remove him from Egypt? he wondered. *Would Mubarak be able to discern Sayed's motives for such an insane plot? I hope so. Would the president shed any light on whether the Egyptians were willing to work with the Americans to find the four men, or would they, as I suspect, work alone?*

Brooks paced around the suite, ignoring the comfort of the cushioned chairs. He wanted to read and relax, but his mind was unsettled. He was to meet Sarah at the Zurich clinic in two days. Questions bore into his thoughts. In a telephone conversation a few days earlier, Dr. Rene Bartot at the clinic revealed to Brooks that Sarah was not ready to return to her home in Sunset Cove. He claimed that her memory of the front-door abduction was still vivid in her mind. She wanted her initial stay in the United Sates to be in a new and safe place. She had made arrangements to stay with her daughter, Lynne, in Texas. This decision surprised Brooks because she had not discussed it with him. He planned to talk with her about it—not to alter her choice, but to understand it better. He had concluded that Sarah did not want to him to travel to Texas with her because, otherwise, she would have asked him. Instinctively, he sensed that she was seeking to keep her distance. That worried him.

Bartot stressed that Sarah had made substantial strides toward recovery; she was healthy and in high spirits. There were no lingering indications of depression or any occurrence of daytime or nighttime terrors. According to him, Sarah was ready to return to a normal life with support from local counselors. Brooks wondered when she'd be ready to return to Sunset Cove and her life in the Bay Area.

Would their relationship continue in the manner it had been preceding her abduction, or was a change in mood and behavior more likely? he wondered.

Normally an optimist by nature, he was on the negative side of this question. He felt she was drifting away from him, and he was searching for what she meant to him and what he should do to return the relationship to its original foundation. His thoughts shifted back to Sayed and his role in disrupting their lives.

Should I show Sarah the note confirming Sayed's responsibility in the plot? Would she be relieved to learn the intention of the Egyptians and Americans to find the rest of Sayed's men? Would that information reduce her fears about returning to normal life?

He brooded over the possible effects of the clinic's program on Sarah. Brooks had agents return to work seemingly unfazed by detention or torture, and others who chose to leave the jobs in the intelligence world immediately. Everyone handled his or her personal crisis differently.

How would Sarah respond? he wondered. *What would Sarah be like?*

His last thought lingered the longest. After a trauma like being kidnapped or tortured, many of his agents had struggled over differences that emerged between themselves and their co-workers and between themselves and their spouses. Little disagreements or quarrels over how to handle the children or manage the family's finances, addressed easily in the past, became major issues. Changes in values and lifestyle often ensued and were the cause of many divorces. Brooks believed he and Sarah were not likely to fall into that trap. He loved the differences between her life and his. Sarah's was quiet, peaceful, and centered around her home. He knew she relished the day-to-day pleasures of Sunset Cove and San Francisco Bay. Rarely did she travel. She introduced him to weekend cycling, quiet evenings reading by the fire, and small gatherings with friends. He found those times most pleasurable. They'd become part of his new life—more local and familial, quite different from before.

Would life like that continue, or would she—would they—want a change in lifestyle?

After two months in captivity, he knew that Sarah, like so many of his agents, would think hard about her life and wonder if she was satisfied with it or want it to change. Through their many conversations, he realized that Sarah thought his life had been overly focused on career and being an active player on the international scene. She represented an adjustment to that, and he welcomed the new dimensions of living she introduced.

★ ★ ★

The next day, Brooks met with President Mubarak and handed him the anonymous message he'd received. Mubarak studied the note for a few seconds, then waved toward chairs in the corner of the room.

"Strange," Mubarak began as the two sat down. "A heart attack is what I've been told. Yet this message infers that someone killed him. You know, Brooks, Sayed was weak. He never did measure up. He was too much the academic, with too few ideas for a real economy. I'd lost confidence in him, and he knew it. So it makes sense that Sayed was behind the kidnapping. He was desperate to get rid of you and to embarrass me."

The president let out a string of curses and waved a hand in anger.

"He had the means with funds he'd hidden in his ministry. I'm sure of that. I also know that he had family connections with the

Brotherhood. Through them, he found a set of hotheaded exiles for the job. He was smart enough to concoct the plan but not effective in the end."

"I mentioned his—" Brooks began before being cut off. It was obvious that Mubarak didn't want to hear his comment.

"Doesn't matter anymore, does it? He's gone and no more a worry to me, to you, or to Mrs. Pierce. Let us talk of other things."

For the next hour, the president pressed Brooks on ideas for accelerating economic growth in the country. He implored him to stay involved with Egypt and to bring him fresh American ideas.

Brooks now understood that President Mubarak, having experienced treachery among his friends as well as adversaries, was not concerned with these heinous acts as long as the culprits were jailed or dead. Sayed was gone, and the president would not mention him again. He'd moved on.

"Mr. President, your openness to my ideas has always been a reward in itself," Brooks said. "But now I must consider that my presence in Egypt, and perhaps throughout the region, has initiated resentment that's caused harm to others—in my case, to a woman who is close to me. I must think carefully on what I do in the future. I've made no decisions. I will inform you of my plans once they are settled."

Mubarak stood and walked Brooks to the door.

"Let us stay in contact," Mubarak said. "Do not make any decisions on your advisory work without discussion with me."

He smiled and offered his hand.

"I have ways to make it very attractive for you."

As Brooks left the Heliopolis Palace, his mind was in turmoil. Mubarak had dismissed discussion of Sayed's plot quickly and devoted most of their time to the value of Brooks' work. Brooks worried that there could be others in Egypt, or in the region, who felt like Sayed and wanted him gone. Part of him had a strong desire to continue his work.

How would Sarah respond to that idea? he wondered.

She had made it clear at the embassy that she wanted to continue the relationship, but on a more open, more honest, basis.

What exactly did she mean by that statement?

His work required secrecy. The confidentiality was consistent with the way he liked to work.

Does she want me to give up my advisory and investment work in the Middle East?

Brooks stepped into an awaiting taxi, his mind torn between the opportunities he discussed with President Mubarak and the concerns Sarah voiced over the dangers of his work in the Middle East. He spoke to the driver in Arabic.

"Cairo International, please. Swiss International terminal."

"What is your destination, sir?" the driver responded in clear English.

"Your English is better than mine," Brooks said with a laugh. "I'm off to Zurich."

CHAPTER 46

Brooks and Sarah

Zurich, Switzerland

Matters concerning Mubarak and Sarah dominated Brooks' thinking as his flight proceeded toward Zurich. On arrival, he fought through the crowds as he walked to the baggage area. He stood next to the carousel for his bag, eager for his luggage and impatient to see Sarah. To kill time, he reached for his cell phone and tapped in some numbers.

At the clinic, Rene Bartot received the call but quickly pulled the phone away from his ear to stem the barrage of questions coming from Brooks.

"Please come by the office today and see the newly restored Sarah Pierce," Bartot said. "She's done extremely well, and I hope you'll agree. On another note, as we're old colleagues and friends, I'll break all forms of my professional protocol and give you an insight on her condition. Just between us, OK?"

"Of course," Brooks said. "I'm all ears. Anything you reveal will help when I see her."

"As I said, she's done well. Her recovery has been as fast as anyone we've had here. That is, compared to others who underwent similar experiences. Here's my private message: You may find her stronger and more independent than the Sarah you knew. We observed her initially as gentle, focused on serving others, a bit hesitant to speak up for herself, reluctant to claim her own territory. We observed that a sense of dependence on others was more in her comfort zone. I think you'll find that has changed."

Brooks was quiet for a moment.

"I think I understand. How will I see it?"

Bartot laughed.

"Believe me—you won't miss it."

"Really?"

"Definitely. After you see Sarah, please come by my office, and we'll have a brief talk."

★ ★ ★

Sarah was alone in a large, private room when Brooks entered. She rose to greet him. Behind her, tall windows overlooked the lawn and gardens, lush from the summer rains. Framed by the windows, she was dressed simply, with a light-blue linen blouse over white pants. Her blond hair glowed in the afternoon sunlight. She wore white sandals with thin white straps that crisscrossed her feet and fastened at her ankles. Brooks wrapped her in his arms, and she yielded to his strength. They kissed softly, gently.

"It's so good to see you," she said.

"Likewise. I've missed you so over these many months but never more intensely than in the last few weeks. It's been hard having you close but not where we were together."

He looked into the pool of her dark green eyes. He felt he could swim in them.

"The docs tell me you've done well and are ready to leave."

"I'm more than ready."

353

"When can you leave?" he asked.

He grasped her hand. She kept her hand firmly in his.

"I know Dr. Bartot told you about my plan to stay with Lynne for a few days. I'm not ready to see, much less stay, at my home again."

"I was surprised we didn't talk about it. I thought we'd plan your return together."

"Did that decision upset you?" she asked.

She looked up at him. Her eyes searched his face.

"Can you stay for dinner? The docs said we can have a quiet table away from the others. We'll have a chance to talk."

"Well, since I'm not traveling with you, I think that's a good idea."

His eyes brightened with enthusiasm.

"I do have more news for you which, I believe, will reduce one of your big concerns," Brooks said. "The mastermind to kidnap you has been identified and is dead."

"Really? My God! Dead? What happened? I want to hear more."

"We'll talk more of this at dinner."

He glanced at his watch.

"It's about an hour before our dinnertime. I need to make a few phone calls to confirm my schedule. Can we meet back here in an hour?"

"What? You're leaving?"

She frowned, revealing her irritation.

"I need to hear about the mastermind," she said. "Are we totally safe now that he's dead?"

"The short version is that I believe somebody powerful in the Egyptian government got to the right man. Our CIA and the Egyptian Mukhabarat—their CIA—are after the four kidnappers. They'll find them. I believe we're very safe from them. I'll give you more details at dinner."

Later, when she greeted him at the reception desk, he noticed what he had missed earlier. The dark circles beneath her eyes were gone. Her cheeks were fuller, although she was still quite thin. Despite the need for more weight on her shoulders and arms, she was breathtakingly beautiful. Her drank in her beauty, then reached for her hand.

"You look exquisite."

"I want to be more than a pretty face, Brooks."

"Oh my God, you are. But...but...your physical presence is arresting. You do know that, right?"

She blushed, the soft pink rising on her cheeks.

"Thank you, but I need you to understand more fully what's underneath. I think we've been a little too superficial in our fast romance."

He laughed.

"Well, as I said before, nothing like a major crisis to make our similarities and our differences very clear. We've had an ideal relationship until the crisis, so what's underneath, to use your language, will definitely emerge."

The receptionist seated them in a quiet section of the dining room at a table with a white tablecloth and sparkling silverware. The waiter poured water into crystal glasses and placed menus in front of them.

"I'm nearby if you have questions," he said.

It had been a quiet week at the clinic. Even with few other diners near them, Brooks and Sarah spoke in hushed tones.

"I want to return to our conversation about your travel back home," Brooks said.

"It's a good place to start, but first I want to hear about the man who wanted you out of Egypt and how and why he died."

Brooks related the history of his interactions with Mubarak and Omar Sayed and his supposition of how Sayed died. She took his recitation of the facts with a calmness that pleased and surprised him.

Clearly, he thought, *Bartot's team had done wonders for her thinking about being kidnapped and the reasons for it.*

When he finished, she reached across the table for his hand.

"Thank you. I understand the situation so much better. I'm pretty much at peace with the ordeal. It was horrific."

She shook her head as if to cast the memories into the air.

"It's not something you'd expect to experience in a lifetime, but I'm handling it better every day. Thank you again for working hard to find me and to follow up with the Egyptians."

She stopped and gave him her dazzling smile.

"Mr. Davidson, you live and work in a volatile world. I want to talk more about that, but I know you want to finish our talk on travel."

"I do. Can we give it a few minutes?"

He sensed her agreement.

"When I got the news from Dr. Bartot of your travel plans, I assumed it was part of your recovery to remain away from me. So I didn't push it, but I am surprised it didn't come from you."

"You said you were busy at Stanford that week, and I couldn't face my home alone."

"But I suggested your friend Jan. Why not stay with her for a few days until I finished my work?"

"I'll tell you more about Jan another time. Why can't you fly to Dallas with me?"

"Once I heard your plans, I made other plans. When some of the folks I work with heard I was in the region, they asked for a meeting."

"Where is that?" she asked.

"It's on the Isle of Man—the UK."

"Jesus! That's the group you work with occasionally on these Arab projects. After all we've been through, you want to talk about more work in the Middle East?"

"It's more than work," Brooks said. "They're my friends. I like to see them. Some of my banking is done there as well. What's more, you should see it. I think you'd love the island. It's unique—quite enchanting in its own way."

"Well, yeah, I can see why you like it. Jabari Radwan said you had millions stashed there. Is that true?"

Her jaw was set, her expression firm. She spoke before Brooks could reply.

"You know, Brooks, during my captivity and at the clinic, I've done a lot of thinking about my life and yours. While we are attracted to each other, we're totally different in what we do and what we want. You have tons of money I don't know about, you told me you were a diplomat, and it turns out you were a CIA agent. Christ! You've hidden these parts of you, so I really don't know what you want."

"Hold on, Sarah. The first part is true. Our careers are totally different. The second part is not. Your daily world is different than mine. I grew to like yours and want more of it. I've come to admire the way we do things locally, like the bike rides, the Marin restaurants and films, reading by the fire. Having a house in a beautiful location that is the center of what we do means a lot to me. I've come a long way toward your way of life."

She placed a hand near her mouth.

"What about the international work and travel, this trip to the Isle of Man?" she asked. "Will you be discussing more risky

357

projects? I don't value that as you do. There's obviously danger in what you do."

His eyes hardened. His words came out fast.

"My work has significant value, and I am paid well. I do love it. And, yes, my colleagues will talk about new projects."

He slowed down and delivered his message more gently.

"They agree with you on the risks, but we also concur on the value we bring to these countries. We plan to talk about what to do, given the growing resentment of capitalists and Western ideas. We're constantly assessing the risks."

"If these talks suggest the risks have become too great, would you stop?"

"Maybe, maybe not."

They talked for another hour about his work, her work, and what they had in common. Sarah toyed with her fork, nudging the last bite of turbot on her plate.

"I think an important difference between us is that you're so private, so self-contained," Sarah said. "I'm so open. And…"

She placed her fork on her plate and pointed a finger toward him.

"…you're very willing to risk bodily harm to do what you want. To get real close to you, someone's got to accept that without question. I guess your wife did?"

"She did, but I might add she often took far greater risks than I regarding bodily harm."

"You like that type of woman," Sarah said, more a statement than a question.

"I admired Clary for her drive to get the big story in dangerous places, but am I looking for that now? No."

Sarah rose from the table.

"Yes, I gather that my lifestyle intrigues you," Sarah said. "But do you really understand it? Eventually it might bore you."

Brooks took her arm as they walked from the dining room.

"Sarah, looking ahead—that is, after you visit with your daughter—why not have Jan stay with you until you're comfortable in your home again?"

She studied his face. Deep inside, she wrestled with his attitude toward work, which, to her, was in conflict with his appreciation of her lifestyle.

"Listen, I don't need Jan to get comfortable with my Sunset Cove home because, given what happened there, I'm uneasy about the place," Sarah said. "Here's a surprise: I'm thinking about selling it. I'm considering a place that is more protected and easier to maintain."

She paused, letting him absorb that piece of news.

"Now here's the next big step: I plan to slowly but steadily close down my clinical practice and give my newfound free time to a nonprofit like Save the Children. I'd like to offer my psychology skills to refugees."

"What in the—?"

"Yes, Brooks, I can make adjustments in lifestyle too."

She raised her hand to arrest further comments.

"You've introduced me to travel, to the value of learning about other cultures, and I plan to do more of it. But I want to restrict my travel to safe places, like Europe, India, other Asian countries where nonprofits are respected and protected. In captivity, I had time to think about many aspects of my life. Thoughts like these rose to the surface."

They walked out of the building. Brooks had called for a taxi to take him to the airport.

They walked to the taxi stand, their hands locked together. As the car approached, he motioned for the driver to wait. Brooks turned to face her.

"Christ, Sarah, that's a ton of new thought. There's a lot to—"

"Brooks...," Sarah interrupted.

She gazed up into his face, her eyes beseeching him to understand.

"We've known each other for six months or so—not all that long. I realized during my prison term and recovery: *You really don't know much about me.*"

She stopped. She was breathing rapidly.

"From everything you do, I believe I won't see much of you. *In fact, I'm wondering if I'll ever see you again.*"

He let go of her hand, then touched her shoulder lightly. He stepped toward the taxi, still facing her, with a slight grin on his face.

"You really don't know much about me either."

He stepped into the taxi and settled in the backseat. He gave the driver the airport information then took a deep breath, thinking – *this is far from being over.*

ACKNOWLEDGEMENTS

Thanks to Charlie MacCormack and Tom Tauras for the incredible journey down the Nile that provided the genesis for this story. And special thanks to those who read early sections of the novel: Karen Price, Janet Warren, Khalid El- Awady, Jeff Slavitz, Seth Howard, Scott Hutchens. And to Rob Brill, Paul Palmer-Edwards, Mike Piekarski, and Jessika Hazelton at Troy Book Makers who brought the project to conclusion.

ABOUT THE AUTHOR

 J.F. Foran has worked internationally as a management consultant for over thirty years. His consulting covered corporate strategy for multinational corporations and public policy for federal and state governments. He was a founder of Strategic Decisions Group and has served on the boards of several public and private companies and also as a Trustee of Save the Children and the Belvedere-Tiburon Library. His first novel, *Angles on a Tombstone*, was awarded Best Historical Fiction in 2019 by the Independent Press Awards. He received his undergraduate degree from Middlebury College and his master's degree from the Wharton School. He currently resides in Mill Valley, California with his wife, Karen.